The Saga of Mary Awiakta

a novel by

Paul Mogolesko

The Saga of Mary Awiakta

Copyright: TXu 2-329-368

Issued; October 25, 2022

Edition: The Saga of Mary Awiakta – rev 20231105

ISBN: 9798352520628

Imprint: Independently published

Paul Mogolesko
Boynton Beach, Florida
November 5, 2023

Chapter 1

My mother did not give me a name when I was born. Later, my grandparents gave me two first names; my Cherokee name of "Ahyoka" and the American name of "Mary". The family name that I chose is "Awiakta". It means "eye of the deer". In a moment, you will understand why my grandparents named me, and not my parents.

The name "Ahyoka" means "she brought happiness". I know that I brought happiness into my grandparent's lives. I gave them a reason for living and enjoying the years of their seniority. When I was a young child, I was called Ahyoka by my grandparents and all of their friends who collectively helped to raise me. The name Mary, well, it was a very common name at the time which referred to a woman of Nazareth, Joseph's wife and Jesus' virgin mother. But, I only learned about the implications of the name later on.

I believe that my mother was mostly of Irish or Scottish ancestry and I believe that my father was Cherokee. My grandparents told me that there was some of the People in my mother's heritage. But, they didn't know for certain. It could just be that they wanted to tie me, culturally, more to the Cherokee than to the white people. All they really knew was that my mother came from somewhere back east. They didn't know exactly where and had no other details of her heritage. All that they knew was that she birthed me, and then, like a ghost, was gone.

My father...well, I believe that he was my father, was always getting into trouble. My grandparents told me that he and his two brothers committed some small-time robberies, but nothing violent. They did spend some time in jail. My grandfather added, with a chuckle, "But, if 'lazy' was a crime, your father and his brothers would have been jailed a long time ago." So, this opportunity, of raising me, gave my grandparents another chance at parenting, having raised three sons who were good for nothing.

To our Cherokee friends, they looked at the child in front of them as being of the People of the Cherokee Nation. They thought of me as one of their own and I am proud to be identified as one of the Cherokee People. Later in life, when I was in the presence of white people, those people looked at me as just a girl with a ruddy red complexion, more Irish than not, especially when my hair was cut short. So, there you are. I am culturally a mixture of both heritages; Cherokee and Scot-Irish. Maybe there was more to it. But, I believe that it was just that mixture of cultures that my parents ran away from. Neither of them wanted me, a half-breed of their own making.

My grandparents inferred that my parents were married but never actually said so. From what I was told, my parents didn't stay together for very long after I was born. I believe, now, that my grandparents had invented that canard about my parents being married and separating after I was born so I would have some excuse as to why I didn't have any parents in my life. They wanted me to have a history, based upon this little lie, so that I wouldn't be embarrassed when other children or adults asked me about my parents. But, I think that I was in good company. There were many other children that I knew growing up that were in similar circumstances.

Frankly, now, I believe that my parents were never married and never together at all. I believe that my mother just gave me up since I was the offspring of an "Indian", as they say, and that I was a bastard. Explaining either or both of those characteristics of my heritage, being a half-breed and being born out of wedlock, would have come at a price to my mother back east. So, my parents, each in their own way, ran away from their own prejudices. They both just gave up on me, not waiting around long enough to take a measure of my character. I guess that neither wanted their child as I didn't fit into either of their worlds. As for me, I would forever be a "half-breed bastard". You see, I had made a name for myself even before I was born.

So, my Cherokee grandparents raised me. They were wonderful people. I loved them dearly. When I think back, I would like to think that I could be as good a parent or grandparent as they were. That would be my fervent wish.

Grandmother and grandfather were born in the 1850s, I am not certain exactly when. But, it was just after the horrible 1,000 mile trek that their parents were forced to take from their native lands in what was called Georgia, ending up in what is now called Oklahoma. More about that later. I never knew when my parents were born but it was likely in the 1870s or 1880s, making them 30-40 or more years old when I was born.

I realize now that my grandparents were very progressive. Oh, I don't mean that they let me do what I wanted without rigorous parenting controls. No, what I mean is that they realized that my life would be difficult being a half-breed. That sounds worse than it is, really. You already know that my parents were of two different races. That's all that the word "half-breed" really means. But, my grandparents knew that in the world in which we lived, being of mixed races would be yet another challenge in life. They tried their best to prepare me to meet that challenge and others.

What I mean by progressive is this. There were some Cherokee that didn't want to learn English. More importantly, they didn't want their children to learn English. They didn't want to adopt any of the foreign cultural practices of the white people. Some others were more than willing to give up their Cherokee culture and adopt the European standards completely; "lock, stock and barrel". My grandparents saw a mid-road. They wanted me to speak, read and write English. They wanted me to understand modern farming techniques, domestic skills such as cooking and sewing and many of the cultural attributes of the Europeans, as well. But, they also wanted me to remain a daughter of the Cherokee Nation and learn and understand those traditional cultural practices. My grandparents were very smart, indeed!

As a child, my grandmother, whom I called "Agilisi", and my grandfather, whom I called "Agiduda", spoke rapid Cherokee, in whispers, when they didn't want me to hear or understand what they were talking about. My Agilisi and Agiduda spoke their native language when they were with their friends. That is not different than in any other culture. But, speaking in English was their rule in front of white people, or Europeans, as we like to call them, even though my grandparent's English language skills were poor.

While I sat on his lap near the fireplace, my grandfather would regale me with traditional tales and customs of our people. I remember it as if it were yesterday. He repeated stories that his parents and grandparents had told him, covering more than the last 100 years of our People's history. And, every once in a while, my grandmother would jump into the "telling" when she thought, I guess, that my grandfather had forgotten something or didn't tell the story quite right. That would usually lead to a dispute of the facts between them. I think that I enjoyed that part of the lesson more than anything else.

Telling me these tales was an effort to bring our culture to the mind of that young child, passing down those traditions to yet another generation. He told me these stories, over and over again, trying to make sure that I knew the truth. It was the continuation of an oral tradition from parents to children that dated back to forever. I am certain that he hoped that I would pass down the tales and that wisdom to my children, when the time would come for that. I told you that my grandparents were very smart.

When I was young, the stories were benign. They were not filled with anything negative, anything frightening. They were the stories that a very young child could relate to and enjoy. My grandfather would be animated using his whole body when telling me these tales. For example, when speaking about buffalo, he would get on all fours and scrape at the floor with his hand just like a buffalo would scrape at the good earth with its "hoof". When telling me about firing an arrow, he would fain putting an arrow into his bow and continue by pulling back on that imaginary arrow in the bow. Then, using all of his powers of expression, including saying "whoosh", he would let the arrow fly. When he was all done, and got up from the floor, with some difficulty I might add, my grandmother would laugh hysterically. My grandfather would get angry at her, and then, they would both laugh together and hug each other with a look that could only be reserved for people that have lived and loved forever.

As I grew older, my grandparents told me more about the lives of our People, about where we lived and where we came from. The stories became more serious and more impactful. Grandfather told me that we lived now in the state of Oklahoma. He said, "You were born in the year 1913. Just before you were born, this place, our home, was not called 'Oklahoma'. It was called 'Indian Territory'." Grandfather stopped talking and took a long drag on his pipe. Then, he turned to me and continued, "Ahyoka…did you know that the name Oklahoma is a name given to us by the Choctaw People?" He waited for a response from me. Of course, I didn't know that. That was not taught in the school that I attended. Frankly, there was nothing in the curriculum of the "Indian School" describing the experience of the native peoples, my People. In school, it was as if the "People" did not exist. But, my grandfather wanted me to know everything. He thought of it as part of my education as a member of the Cherokee Nation.

Grandfather continued, "In the Choctaw language, 'Okla' means 'People' and 'Humma' means 'red', hence 'red people' or 'red men'. Just a few years ago, that 'Indian Territory' and the 'Oklahoma Territory', together, became the State of Oklahoma." I was confused. I said, "If you take the name Oklahoma Territory as "Red Man Territory" and the "Indian Territory" as the place where the red men lived, it sounds to me as if there were two places with the same name, a redundancy." Grandfather didn't respond to my question. I'm not sure that he understood my point. But, he did tell me that the two places were certainly not similar in nature.

He told me that, "The American government in Washington signed peace treaties with the 'Five Civilized Tribes'; the Cherokees, Chickasaws, Choctaws, Creeks, and Seminoles. At first, the governments of Presidents Washington, Jefferson, Adams and Madison tried to uphold those treaties. But, then, as the European population swelled and its need for more farm land grew, the government was unable or unwilling to fulfill the requirements of those treaties. Written promises were made. But, those written promises were not kept. The treaties be damned. They were ignored. Displacing our people was what resulted." Grandfather exhaled very loudly. He was hurting inside just telling me the story.

"With the purchase of a large amount of land from the French, there was a place, a big place, for the white people to relocate our People so that they could have more room for their farms in the east and south. They wanted to move our people out of the south where they could use their African slaves to grow and harvest more cotton for trade with England, enriching themselves. Incentives were offered to our People to move west so the white farmers could cultivate more and more land that was ours. Some of the People did take the incentives and willingly moved westward.

"By the time that Andrew Jackson became president, our People's fate in the east was sealed. Jackson was known as the 'Indian Fighter'. He and Congress were committed to remove any 'Indians' from east of the Mississippi River. It turns out that these people just made up laws to do whatever they wanted with our People. So, in 1830, they wrote the 'Indian Removal Act'. At about the same time, gold was found on our ancestral homeland in Georgia. That just added to the pressure for the white people to rid the state of the Cherokee People. The state even held lotteries for white Europeans to own Cherokee land and gold rights. Laws written by the Cherokee Nation, for their own government, were voided by the white people. Tribal business;

contracting, mining for gold and all the rest, was no longer allowed."

Grandfather shook his head up and down and left to right to emphasize the key points of what he was telling me. He continued, "Petitions were signed by over 15,000 Cherokee against that 'Indian Removal Act'. In 1832, even the Supreme Court of the United States ruled in favor of the Cherokee, and other Peoples, saying that we were sovereign nations and could not be forced to move from our lands. President Jackson ignored the Supreme Court ruling and enforced the 'Indian Removal Act'. As I said, our fate was sealed."

Grandfather took a deep breath and let it out with a deep sigh. Sadness was expressed by the tears welling up in his eyes. Then, he resumed his lesson. "But, it didn't stop. In 1835, the American Government found 500 Cherokee in Georgia that were willing to sign the 'New Echota Treaty' which required the Nation to move west. So, listen to me, little one. They enforced a treaty supported by 500 when they ignored petitions signed by 15,000 and a Supreme Court decision." He emphasized "and". "Of course, the New Echota Treaty was a sham. This is the type of people that they are. Don't ever forget that."

"My parents, your great-grandparents, were only a few years old when our people were forcibly moved from Georgia to the Indian Territory. More than 60,000 of the People were forced to march over 1,000 miles. And, if they refused, they were taken to jail or worse. Eventually, most everyone stayed together and joined the march. Four thousands of the People died on that march. That trek was later named the 'Trail of Tears'.

"But, even the land that our People were being sent to live on couldn't be left to our tribe. 'The Dawes Act' eliminated tribal lands held in common by these sovereign nations like the Cherokee. That law required the head of each household to file for their right to individually own only 160 acres. And my dear daughter, that is the land that we now live on. But, the land that the People lived on before that Dawes Act was much greater than what we have now. The leftovers were given to white settlers.

"The white government used any and all excuses to keep moving our People further west, pushing and squeezing us into smaller and smaller spaces. There was no end to their deception, lies and…" His voice trailed off. "By around 1890, my home was then in the 'Indian Territory'. And, just a few years before you were born, in 1907, that territory became part of the State of Oklahoma."

Grandfather always finished telling me the story with tears flowing from his well-hooded eyes. And, at the end of every lesson, my grandmother would look into those eyes and tell my grandfather, "That's enough for one day." He seemed relieved. She was relieved that he would stop, knowing how the retelling of the story was painful to her husband.

Grandfather told me these stories so many times that I knew all of the details by heart. I thought a lot about what he was telling me. What did it all mean? As a child, I didn't understand why the white people did these things to our People. As an adult, I know that all people, including my People, are sinful. But, I still wonder why they couldn't allow us to be at peace.

For her part, grandmother taught me about the domestic responsibilities that a Cherokee woman had, and still has, as a member of the Nation. She taught me to forage for firewood, build a fire, cook and clean, sew both hides and European style fabrics and even taught me about natural medicines that can be found in the woods. She told me about yarrow which is applied to open wounds to clot the blood. Then, she ran through the list of other medicines that she knew about. She said, "Sumac relieves sore throats and helps with diarrhea. As a tea it reduces fever. People believe that it can also help to treat blisters and colds." She added that, "Blackberry and mint are good for upset stomachs. Rosemary is good to soothe sore joints. Honeysuckle works for respiratory infections, even pneumonia. Willow bark is a painkiller."

Some days, when she had the time, grandmother took me into the nearby woods and located some of these plants, reviewing again, what their medicinal effects were and how to apply them. She brought some willow stems and bark back home. There, she showed me how she strips the bark and then applies it to a painful location on the body. She even showed me how to boil the willow bark in water. And, after the removal of the bark from the water and filtering it through a piece of cloth, the liquid can be used for general pain relief anywhere in the body. She also took the willow bark extract and used it as part of a broth made from chicken.

While grandmother was teaching me about these domestic skills, grandfather would go back to his hobby of leather working. He had several handmade knives and tools that he would use to cut and shape leather. Then, he would cut a pattern into the leather with ornamentation. He candled the leather so that the black soot from the candle would fill the cuts. Once he was satisfied, he would wipe the surface of the leather leaving the black soot highlighting the patterns that he had carved. Most of his work resulted in being made into belts with leather tassels at the ends to be tied together. Then, he would make gifts of these treasures.

While my grandparents wanted me to maintain our Cherokee heritage, they also knew that I would soon be on my own and that my future would be more successful if I knew English. They taught me what English that they knew so by the time that I was ready to go to school, I would be bi-lingual. That is what they wanted for me. They wanted some assimilation while maintaining the Cherokee culture.

Grandfather noticed my interest in reading English. So, on more than one occasion, he purchased books for me. My grandparents looked at it as an opportunity for me to better learn the English language. One of my favorite books was the "Wonderful Wizard of Oz", by Frank Baum. It was so exciting that I just couldn't put it down. I imagined myself living in Kansas, having the same adventures as Dorothy. She was a farm girl just like me. I read it, again and again. My grandparents thought of the story as just that, a story about a farm girl and her dreams, her fantasies. But, they didn't know the character of the man who wrote it. I didn't either. But much later in life, I found out that Frank Baum was a racist. He wrote that the only way to protect the white settlers was for the genocide of the "Indians". But, at the time that I read this wonderful story, I was a child, I was innocent. I only knew of the immediate world around me and that was filled with love. I knew none of the subtleties and dangers that were lying there, just outside of our home. I was soon to go there, outside of our home, and understand those subtleties and much more.

Chapter 2

The federal government had funded more than 300 "Indian Schools", many of them across Oklahoma and Kansas, but also in other areas across the west where there were "Indian" reservations. Most of these schools were run by religious orders of one type or another. But, even though the school that I attended was close to my grandparent's home, I had to live at the school after my first year. I was fortunate that I was still able to see my grandparents, once in a while, and during the summers. Some other Cherokee parents didn't want their children to learn English and to be contaminated by this foreign culture. In many cases, those children were taken from their parents, against their will, and brought to even more distant schools. Many times, their children were never to be seen again.

When we started school, most of the children were given new names, Christian names like "Mary". Well, my grandparents had already done that. I had the name of "Mary". At school, we were forbidden to wear traditional dress and they removed the ornaments that we wore. They didn't even allow us to continue our dancing and singing traditions. They cut our hair short. And, with my hair cut short, having no ornaments, and wearing the uniform that they made me wear, I looked more like a "Mary" than an "Ahyoka".

My grandparents hoped that going to school would open up opportunities for me, adding the foreign culture to my culture. But, from the moment that I started in school, everything was done in the European fashion. There was no mixing of cultures that my grandparents sought for me. The teachers and the pastors denigrated everything that our culture stood for as if it were a plague upon our People. To them, we were heathens, people who lacked culture or moral principles. Frankly, there was nothing taught about "Indians" apart from their welcoming of the white explorers when they came to this land. There was nothing about what the white people did to the "Indians"; nothing about them stealing our land, nothing about the "Trail of Tears", and nothing about their attempt to wipe away the traditions of the Seminole, Choctaw, Chickasaw, Creek and my people, the Cherokee. I never heard of our traditions from any teacher, or in any books, or at church. I only learned about those truths from my grandparents when I sat with them around the fireplace. Looking back, I don't believe that my grandparents would have willingly let me go to the "Indian School" if they knew that these people, our teachers, literally wanted to wipe out our culture; the tales, traditions, religious experiences and all of the other things that Agilisi and Agiduda had taught me.

At school, we were trained, just like show dogs, to respond to the bells that they rang for this or that. Even when we ate our lunch, we could only begin eating after they rang a bell. And, we couldn't eat without saying a prayer to this God that we knew nothing about and certainly was not part of our tradition.

In our classes, there was allusion to the romantic push of the European explorers, sailing the vast oceans, reaching the Americas. We were told that when they reached these places, they found spices, raw materials and gold. The gold was the most important "finding". They brought back those treasures, enriching those Europeans with wealth from the "newly discovered lands". I must have laughed out loud one day when I heard the teacher say something about the "newly discovered lands". They weren't "newly discovered" to the People who raised me. Gold wasn't a new discovery. Our people had gold and lived on the land from which it came. The Europeans took it away from them. But, when the teacher heard me laughing out loud, he took his stick and smacked me several times across my hands. The teachers did that for any infraction of their rigid rules. Sometimes, I think that they just wanted to beat us so they found reason enough to do it on any given day.

Our teacher taught us about Lewis and Clark exploring a water passage to the northwest. We were taught that one of the purposes of their exploration was to tell the "native peoples" along the Missouri River Valley that the great white father in Washington was now their leader. We were taught of these events as examples of bravery. Imagine, that is what they taught us. But, these teachers, white people all, couldn't conceive that these events were the onset of a tragedy for the People of the Great Plains and Northwest.

When I think back about the exploration by Lewis and Clark, I could only believe that their message about some great white father in Washington was not received well by the People that they encountered. I don't think that those Peoples could even conceive of what Washington was or is. They couldn't conceive of a government with as much reach or size of the United States, even in the early 1800s. Centralized governments, weapons and technology were all beyond the comprehension of our tribes and leaders. Those three; centralized government, weapons and technology were the elements that allowed for the European conquest of the landscape that later became known as America.

The white people just thought it was their prerogative, their destiny, to occupy the entire land. In the process, they displaced us, denigrated us and even killed us. We were just in their way. From a European experience, it was the successful and almost romantic push of settlers westward, of fighting wars against my People. From the native people's experience, it was the displacement and concentration of those original settlers, the People, by the interlopers. I know that you are not taught this in your schools, but it is our collective history.

I guess that I am being cynical now when I describe a little of what we were taught and my reaction to it. It could be that I knew too much. My grandparents had already educated me to truths that were ignored by the white people.

School also included religious indoctrination where we were taught that what our parents, grandparents in my case, had taught us was a lie. These "good people" wanted to "Christianize" us, enlightening us to the way of their Christian God. In the process, they wanted to eliminate any religious notions that were part of our oral tradition and history. In a way, I felt betrayed by these teachers. They didn't want the continuation of these very traditions, tales and language that my grandparents wanted me to know and to pass down to my children. From a broader perspective, I really didn't know what they wanted of us. In one sense, they wanted us assimilated so that we could become part of the broader American society. We had to dress, speak and pray like all of the Europeans. Yet, on the other hand, these same people didn't really want our people to be integrated with white people any more than they wanted the recently freed African slaves to be integrated within white society. They didn't know what to do with the former slaves. And, they didn't know what to do with us. The only thing that they seemed to know for certain was how to find ways and means to strip us of our land, our dignity, and anything else that they wanted. All of this "schooling" left me angry. It also left me with a lack of confidence in who or what I was.

The school that I lived at was run by Christian missionaries. We had to go to church services every Sunday. They taught us that if we didn't go, we would "rot in hell". None of us knew what it meant to "rot in hell". We had no idea of where or what hell was. I guess that I got used to the idea of "rotting in hell" because it was always the reason that they gave us for hitting us with their stick. And, hitting us was an everyday reality. Frankly, I was more concerned about their sticks than of "rotting in hell". I thought of "rotting in hell" as a possibility for later.

I was raised as a Methodist, although I really didn't know, at the time, how that distinguished me from Presbyterians, Baptists or Catholics. Anyway, I really wasn't given a choice. The pastors taught us about Jesus Christ and the "one true religion". I was always taught that there is only one Christian God. I wondered, how is it that there are so many different churches that claim to "own him"? I learned later that each Christian church had their own view of prayer within that "one true religion". I continue to wonder...

Even with all of this anger within me about what they taught us, there were many things taught that were invaluable. Historically, our people were hunters and gatherers. And there were times that the hunt was not successful enough to feed the tribe. Some people starved. Others were malnourished. For quite a long time now, our People and the other Civilized Tribes had adopted European farming techniques which helped to better feed our people. In school, we learned European domestic skills. We were taught how to spin, weave and stitch cloth which was much easier than using animal skins for clothing. All of these were skills at which the Europeans excelled. I knew immediately that I had to learn these skills.

Although my grandparents never talked to me about specifics, their abiding hope was for me to be a modern woman with knowledge that we learned at school and for me to still practice and pass down the traditional Cherokee culture so that it wouldn't be lost like a fading sunset. I told you before, my grandparents were very smart, indeed!

I think that I was about 12 or 13 years old. I was at school when an old family friend by the name of "Yona" rode up on a buckboard. I didn't see him arrive. He must have spoken to the school headmaster because they both came to my school room together. The headmaster spoke to the teacher whereupon he called out my name and told me to go with these people. Of course, I did as I was told. Once we were outside of the school room, the headmaster said that this person had something to tell me and that I should listen to him. I was surprised to see Yona at my school. I hadn't seen him in years. So, when he appeared, I was concerned. But, I behaved as my grandparents would have wanted me to and merely said, "Hello, Yona. It is so good to see you." He said, "It is also good to see you, my daughter." Then, he grabbed both of my hands and looked straight into my eyes. "I am sorry to have to bring this sad news to you. Your grandmother has died." He said nothing more. I knew that my grandparents would have wanted me to behave properly. So, I controlled a tear that had collected in my eye and desperately wanted to fall upon my cheek. I turned to the headmaster, took a deep breath, and asked him if it would be okay for me to leave school to be with my grandfather for a few days. When I look back, I believe that he was both impressed and pleased with the maturity of my reaction to the sad news and of my request. He replied, "I think that we can arrange for you to go home for a few days". Yona was allowed to take me back with him.

When I returned to my grandfather's farm, I collapsed into his arms. It was only at that point that I let my emotions go. My body began to shake and my tears flowed down both checks. The more that grandfather tried to comfort me, the more that I shook with emotion. I don't think that it was only the loss of my grandmother that I was bemoaning. I think that it was more than that. It was the loss, to my generation, of the Cherokee culture that my grandparents tried so hard to impart upon my soul. All of those fireside talks would be, could be, no more. Those tales were now ignored by my teachers and pastors. It was all being taken away from us and there didn't seem to be anything to be done to stop it.

My grandmother was about 65 years old when she passed away although I am not sure if that is correct. There were no records. She was prepared for burial by the local women. They scented her body, wrapped her in a cotton sheet, placed an eagle feather on her chest and wrapped her hands around it. Eagles are considered sacred by many of the tribes.

The shaman knew her well. He offered prayers and blessed my grandmother. All the while that he was talking, he was looking at my grandfather and at me. He talked about all of the love that my grandmother had for us.

During the funeral, I held tight to my grandfather's hand trying to comfort him, trying for the impossible. But, it was my grandfather that comforted me. As I sobbed, he wrapped his large hands around me and said, "Agilisi would not want you to cry. She would want you to be happy. She is at rest and in harmony and balance with the great spirit and the world that we rely upon for our very lives." I cried even more with my body shaking. Grandfather squeezed harder and said, "Now, there, please, please don't." After a moment or two, I quieted down.

Grandmother was buried under the shade of a large flowering dogwood tree. It wasn't in bloom at the time of the funeral, but it would be during the spring. My grandfather will go there, when the tree is in bloom, and think that the beauty of the tree and its blossoms was the result of my grandmother being buried beneath. For, it is part of the Cherokee custom to believe that the deceased body feeds the earth with nutrients. Faith! The truth of the matter has no relevance.

For the next seven days, there were prayer services led by the shaman. The purpose of those prayers was for the survivors and the house of the deceased to be cleansed. And, after the seven days, the shaman took us to a local river to be "baptized" seven times, and then, it was done. Those that were in mourning could come back to the living.

The Cherokee would not have used the word "baptized" as the tradition did not have a word like that. But, now I was being indoctrinated in the Christian culture. That is probably what my pastor would have called that experience.

I felt empty inside as I left my home and said goodbye to my grandfather. The tears that I shed were for more than my grandmother. Because, as I left home on Yona's buckboard to go back to school, I feared that I would not see my grandfather alive again. But, I did see my grandfather several more times over the years for a few weeks each summer. But, every time that I left him, I cried, because I felt that it would be for the last time. You see, I was mourning the loss of my grandfather each time that I left.

As the view of my grandfather's farm faded from view, I realized that there are some things that you can't control and after some time of adjustment, you have to let it go. I let go of my grandmother. But, I will always feel her warmth. I returned to school.

It was not very common for girls to go to high school, but there were a few of us at that level. So, my education continued at Sequoyah High School. The town of Tahlequah, Oklahoma, where the high school was located, was also the capital of the Cherokee Nation. The school was named after the Cherokee man that invented a written form of the Cherokee language about one hundred years ago.

You would think that with all of this oppression that my Cherokee People have experienced, over these hundreds of years, that I would have been embittered in my attitude toward these white people. But, you see, I am half white, and yes, I ended up marrying a white man. So, I guess that there can only be a little room in my head and heart for anger and hatred.

Chapter 3

Lucas Taddum's wife, Dolly, became ill. Her illness prevented her from working alongside him. Lucas realized, probably for the first time, just how much of a contribution Dolly made every day at their farm. Without her there to do her chores, all of the work rested upon his shoulders. Yes, you can always hire migrant workers, but at the end of the day, the burden of running a farm still falls on the farmer himself.

Lucas certainly wasn't a lazy man. But all of it, now including taking care of Dolly, became too much. It would have been too much for any person. A few of his neighbors stopped by to look in on Dolly. He got help from his neighbor and good friends, the Clarks. Their son, Jack, came over every morning, to milk the cows and do some other chores. But, Jack could only spend so much time helping out because he had responsibilities on his own family farm, working alongside his father, Jim. Helen Clark cooked many meals for the Taddums and stayed with Dolly talking about this and that. But, Dolly was in decline and needed more than pleasant conversation. Also, Lucas knew that he had already stretched the limits of his neighbor's good will enough. He didn't want to lose their friendship. So, he decided that his situation needed to change.

After church services the next Sunday, Lucas waited around for his pastor to receive his parishioners. Then, he spent some time with him, sitting together in one of the pews inside the small church. After hearing what Lucas had to say, the good pastor recommended that Lucas put an advertisement for help in a local church newsletter. The newsletter was circulated throughout the congregation and the town of Muskogee, Oklahoma. Some people spoke to him over the next few weeks asking about Dolly. But, none offered the name of anyone who might be suitable to help out.

Somehow, I am still not clear exactly how this happened, that newsletter made it to the church that I attended in Tahlequah. Our Pastor Smyth, had exchanged letters with this farmer's pastor by the name of Berkley. Our pastor told the farmer's pastor, in a letter, that there were several girls that attended his church from the nearby high school that might be suitable.

In several exchanges of letters, Pastor Smyth was told that this farmer had a good reputation, having been married for a few years, with no complaints from anyone as far as he could determine. Then, satisfied that this was a serious inquiry that would not endanger any of the girls from his community, our Pastor Smyth spoke with the headmaster of my school in the hope that one of the girls would be willing to leave school and take on this job. At the time, I was in my second year at Sequoyah High School.

You know by now that if all of this didn't directly affect me, you would not be hearing about it.

For the most part, we weren't really spoken "with" by our teachers or the headmaster. We were spoken "at". We were told what to do and we were expected to do it, period, no questions or challenges. Those who didn't obey, and obey quickly, would receive a wack across the knuckles or worse. But, the headmaster liked me and that is why he took the time to explain the world, my world, to me that very day. It was certainly one of the most revealing and traumatic days of my young life. I was sixteen.

The first that I knew about the proposal was when the headmaster called me away from my classmates as we were leaving class to go back to the dormitory. The headmaster sat me down on an outside bench. He said that he needed to speak with me about something that was very important. He told me that he knew all about my history. He knew that my parents had abandoned me at birth. Then, he talked about things that I had never thought about, things that wouldn't have been obvious to me to even think about. He started by telling me how old my grandfather was. He didn't know for certain but he said that he was well over 70 years old. I didn't like that the headmaster was bringing my grandfather's age up to me. Yes, I had thought at the time of my grandmother's death, and every time that I left him after summer vacation, that I wouldn't see my grandfather again. But, I had never calculated grandfather's age or thought in terms of the limitation of a human lifetime. That sort of thinking was well beyond anything that I could fathom at my age. Even if I could, it was not something that I wanted to think about, my grandfather's death, that is. But, as I listened to what he had to say, I began to understand his perspective. Then, he said, "You have to start thinking about your future". I hadn't. Future? I thought mostly about today and a little about tomorrow. That was the future that I thought about. Next year never even entered my mind. He said, "In a little more than two years you would be completing high school. What then?" Of course, with my shortsightedness, I had no idea.

The headmaster said, "You should know that your grandparents never adopted you. Do you know what that means?" I replied, "No, I never even thought about such things." He continued, "Well, unfortunately, that means that once your grandfather passes, his farm, the one that you grew up on, will go to your father and his brothers. They might take you in but it is not likely that you would be allowed to stay for long as they have several children that they call their own and the farm can only sustain a …."

As the headmaster was speaking, I withdrew into my thoughts. My head began to spin. If I really believed that I wouldn't see grandfather again, then where would I live after school? How would I live? I didn't have any parents, not really. I didn't have any brothers or sisters. I was going to be all alone with no money and no home to go back to. Home…the headmaster was now bringing this into focus. Listen to the headmaster…

He stopped talking for what seemed like the longest of moments. Then, he said the exact same thing that I was thinking. "Mary, you might have no place to go after you leave here. You need a plan for the future that includes a roof over your head and some food on your plate. These are the minimal requirements. I know that you are very smart. I know that you do so well in our school. But, you must understand that this is your reality." He was speaking to me as if I was already an adult with the life skills and knowledge to really understand the implications of everything that he was saying to me. But, the only thing that I was certain of was a feeling of insecurity. That was new to me but would never leave me. And, in one way or another, that feeling of insecurity would haunt me and drive choices that I would make my entire life.

The headmaster rose up from the bench and said that we should continue our discussion in his office. So, I followed him back there. He offered me a chair across the desk from his. The walk back gave me an opportunity to absorb the information a little bit better. But, I was still stunned. I was not readily able to form cohesive thoughts about what it all meant to me now.

Then, the headmaster started talking again. I could see his lips moving. But, I don't believe that I heard him as my head was still in the clouds. He said, "I have a proposal for you." Listen to him! He said, "There is a family not very far from here. Well, not really a family. There is a husband and wife. They live on a farm with a two bedroom cabin. The wife has been sick for a while. The husband does what he can to take care of her, but with all of the farm work to be done, it is a real challenge for him. He has his normal farming work. Now, he is taking care of the barn and the vegetable garden and is also taking care of his wife. He has some help from his neighbors. But, they have to get on with their own lives. And, frankly, there are some of the duties that the farmer has to do as part of taking care of his wife that make him uncomfortable. You know what I mean." I didn't know what he meant. I had no idea what he was talking about. A proposal?

I sat back in the chair. I didn't see or hear anything for a moment. I almost felt as if I was going to pass out. I was still thinking about the farm that I grew up on and the village nearby. Then, my head came out of the fog that it was in and I realized that I was not like most of the other children in the school. They had families to go back to, farms to work on, and yes, they would eventually inherit the land and house or marry into another farm family. They would have a place to call home. I said to myself, "Sure, they had parents, they had a family. But, I had the very best people raising me." I realized that might not be enough.

The headmaster decided to take a step back and tell me how he found out about this possibility, telling me about the sequence of events starting with the pastor at this distant church and the newsletter advertisement. When our Pastor Smyth told my headmaster about the opportunity, he had told the pastor that he was immediately thinking of me. "But", our pastor said, "if not Mary, possibly you could recommend someone else."

I said, "Recommend me for what? What is this all about?" My immediate response was almost shrill. I still didn't get it. I was still thinking about what he had told me so far. I hadn't caught up. It should have been clear. I didn't have a secure future. This was a way to secure my future.

The headmaster had already made all of those facts about my future abundantly clear. Why couldn't I see where he was going? I was naïve. Frankly, there was a lot, a great deal, that I didn't know or yet understand in life. He continued, "The farmer is looking for someone to help out; take care of his sick wife, work with the animals and tend the garden." I guess that I still sat there somewhat dumbfounded. I asked myself whether this was real or just a bad dream. Wake up!

All sorts of things went through my mind. Just a little while ago, thirty minutes or so, I was this high school student enjoying my lessons even though my knuckles were red from where they got thwacked. By now, even with the punishments, school was my cocoon. I was enjoying being with my girlfriends. And now, here I was, in the office of the headmaster, talking about my future, about some farmer, someplace else, of leaving school…of leaving school! A chill went through my back. Immediately, I tried to look for a way out. I needed to tell the headmaster something, anything, as an alternative…"No, please, sorry, I already had plans after school to ahh…open up a dress shop…or…a restaurant…or…something else." But, no, I didn't have any of those plans, or any others, period. I didn't have any money to do any of those things. Maybe, I could work in a dress shop or in a restaurant. That would be about it!

I tried to focus upon what the headmaster was saying to me. But, I was in a panic. I had a lot of emotions racing around in my head. I guess just raw fear would be the first one. I was frightened by the prospect of leaving school. Then, if I went to this farm, how would I be treated? Would the farmer try to take advantage of me? Would he abuse me? Would he hit me if I did something wrong? And, I am not thinking about only a rap on the knuckles. What do I know about such situations? The more that I thought about these questions, the more my heart was racing. I said to myself, "Just stop it! Take control of your emotions." Then, I settled down a bit and said to myself, "Seriously, would I be able to take care of this sick woman? What would it be like? Would I have enough food to eat?" I knew so little about farming. Yes, they did teach us farming skills at school, but that was not like being on a farm, having all of those responsibilities. I understood from an early age that there is a big difference between thinking that you can do something and actually doing it. Practice does make perfect.

The headmaster knew exactly what to do at that moment in time. He needed to ground me, to settle me down, and that was what he did. Out of nowhere, the headmaster handed over a fistful of bank notes and coins. There were several five dollar bills along with many singles, some paper twenty-five cent notes and a small handful of nickels and pennies. The pennies were a mixture of Indian and Lincoln Heads. I had never seen a five dollar bill with the picture of President Lincoln on the front. I had seen and held dollar bills and the rest. I looked at everything that was in the palm of my hand. Quickly, I moved the money from one hand to the other, mouthing to myself, as I counted. All told, there was more than twenty-nine dollars.

I asked the headmaster, "What is this for?" He told me that it came from my grandfather. I asked, "Why would grandfather give me so much money?" The headmaster, with a knowing look on his face, responded, "I discussed this proposal with your grandfather." I thought, why didn't he say that to me in the first place? "Your grandfather told me that he and your grandmother had talked about their concerns for your future many years ago and he still has those concerns. They knew that school would come to an end and they wanted you to be prepared to take your place in the wider world. That is why they wanted you to learn to speak, read and write English, yet to maintain their culture in your heart. That is what he told me." That was the very first, and only time, that any of the white people at my school had ever mentioned anything about my Cherokee culture. That made me think better of the headmaster; first, because he actually had spoken to my grandfather about this proposal, and second, because he repeated words to me, that I knew, for certain, came from my grandfather. I could hear my grandfather say those very words in my head.

The headmaster paused thoughtfully and said, "When I told him about this proposal, your grandfather told me, '…this is a good opportunity for my daughter.' Yes, he called you, 'my daughter'. That is what he thought of you. Your grandfather said to me, 'It will give her an opportunity to succeed as an adult in this world. From doing this, she could gain a good reputation in the white community.'" My grandfather had always told me that half of my very being was white, so I had to consider being part of the white community as much as being part of the Cherokee Nation.

"Mary, your grandfather told me that your future might be difficult in the Cherokee world being that you are half white and educated in the ways of the white community. Then, he told me, sadly, that you might have trouble being accepted in either community." After a moment, the headmaster said, "He gave you all of the money that he could spare so that you would have something in case things don't work out well for you. He wanted for you to have something to call your own. He loved you that much."

I began to think more clearly. With the knowledge that my grandfather thought that this was good for me, I began to think seriously about the proposal and decided to be bold and ask some questions. With all of this money in my hand, I asked the headmaster if I would be paid for what I would be doing. He said that it was his understanding that initially there would be no salary other than room and board. Then, if the farmer were satisfied with my work, he would pay me what he could. I asked a few more questions. But, with my grandfather's support, my mind was already made up. It's funny how shocked I was at first. But, once I heard the words of my grandfather, I knew that this was my future, my fate. I told the headmaster that I would accept the position. He told me that the pastor from the church in Muskogee would want to meet with me before any final commitments were made. I thought, "Muskogee". I'd never heard of it.

And so, our headmaster responded to Pastor Smyth who got into touch with Pastor Berkley in Muskogee. A few weeks later, Pastor Berkley came to Tahlequah. First, he spoke to the headmaster who told him of my good grades and pleasant personality. Then, the three of us met at the church with Pastor Smyth. Pastor Berkeley wanted to understand everything about me. I told him everything…everything. After all of the talking, he told me to be ready to leave in three days' time. I agreed. He left to go back to his parish in Muskogee.

I was about to leave this rather comfortable cocoon, going off to a new stage of my life. Like when I first came to school, I was apprehensive. But, with the words and the money from my grandfather, my courage was regained. Grandfather's love had given me confidence that I could handle anything that came along.

I had only those few days to complete some work for school, pack the small number of things that I called my own and say goodbye to my friends. I tucked the paper money that I had been given by my grandfather into my underwear. The change remained in my pocket.

By the time that I told my girlfriends what was going to happen to me, I was already resigned to that unknown future. I had already begun the mourning process. I started that process the moment that I told the headmaster that I agreed to take the position.

My girlfriends were rather giddy about the direction that my life was about to take. For some of these girls, their futures were secure. For some of the others, they had yet to face their own realities. I didn't want to give them any reason to be concerned. We shared hugs and there were a few tears. After all, I had been with these girls in our classes and in the dormitory for almost two years. And, I knew most of these girls from the previous school before attending Sequoyah High School.

The third day came to be. By midday, I was told to wait in the headmaster's office. There, I held my small bag of items in my lap; mostly underwear, a few school uniforms, a tooth brush, some toothpowder, a hair brush and a washcloth. The headmaster was sitting across the desk reading some papers. He stopped what he was doing and stood in front of me. He said, "Mary, you have been a wonderful student here. Your good grades are only the beginning of your strengths. I know that you will do very well. I know you will behave in a reserved manner and make us proud of your accomplishments." I smiled at his compliments. That was all that he said. He sat back down.

After a short time, this tall man walked into the headmaster's office. The headmaster rose and introduced himself. The man said, "I am Lucas Taddum. Do you know why

I am here?" The headmaster replied "Yes, I know why you are here." Then, the headmaster turned to me. He said, "This is Mary." He never said my last name. I added that. "My name is Mary Awiakta." Lucas stood there dumbfounded at hearing my voice. I suppose that I shouldn't have said anything at that moment, but I wanted to be recognized by my Cherokee family name. I didn't want any confusion about that. I am a daughter of the Cherokee Nation and I wanted him to know that right away.

Lucas turned and left the office. The headmaster wished me well as he took my hands in his. I think that he really meant it. I didn't want for him to see that little glint of a tear forming at the bottom of my eyes, but he had to. Well, no shame in that. I turned from him and said goodbye at the same time. I picked up my few things and literally ran out of the office.

Lucas came to my school on a buckboard pulled by a single horse. I climbed aboard holding my bag tight. Then, Lucas said this one thing to me. "It's a long ride to the farm. You should put your bag in the back. Tie it down real good so that it doesn't fall out." While he was talking he didn't even turn to face me. I jumped down and placed the bag in the back. I tied it down with a single lash of rope that was there for such things and then, I climbed back on board.

I would have liked for my friends or the headmaster to be outside so I could have waved one last goodbye to them. But, alas, it wasn't to be. Frankly, leaving school did leave me with an empty feeling in my stomach.

With a snap of his wrists, Lucas signaled the horse to go forward. I was now onto the next stage of my life. Our journey to his farm began just that way. Lucas sat in his seat looking straight forward, not looking at me or talking to me. The horse did the same thing, going about its business, pulling us along. It didn't turn to acknowledge my presence either. I was invisible.

The trip in the buggy to the farm took about four hours. A truck would have taken half that long. I never knew why he took the buckboard rather than a truck. During the first half of the trip, Lucas didn't say a word to me. He just continued guiding the horse with a little nudge here and a little nudge there, first guiding him to the right and then guiding him to the left. I think that the horse would have found its footing without the nudging, but it gave Lucas something to do other than just sitting there mum. I was thinking about starting a conversation, but I thought better of it and remained silent.

Then he said, "You know…" That was all that he said for a minute or two. He was probably collecting his thoughts before he said anything more. Or, maybe, that was all that he had to say. It was obvious that Lucas was uncomfortable talking to me. I didn't know if it was his discomfort with me, in particular, or his being uncomfortable talking about his wife. But, sooner or later, he would have to tell me about his wife so I would be able to tend to her as soon as we arrived at his farm.

A few minutes later, Lucas started talking to me, telling me about his wife. He said, "You know…my wife, Dolly, is ill. She is very ill. Dolly is in some pain. Not all of the time, but every once in a while. I hear her moan in her sleep. Sometimes, I see her wince. I think that she is in pain when she does that. I don't know. But, it isn't good. She won't talk with me about it." He paused. I think that I saw tears well up in his eyes.

"Some nights she doesn't sleep very well. She rolls around trying to find a position that allows her some comfort. She sleeps during the day for an hour or two but she always seems to be tired. She can walk to the outhouse in the morning but I fear that she will not be able to much longer. We will have to figure something out when that happens." Then, he stopped and asked me if I knew how to take care of an outhouse. I wanted to laugh but I realized quickly that he was very serious. I said, "No, but I can learn." That might have been the first thing that I ever said to him other than my name. He chuckled, probably because of what we were talking about…the outhouse.

"More and more..." He paused. "I know that Dolly tries to do some things every day. While she continues to do some of her chores, it is getting more and more difficult for her to even take care of herself. More and more, she is no longer in any condition to help me on the farm or in the house and I am not able to do everything that I have to do to keep the farm going; feed and tend to the animals, cook, clean and tend to her. I am bringing you to the farm to help Dolly although there will be other chores. I want her to stop worrying about me and the farm. I want her to know that everything will be okay even if she can no longer help me. But, mainly, I want her to be comfortable.

Then, he seemed a little more relaxed. He told me that he and Dolly had been married a little more than three years. They had no children yet. That was all that he said that was personal in any way. He didn't tell me how and when they met or anything about his or her background. He didn't seem to care about me or my history. I had an initial sense that he didn't think of me as a person apart from my responsibilities. I hoped that would change over time.

Lucas started talking again, "A few times, Dolly has had trouble keeping her food down. I don't know if it is related or not. But..." Another pause. "She is losing a little weight." That tear was now growing in his eye. I was surprised. White people had always seemed so cold in their nature and calculating in their actions. That was my experience in school. So, this man's empathy toward his wife's illness was unexpected. I thought that maybe my first impressions were wrong. We'll see.

"You will sleep in the bedroom with Dolly and tend to her. I will sleep in the other bedroom, tend to the fireplace and keep it going throughout the night to make it more comfortable for Dolly." He never said that it would be more comfortable for me, as well. After a pause, he continued, "You will keep the fire going throughout the day and chop wood for the cook stove. The wood pile is just to the right side of the barn. The chopped wood is kept inside the house. The well is just outside of the house. You will draw water for the house. You will cook and keep the house clean." That was it. There was so much more to be said, but I didn't say anything. I didn't ask any questions although there were so many floating around in my head. They would have to wait for the right time.

Given what I knew, now, I didn't believe that Lucas had really thought through all of the things that needed to be done for Dolly. He just had a general sense that he needed help taking care of her.

We pulled up to the farmhouse. Lucas jumped down from the buckboard and went around to the back to gather my bag. I jumped down and took my bag from him. As we walked into the farmhouse, I could smell bad odors emanating from the bedroom.

Chapter 4

Lucas led me into the bedroom. Clearly, Dolly had soiled herself. I knew instinctively that I had to ensure that this woman's pride was maintained. I also knew that the relationship that I was about to embark upon with this woman was to be more personal than even that of most husbands and wives. I had to gain her confidence in the matter before me and so many others. I decided quickly that I would work around the cleanup trying not to embarrass her.

I could see that she was having a little difficulty sitting up in bed. Maybe, it was just that she just woke from a nap. I saw an opportunity and took it. I quickly moved behind her and supported her weight as she moved back. I straightened the blankets out. Then, I moved away from the bed and folded my hands behind my back. Dolly smiled pleasantly while looking at me. Lucas said, "Dolly, this is Mary. She's going to help out." Dolly said, "Hello Mary. It's nice to meet you. I can already tell that you will be a great help to me and to my husband."

Lucas said that he had work to do and left. Dolly said to me, "Please sit with me for a minute. We'll work together. There is some time." I brought a chair next to the bed. Dolly asked me to tell her about myself and so I did. I knew that she knew about me before I had even been chosen for this job. But, I continued anyway, telling her about my grandparents, their farm, my schooling and all of the rest. Then, she asked me about my parents. Even though everyone knew about my parents abandoning me, it was still embarrassing telling someone who I had just met and didn't know. So, I took a deep breath. I told her what I knew. She said simply, "I'm sorry". I responded, "Thank you, but please, my grandparents were the most wonderful 'parents' that any girl could want." Then, I told her about the loss of my grandmother. Again, she said that she was sorry. I just shook my head up and down. There was silence.

I asked Dolly how I could help. I had expected that she would have said something about her needing to be cleaned up. But, she said, "Let's make dinner together. I will teach you some of Lucas' favorite dishes." Dolly tried to get out of her bed. She was struggling a little. I got behind her and aided her in getting to a sitting position by the edge of the bed with her feet dangling down. As she settled, her blouse opened up just a little exposing one of her breasts. That's when I saw what might have been the root of her problems. There was a large raised area on her breast with what looked like a bleeding sore on the surface. Dolly noticed that I was looking and quickly covered up. I didn't say anything about it and just looked away.

I think that Dolly was struggling with what to say. There was no way around it. So, I said, "I would like to get you into some clean clothing and clean up the bed before we prepare dinner." She smiled and agreed. She pointed to a cupboard in the corner of the bedroom where there were fresh clothes and bedding. I found a pitcher of water and some towels. I sat her up in a chair near to her bed, washed her and got her into the fresh clothing. She smiled. I believe that being cleaned up brightened her day. I told Dolly to just relax for a little while I tended to the soiled clothing and bedding.

I took everything that I used to clean her, soiled clothing and linens, outside to the two wash tubs that were there. I soaked everything in the wash tub along with a little bit of soap powder that I found. Everything certainly needed more than a rinse.

Dolly and I went into the kitchen. They had a good sized cook stove and a large supply of firewood. Dolly sat in a chair near the table. She told me to get a good fire going. I added more kindling and stacked some additional wood in the stove. I felt good that I could put those skills that I had learned at school to good use here in my new life. The fire became good and hot.

Dolly told me about one of Lucas' favorite dishes. It was a casserole. Like all of the dishes that Dolly taught me to make over the months, this one was quite easy to prepare. I cleaned some potatoes and cut them into small pieces. They were put into a baking dish and covered with cheese, ham and onions. That was placed into the oven for about a half hour. Then, eggs, milk, pepper, and salt were whisked together and poured over the potatoes and the rest. Everything was put back into the oven and left there for about an hour until cooked through and through. Then, Dolly said that we should make an apple pie. I said, "…mmm, that sounds wonderful!" I had never had apple pie. She sat there and guided me through the preparation starting with the crust; a few cups of wheat flour, water, a touch of salt and some lard. The dough was split in half and rolled out into two disks, one for the bottom and one for the top. The apples were cut up into small pieces, soaked with a little water and sugar and a touch of salt. All of it was mixed up well and poured into the dough shell. The other shell was put on top of the bottom shell that had been filled with the apple brew. The edges of both dough shells were pinched together. Dolly told me to take a fork and puncture the pie all around. Then, I put the pie into the oven for an hour or so until the insides were bubbling. Dolly looked at it and then, as if by magic, she told me to take it out of the oven to cool. The shell was darkened and crisp. Both the casserole and the pie were left on the table to cool.

I think that all of this activity was tiring to Dolly. She asked me to take her back to her bedroom. I did. Then, she told me to take a walk around the farm yard and barn.

Once I was done with my short tour, I came back to the house. I hadn't thought about it at the time, but that house, that farm and that barn was to be my home for the future, a future that had no time limits or definition. It's interesting to me now, that before the headmaster told me about this opportunity, I had no thoughts of the future, my future. At sixteen, you don't think much about the future. But, here and now, I was already exploring, in my mind, just how long this particular "future" was to be and what the next "future", beyond this one, might hold for me.

I walked into the bedroom. Dolly had a smile on her face. She told me to cut a piece of the apple pie for myself and to bring a small slice back to her. I did and we ate the pie together. I didn't know that apples could taste that good. It was wonderful.

It was time for dinner. Dolly pointed to a bell near the front door. She said that Lucas will be able to hear the bell regardless of where he is on the farm. So, I rang the bell, banging it back and forth as loudly as I could, thinking that it was an awfully small bell to be able to be heard across a farm. But, it worked. Magically, Lucas appeared at the door. I laughed to myself. It reminded me of school. There, I thought of the students responding to the bell as if we were trained circus animals.

I served dinner to Lucas and Dolly. I was feeling comfortable with Dolly. Other than the ride to the farm, I hadn't seen Lucas all day. He was still an unknown to me. After they finished, I settled Dolly down for the night and then ate dinner myself just before cleaning everything up. After I finished, I went into Dolly's bedroom, talked with her about what needed to be done for breakfast. I washed up myself and checked on Dolly, again. She seemed to be comfortable.

After dinner, Lucas remained by the fireplace smoking his pipe. Once he finished with his pipe, he peeked into Dolly's bedroom to say goodnight. In a way, it was just like my grandparent's house. They would always say good night and wish each other a good night's rest.

I settled into my new bed, a straw bed, located in the corner of the same room as Dolly. I laid there in the light of a single candle. It had been years since I had to use candles for light except for the days that I was able to return to my grandparent's farm. In fact, most farms in the Midwest did not have electricity. Lucas' farm would have to wait another five years or so.

Within that first day, the apprehension about what this new adventure might hold for me started to evaporate because I immediately enjoyed being with Dolly. There was something about her that made you want to help. And, Lucas made it very clear that Dolly's comfort was the main reason that I was there. I said to myself that I would do everything that I could to make her comfortable. Yes, I already sensed from what Lucas had told me that Dolly's future would hold dark moments. But, for now, I had to put that out of my mind.

Dolly let out a soft moan and then rolled over. It frightened me. I jumped out of my bed and went over to check on her. She settled and was breathing normally. I thought to myself, "OK, she's okay. But, maybe those dark moments are not so far off in the future". I blew out the single candle and settled back into my bed and fell asleep.

I woke up well before sunrise. First, I checked on Dolly. She was resting comfortably. So, I ran out and took care of my personal needs at the outhouse. On the way back, I stopped at the well pump, washed up in the cold water, filled a large bucket and brought it back to the house. Quickly, I went back to the bedroom, straightened out my few things and checked again on Dolly. Then, I lit the fire in the kitchen stove. I needed to get breakfast for Lucas. I didn't want to disappoint him. I prepared enough oatmeal and coffee on the stove top for the three of us. Just when I finished preparing his breakfast, he appeared, almost like an apparition. Again, he didn't say a word. He just sat down and ate what I had made for him. Then, he rose up and left without saying a word. No, he didn't need to thank me for breakfast. That was my job. But, I would have expected at least an acknowledgement that it was a good morning. Something, anything, would have been nice.

During those first few days, I exchanged few words with Lucas. I quickly learned that he was a man of few words.

I cleaned up and went back to Dolly. She was stirring when I got back. She opened her eyes as I stood over her. I asked her, "Did you have a good night's sleep?" She smiled at me and nodded in agreement. I asked Dolly if she needed to go to the outhouse. She nodded again. I asked if she was ready. A third nod, not much more. I helped her up and out of the bed. I wrapped her in a shawl and supported her as we walked out to the outhouse. She called out to me and I opened the door. I placed my arm under her shoulder and stood her up. I sat her down on a chair outside of the outhouse, scooped some lime out of a pail and sprinkled it in the hole in the ground. Lucas had told me to do that because it neutralizes the odor.

At school, and before that with my grandparents, we talked all of the time while eating. With the other girls at school, it was always silly talk about other girls or the teachers or other people that we knew. Here, with Dolly, we talked about food preparation. We sat together, ate breakfast and chatted away. It was important for me to talk with her because I was still a little nervous. But, it was more than that, almost immediately, I enjoyed talking with her. I didn't know it at the time, but Dolly was to become my new teacher and much more than that.

After breakfast, I cleaned up. Then, I walked Dolly out to the porch. I thought that it would be good for her to sit outside in the sunshine as much as she could tolerate. Dolly told me, "There are chores that I had done on the farm in the past that I can no longer take care of." She didn't tell me the specifics of the chores right away. Then, Dolly said, almost philosophically, "You know, most people in my hometown, back east, think of farm wives in places like Oklahoma as just the same as themselves except that they were 1,000 miles further west. That is what my friends from school would have thought. That's what I would have thought. Of course, we were wrong! While farm wives do the same chores as town wives, they do so much more here on the farm. There is so much more to do on a farm.

Dolly stopped talking and after a moment or two of silence, she asked me, "Mary, I know so much about you. Would you like to know something about me?" I was very interested. I felt that knowing about Dolly would bring us closer together. So, I shook my head.

"Mary, where I grew up in Asheville, North Carolina, I had no idea what farm wives did. There were farms around but we lived in town." She paused, then said, "Mary, have you ever been in a town like Asheville?" I responded, "I've never even heard of Asheville. The only thing that I know is that some of the Cherokee people came here from places like Calhoun in North Carolina. I told Dolly a little about "The Trail of Tears". I told her what my grandfather had told me time and again. She didn't know. Then, she took a big breath and said how sorry she was for what had been done to the "Indians". I felt that her apology, although unnecessary, was sincere and that she had empathy for my People. That was good for me to hear.

Then, Dolly chuckled and began telling me more about herself, "Mary, you would not have any idea of what a town like Ashville is like. It is so large and has so many people that you can get lost. I think that is what happened to me. But, I don't mean lost as if you can't find your way to your home. I mean it in a different way.

"My dad wasn't a farmer. He worked in a tobacco store right in the middle of town. Unfortunately, he didn't own it. If he had, he would have been much better off; we would have been better off. My mom stayed at home. I knew that things were difficult for my parents. We didn't have a lot of money.

"My friends all had nice clothing. I had 'hand me downs' from my oldest cousin. I told my parents that I wanted to leave school and go to work so I would have some money of my own to buy new clothing. That was pretty selfish of me, only thinking about myself. But, even though we could have used the money, my parents insisted that I stay in school. They always wanted what was best for me. I stayed and finished high school." Then, a blush came over her face. I believe that she realized, at that very moment, that I didn't have an opportunity to finish high school. That I had left high school to work at her farm.

Then, she continued, "I didn't have a boyfriend in school. None of the boys came calling. My girlfriends told me that many of the boys in my class talked about me behind my back. After my friends told me about what the boys were saying, I tried to get close to a group of them. And, one day, I was able to hear some of them talking about me. I heard enough. I heard them say that I was 'as plain looking as homemade pie'. That said everything. It didn't matter whether I was smart or pleasant or well-mannered. My face was all that they cared about. I ran away from them and cried my eyes out."

Dolly started to move around in her rocking chair. I didn't know if she was in pain or just uncomfortable with what she was talking about. So, I asked her if she was alright. I think that she was annoyed at me for asking. She took in a deep breath and continued talking without answering the question that I had posed to her.

"After high school, many, if not most, of my girlfriends got married and started families of their own. Then, they were busy raising their babies. Those girls got together all of the time to share their experiences, all of those experiences that I didn't have. I was invited to be with them. But, after a little while, I felt completely out of place. Sure, they were nice enough, but I no longer had anything in common with them. As it turned out, I would never be with them again. We lived different lives. Now, I can barely remember their names.

"As I said before, I was lost. I had no direction. "I didn't know what to do with my life. I didn't like what I saw as I looked into the future, my future.

"My father helped me get a job in one of the large general stores in downtown Asheville. My specialty was women's clothing. That was about as close to a new wardrobe that I would come. In the store, these 'women of comfort' would come in and

I would attend to them." I guess that I looked confused so Dolly clarified what she was saying. "No, Mary, these were not 'women of the night'. We called them 'women of comfort' because they had enough money to come in and shop as if they were a queen, not being concerned, at all, about the price of what they were buying. They didn't even ask what a dress might cost. Well, maybe, just maybe, as I think about it, maybe some of them were 'women of the night'." Dolly stopped and began laughing. Her laugh was joyful. It filled the air like a contagion. It did both of us good to hear her laugh like that. My face grew scarlet because I didn't know what she was laughing about. Every time she tried to stop, Dolly would giggle a little more and that, finally, started me off laughing with her. Once we settled down, I asked her what a "woman of the night" was. She patiently explained it all to me. I tried to be ladylike. I cleared my throat, trying to behave in a reserved manner just like the headmaster said. But, then, I started giggling myself with my hand over my mouth. Well, that started up Dolly again. And then, I became hysterical. You can imagine!

After another minute or two, we settled down. Dolly started telling me some more of her history back east. "I didn't have many offers for dates. Every day was like every other day. I got into a rut. Then, all of a sudden, without me feeling the passage of time, I was almost twenty and still unmarried. An aunt of mine, my mother's sister, Ethel, said to me that I was going to be an 'old maid'. She said it to me so many times. I knew what she meant. It hurt my feelings. Alas, it no longer took my aunt to tell me that I would become an old maid. After a while, I was telling myself the same thing.

"I spoke to my parents about what my aunt was saying to me. Of course, it was not the easiest discussion to have. Those feelings and concerns shouldn't escape your own thinking, your own heart. Initially, my mother was visibly upset with her sister. But, of course, my parents were already thinking the same thing. It's just that they were reluctant to bring it up to me. It would have been too embarrassing to me, and to them, to talk about it face-to-face.

"My mother just said that everything would be alright. That is what mothers do, I think. Shortly, thereafter, my mother and her sister, Ethel, started working together on 'my problem'. Sometimes, they would discuss my situation right in front of me. They would talk about me as if I was some cow or rooster at an auction. That hurt me even more than just being called an old maid.

"Then, the worst thing happened. It was the worst thing that could happen to any young and vulnerable girl. It was the worst day of my life. My father dropped dead. He died right in the middle of a street, in the middle of Asheville, North Carolina. No one knew why he died. Oh, Mary, it was awful! Imagine being told by the store owner where I worked that my father was lying dead in the street. I ran out. When I got to him, there was already a doctor listening to his chest with a stethoscope. The doctor looked up at me and asked if I knew the man. I shook my head. 'Yes. He's my father'. He shook his head back and forth while removing the stethoscope from his ears. Then, with the saddest expression on his face, the doctor said that he was sorry.

"The next few days were a blur. The haze of my loss, my mother's loss, lifted. But, the emptiness of our loss remained. And, every time that I thought of my father, I started crying again. He was so nice. He was well liked by everyone that knew him. I still miss him.

"But, once the funeral was over, the reality of our situation came into clearer and clearer focus. Our bread winner, our father, was gone. His salary, what we lived on every day, was no longer. We were as poor as proverbial church mice.

"My aunt Ethel lived in a house along with her husband and daughter. She offered to take my mother into her house. My aunt said that I could stay for a while, in the same room as my mother, but there would have to be an end to it. My mother was so weak. My aunt was not. There was no room for me."

Then, in the middle of Dolly's story, someone drove up. She went around the back of her buckboard and gathered up a covered tray. She walked toward us, calling out with a joyous voice and a broad smile, "Hello, Dolly". Then, she looked my way. I don't know if she knew about me. Dolly, seeing Helen's reaction, said, "Helen, this is Mary. She is here to help out. She is going to help take care of me." Helen said, "Oh, you did mention that you were getting some help. Mary, it is so nice to meet you…" Then, Helen said, "Look at what I brought you." She pulled back a cloth covering from the two dishes that were sitting on her tray. One looked like a stew. The other was a wonderfully good smelling loaf of bread. I looked over at the bread, inhaled the wonderful fragrances and said that it smelled so good. I took the dishes from her and walked them into the kitchen allowing time for Dolly and Helen to gossip about me. Then, after a few minutes, I walked "loudly" back outside. Dolly said, "Mary, please cut a large piece of that apple pie that you just made and give it to Helen." So, I did. I put it on a plate and covered it up with a cloth. Helen was grateful, adding that it smelled so good and that she couldn't wait until she got home to taste it. I said, "Please stay right there." I walked back into the kitchen, cut another slice and took the plated pie and a fork back out to the porch and offered it to Helen. I think that she was both pleased and surprised that I would have that much poise and confidence to take such a step. She started eating the pie, looked at it closely as if inspecting it and she smelled it. Then, she said nice things about the pie. "Oh, the crust is so flaky…the apples so tender…it's so fragrant", things that you would have expected. Has anyone ever tasted something under those circumstances, and said anything less than how wonderful it is regardless of their true opinion? Helen left after another 30 minutes of chit chat, taking the other piece of apple pie, mounting her one horse buckboard and waving good-bye.

Dolly told me that she was tired and would continue her story tomorrow. So, I helped her get back into bed. With every move that she made, I could see a small grimace on her face and the moans that she tried to suppress. Once she got into bed, she told me that she needed to take a nap. I stayed in the bedroom with her until she settled and was gently snoring.

I didn't know exactly what was wrong with Dolly, what she was suffering from, but I knew that she was in some pain and that the sore on her breast looked infected. So, I left the house on the hunt for some medicinal remedies that my grandmother had told me about when I was a child. I thought that I might help Dolly by treating the breast and also reducing her pain. I didn't want to tell her what I was contemplating. I feared that she might not trust me or want the help. After all, we had just met. I had no idea what Lucas might say. He might think that I was crazy and just kick me out.

I took a long walk into the woods adjacent to the farm house, stopping here and there, looking at what was available. Finally, I was able to find yarrow. I remembered my grandmother telling me that yarrow could heal sores and clot blood. I thought that the yarrow could help if I put it on the sore in Dolly's breast. So, I gathered as much as I could find. I also gathered a great deal of small branches of willow bark. I knew that willow bark is used to reduce pain. I brought everything back with me to the kitchen.

I cut up the yarrow stems and cooked them up in a small amount of water, stirring and crushing the stems as they softened to make a paste. I wanted to coat the inflamed area of Dolly's breast with this paste in the hope that it would help. I let the yarrow paste cool and I settled the paste from the remaining stems. When it was cool, I took the paste and walked into the bedroom. I probably woke Dolly up when I opened the door. I stood next to the bed to see how she was. She smiled at me without saying a word. I told her about the natural medicines that my grandmother had taught me about. Then, I told her about the yarrow paste that

I had just prepared and asked her if we could try it to see if it would help. Dolly was reluctant. I believe that she didn't want me to see or treat her breast. She said, "Thank you, Mary, but I don't think so." Then, she looked down at her blouse. The oozing from her breast had soaked through and presented as a small stain on her blouse. When she saw it, she looked up at me, realizing that I had seen it, as well. Her face turned red. I said, "Dolly, please don't be embarrassed." She looked up to me again, hesitated and then said, "Yes, please, see if it will help". I walked to the kitchen to get the yarrow paste. When I came back she had her blouse partially opened exposing her breast. I said, "Are you ready?" She shook her head up and down slowly. I could see that she was nervous. I took up some of the paste in my hand and carefully applied it to the area around the sore. Then, I coated an even larger area, the entire area that was inflamed. She had no discomfort from the application. I placed a small wet towel on the area that I covered with yarrow to ensure that the paste would not be removed by her movements or rubbing against the bedding. Then, I closed up her blouse. Dolly thanked me.

    I left Dolly in her bed and went into the kitchen to prepare dinner. This time, it was the stew that Helen had left with us. I put the stew into the oven and the loaf of bread on top to warm it up. I went into the root cellar to get some butter. It was the first time that I really looked into the root cellar. It wasn't a typical root cellar, some smallish underground room used to keep perishables from spoiling. This was a huge and deep shaft. I couldn't even see where the shaft ended, it seemed to go on and on. I grabbed an oil lamp and lit it to provide some light. I walked further and further. Only the first ten feet of the shaft was used for food storage. I noticed that the further you walked into the shaft, the cooler it became. It made me think that we should be storing the food stuff further back. I also saw what appeared to be jugs of liquor in the very back. I left the root cellar, shutting down the oil lamp and placing it in a safe place near to the door.

When I brought the butter back, the bread was already warmed. I checked the stew. It was hot. Ready to go. I rang the bell and Lucas showed up. While Dolly and Lucas were eating their dinner, I took some of the willow bark and boiled it in a small amount of water. After a few minutes, I poured off the water. Then, I passed the brew through a piece of cheese cloth. That took out any residual bark pieces. I made enough of the willow bark brew for many servings of tea. I made tea for Dolly from the willow bark brew. According to grandmother, the willow bark extract should act as a painkiller. We'll see. I made coffee for Lucas.

Once again, Lucas had little to say during dinner. So, I decided to ask him about the root cellar. "Mr. Taddum. I went into the root cellar and found that it goes way back. I also found that the further you go in, the cooler it is. Was the root cellar once a mine shaft?" He answered, "Yes." He smiled. That was a first. He said, "When I was a young boy, I had heard that my father and many of the other farmers around here thought that there was gold in these parts. That's what it was for. It's a bit of an embarrassing story. You see, there was this guy, a local farmer, who spread a rumor about a gold strike. This was just before he sold his farm and home. My dad, like several other farmers in the area, was bitten by the rumor and started digging. It turned out that the farmer started the rumor so that someone might want to pay more for his land because of the reported gold finds in the area. Well, he sold his farm for a lot more than it was worth. Of course, there was never any gold. For the rest of the farmers around here, they just wasted their money, and their time, digging for something that never existed. They were all deceived. But, I guess that there was a silver lining. My daddy dug and built one of the world's largest root cellars." Lucas started laughing. It might have been the first time that I had seen or heard him laugh. He said, "I'm just joking about it being one of the largest. But, you have to admit that it is big. When I was a kid, I wouldn't even go in there with my father. I was always worried about what was there, hiding in the darkness. I have to say that I never appreciated that it is cooler the further you go in. Maybe, we should be storing our foods further back so that they keep even longer. Dolly, what do you think?" Dolly just shook her head up and down. She knew the story. She didn't seem terribly interested.

    I got Dolly into bed about an hour after dinner. Then, I cleaned up the kitchen. Another day. But, then, Lucas showed up in the kitchen. He moved so quietly that I didn't know that he was there watching me clean up. Then, he made some noise so I wouldn't be frightened by his presence. He waited for me to stop what I was doing. Once he had my attention, he said, "Mary, tomorrow, I would like for you to come into town with me to pick up some things for the kitchen and anything that you may need for Dolly." I responded, "Yes, Mr. Taddum." He walked out as quietly as he had walked in.

Chapter 5

I was up very early the next morning because I had to get ready to go into town with Lucas. Dolly was sleeping quietly. So, I went to the well to wash up and then, as I was about to return to the front door, I saw a shadow dismount a horse and move across to the barn. I didn't know who or what that was. I do know that it frightened me. When I got into the house, I ran back into the bedroom seeking its safety. Dolly was awake. I collected my thoughts and asked her how she was feeling. She responded that she had a wonderful night and felt very good this morning. I was pleased. I hadn't told her about the willow bark extract that I had used for her tea the night before. I hoped that its use to relieve her "discomfort" might have been a factor in Dolly having a good night's rest. Also, I didn't want to mention anything about the shadow that I had seen crossing the yard for fear of adding to her burdens. After all, maybe, it was just my imagination.

At the time, I had thought that the problem with Dolly's breast was an infection. It just looked that way. I really didn't know. But, that was why I had applied the yarrow patch. From that concern, I also knew that it was important to keep Dolly clean to avoid any additional infections or rashes. That was why I was so focused upon taking her to the outhouse. I didn't want her to soil herself again. And, fortunately, she was already comfortable with me taking care of her even though I had been there for only a few days. Maybe she felt comfortable with me taking care of such intimate issues because I was a stranger. I didn't know anyone in the area, so there was no one to share any gossip with. I wouldn't have done that anyway. It just wasn't who I was.

I helped support Dolly as she got out of bed. The linens were not soiled. I asked her, "Are you ready?" She said, "Yes." I supported her as we walked to the outhouse.

I took Dolly back to the house and settled her in a chair in the kitchen. I proceeded to make breakfast for Lucas and Dolly including frying some eggs in the fat from the bacon that I had prepared. I took a chunk of the bread that Helen had made for us, heated it on the stove and put it on a plate with a slab of butter. When Lucas showed up, we all ate together as I had to be ready to leave once Lucas said that it was time to go into town. I didn't ask, but they seemed okay with me eating with them.

After breakfast, Lucas said to me, "Whenever you are ready to go just ring the bell and I will return." So, after cleaning up and taking care of Dolly's needs, I rang the bell. As he always did, Lucas just appeared out of nowhere. I walked out and climbed aboard the buckboard. He gave the horse a little nudge with his whip and off we went. I hadn't been to town before.

On the way into Muskogee, Lucas said, "Dolly told me about the remedy that you had applied. What was it?" I told Lucas about the yarrow and my grandmother's explanation of all of the natural remedies that can be found if you know what to look for. I also told him about the willow bark. I wanted to see his reaction before I told him what I had done with the willow. He shook his head up and down in acceptance of what I had told him. Then, I said, "I used the willow bark extract last night in the tea that I prepared for Dolly. She had a very good night's rest. I hope that it was the willow that helped relieve her 'discomfort'." I didn't want to use the word "pain". He responded, "Anything that you can do to make Dolly more 'comfortable'…I hate to see her…" He didn't need to complete the sentence. After a moment's pause, I asked Lucas what ailment she was suffering from. His head dropped like a rock. It was as if I shot him with a gun. I had thought that it was that infection in her breast. He took a deep breath and responded. "The doctor told me that she has a 'cancer'. I didn't know what a cancer was until the doctor explained it to me. He told me that it is in her breast, maybe elsewhere. He also told me that it was very unusual for a young woman to have such a cancer, but he was certain that was what it was." I asked him, "What can be done about it?" Lucas hesitated for a moment and then said,

"The doctor here in Muskogee, Doctor Held, wanted her to go to Oklahoma City where they have facilities, surgeons, and the like. We did. But, after examining Dolly with their instruments, the doctors in Oklahoma City told us that they can't do anything for her." He stopped talking. I think that he was waiting for me to say something. I didn't know whether that infection in her breast that I was treating with yarrow was the cancer or if it was something else that was plaguing her. But, the statement of fact that there was nothing that could be done for Dolly put a punctuation mark on her life. That, I hadn't known. I hadn't even thought about her being <u>that</u> sick. How could I know anything of that nature? I was sixteen. I tried very hard to maintain my composure for his sake…mine too. With this news, it wasn't easy to be calm.

Lucas continued, "The doctor in Oklahoma City knew about some new treatments that they were doing back east but he told us that the cancer was so large in Dolly's breast that he recommended just to keep her as comfortable as is possible until 'the end'." He just shook his head sadly and told me that it was "too late". I had never heard of something called a cancer.

Lucas was focused straight ahead upon the road. A tear welled up in his eye as he was telling me about Dolly. I thought that if he turned toward me that he might break down and cry.

I was trying to absorb what he told me. But, these words, "the end" and "too late", shook me up. Until that point in my life, I had only known of death after it happened. But, this wasn't going to be like my grandmother who was already deceased when I found out. Now, based upon what Lucas told me, we were waiting for it to happen. The time between now and when Dolly died was what was on my mind.

There was only silence for the rest of the trip into town. There was nothing more to be said at that moment.

The sense of knowing when you can control something, and when you can't, served me well my entire life. There are times when you just have to let it go… I quickly understood that, one day, I will have to get through Dolly's death, like that of my grandmother, no matter how much I had become attached to her. That was a frightening prospect!

When we arrived in Muskogee, Lucas pulled the buckboard onto a side street and climbed down. As we walked around to the main street, called Chandler Road, he told me that we would first go to Tanner's General Store. Lucas said that we can find almost everything that we need right there. We walked into the store. There, he stopped and looked at me. It was probably the first time that he actually looked at me. He said, "Mary, I have only seen you in those school uniforms. Do you have anything else to wear?" I was somewhat embarrassed, as if I should have had more clothing. Then, I remembered Dolly's story about wanting more clothing herself. That buoyed my confidence in myself. I said in a strong voice. "Mr. Taddum, the two school uniforms, a nightgown, some underwear and a winter coat is all that I have." Lucas said, "Well, we need to buy you a proper dress for church and all. Can you sew? I mean, can you make a hem? If not, maybe Dolly can help you." I said, "My grandmother taught me how to sew although she still used a needle made from bone. But, in school, they taught us how to use metal needles and thread." He said, "Good." Then he added, "They have nice overalls and rough shirts to wear beneath them. That is what Dolly always wore while working outside before she took ill. Get a couple of them. And, please, I don't know what else women need so if there is anything else that you need for yourself, please gather it up." I thanked him.

I saw Lucas pick up a ten pound sack of rice and another sack, about the same size, of dried oats. He placed them on the counter. He seemed to know his way around this store as he went on a straight line quickly picking up four cases of canning jars and wax, a large box of candles, matches and tobacco for his pipe. Then, he seemed more relaxed probably because he had already collected the essentials. He started wandering around, picking up this and that, examining them and then returning them to their position on the shelf. I followed him around. I enjoyed looking at all of these things, many of which I had never seen before. Then, when he stopped to look at the jars of honey, I went over to the dresses. I could see that they were nearby. There were three colors, white, black and a dark blue. The black dresses seemed appropriate for a funeral. There would be a time for those. But, not now. I went through the white dresses until I saw one that looked right for me. The one that I chose was more plain than fancy. I thought the fancy ones were more suitable for a wedding. I held the dress up to my shoulder and looked into a mirror that they had in the corner of the store. The dress was a little too long but otherwise it seemed as if it would fit me well and it was very pretty. I took it and placed it upon the counter next to where Lucas had put the rice and oats. When I was at the counter, I asked Mr. Tanner, the store owner, where he had overalls and shirts. He called out to his daughter, Aida, to help me out. She appeared and walked me to the location and said that if I needed anything else that she would be very happy to help. I held the overalls up to my shoulder line to check for size and decided that they also would require some hemming. But, otherwise it would be just fine. I added another one of the same size. I checked the rough shirts for size, picked out two of them and brought all of it to the counter. Lucas was at the counter when I came back. He asked me to show him the dress that I had picked out. I picked up the dress that was lying on the counter and showed it to him. He looked at it, thought for a moment, and said, "That's very pretty, but one dress is not enough." He said that there were times when I would need a change. I was surprised that a man like Lucas would even have that sense of such things. So, I went back to the dresses and chose a simple dark blue dress. I had never had a dress, let alone two dresses, along with the other outfits. All of this was very generous of Lucas. I told him so. He just smiled.

I needed a lot of cloth to make rags for Dolly's care. I found soft cloth. I added it to the pile on the counter. I also picked up some cheesecloth for the same reason. Then, I asked Mr. Tanner if he had needles, thread and scissors. He said, "Young lady, my name is 'Isaac', but you can call me 'Ike' if you like." I didn't want to call him "Ike" because that seemed too familiar. Maybe, someday I will, but for now, I will call him "Isaac". I said, "Ok, Isaac, please call me Mary. Can you show me the needles, thread and scissors?" He walked me over to the area where they had the sewing supplies. I picked up a spool of white cotton thread, one of blue, a few needles of different sizes, and a small scissor for the thread and a larger scissor for the fabric.

Then, I had to look for one last thing. I didn't want to embarrass myself by asking where I could find what I needed, so I rooted around the store by myself to see what they had. I couldn't find one. Lucas saw me looking around and came over to me to ask if he could help. I whispered quietly, "I need to get a 'honey bucket'." He looked at me quizzically. I added, "From what you told me about her illness, we don't know how long Dolly will be able to walk to the outhouse. So, I was thinking about a honey bucket as an alternative". My hands raised up as if I had achieved an epiphany, a revelation from God. I was just pleased that I was thinking about ways to help out. Lucas thought for a minute and realized what I was saying was probably true. He stared at the floor, searching his memory of the store in an effort to find the location of where they might have "honey buckets". He probably couldn't think of where they would be so he said that he would help me look for one. We walked around but couldn't find anything. Then, Lucas asked Isaac what I was too embarrassed to mention. The manager told us that he didn't have any. Lucas asked if Isaac knew where one could be purchased. Isaac had no idea. You could tell that Lucas was thinking. Then, he walked around the store once again and came upon a large metal bucket and brought it to the counter. He said to me, "Mary, if you're finished, let's go back to the farm." As it turned out, I was getting ahead of myself looking for a honey bucket.

Lucas went over to Isaac and asked him to total the cost for everything on the counter, now including the bucket. Isaac totaled to $32.75. Lucas slowly and carefully counted out the money that was required. Isaac counted along with Lucas. When the three quarters were finally put on the counter, Isaac said,

"Thank you." Lucas collected the larger items, the rice and oats. He put the rice and honey into the large bucket. He balanced the oats on top. I grabbed up the dresses, the other clothing, the fabric and the sewing equipment. We walked back to the buckboard and loaded everything into the back, tying it down so that it wouldn't just fly off. Lucas helped me up into the passenger's seat and went around to the other side, climbed in and took the reins.

We started to leave town when we came to a large fairground. There were tables all around but there were no people. Lucas stopped his rig and said, "This is where the Country Fair is held every Saturday. We mostly call it the "Saturday Fair" or just the "Fair". This is where we sell our goods. It's Thursday now. I will be here on Saturday. In the past, Dolly was the one that took care of this. Now, she is unable. Then, he waxed philosophically. "Yes, there were many other things that she took care of at the farm. I didn't appreciate just how much she did until she was no longer able to do her chores. We shared the work. I take care of the main crop of the farm. Mostly, she did the rest." He paused. Then, he said "I would like you to come with me to the Fair this Saturday if you think that we can leave Dolly alone for a few hours?" Then, he thought better of the idea. "Maybe, I can ask Helen to stop by and keep her company. She doesn't usually go to the Fair. Her son, Jack, takes care of that for their farm..." He stopped himself in mid-sentence. "No, it's already Thursday. I can't ask Helen for the day after tomorrow. I'll ask her for next week." I told Lucas that, "Dolly should be able to be alone for..." I thought for a moment. "...possibly, three hours, but not much more." I certainly didn't want Dolly to be stressed or to soil herself. Lucas said, "That should be enough time for you to see the Fair and help out a little. Can you ride a horse? I mean, if you can only stay for a few hours, it would be best for you to have a way to get back to the house by yourself to tend to Dolly. Do you think that you could do that?" I reminded Lucas, "I am part Cherokee. Of course, I can ride a horse. My grandparents taught me. In fact, I ride very well." I might have been too expressive. I might have been too proud of my heritage and of my riding skills. But, my outburst affected Lucas in a peculiar way. He was embarrassed. His face turned red. He shook his head up and down.

We continued the ride back to the farm. Not another word was spoken.

When we got back to the farm, we unloaded everything. The clothing, sewing goods and cloth came into the house with me. I went immediately to see Dolly. She was awake and gave me a slight smile. She said, "What did you get? I hope that Lucas told you to buy a dress." Ahh…with that I knew where that idea came from. I said, "Yes, Dolly, he was very generous. Mr. Taddum bought me two new dresses and two sets of overalls with rough shirts and sewing goods." Dolly said, "That's wonderful. I see that Lucas took some initiative. I had told him that you needed a dress. He told you to get two of them. Good for him! I told Dolly that I will have to hem everything. She said, "I have needles and thread here." I was somewhat embarrassed as I might have spent money that didn't need to be spent on needles and thread.

I prepared a simple lunch of some bread and honey topped off with a cup of coffee and what remained of the apple pie. After lunch, I set Dolly up on the porch in a rocking chair, covered by a shawl, as I did before. She said that I should bring out my new dresses and the scissors, needles and thread. She was going to help me fix the hems. I left her there in the sun.

I quickly gathered up what was needed. When I got back to the porch, I slipped the white dress over my clothing. Dolly looked at me as if it were for the first time. Then, she said, "Do you know that you are very pretty?" Without waiting for a response, she said, "Please stand on this chair next to me so I can set the hem for you." I didn't respond to her comment about my looks. No one had ever said that to me before. Frankly, I didn't know what to say. So, I ignored what she said. She grabbed up the hem of my dress in her capable hands and then "tacked" the hem line with only one or two stitches each. I turned so she could tack all around. She was done in no time at all. Then, she said for me to take off the dress. She fed the needle's eye with more cotton thread and showed me the proper stitching for a hem. Once she did a few stitches, she said, "Here, now you try it." I had done some stitching work for my grandmother. But, that was crude work. I had also done some in school but never on such an important garment. This had to be perfect or the hem would pull and not look right when I wore the dress to church.

As I carefully stitched up the hem, Dolly looked over what I had done so far. She seemed pleased. Then, as I was doing my stitching, she said, "You remember when I told you about my life in Asheville." I said, "Of course." I told her that I found it very interesting. She shook her head up and down as I responded to her. Almost temptingly, like holding a gift just too far from a child to grab ahold of, she said, "Would you like to hear more?" I said, "Of course, very much so."

I continued to stitch the hem as Dolly repeated some of what she said earlier. "I think that I left off as I told you that my father had died right there in the street, just a small distance from where I was working at the time." She stopped to figure out how to restart her story. "…Mmmm…my mother had never worked. Ah…yes, about my father…my father had left just a little bit of money. We didn't own a farm and we didn't own a home. We barely had enough money to bury my father. After all of that, we were nearly destitute. My small income from working in the General Store was all that we had to live on.

"I was unprepared for my father's death. Oh, that sounds so awful. Of course, I was unprepared for my father's death. What I really mean is that I was unprepared for the consequences of his passing, especially the loss of the money that he made and that we lived on every day. Back then, I didn't think much about money, where it came from and how much you needed. My father took care of everything. I quickly understood that I had to do something but I didn't know what."

Although Dolly was still talking to me I didn't hear her words. Her voice faded from my sense of reality. In my thoughts, I knew that this would be a difficult time for me. Yes, I was enjoying being with Dolly now, but with what Lucas had told me about this cancer, I began thinking of Dolly's degrading health and what the future may hold for me. That was selfish just thinking about the consequences for me. But, I was worried that I might be overwhelmed. There was no preparation that I could make to be ready for what was coming. I wasn't thinking about the honey bucket. No, that was only one small issue that I would have to deal with. I knew that there were so many other small issues that would come up which I couldn't even conceive of at this moment in time. But, they would come up whether I was prepared or not. How would I deal with them? Then, Dolly. Would I feel, once Dolly leaves this earth, that I had done everything within my power to help her, to soothe her? I may fail this woman who I had already taken a liking to. And what about Lucas with such a transition?

...my focus came back to what Dolly was saying to me.

"People, men, that is, tried to attract women to the mid- and far- west, because the ratio of men to women in those locations was very high. If men wanted to start a family or to have support on the farm, they needed a means to bring women to the area. So, my aunt started looking at advertisements in local newspapers. I guess that I could have done these things, read the newspaper personal sections, responded to advertisements and the rest. But, I found it all too embarrassing. My aunt did it all. She found a few men in the advertisements that seemed like possibilities. So, she had me write letters to them. I was not too enthusiastic but I did what I had to do. When I received their responses, I found that these men were barely literate. I just didn't want to be with a man who had so little education that he couldn't write a proper sentence. It reflected poorly upon them.

"Then, we spoke with my pastor in Asheville. As it turned out, he had received many letters that were passed through various parsonages. They were from places like California, Ohio,

Nebraska and, yes, Oklahoma. The pastor asked me if I wanted to see these letters. I read them through and asked the pastor if I could keep a few. He agreed. After reading them over again with my aunt and my mother, we thought that two of them merited a letter back from me. So, I wrote two similar letters and handed them over to our pastor. He mailed them to the pastors out west. Then, after about a month, I received a letter back from Lucas and then a week after that from another gentleman. My pastor, my aunt, my mother and I got together to read the letters. We all thought highly of Lucas' letter. We were less impressed by the other letter. We exchanged one more letter and continued to be pleased with what Lucas told us about himself. He seemed stable, had a small farm, he was a regular church goer and the pastor thought that he was a decent God-fearing man.

"So, with the help of our pastor, we arranged for me to travel to Muskogee and to stay with Pastor Berkley and his wife, Sally. And then, after a few days, the pastor arranged for me to meet Lucas at church. If I found the initial meeting satisfactory, then the pastor was to invite Lucas over for dinner so we could spend a little more time together. You know, in order to get to know each other. The pastor didn't want to invite Lucas to dinner too soon after we had met for fear that it would indicate that I was desperate. Well, maybe I was desperate. I don't know. But, I listened to the pastor's advice. I agreed. After all, I immediately found the pastor to be a good and trustworthy man! In all of the days since then, he has never betrayed the trust that I had placed in him.

"When we met in church, Lucas didn't have too much to say. But, that was at church where our focus was to be upon God and our prayers. Dinner was the perfect place to have a decent conversation. Lucas didn't have too much to say at dinner either. He seemed shy, like me. From what he did say, he seemed kind and hardworking. He did like to drink a bit and he smoked a pipe after dinner. My father had done both during his life, so I didn't find either one of these habits objectionable.

"We continued meeting at the pastor's house for dinner and then occasionally, we went out for a buggy ride with Sally Berkley in attendance. After a while, the pastor allowed us to take those rides without a chaperone. As we rode together, Lucas opened up more and more. Don't get me wrong. He doesn't like to chit chat about silly things. But, when he has something to say or to discuss, he is quite the conversationalist.

"During one of those rides, Lucas took me to his farm. He toured me around the house and barn and told me about what he grows. We left the farm and headed back to the parsonage. Then, after a Sunday dinner, Lucas asked me to take a walk outside with him. I agreed. It was during that walk around of the parsonage that Lucas asked me to marry him. I was prepared for the question although it had never been posed to me before. I said, "Yes". We were married by the good pastor in the parsonage house on March 25th in the year 1926, just over three years ago.

"When I lived in Asheville and even after Lucas toured me around, I never knew what the wife's responsibilities were on a farm. I just hadn't been exposed to a farm before coming here. I can tell you that farm wives are much more than an ornament, something to appear on the arm of the farmer at church or during square dances or in town. That is what wealthy town wives, those 'women of comfort' in Asheville are...ornaments.

"It wasn't too long before I learned how to run everything that Lucas needed for me to do. I tended to the milk cows. That includes feeding, milking, skimming cream, churning the cream into butter and making cheese. I tended to the dozens of hens that we have; harvesting, candling their eggs and preparing them for the market. Then, I tended our table at the Fair where we sell most of the eggs, some milk and cream, along with a lot of the butter and cheese and the fresh chickens.

"I've also maintained a garden plot where I grew green beans, beets, lettuce, cabbage, cucumbers and potatoes and other vegetables. All that is not eaten is stored in sealed jars and put on shelves in the root cellar to keep it as fresh as possible." She stopped herself and chuckled…"Oh, yes, I cook all of the meals." Dolly laughed even louder. "My mother would have stopped right there. All of the rest that I have told you about would have been foreign to my mother as it was to me when I first arrived. My mother would have difficulty living on a farm. She never worked. She had no skills. Frankly, I didn't either when I got here. But, I've learned and I've contributed.

"Mary…a farm wife forms a partnership with their husbands without which the farm could not survive. Sure, neighbors help as much as they can when there is a need. In fact, over the last few months, we have had Helen's son, Jack, helping out in the early mornings. But, he has his own chores on his father's farm. His helping here means that he has less time to work on his own farm. Frankly, it is a strain on our friendship which should only be tested so much. They have their own farm to run." With what Dolly said, I realized that the shadow that I saw moving across the barnyard must have been this Jack that Dolly mentioned.

"Did your grandparents have a root cellar on their farm?" I thought and thought, but then I realized that I just didn't know. I told Dolly that I had left my grandparent's home for school when I was a young child and came back in the summers for a short period of time." "Well", she continued, "You've seen our root cellar. We store everything that we can as deep into the root cellar as possible because during the winter, anything stored near to the doorway will freeze and then rot. Anything near the doorway during the summer will get too hot and rot out, as well. The root cellar is God sent. It keeps everything just right, year around. You should know that the root cellar is also where Lucas stores his hard liquor that he makes for himself. It's way in the back." I didn't want to interrupt Dolly but when she had completed talking, I told her that, "I already walked deep into the root cellar with an oil lamp. I saw the jugs of liquor there."

Dolly ignored what I had said and kept telling her story, "So, when I took ill, it was a challenge for Lucas no different than if Lucas took ill. Each of us has their role in the success of the farm. If we had children, they would help out. But, Lucas and I have no children. So, with me ill and spending so much time in bed and everything else that you now know, Lucas understood that he needed help. And that is why he contacted our Pastor Berkley. And thankfully, you are here."

As Dolly was finishing up her story, I finished hemming the dress. She told me to put it on. I put it on again over my clothing and stood on the chair next to her so she could get a better look at the handiwork that I had done. She looked at the hem, squeezing it with her hands here and there to make a crease. Then, she said, "Take the dress off. We need to make a better crease at the hem line. I have an iron. Please heat up the kitchen stove. The iron is on a shelf right above the stove. Heat it up." She repeated herself. Dolly asked me to take her into the kitchen so she could watch over me as I ironed the dress. I did as she told me. I had learned how to iron in school as part of the domestic training that we had there. Dolly told me to be very careful not to leave the iron in one place too long or it would burn the dress. I was very careful, finished ironing and tried on the dress one last time there in the kitchen for Dolly to see. She had me twirl around with the hem of the dress lifting in the air like the wings of a bird. She seemed pleased. "Now, Mary, please take that dress off or you will get it dirty. Put it in a place where it will stay as lovely as it is now. You will wear it Sunday for church. Then, Dolly said that we should do the same thing with the blue dress and the coveralls. And we did. That was my first Thursday. There was a lot done. It was good.

Chapter 6

The next morning began my first Friday at the Taddum Farm. I got up early which was now part of my daily routine. I fed Lucas so that he could get back to the fields.

At breakfast, Lucas repeated that he wanted me to come with him to the Saturday Country Fair. He added that I should work with Dolly so that I can prepare the food for the Fair. After I prepared breakfast for Dolly and the dishes were cleared, she and I went into the barn. I settled her in a chair.

She started my farm education with the eggs. There were several baskets of eggs on a table. Next to the baskets were large candles. Dolly said, "All of the eggs have to be candled to make certain that they're sterile and that a chick is not developing inside. Since the new eggs are checked daily, we only have to check yesterdays and what was laid today." Dolly guided me through the candling of the recent eggs. I discarded the few that weren't appropriate for sale. Then, Dolly told me to go to the root cellar and wrap some of the cheese in paper, preparing it for the next day. It was going to the Fair.

Saturday, the day of the Fair, was upon us. I started off my day a little earlier so I could get everything done before we would have to leave for the Fair. I dressed in one of my new overalls with a white rough shirt. Dolly looked at me and told me how beautiful I looked in my new outfit. I rang the bell for Lucas. When he came into the house, he just looked at me. As we were finishing breakfast, there was a knock at the door. The door opened and in walked Helen's son, Jack. Other than his shadow, I had never seen him before. He was almost six feet tall and quite good looking. Lucas introduced me to him. I said hello and then offered him a cup of coffee. He declined the coffee. He seemed anxious. Then, he said to Lucas that they needed to go if they were to get their usual tables at the Fair. They both got up from the table.

By that time, Lucas had already loaded up the buckboard with the hundreds of eggs, eight five-gallon cans of milk, cheese, butter and four crates of chickens. Our agreement was that Lucas was to set up the tables at the Fair. I was to delay and then ride by horseback myself so I would be able to return in time to take care of Dolly.

Lucas set off to the Fair. He told me to wait a half hour and then to come. After the time passed, I mounted the horse and rode to the Fair by myself. It took me about 20 minutes to get there. I brought the horse into a local barn and walked back over to the Fair. I saw Lucas standing behind the tables that he had filled with his goods. When he saw me, he waved for me to come over. I did. Jack, Helen's son, was at the next table selling goods from their farm, as well. Jack walked over. I stood behind the table with the two men chatting for a while about absolutely nothing of importance. After a short time, Jack went back to his own tables.

Lucas said that selling our goods at the Fair was one of the chores that Dolly had done. He had already told me that. Then, he said that he wanted me to learn about all of the prices and how to sell everything by myself. Of course, I had no idea what eggs or chickens or cheese should sell for. I felt so ill at ease. I told Lucas just that. He chuckled and said, "Of course. Why would you know what these things sell for? I believe that you've never had to buy a single egg. Is that right? Well, let's start right there, with the eggs, OK?" I shook my head. I was still embarrassed about my complete lack of knowledge. I hoped that my face was not very red. Lucas said, "You've seen our hen house. We have six dozen hens, more or less, right?" I shook my head. I didn't know. I hadn't counted them. "Well, typically, each hen produces an egg a day. Some days, a hen doesn't produce any eggs. But, mostly, an egg a day for each hen. That gives us six dozen eggs a day. Every week, we bring what we don't need at the house to market. So, that's about ..." Just then, a woman walked up to the table, faced me and said that she wanted two dozen eggs. I think my heart stopped for a second. I didn't know what to say in response. Fortunately, Lucas took over. He said, "Ma'am, the eggs are 49 cents a dozen this week. Is that alright?" The lady said, "That's a little high. Can you do any better?" Lucas smiled and said, "Well, I can do a little better if you are willing to buy three dozen." Lucas broadened his smile. There was a twinkle in his eyes. I didn't know this side of Lucas. Of course, I really didn't know any side of Lucas. I only knew him for a short time.

They settled on three dozen eggs at 46 cents a dozen. Lucas asked me to package the eggs in three brown paper bags. He had a stack of them next to the baskets of eggs. I placed the three bags of eggs in front of the woman. She counted out the money and looked at who to give it to. Lucas pointed to me. The lady gave me the money and left with her eggs. I turned around and gave the money to Lucas. He said, "Hold it for now. Hey, we need to get you a purse. You will be here most weeks selling by yourself." That prospect was frightening. I didn't know anything about selling. But, now, I understood that I would be the person at the Fair, selling everything before me. I needed to learn fast.

Jack came back over to our stall and asked me how I was doing. I said, "Well, I know some about selling eggs but I certainly don't know anything about hens and how to take care of them. There is so much to learn". He offered to help. I looked over to Lucas to see if that would be okay. He smiled and shook his head just a little as if his approval were a secret. I responded, "Yes, Jack, but, I don't want to take you away from your chores." Jack thought for a moment and looked over at Lucas as he spoke. "Well, tomorrow...ahh, but, there may not be enough time to show you anything tomorrow with chores and church and all. Maybe, another day." I was just looking to have something to say to him. "Oh", I said, "I think that I saw you the other morning in the barnyard. I thought of you as just a shadow, a ghost-like figure." Jack had a twinkle in his eye, "Well, that was probably me. But, I don't think of myself as just a shadow and I don't believe in ghosts." "I didn't mean to say that exactly." His face lit up in a wonderful smile. He was having fun at my expense. "I was only telling you of my impression at the moment." Jack let it drop, "Okay. Will you be going to church with Mr. and Mrs. Taddum?" I said, "Yes, I think so". He continued, "Then, I will see you at church tomorrow. On Monday, I will be back to help out. Once you take care of Mrs. Taddum and I do my chores, I can begin to show you what needs to be done, what Mrs. Taddum has always done. She can also help you. Speak with her. She knows it all…there is a lot for you to learn." Again, we both looked over to Mr. Taddum. And, once again, he shook his head and smiled.

Then, after selling eggs and the other items with Lucas' help, he suggested that I take a walk around the Fair since this was my first time being there. I took all of the money in my pocket and handed it over to him. He looked at what I had given to him and counted out fifty cents. Lucas said for me to buy something that I had not had before. I thanked him and quickly left. I knew that I didn't have a lot of time, maybe about one more hour before I would have to leave to get back to Dolly. And, I surely didn't want to disappoint Dolly by being late. But, I was excited to look around.

I stopped by many of the food stalls to see what they had. There were wonderful foods everywhere. Everything smelled so good. I came upon a cart that had some type of machine that kept making popcorn. I asked the man how much for a bag. He told me that they have two sizes, a small bag for a nickel and a larger bag for ten cents. I asked him to give me a small bag. I handed over five cents. I gobbled down the popcorn as I walked around.

There were stands selling cold drinks with ice. There was ice cream. I had ice cream only one time before in my life. The same stand that had the ice cream also had shaved ice covered with sweet cherry syrup. I had to decide. So, I asked for a cone of shaved ice with cherry syrup. I had never had that before. I gave the man five cents as he handed me the paper cone filled with ice and covered with cherry syrup. I didn't know whether I should lick it or take a bite. I was just looking at it trying to decide, when Jack came up behind me and said, "Good choice. I like the cherry ices myself. You look like you are having a problem." I said, "I don't know whether I am supposed to lick it or to take a bite." He told me that it didn't really matter. Then, he added, "But, if you wait too long, the ice will melt and you will have a mess. It will drip onto your overalls. If the cherry syrup gets onto that white shirt of yours, it will never be white again. Eat up quickly." I did what he said, licking and then biting small portions of the ices. I kept an eye on the bottom of the cone being careful not to let any of the drips hit my clothing. I finished my ice while walking around, taking in the sights of the Fair. I came back to Lucas with my hands stained red from the syrup.

When I got back, the eggs were almost gone as was the milk, cheese, butter and chickens. I told Lucas that I would be leaving to get back to Dolly and thanked him again for the money. As I was talking with him, I handed him what I had left in my pocket. Lucas said, "No, keep the money". I held it in my hand and offered it to him again. I saw that he was not going to take it so I put it back into my pocket and said, "Thank you." I left the Fair going back to the barn to get my horse. I traveled back to the farm in plenty of time to take care of Dolly.

When I got back to the Farm, Dolly was sleeping on the settee. But, my presence caused her to stir. I stood over her as she opened her eyes, stretching out her arms just like an alley cat. I asked her how she was feeling and she replied that she was comfortable. I suggested that we get her up and have something to eat. That is what we did.

Lunch was a simple affair, some bread and honey and some tea, again, using the willow bark extract in the brew. I asked Dolly, with some trepidation, if I could change the yarrow paste and towel on her breast. But, she was receptive. So, as she sat in the kitchen, I asked her to open her blouse. She did and I cleaned her breast, dried the area and reapplied yarrow paste and a fresh small towel. Unfortunately, the area didn't look any better than it had before. I thought to myself that the yarrow paste may not be having the effect that I had hoped for. After lunch, Dolly asked to sit out on the porch to enjoy the sunshine. As we did for the preceding days, I sat her down and covered her shoulders with a shawl. She was thankful. Then, she said, "Please sit and tell me all about your time at the Fair. What did you have to eat, was there any music, who did you speak with…was it wonderful?"

I told her that there were some singers who sang in harmony that I had never heard before. She wanted to know if I liked it. I told her that I did and went on and on about the lyrics of one of the songs. Then, I said, "The men that sang were dressed differently from all of the others. Most of the men just wore coveralls, similar to what I wore. But, these men all wore a vest, a bow tie and a straw hat. Lucas told me that style of singing is called a 'barbershop quartet'. I had never heard of such a thing but they were very good, indeed."

I sniffed the air and described the many odors emanating from the stalls that were offering all sorts of foods, many of which I had never seen before in my life. Then, I told Dolly about the ices with cherry syrup. Dolly seemed to relish in my experiences as if they were her own. Talking with Dolly was just like talking with my friends at school.

Enthusiastically, I said, "How can I forget? Jack was there. Now, I know that he is the shadow that I see moving around the barnyard early in the morning. He seemed to be watching over me as I wandered around the Fair. I didn't feel that there was anything for me to be afraid of but he stayed pretty close all the while. He also offered to teach me everything, all of the chores …" I stopped myself. Dolly said, "I know. You were about to say all of the chores that I did before I became ill. I know…"

I could readily understand that these would be my chores before too long. I believe that Lucas hadn't told me about all of them yet because he just didn't want to overwhelm me and possibly scare me off. If I didn't like Dolly so much already, the amount of work required might have scared me off. Truly. Of course, scared me off to where? To what? I certainly wouldn't be allowed back at school if I abandoned my job here at the Taddum Farm. Frankly, I didn't want to leave this farm. I didn't want to leave Dolly.

Then, Dolly looked at me with a curious smile and broke the silence, "So, Jack was taking good care of you...was he!" I said, "I think that he was just making sure that I didn't get lost or meet up with some of the rougher crowds of boys that were roaming about." Dolly's smile grew. She looked at me with a bigger and broader smile than I had seen in the few days that I had been at the farm. "Mary, Jack knows that I can show you everything here. Jack...hmmm...Jack is going to show you how to do everything because he wants to see you. He wants to be with you." "What? I don't understand." "Mary, I think that you do understand. Jack is no longer a boy. He is a grown man and you, my dear, are a grown and very beautiful woman". I never thought of myself as beautiful or as a woman. I have always thought of myself as that little girl sitting on my grandfather's lap listening to all of the stories and traditions of my People. But, here and now, Dolly was calling me a very beautiful woman. When did I become a woman? How did that happen?" Dolly continued, "You know, Mary, a worker bee tries very hard to help build the hive. But, when it comes down to it, the worker bee only comes to see and serve the 'queen'. Mary, you are the 'queen'. Jack wants to teach you what I do for several reasons. Yes, he wants to help out by having you be able to take on some additional chores. But, also, because he wants to be with you. It's that simple." I guess that I was sort of dumbfounded listening to what Dolly was saying. Then, coming from all of my insecurities, I blurted out, "Why would he be interested in me? I'm a half-breed Cherokee girl who was probably born without my parents being married. That makes me a 'bastard', an outcast". "Mary", Dolly continued, "Please. We knew all about you before you came here. That didn't stop us from asking for you. We chose you! I know that you are a Cherokee woman. You are also a woman whose mother was probably Scot-Irish, just like Lucas or I. So, you are both, a child of both cultures. You are not the only one. As far as the issue of whether your parents were married or not, it doesn't change who and what you are. Let me tell you what and who you are even though we only know each other for a few days. You are obviously very smart. I know that from what we found out from your school headmaster. I also know it from the very way that you behave and speak. You are compassionate. I know that from the gentle way in which you take care of me. You probably didn't think that I noticed, but I did. And finally, you are beautiful. I know that because I just need to look in your direction. You glow. I am telling you the truth. Now, do you really not understand why Jack is willing to come over here and help you out?"

I was flustered. I didn't know quite what to say in response, if anything. But, what Dolly said to me sounded so nice. It made me feel good about myself. It helped my self-confidence, something that the teachers at school had all but stripped away. I think that I stuttered when I started to respond. "Buuuut..., Dolly, there are always the 'looks' and sometimes words from white people who make me feel like I am Cherokee. That is okay with me. But, from their 'looks', it probably isn't okay with them." I stopped myself and chuckled. "Then, there were the 'looks' that I got when I was in school from some of the other Cherokee girls. They were thinking that I didn't belong because I was half white. They probably also knew that I was a bastard. All of that is my burden in life."

"Mary, I know that this is very personal. Of course, it is. But, I need to speak with you about it. There will be people that don't like you for any or all of these reasons. There are people who don't like other people for a variety of reasons having nothing to do with their birth. Some people back in Asheville didn't like me because I was plain looking. What did they used to say about me? 'She's as plain looking as homemade pie'. So, I think that I know a little about people's prejudices, about people being mean-spirited. But, I can tell you that Jack is not one of those people. We know him very well. He is a good and kind person. And, his mom, Helen, already likes you from that single time that she met you. So, you cannot allow what your mother and father did, or didn't do, sixteen or seventeen years ago, affect your entire life, your understanding of yourself. 'Bastard' is just a word. If your parents had been married, they would have had a piece of paper, a marriage certificate. Would that have changed who you are? You are who you are. Your parents do not deserve the credit nor the blame for who you have become. You are responsible and deserve the credit for you, and for all of what you do. If you do not remember anything else that I have told you, remember this...the life choices that you make are yours to make. And, the consequences of your choices or decisions are yours to endure. Your choices...your consequences. It is a life lesson that I had to learn. It really is that simple. My recommendation is to learn it and live it. Stop worrying about your parentage. It is what you do with your life, your choices that will determine who you are. And the consequences of your choices, that you will have to live with, have nothing, at all, to do with your parents. Don't use them as an excuse."

Dolly looked at me in the hope that I absorbed everything that she had said. Up to that point in my life, I had always been subject to these words, these definitions, which people had labeled me with. Dolly was trying to liberate me from the words, from the names that had nothing to do with who I was.

There was nothing more to say. Yet, I felt in my heart that I wanted to spend more time talking with Dolly. Every time that I had a conversation with her, it made me feel better. It made me feel like there was a future to look forward to, who knows. But, one thing that I knew almost from the start of my adventure with Dolly was that she felt more and more like a mother to me. Yes, she was only six or seven years older than I. But, she knew so much more about life and people and about feelings.

Then, Dolly broke the mood that I was in. In a completely different tone of voice and a bright smile on her face, she said that Saturday nights were usually a time to get together with friends, the Clarks. She said, "This evening, Helen, her husband Jim, Jack and their daughter Betty are coming over for dinner. We have a lot of work to do…we'll do it together. I would love for you to join us. You are part of the family." Dolly was telling me that I was more than just a servant. That made me feel very, very good, indeed.

Dolly continued, "Helen's husband, Jim, is exactly the opposite of Helen. She is so gentle, kind and considerate. Jim, is…well…he is not as pleasant. He is a bit intense. And, sometimes, over dinner, Jim and Lucas disagree about what is going on in the world. They can have quite a quarrel. Betty, their daughter, is about 14 years old. She is still a child. She rarely says a word. Well, I'd say that you already know Jack." She smiled and waited for me to react. "Mary, they will be here in a little more than three hours. As I said, we have a lot of work to do between now and then. Are you ready?" Dolly chuckled saying, "Ok, you will be doing most of the work but I'll be there to help where and how I can." That chuckle became a torrent of laughter. Dolly had a wonderful laugh. It was infectious.

We spent the next three hours together preparing dinner. Dolly instructed me how to prepare her favorite dishes. She claimed that she made the very best roast chicken in the world. It was based upon her mother's recipe. She asked me to pull out this pan that she always used. She claimed that the reason that her chicken was so good is because of the pan. She said that no other pan will do. I don't know. But, that was her claim. So, I followed her directions. I took a chicken out of the root cellar along with some snap beans. The chicken had been slaughtered in the morning and drained over the day. I plucked the feathers and burned off any residual small feathers or stems over a large candle flame. Then, I placed the chicken in the pan. I rubbed the spices that Dolly dictated all over and added a small amount of water into the pan. I added more wood to the stove. Once it caught fire, I put the chicken on the other side. Then, I set my eyes on cooking the beans and making muffins. Dolly told me that the apple pie that I had made earlier in the week was a big hit so she thought that we should make another.

We let the chicken cook for about an hour and then put the freshly prepared apple pie next to it. Finally, the muffins were added. Dolly sat near to the oven checking the chicken, the pie and the muffins every fifteen minutes, or so, making sure that nothing was burned or wasn't cooked enough. I watched her every step of the way so I would be able to do exactly what she did in the future. While she was sitting watching her masterworks in the oven, I swept the floor, set the table, went to the root cellar to retrieve a couple of bottles of milk, butter and some cheese. I was learning. I was also learning that it was a lot of work.

Near to five o'clock, our neighbors walked into the house. Lucas greeted Jim, Helen, Jack and Betty Clark and asked them to come in. They greeted Dolly. I stood behind her, trying to stay in the background. Jack said hello to Dolly and circled around to me. He asked how I enjoyed the Fair. I told him that it was very exciting for me. I added that there was so much to learn. Jack introduced me to his sister who was pleasant enough. Finally, Jack introduced me to his father, Jim. He was less than pleasant, barely saying hello to me. Seeing his father's reaction to me, Jack shrugged his shoulders. Dolly saw what happened.

As a diversion, Dolly suggested that we all sit down to dinner. The kitchen was warmed by the oven and the glow of the sunlight outside filtering through the curtains drawn loosely across the single window. Everyone stood by their chairs. Lucas sat first followed by Jim Clark at the two heads of the table. I settled Dolly into her chair. Then, Helen and her children sat down. The chicken had been cooling on top of the oven for a while as the burning wood lost its heat. The beans were cooked and tender. I drained them and placed them on a plate. The muffins were already on the table along with a slab of butter. I brought the chicken, still sitting in its juices, to the table and placed it in front of Lucas. I handed him a large carving knife, fork and ladle. He immediately picked up the knife and fork and began the process of carving the chicken breast into slices and let them rest in the juice to add to their moisture. Then, he cut off the wings and legs and the rest. It was done.

I brought the plates to him as he asked each one of our guests which part of the chicken they preferred. As he placed the chicken on their plate, he ladled some juice on top, added some beans, a muffin and a slice of butter. I took the plated food from him and placed it in front of each of our guests beginning with Jim Clark. Then, he served Dolly, Helen, Jack and Betty. Finally, he asked me what I would like. I thought that was very nice of him. Then, Dolly suggested to Lucas that they start with grace. Everyone bowed their heads. Lucas began, "Heavenly Father, bless us and these Thy gifts which we receive from Thy bountiful goodness, through Jesus Christ, our Lord. Amen." Then Lucas said, "Mmmmm...Let's eat dinner".

Everyone began to eat. There was a hush, with the only noises being those of clanking utensils and smacking lips. Then, Jim started talking about current events. Dolly had prepared me for this "discussion". Jim talked about the recent tornadoes in Arkansas that killed six dozen people. Although terrible, I didn't know why he was talking about something that happened so far away. We had tornados right here in Oklahoma. Then, Jim broke into my thoughts. He said, "I was at St. Mark's Farm & Feed earlier today. The guys there were talking about the Scopes Monkey Trial." Lucas broke in and said, "The what? Do they have nothing better to do? Now, they're putting monkeys on trial?" Jim said, "No Lucas, this was very important. It's not about monkeys. It's about God and this thing called 'evolution'. Lucas, your people came from Tennessee, didn't they?" Lucas shook his head, asking "What does Tennessee have to do with monkeys." Jim had already accomplished his primary goal of looking down on Lucas. "Well, there is this law in Tennessee, and I think in other places, as well. The law says that you can't talk about evolution in school classrooms." Lucas asked, "What's e-vo-lu-tion?" Jim thought for a moment and then responded, "Well, according to what they were saying in town, 'evolution' is that human beings came from great apes." Jim was clearly winning the competition. You could tell by the looks on the men's faces. Jim continued, "But, that goes against the biblical fact that God created man. You know...you remember...it's in the Bible, Genesis, I think. That's where God creates everything in six days and then rests." Lucas said, "Yes, that is where God said 'Let there be light' on the first day...and there was light. Then, day two, God created the firmament, separating Heaven and earth. The third day..." Lucas continued through all of the biblical days finishing with "And on the sixth day, God created man in His image and man created woman. And God looked over everything that He had made and it was very good." Jim appeared shocked, surprised, to say the least. Apparently, he never thought that Lucas knew his Bible. This was one of those surprises that Lucas gave us. On one hand, you don't think of him as that talkative or knowledgeable. But, it was clear, as night is from day, that he knew his Bible, and knew it very well.

Jim said, "Lucas, everything that you just said was on trial in Tennessee. The atheists are saying that there is this thing called evolution and that we came from apes. But, as you said, we know from the Bible that we were created by God on the sixth day. No question about it! So, we couldn't have come from apes. And, so, to prevent the teachers from instructing their students about this crazy idea, a law was passed. This teacher, by the name of Stokes, violated that law, teaching his students about evolution. Then, he was arrested and put on trial. Fortunately, the teacher was found guilty. Thank God! The Bible won!! Now, they can't teach that evolution stuff in their schools."

As for me, I know the Bible, so I knew what Lucas was saying. But, I had no idea what Jim Clark was talking about. I wanted to ask what "atheists" were but I maintained my silence.

The men seemed to have exhausted the subject. So, not to be rude, I had waited for that quiet period to get up and brew some coffee. Then, Lucas spoke up again and started talking about the prices of soybeans and winter wheat. Jim had some comments to make about the prices and how difficult it was to make a living. The discussion died down once again.

From that first formal dinner at the farm, I came to realize that silence is very difficult to deal with. It makes people uncomfortable. And, many times, people look to fill the void, the silence, even with things like a trial that had happened years earlier. I came to realize that Jim and Lucas were just looking for something to talk about, to impress one another, to fill that void. That's all. I don't think that they actually cared about that trial.

But, I also realized that night that all of this was new to me. I had never heard the words "evolution" or "atheist" in my life. I was afraid to ask. Other than the eggs that I sold at the Fair that day, I didn't have a feel for the price of the crops at the farm or anything else. I knew that it was all important. But, it was all over my head. I wondered whether Dolly and Helen or Jack and Betty really understood the discussion. I was too embarrassed to ask. If they did, I would have blushed even more. I knew from that very moment that I needed to study many new subjects, possibly more than I had ever learned about at school. Now, this farm, this new world of mine, was to be my real school.

Once everyone finished dinner, I got up and cleared the table. I brought the apple pie and coffee back with me. I served the pie and poured the coffee. Everyone dug into the pie and seemed to enjoy it. Then, Dolly said, "Mary, this pie is as good as the last one. Dinner was wonderful. Jim and Helen, did you know that Mary made the entire dinner herself?" Helen responded by saying how wonderful everything was. There was no response at all from Jim.

This 'Helen', before me, was a completely different woman than the one that I met when she came over to visit with Dolly by herself. I thought long and hard about why there was such a difference in her aspect. I came to realize that it was probably having Jim there. Their relationship seemed cold. There was barely a word spoken between them.

Betty helped clear the remaining dishes. While she was doing that, Dolly and Helen chatted away about all of the local gossip. I heated up some water and added a little soap to clean the dishes in a few trays. After they were washed, I set them aside to dry. Helen helped Dolly into the main room sitting her near to the fireplace. Although it was late spring, there was still a chill in the air. It was cold enough for the fire to be lit. Jim and Lucas went outside to smoke. Then, they went to the root cellar and from there to the barn. The root cellar was where Lucas had his, not so secret, stock of alcohol. The barn was where they imbibed in these illegal spirits.

With Dolly settled and talking with Helen, I went outside to the porch. It was good to just be by myself for the moment. There were so many thoughts rattling around in my head. I wasn't there for more than a few moments when Jack showed up and sat beside me without saying a word. He waited for a moment. Then, he asked me what I was thinking about. I couldn't share my thoughts with anyone, certainly not someone that I had just met. I said, 'Nothing special." I stared into the wonderful starlit sky. I continued, "Jack, isn't it a wonderful day? The weather is just perfect." He agreed. I think that I said these things to fill that void of silence which was so uncomfortable, even for me. Again...silence. We sat there together feeling the intimacy of sitting so close without touching or saying anything. He appeared to be searching for something to say. He looked down and then at me, then down again. I wish I could have helped him but I was as unaccustomed to speaking with a boy, a man, as he was clearly uncomfortable speaking with me. After a few minutes, I realized that we didn't need to say anything. It was alright to just be together on that porch in the cool of the night.

Jim and Lucas came back from the barn where they had imbibed some of that homemade brew that Lucas distilled. From halfway between the barn and the farm house, Jim shouted out, "Okay, we're leaving." He continued walking as he was shouting to no one in particular. But, everyone could hear him. As he walked into the house, he glanced sideways at Jack and me sitting on the porch together. Then, he glared back at Jack. He and Lucas walked inside. Jack followed me back into the house. Goodbyes were said all around. Once again, Jim barely recognized me. Helen said that she would see all of us at church in the morning. As she said it, Jack glanced at me and gently shook his head up and down indicating to me that he also looked forward to seeing me there. I could tell.

As the Clark family left, I walked over to Dolly and told her that it was an interesting evening. "I have never heard such an interesting conversation as was had at the dinner table. Is it always that interesting when they come for dinner?" She looked at me with a curious smile, "Yes, well, it was more than just a conversation. It's never just a conversation. Those two men always try to outsmart one another. They are always competing. I believe that it is in their nature. Maybe it is in the nature of all men." Then, Dolly looked into my eyes and asked me if I had a good time. "Yes, it was very interesting." She said, "I know that you thought that it was an interesting conversation. You have said that already." She seemed almost insistent that I open up with my real feelings, not some benign comment. She said, "I didn't mean that. I think that you know what I mean". I must have blushed. She let it drop. She said that we should get ready for bed. And, in the light of a single candle, we prepared for sleep. With Dolly settled, I took care of my needs and laid down listening to Dolly's gentle snoring indicating to me that she was comfortable. I had a lot to think about that evening and had difficulty falling asleep.

The next day, Sunday, started early for everyone. We had to get everything done prior to going off to church. I knew that Dolly would be climbing up on the truck, climbing down and walking a lot. Then, there was the sitting and rising in church itself. I know that her spirit would not let her miss any of the services, even the singing. So, I prepared more of the willow bark infused tea in the hope that it would help relieve some of her discomfort.

Jack was over very early to milk the cows and feed the chickens. Everything else would have to wait. He left to get ready himself. We were going to church. After Dolly was dressed and prepared for the trip, I sat her on the porch in the sunshine. I went back to the bedroom and put on my new blue dress and added the shoes that I wore at school. At school, they had our hair cut very short making us look like boys rather than girls. But, now, my hair was just beginning to grow out. Maybe it was only in my imagination. Anyway, I ran a brush through it. When I walked out onto the porch, Dolly looked in shock as if she had been told a long kept secret. She stared at me and said, "Mary...you are even more beautiful than I thought." She always had the nicest things to say. Lucas joined us on the porch. Dolly repeated what she had said to me. "Lucas, isn't our Mary just beautiful." Lucas said nothing. I am fairly certain that it was not the type of compliment that he had any experience responding to. He was much more comfortable talking about soybean prices than how beautiful a woman was or wasn't. In that regard, he was exactly the same as most farm men.

Lucas set a wooden step that he had fashioned alongside the truck and we helped Dolly get aboard. I picked up the step and put it in the back, securing it with a lash. Dolly sat alongside Lucas and I sat on her other side. We were off. The trip to the church in Muskogee took about fifteen minutes. Lucas pulled up in front of the church. I jumped down, ran around to the back and retrieved the step. I placed it so Dolly could climb down. I helped her down and into the church, settling her into one of the pews. Lucas parked his truck and joined us in the church.

As the parishioners gathered in the church, there were a lot of looks coupled with hushed comments. The few that I was able to hear focused on me, wondering who or what I was. Once everyone was seated, Pastor Berkley started with an opening prayer and a greeting. Then, as everyone was greeting each other, the pastor said that we have a new parishioner in the church. With that, he took the time to introduce me to the congregation. He asked me to stand up for a moment. I did. There were more hushed comments and looks. I didn't know whether I should feel good about the looks or feel threatened by them. I sat down and the services resumed.

Pastor Berkley's sermon addressed how people reacted to one another. His point was that the way that you treat or mistreat other people should not be a reflection of them or their behavior. It is a reflection...of your own behavior, of your own spirit and humanity. He continued, saying. "There is no question that some people are mean-spirited, they could be without merit of any kind. You might think that you can treat them poorly, give them less of your time or ignore them altogether. However, their behavior or actions do not give you reason to treat them poorly. The way that you treat others is a reflection of your value, of your integrity, of your Godliness." He kept emphasizing the word, "your". I couldn't believe it. That was exactly what Dolly and I talked about just yesterday. Was he clairvoyant?

What he said rang true. It resonated with my spirit. I wish everyone would behave in that way. I have to say that I enjoyed the services. Pastor Berkley knew his congregation well.

The services ended and we began to walk toward the doorway. We didn't get far before many of the parishioners came up to me to welcome me to the congregation. A few of them offered any help that I needed. They probably knew about Dolly's illness. I thanked them and moved on. At the doorway, Pastor Berkley greeted us and asked me how I was. Of course, I answered that everything was wonderful but that I had so much to learn. I thanked the good pastor for his sermon and told him that it was very meaningful to me. We parted. Dolly, Lucas and I continued down the walkway until we found a bench. I had Dolly sit down and rest until Lucas could retrieve the truck. Then, as we were sitting there, we met up with the Clark family. Helen greeted Dolly and me. Betty just stood shyly alongside of her mother. Jim said "Hi" to Dolly, ignoring me. Jack took notice of his father's slight, once again, and immediately said hello to me. He asked me how I liked the church service. I told him of my appreciation of the pastor's sermon. While I spoke to Jack, I saw that he couldn't take his eyes off of me. His father, Jim, noticed his son's attraction. I didn't think that he was very happy. I started to think that Jim Clark didn't like me very much even though he didn't know me at all. I thought of the pastor's sermon as fitting given Jim Clark's reception. I quickly understood that Jim Clark didn't appreciate or didn't understand the meaning of the pastor's words.

Jack said, "I was thinking that you can go around with me as I do some of the chores tomorrow morning." I turned to Dolly. "What time would be good for you?" Dolly responded that

Jack would be there from very early in the morning. She said, "We will figure it out in the morning. OK?" Dolly was changing the course of the conversation. Of course, we all shook our heads. We were all uncomfortable with the unspoken issue of Jack's ulterior motive of spending time with me and of his father's obvious displeasure with everything that he saw before him.

Jim Clark came over to his son Jack and gently nudged him away from me saying that they had work to do at the farm and they had to leave. As Jack was leaving, I turned to Dolly. She said that she looked forward to working with Jack to teach me how to do everything. I shook my head. I knew that I would be taking care of these different chores as soon as I could learn what was required.

Before yesterday, sitting with Jack on the porch. I had never been with a boy...never. I had barely even spoken to any boys. So, this was all new to me. It felt good even though there was nothing to it. It was all unspoken feelings. It was harmless. Well, that just wasn't completely true.

Chapter 7

I got a real early start on Monday. The morning regiment with Dolly had been well established. After everyone ate and was ready, I sat Dolly comfortably in the cool of the barn. Jack was already working his chores for Lucas. Once he saw us come into the barn, he stopped and walked over to us with his hands on his hips and said, "Good morning. Are you ready?" I shook my head.

Dolly immediately took over the lesson. She said, "Let's start with the hens and their eggs. Mary, egg laying hens produce about one egg a day. While they live about eight years, these hens are only productive laying eggs for about two or three of those years. After these hens are beyond their egg producing years, they are too old to eat. Most chickens that we raise or purchase to eat are only about three to five months old. The meat of those young chickens is much tastier. The older hens' meat is gamier. People don't like eating these older hens. Okay?" I shook my head. Dolly continued. "There are only two ways to deal with hens that are beyond their egg producing time; kill them or sell them to pet food factories. That is what we do, we sell them for pet food." I guess that I never thought about it. When you look at an egg, you just see it as an egg. You don't look at it as one part of the life of a mother hen. But, there you are.

Jack stood by, waiting to make his contribution. He told me about feeding and watering the hens and cleaning out their cages. Then, he told me about candling the eggs to make sure that they were not fertilized and in the process of a developing chicken. I had already learned about that but didn't stop him from teaching me. Jack said, "And that's all there is to eggs."

Dolly told Jack to take me to the milk cows. As we walked over to the milking stalls, he explained that the Taddum Farm has about ten milk cows. I was confused because I knew that they were not milking ten cows. With that quizzical look on my face, Jack said, "Okay, here it is from the start. Young cows are inseminated at about 13 months. It takes about nine months for a cow to birth their calf. The calf is separated from their mother after only a few days. The milk cows lactate for about 10 months and then they are inseminated again and the cycle for the cows begins again." I shook my head as if I understood what "inseminated" or "lactate" meant. More words that I had to learn. Jack continued, "Each cow can produce six to eight gallons of milk, every day. If you want to think about it, here at the Taddum Farm, there are mostly four milk cows that produce about thirty gallons each day. And, that's a lot of milk. At our farm, we have even more. Farms that have electricity have milking machines. Since neither of us has electricity, we do all of the milking by hand. When we were at the milking stall, Jack showed me how to milk a cow saying, "It's a lot of work milking even four cows, twice a day.

"We can't readily pasteurize the milk here at the farm. So, Lucas takes most of the milk to a local pasteurizer. Selling it at the Fair is more profitable than selling it to a pasteurizer. So, we sell the raw milk, cream and skim milk that we collect on Thursday, Friday and Saturday mornings at the Fair. We also make butter or cheese out of enough of the milk to satisfy our needs and our customers at the Fair. I thought, boy oh boy, it is complicated. I guess that I looked like I felt. Dolly said, "Mary, don't worry. It will all be clear to you after a while.

"Jack has been helping with the morning milking and with the eggs and sometimes other chores. Lucas has been taking my place milking in the afternoon and making the butter and cheese. It's been a big burden for him adding to his other chores."

Then, Dolly proceeded to show me the process to make butter from the cream and cheese from milk. She asked Jack to get her some cream that had separated out from the skim milk and a bit of butter milk that was stored in the root cellar. She added a touch of buttermilk to the cream and asked me to pour it all into the butter churn. She asked Jack to churn because she didn't have the strength to do it. Jack obeyed and after a few minutes the churn was opened. The cream had magically turned into butter and buttermilk. After some washing of the butter, Dolly showed me how to transfer it to wax paper. That was it.

There was still so much more to learn. But, I knew about egg laying hens and how to milk the cows and how often. I knew how to make and store butter. That wasn't all that there was. But, it was a start.

Then, Dolly said, "Mary, I know that you and Jack did all of the work, but I'm the one that is tired. Please take me back to the house. I need to rest." That's what we did. I took Dolly back to the bedroom. She laid down. I started to leave the room when she said, "So, what do you think about what you learned today?" She was always asking me what I thought. I said, "What I realized today is how much I need to learn if I am to be of any help on your farm. Today was only the start." I hesitated, but then I blurted out, "I'm embarrassed to ask, but…what does 'pasteurize', 'inseminate' or 'lactate' mean?" Dolly broke out in a smile and started laughing. But, she wasn't laughing at me. I knew that because as she was laughing, she reached out her arms and waved her hands in the air beckoning me to draw near to her. I came into her embrace. Then, I sat on the bed and leaned over to her as she whispered, telling me about what those words meant. Pasteurize was easy to understand. The other words were an education of another kind. I guess that I blushed. Dolly said that I shouldn't be embarrassed. "These words and their meaning are normal parts of our life. They're certainly part of farming." She repeated, "Really, they're not something to be embarrassed about." I felt a little better although I didn't think that I could ever say those two words to anyone other than Dolly.

Even these early days of my life on their farm, I was looking to make a contribution, to be more valued than just a worker, taking care of Dolly. Of all things, I thought of the cheese that they sold at the Saturday Fair as one way of achieving that goal.

I had always loved cheese, although the cheese that Dolly and Lucas made, Farmer's cheese, is not very flavorful. At school, cheddar cheese was occasionally served with our lunches. And, as part of one of our homemaking classes, we were taught how to make it. I always loved what I made. I thought that Lucas' customers at the Fair might enjoy it as much as I did. And, we could sell it for much more than the Farmer's cheese.

With Dolly resting, I walked into the barn and started to look for something with which to make some cheddar. I wandered around and came upon that large bucket that Lucas had bought at the General Store. It looked to be five gallons, more than enough to make a large trial batch of cheddar.

I took the bucket out to the well pump and gave it a good rinse. When I got back to the barn, Jack was still milking the cows. I hollered at him, "Hey, Jack. I need that fresh hot milk". He looked at me curiously but stopped what he was doing. I said, "I'm going to make some special cheese and I need the milk to be hot. This cheese is going to be as fresh as anyone could think of, taking the milk directly from the cow's udder."

Jack milked the cows, filling my bucket. I thanked him for the milk and tried to pick up the bucket. I could barely get it off of the ground. Jack saw me struggle and brought the bucket of milk near to a small table so I could work on it. I ran to the root cellar to get the milk cultures and rennet, starting the process. I was so excited that I woke Dolly up and told her all about the cheddar cheese. She thought for a moment and said, "Make your cheddar and we'll see if we like the taste." Then, Dolly added, "Don't you have to age cheddar? How can we sell it if we have to age it?" I said, "Dolly, you're right. At first, we will sell it pretty much as we make it. But, then, we will age some of it until…well, once we get going, we will be making cheddar for sale in three months. Do you understand? After a while, there would be no difference." Dolly shook her head. I think that she understood. Well, maybe not.

By the end of the day, I had cast my first wheels of cheddar cheese. The cheddar that I made was very fresh, not aged at all, but I took a small bite of what I had made. It was delicious. So, I cut off a little piece and brought it back to Dolly. She smiled, saying "It really is very good. Go find Lucas and have him taste it."

I found Lucas out in the fields. I told him what I was doing. I offered him a small piece. He shook his head and said that it was very good. I related that we needed the cheese to be aged for at least 90 days for it to be best and that we need more space in the root cellar to age the cheese. I had done my calculation and asked him, "Could you build five 10 foot long shelves in the root cellar for the cheddar to age?" He chuckled. I didn't think that he was laughing at me. I just think that he was amused by my childish enthusiasm. He said, "Of course. I'll do it."

My schooling continued. Several evenings that week, after dinner, Lucas taught me about everything that was sold at the Fair and how to "haggle" with the customers just like I had seen him do with the woman who wanted a lower price for her eggs. Dolly sat on the settee listening and adding her advice to complete my education. I wrote down every word of what he and she told me so I wouldn't make a mistake. I studied my notes just like I did in school. By Friday evening, I had memorized everything that they had told me.

That Saturday, Lucas and Jack helped load up the buckboard for me to take to the Fair. Lucas saw how stressed I was. He told me not to worry, but I did. To relax me, he made it clear that he would be okay with whatever I did at the Fair. This was so totally different from my experience in school where any infraction was punished. Regardless of what he said to me, I didn't want to disappoint Dolly or Lucas. I was both nervous and excited.

Lucas put about a dollar's worth of coins in my purse so I would be able to make change right away. I had to be very careful to make the correct change. I didn't want anyone think that I had cheated them out of a few pennies. Then, Lucas grabbed my hands in his and said, "I'll watch over Dolly. I know that you will do great. Don't worry so much." Jack smiled and said that he would be there shortly after he picked up his goods. I was glad. I realized at that moment that I enjoyed being with him.

So, ready or not, I was going to the Fair, ready to haggle with the customers and sell everything all by myself. When I got there, I unloaded everything. The milk containers were heavy, more than forty pounds each, but I managed. The eggs, the chicken crates, the butter and the cheese were all off loaded. Then, I moved the buckboard out of the way to an area where the horse could graze and there was a source of water. He would be okay.

I got back to the table and greeted the people with a broad smile as they passed by. I immediately found that I enjoyed selling, talking with people and haggling over pricing. Selling seemed to be in my blood. I had no idea. I had learned my lessons well.

After more than two hours into this new adventure, as sales were slowing, I heard what sounded like an argument at a nearby vendor. It was hard to tell due to the distance, but it sounded like the woman was speaking in the Cherokee language. It had been a while since I had spoken more than a few words in Cherokee. It was discouraged in school. No, that is not correct. What I mean is that if we tried to speak in the Cherokee language at school, even in our dormitories, we were hit and punished. So, I had only spoken Cherokee when I went home to visit my grandparents. But, back to the customer. I believe that the customer said, "Hi-la-go hi-la-go da-gv-wa-lo-dv na-s-gi-na-l tsu-we-tsi". "How much for eggs?" Along with the lady's pointing, I was pretty certain that was what she was saying. I walked over, leaving my table. As I got closer, I heard the woman ask the same question. Then, the vendor just threw his two hands up in the air and said something disparaging like, "Damn Indians, why can't they learn to speak English." Well, I guess that he "got my Irish up". At least, that part of me that was Irish. I was angry. In school, I learned quickly that becoming angry, and acting out, only got you more severe punishment. But, my anger was seemingly always there in the background, just below the surface. While I knew that I was not going to rid this one man of his prejudices, I needed to focus on this one woman's needs and help her out.

I said to this woman, "Tsu-we-tsi?" She responded back in the Cherokee language, "Yes, I just wanted to know the price of eggs". I repeated that to the vendor. He responded in a nasty voice, "Tell the woman that they are fifty-two cents a dozen and I only sell them by the dozen." I could have told her that I sell them for forty-seven cents a dozen but quickly realized that would start a war with this vendor. I didn't want to do that. So, I tried my best to tell the Cherokee woman what the vendor told me. She responded that she would take a dozen. I repeated that to the vendor. He said, "OK, but I want the money first." I asked the woman for the fifty-two cents and handed it over. The vendor handed me the eggs in a box. I handed the box over to the woman. The sale was completed. The vendor was so obnoxious.

As I walked away, I felt my blood surging through my temples, once again. I guess that I ignored the pastor's sermon. I stopped, and turned back to the vendor. Losing control, I said to the vendor in a really nasty voice, "Ya, know...not everyone speaks English, even white immigrants." He said, "Yeah, yeah", you're right. It bothers me when they don't speak English either." I threw my hands up in the air and walked away. It was no use to try to change this guy's attitude!

As I walked back to my table, I realized that this Cherokee woman had followed me. She tried to strike up a casual conversation in Cherokee. It was difficult for me at first. But, the more that I spoke the language, the more that it came back to me. We spoke for a while and revealed our backgrounds to each other. It felt good to speak the language again.

She said that she was new to the Fair and didn't appreciate that she would have to speak English to buy from the vendors. I thought that was quite naïve of her but kept that feeling to myself. I gently said to her that learning English would help her here at the Fair and really, everywhere else. I explained to her how my grandparents wanted me to maintain the Cherokee traditions yet to learn to read, write and speak English. I continued, "They had told me that I must live in the two worlds to be successful." She smiled at me.

The woman said that she would be back and would bring all of her friends to shop at my table. I thanked her for that, although I knew from my reception as a child by members of my own village, that prejudice is wrong regardless of from whence it comes. So, I explained to her that it would make things worse for the Cherokee if she bought only from me because I was Cherokee. Then, she said that they would do it only because they could communicate with me. I thought about it. I realized that there might be some validity to that argument. Ugggh. Why does everything have to be this complicated?

I finished selling. I packed up the egg baskets, the chicken crates and the other materials that I had brought with me from the farm. I brought the buckboard around and packed everything in the back.

I was about to leave the Fair when I saw Jack standing in back of his table. I wanted to talk with him but I had no experience in the game that boys and girls play, looking for reasons to talk to one another. But, I tried. I walked over to his table and asked him how his sales were going. He told me that he had done well. I told him that I had sold out. He was impressed. That back and forth was my first foray into that game. Then, Jack asked me what happened with the Cherokee lady. I explained. He said, "Do you remember Pastor Berkley's sermon last week? Ya know, people should just treat other people fairly." Well, I surely did remember. I responded, "Jack, I don't believe that the vendor could even understand what Pastor Berkley was talking about." Jack just shook his head in agreement. I was happy with his response. He wasn't placating me.

We talked a little more and then I said that I would see him back at the farm tomorrow morning. To me, at that moment, Jack had transitioned in my mind from being just a shadow walking across the barnyard, in the dark, to a person that I wanted to see, and be seen by, in the daylight.

As I was about to go back to the farm, I picked up a newspaper from a table nearby. I thought that Dolly would enjoy reading something to occupy some of her time. I asked how much they were, placed the three cents on the table and bought the newspaper.

I returned to the farm and off loaded all of the baskets, crates and other materials that held the products that I had sold. I was "over the moon". I had made a real contribution. After all, even though Dolly thought of me as a woman, I still felt and acted like a child.

I walked into the house, excitedly telling anyone what had happened at the Fair. Helen was there visiting with Dolly. Both of them were happy for me and appreciative that I had rapidly picked up on what needed to be done. Helen questioned me regarding what I mentioned about the Cherokee woman. I filled her in. She thought that I was quite smart to use my language skills in that way.

In my excitement, I almost forgot about the newspaper that I had brought back. I handed the newspaper to Dolly. She seemed pleased. I asked her if she would want me to get one each week that I attended the Fair. She thought that it was a great idea and thanked me.

I made lunch for Dolly, Lucas and Helen. When Lucas came in from the fields to eat, he asked how it went at the Fair. He seemed so relaxed about something that I had been so nervous about. I excitedly went through the entire experience at the Fair once again. He seemed pleased as I went through everything, although I probably included too much detail. I had already developed a sense of Lucas as a guy who didn't have patience for details. But, then, as I finished, a big smile lit up his face which validated everything that I had done.

When I told Lucas about the newspaper, he hesitated, seemingly not very interested. But, then, he grabbed at his overalls. His face slowly rotated around his neck. He admitted, reluctantly, that he had never read a newspaper in his life. But, then, he said definitively and forcefully, "Why not?!" Lucas looked directly at Helen Clark. "It will keep me up to date and I'll be in a better position to respond to Jim Clark when he starts talking at dinner. And, boy, he does like to talk! I bet ya that he reads the newspaper." Lucas was looking for a competitive edge in his battle with Jim Clark and he might have just found one. And so it was.

I said, "I almost forgot...Mr. Taddum, here is the money, less the three cents for the newspaper. He took the purse from me, counted the money, smiled, and handed me back the purse with about a dollar's worth of change left inside for the next week's Fair.

From that one single experience, I had already developed a rhythm regarding the Saturday Fair. There was nothing about it that remained a mystery. I liked selling at the Fair, especially since Lucas had entrusted me to do everything by myself after just one week, some instruction and a lot of studying. I was learning. However, I did have a concern about leaving Dolly alone for so many hours, week after week. So, after Jack picked up Helen, I expressed that concern to Lucas. I had forgotten that Lucas told me that he was going to ask Helen to visit Saturday mornings. "Mary, Dolly and I have already spoken with Helen. She's agreed to come over every Saturday morning with Jack and stay while you are at the Fair. The ladies enjoy each other's company and this gives them a good excuse to get together, just the two of them, without the men folk or the children around. Then, Jack will come back after he returns from the Fair to bring Helen home. Also, I'm here if there is anything Dolly needs. It will work out well...so, don't you worry about leaving Dolly for the morning." He looked over at Dolly. She nodded her head in agreement. But, then, Dolly stared at Lucas, and stared and stared. I didn't know if she was unhappy about something that he said.

Then, Lucas cleared his throat, "Ahem...Mary, do you remember what your headmaster and pastor told you when you asked if there were to be a salary for your work here. I believe that they said that there would be no salary, initially, but that we would see if that could change. Well, you have done so well, taking care of Dolly and now, taking over everything related to the Saturday Fair. You learned everything so quickly. You have done everything that we could have wanted and more." Lucas stared into my eyes. "What do you think about thirty dollars a month?" Well, I was flabbergasted. I said...I didn't know what to say, but I blurted out. "Mr. Taddum, that would be wonderful. Thank you so much." I didn't really have a full understanding whether that was a lot of money or not. I only knew what my grandfather gave me. That was more than twenty-nine dollars. This would be thirty dollars every month. And, I didn't have to pay for food or a room. When I realized how much it would be compared to what my grandfather had given me, I gulped. I repeated my thank you. Then, Lucas said, "And listen, I don't want you calling me Mr. Taddum ever again. My name is Lucas and your name is Mary. That's the way it ought to be. Okay?" I said, yes, thank you, Mr. Tad...I mean Lucas."

Chapter 8

It was the end of September. The summer weather was waning. There was a chill in the air. I lit a fire before Dolly woke up. After taking care of my needs, I prepared a simple breakfast and coffee for Lucas. Then, I took a cup of coffee and settled into a rocking chair on the porch. I needed a moment. Quickly, I was lost in my thoughts as I sat rocking gently back and forth watching the steam come off of the coffee cup, taking very small sips of the hot brew. I thought that I was fitting in more and more in the Taddum household finding value in my contribution not only for taking care of Dolly but for my work at the weekly Saturday Fair with the Cherokee and white customers, and now tending to the winter storage of the beets, beans, squash, tomato sauce, corn and everything else. But, while I enjoyed my life at the Taddum farm, in the back of my mind there was always this nagging, and now growing, concern about my future should Dolly pass away. Or, should I say, when Dolly passes away. What would happen to me? I had some money of my own. So, I would be able to survive in town for a while if it came to that. But, there would have to be more, more of something, to thrive. I thought of various options but they all needed money or a connection. I thought that it would be great if I could open up a dress shop but that takes a lot of money and I had just enough money to survive for a little while. Thoughts…thoughts…no plan…no idea even how to have a plan.

    I went back to the bedroom. Dolly was already up and had a nice smile on her face. We worked our way through the usual preparations for the day. Then, out of nowhere, there was a holler, "Dolly, Lucas…are you there?" I didn't recognize the voice. Dolly did. I went to the door and saw Pastor Berkley and his wife, Sally, standing there. I assumed that they were here to check on Dolly and offer her some comfort. I asked them to come into the house and to have a seat while I got Dolly ready to receive company.

    When Dolly was ready, we walked back and greeted the Pastor and his wife more formally. I offered everyone a cup of coffee or tea. No one wanted anything other than a glass of water. I added some wood to the fireplace to warm up the room. Then, I sat next to Dolly. The chit chat continued for a few minutes. Lucas suddenly appeared at the door. A large smile spread across his face as he welcomed the pastor and his wife. Lucas asked me for a glass of water and I brought it to him and sat, once again, next to Dolly.

Before I realized it, the discussion turned to me. Dolly told the pastor about my making cheddar cheese. His interest seemed real as he asked me how I got the idea. I told him about how we made cheddar as part of our schooling. He listened patiently. Part way through my description, I realized that he was just waiting for me to finish.

Then, the discussion switched. Sally Berkley, the pastor's wife, had heard about my developing a large and loyal contingent at the Fair, now including many Cherokee women. Obviously, I was developing quite a reputation. I described the problems which the local Cherokee families were having including; difficulty with the English language, getting a job, money and being accepted by the town's people. Then, I stopped. I didn't want to make too big of a deal of the local Cherokee issues. Yes, it was important to me. But, I thought to myself, if I made too big of an issue, then it might have appeared to be an attack on all white people, including my farm family and the pastor himself. I knew of him as a good person who had compassion for everyone. Then, he woke me out of my thoughts and regrets when he said that he would have something to say about those problems that I had mentioned in his sermons. "Furthermore", he said, "I will welcome the Cherokee people into the congregation with open arms." I knew that he was a good man, but even that good man shocked me. He was willing to risk losing the loyalty of his white congregation, well, except for me. He would be taking a great risk. He was amazing!

Then, with all of the chit chat finished, the pastor turned to his wife Sally. Both of their faces turned down, sullen and saddened. He reached into the inside pocket of his jacket and took out an envelope. He held it out in front of his legs with stretched out arms as he sat across from Dolly and I. He looked at the envelope and remained silent for a moment. Then, he raised his head just enough to look me in the eyes and slowly stood up without taking his eyes off of me. He handed me the envelope that he had held so tightly in his two hands.

I looked at the envelope with some trepidation. I looked up toward the pastor. He didn't say a word. I opened the envelope and took out the letter. There was an eagle feather inside the folds of the letter. Once I saw that, I knew, instantly, what it meant. You see, my grandfather's name was "Wohali" which means "Eagle".

I held the feather tightly in one hand and the letter in the other. The letter was written in English and was addressed to me. I started to read the letter as tears filled my eyes. The pastor and his wife, and Lucas and Dolly couldn't take their eyes off of me. With all of them around me, I said, "If you would like, I will read this letter out loud." They all said, "Yes, please…", almost in a whisper.

I began. "The letter was written by a man named 'Waya'." I stopped myself. I said, "His name means 'Wolf'." Then, I continued, "I remember a man by the name of 'Waya' or 'Wolf'. He was a close friend of my grandfather.

"The letter is addressed, '*Dear Ahyoka*'. I stopped to explain that I was given two first names by my grandparents, Mary and 'Ahyoka'. 'Ahyoka' is my Cherokee first name. It means, 'she brought happiness'." I stopped to see the reaction to a name that I hadn't shared with them before. I read on…

"*Dear Ahyoka-*

I hope that you remember me. I was a good friend of your grandfather and my wife was a good friend of your grandmother."

When I read that he use the word "*was a friend of your grandfather*", I knew immediately that my grandfather had died. I continued, as a few of the tears that had filled my eyes began to roll down my cheeks. I didn't try to stop or stifle the tears. They needed to flow. I continued reading what Waya wrote;

> *"Your grandfather has passed away. He was very ill for several weeks prior to his death. During that time, with your grandmother having already left us and their sons nowhere to be found, my wife and I looked after grandfather during his difficult days and nights.*
>
> *"Your grandfather couldn't write to you, himself, as he never learned to write in 'Tsalagi', or in English, for that matter."*

I stopped reading and said that "'Tsilagi' is the name of the written Cherokee language.

> *"So, he asked me to write down his words. I was worried that you would not be able to read 'Tsalagi' either since you were taken away to the white people's Indian School at an early age. I know that at the Indian School they taught you only in English."*

I stopped once again and told everyone that because of my practice at the Saturday Fair, I was, once again, fluent in the spoken Cherokee language. But, I didn't learn to read or write in "Tsalagi".

After a space on the page, my grandfather's words appeared before me. My voice was almost taken away from me. After a few moments, when I was able to speak, I started reading my grandfather's last words to me.

> *"My Dear Granddaughter, My Dear Daughter;*
>
> *"I asked Waya to write down my words. He is a good friend.*

"By the time that you receive this letter, I will be gone. I am sad that I will never see you again in this life. I hope that I will meet you in the next life. But, I do not want for you to rush to get there. I want for you to live a very long life in this world, wherever you are, enjoying whatever you are doing.

"I remember all of the wonderful moments that we spent together with your grandmother by our fireplace. I remember telling you our People's stories and traditions. I hope that you remember what your grandmother and I said and will someday pass those stories down to your children and grandchildren.

"I knew when you went off to school, or even earlier, that your life would be difficult. The farm that you grew up on can never be yours. By all of the rules of both the Cherokee Nation and of the white man's world, the farm must go to my good for nothing sons. I haven't seen them in many years. But, I feel that once they hear that I am no longer of this earth, they will come and pick over my bones. In this case, the bones of my body will be worthless, but the farm will not. They will own the farm and I fear that there is nowhere, no place, in their hearts for you, my child.

"When you left school to work at that farm, I sent as much money that I had to you. I hope that it was given to you."

I stopped reading and whispered, "Yes, grandfather. Thank you." I continued reading from the letter;

"There wasn't much money. But, I gave you all that I had saved. I wish that it could have been a lot more.

"Grandmother and I knew when you left for school that you would have to be very strong. You must be very strong and very smart to succeed. You always were very smart in school. I hope that you use what you learned and what you know to be true. The truth will never fail you.

"You came to us in a very special way. You were like a gift from the gods. You made our lives a joy. You were always very compassionate. You were always very loving. We felt your warmth, your love. We, I, felt as one with you and still do. When we said your name, it made us smile even when you were no longer living with us.

"I asked my friend Waya to find two eagle feathers for me. One of the feathers will be buried with me just like we did for your grandmother. The feather will be placed in my hands. It will be with me as I travel to my next life. Maybe, I will come back to this earth in the body of an animal. Maybe, I will continue on as a spirit. I hope that I will become a spirit so I can look over you as you live your life. Maybe, I can protect you from bad spirits and difficult times.

"I placed another eagle feather in the envelope that will hold this letter to you. I hope that it finds you. It will be our connection, forever, as it will be one of the last things that I touch. I hope that you bury this eagle feather near to where you are so that I might stay close to you and remain in your heart.

'My daughter, you brought joy to us and to the world. Continue bringing joy to all that you meet. Be loving, be faithful, and be as wonderful as you were when we knew you.

Know that you were loved,

Grandfather."

I folded the letter and held the eagle feather in my hand. I raised my head and said to all, "Now, when I think of my grandparents, I feel their unconditional love for me. Their love was so great that I never had feelings of sadness about my own parent's abandonment."

The small flow of tears coming from my eyes grew to be a river. I shook with sadness. Then, Pastor Berkley and his wife,

Sally, came over to me and hugged me. Lucas and Dolly followed, joining the circle of love. They held me until the tears of sadness were replaced by smiles. Then, the pastor asked me what my grandfather's and grandmother's names were. I had to stop and think. When I was a child, I only called them grandmother and grandfather. But, it only took a moment for me to remember. I said proudly, "My grandmother's name was 'Adsila' which means 'Blossom'. My grandfather's name was 'Wohali' which means 'Eagle'." I thanked him for asking. He just shook his head gently up and down. I smiled and then closed my eyes and lowered my head wanting to savor the moment.

I was so grateful for the letter that the pastor brought to me. I was equally grateful for the kindness shown to me by Pastor Berkley, his wife Sally, along with Dolly and Lucas. I had seen little emotion from Lucas toward me until that very moment. But, his warmth and hugs made me very happy. I believe that I saw a tear forming in his eyes as I read my grandfather's letter. I had seen his tears before only when he told me about Dolly's illness.

Then, Lucas surprised me once again when he said, "Mary, 'Ahyoka', would you like to bury your grandfather's feather here on the farm?" I started to cry once again. I tried to control myself. I said, "Thank you. That would be wonderful". But, in my heart it was more than just nice. It was respectful of a culture that they didn't really understand. Yet, more than their understanding of my culture or anything else, they wanted for me to feel their love.

I asked Lucas if I could pick out a place to bury the feather. He agreed. I knew of such a place underneath a large oak tree on the hillside just above the root cellar. I knew that oaks are strong just like my grandfather was. I told Lucas about the location. He said that he knew where I meant. The pastor asked if he could join me as I buried the feather. Dolly looked at me and said that she would like to be there but didn't think that she could make it up the hill. I had to agree. Sally, the pastor's wife, said that she would stay with Dolly.

I held the eagle feather in both of my hands as Lucas, the pastor and I started walking out of the house. Then, Lucas said that we should wait there. He needed to get a shovel from the barn. When he was in the barn he came upon Jack doing chores. I overheard them talking. Jack came out of the barn and said that he was sorry for my loss. Then, he asked if he could join us. I said, "Of course". Lucas agreed. We all walked slowly up the hill to the place where my grandfather's memory would be held for as many years as it can be remembered.

When we got to the spot, Lucas asked if he could dig a grave for the feather or if I wanted to do it. I thought it best if he did it since he had offered. When the digging was completed, I stood over the hole for a while because I realized that once I put the feather into the ground, the reality of my grandfather's passing would be complete. As if, by not placing the feather into the ground, my grandfather would be still alive. I know that is not rational. But, it was an emotional time for me, an end of a portion of my life that could never be recovered.

Then, the pastor asked if I wanted him to say a prayer. I thought that it might be something that resonated with me. I asked him to recite a few verses of Ecclesiastes. He folded his hands together and recited from memory;

*"There is a time for everything,
and a season for every activity under the heavens:*

*a time to be born and a time to die,
a time to plant and a time to uproot,
a time to kill and a time to heal,
a time to tear down and a time to build,
a time to weep and a time to laugh,
a time to mourn and a time to dance..."*

The Pastor's voice faded into the background of my consciousness. I thought about my childhood, sitting on grandfather's lap as he told me about the People and their travails, stories of our heritage. "Mary, Mary, mmm Mary." The pastor said, trying to get my attention. He asked me if I wanted him to recite anything else. I responded, "Yes. Pastor, please recite the 23rd Psalm of David." The Pastor closed his eyes and began...

"The Lord is my shepherd; I shall not want..."

His voice faded again. I thought to myself of how wonderful it was of the pastor to do this for me...

"...and I will dwell in the house of the Lord forever."

Then, the pastor added closing remarks of his own choice;

"We pray that your grandfather rests in peace and may his memory be a blessing to you and to all of us."

The recitation of these ancient prayers made me feel better. I was blending the two cultures of my heritage. I placed the feather carefully in the grave. I picked up the shovel and placed a small amount of dirt on top of the feather covering it completely. Then, I handed the shovel to Lucas. I asked him to place a small amount of dirt in the grave. He then handed the shovel to Jack who did the same and finally, to the pastor who blessed the ground and finished filling in the "grave". It was over. I was saddened. But, there was so much good that had come out of this experience.

We walked back to the farm house together. I felt that this experience had made me a part of this circle of friends and neighbors. I no longer felt like a stranger, a servant, even an outcast. I was at peace.

When we got back together with Dolly and Sally, the pastor described the ceremony just completed. Dolly repeated the final blessing,

"Mary, may your grandfather rest in peace and may his memory be a blessing to you."

Two days later, Jack walked from the barn to the farmhouse after finishing his chores. He called out my name, "Mary...Mary. Are you in the house?" I responded, "Yes, I'm taking care of Dolly in the bedroom. What do you need? What can I do for you?" He responded that he would wait on the porch until I had a few minutes for him. Once Dolly was comfortable, I went to the kitchen and washed in the water that we kept there in a large jug. When I was presentable, I walked out to the porch. I smiled as I was glad to see Jack. He seemed very excited. He asked me how I was and if I had a few minutes to be with him. I found myself happy to be with him so I would make the time. He was talking very fast.

Jack asked for me to go with him. I said, "Of course. Where are we going?" Jack said, "Just come with me". He reached out his hand as we walked away from the farmhouse. My heart skipped a number of beats. I didn't know what to do but I had only a second or two to decide. So, I grabbed his hand as we walked up the hill, above the root cellar, to where my grandfather's feather was buried under the oak tree. I didn't look at him and he did not look at me. No words were shared. Then, when we were at the top of the hill, I saw a large piece of shale erected at the place where my grandfather's feather was buried. It was about a foot wide and two feet tall. It appeared like a crude grave marker. As I got closer, I realized that there was writing on the stone. Jack told me that he found this large piece of shale on his farm and thought immediately that my grandfather's "memorial" needed a marker. He called it a "memorial". Jack had carved "Wohali" near to the top of the stone. Just below, he carved "Eagle". Below my grandfather's names was carved the year that he died, 1929.

Wohali

Eagle

1929

The writing was crude. But, it literally took my breath away. I had been doing more than my share of crying over the last few days. This was yet another occasion. I wasn't sobbing. Not really. My tears were falling down and dropping onto the ground. It was as if my tears were watering the grave of grandfather's eagle feather.

Jack said, "I'm sorry that the writing isn't better. I didn't have the right tools." I looked at him, straight on, and gave him a hug without saying anything. I looked at the marker. There were no words that could have captured my feelings. My tears turned to a smile. Sometimes there just are no words. We left the hillside. Jack went back to the barn. I came back to the house. When I walked into the kitchen, Dolly looked at me. I guess that my face was red from crying, once again. She asked, "What did Jack want?" I told her what he had done and how pleased I was that he did that for me. I didn't tell her about holding hands or the hug that I gave him. Dolly said, "Remember what I told you about the worker bees doing what they had to do to build a hive. But, they really do it all for the pleasure of the queen. I think that Jack has taken a liking to you." What could I say? Could I say that she was wrong? If she was right, Jack was the first boy that had taken notice of me. Were there others? I couldn't think of any. Should I tell Dolly that I have taken notice of Jack? I said, "I think that Jack is just very considerate. He probably thinks of me as a sister." I thought for a moment. "Dolly, I have never had any boy take notice of me." Dolly replied, "I know that it is difficult for you to accept. Jack may be the first but he will not be the last. You have too many fine qualities not to be noticed. And, as I have told you before, you are very pretty. Why wouldn't any boy, or man, for that matter, take notice of you?" When she said "man", it took me by surprise. I blushed once again. I seemed to be doing a lot of that, blushing, that is. But, I was only sixteen. I only knew men like my grandfather or his friends when I was a child. Now, I knew Pastor Berkley and Lucas and a few others from town. I said to Dolly, "I don't know any men in that way." She said, "You will. It will happen to you before you know it." I thought that Dolly was talking to me as my mother might have, if I had one, or rather as an older sister. Even though it was difficult, it felt good to have someone to talk with about these types of things.

    Everything that had happened since the letter arrived from Waya left me with a rainbow of emotions. I was sad about the loss of my grandfather. He was my most favorite person in the whole world. He was the link with my Cherokee past, my traditions. But, it was more than his stories and legends. It was him. It was his spirit, his life. I was glad about the warmth and blessings from having a circle of friends starting with Dolly and Lucas, and now, Pastor Berkley and his wife, Sally, and, of course, Jack. And, yet, at times, I felt alone even though I was in the midst of all of this love.

    For the next few days, my thoughts were focused upon the loss that my grandfather's passing represented to me. But, thinking about all of the good times that I spent with grandfather made me smile.

Chapter 9

More schooling. Lucas taught me about the crop rotation that he plans out. Each year, each season, he makes the decision as to whether he should plant two wheat crops or one wheat crop and one soybean crop. He bases his decision upon current and future crop prices. This fall, he will be planting winter wheat. And then, just before Easter time, he will look at all of the "futures" pricing information that he gets at St. Mark's Farm and Feed and make the decision in good time to get the seed that he needs for spring planting. It is with the sale of these wheat and soybean crops that keep the farm going. The garden, the cows, the chickens and the eggs are all there to feed the farm family and now, that includes me. Any sales at the Fair is a help, but the crops are the foundation upon which the farm survives.

For every planting, Lucas hires quite a few migrant workers to help in the field. These people stay for as long as they are needed and leave when the work is done. They come from somewhere else and are quiet and respectful when they are here. And then, they leave as quietly as they came.

The days passed quickly. I was learning more and more about the chores that I had to take over from Jack and Lucas, chores that had done by Dolly prior to her illness. One day, Lucas asked me to go to the root cellar to get something for him. Sending me to the root cellar for that something was just a canard to get me to go there. I went and saw Lucas' work. Seeing the new shelves that I had asked him to build was the real reason that he sent me into the root cellar. I excitedly gathered the aging wheels of cheddar and stacked them on the shelves. I took a heavy wax pencil to mark the edge of the cheddar wheels with the date that they were stored.

I went back to the barn to thank Lucas. I started to say thank you…then I saw him in front of a large work table. Jack was in the background. In front of the table was a chair. There were also four new five gallon buckets for preparing cheddar cheese. None of this was present just minutes before. I said, "What?" Both men smiled. Lucas said, "I know that you have been struggling with your cheddar cheese production. This is your new work table. This should help. I also got you some more five gallon buckets so you can prepare several batches at the same time. The only thing that I could think to say was, "How wonderful! Lucas, thank you so much." He had done everything that I asked for and more.

Then, it was the very beginning of November. It had been more than three months since I put the first wheels of cheddar cheese into the root cellar for aging. Now, the first of these aged cheddar wheels would be available for sale. And each week I would be selling at least seven or eight wheels of the aged cheese. That is, if the people at the Fair really like it. I hope so.

Well, it wasn't too long before we found out. By this point, I had made about sixty wheels of aged cheddar, each one weighing in at about five pounds. I enjoyed the cheddar even before it was aged. Now, I couldn't wait to have a taste of the final product. So, I took one of the oldest wheels and took the smallest of pieces and tasted my creation. The cheese literally melted in my mouth as I sucked all of the flavor out of it. I was so excited. I had to have Dolly taste it. I ran back to the house, large cheese wheel in hand.

I burst through the door without opening it properly, shouting, "Dolly, it's time. It's wonderful!" Frankly, I was behaving like the child that I was. She said, "What's going on? Are you alright? What's wonderful?" I said, "Dolly, it's wonderful!" She said, "You have said that twice. Now tell me, what is wonderful?" I said, "The cheese…the aged cheddar!" Dolly threw up her hands into the air and said, "Oh, is that all? What is so exciting about a wheel of cheese?" Excitedly, I said, "Dolly, please taste it and let me know what you think." She did. All she had to say was for me to find Lucas and get him to come back to the house. I went to the door and rang the bell. In just a minute or two, Lucas came to the door and asked what the matter was. I think that he was afraid that Dolly had taken a turn for the worse. But, once he came through the door and saw the smile on Dolly's face, he knew that everything was good. Dolly saw the look on his face and said,

"Lucas, Lucas, everything is okay! You have to taste the cheese that Mary made." I broke off a piece of the cheddar and handed it to Lucas. He looked at it and smelled it as if he were a connoisseur. I quickly realized that foods do satisfy the entire palate which includes the odor, the tactile feel and then, the taste. I was more impressed by Lucas because of the way that he approached my cheddar. Lucas finally tasted the cheese. He let it melt in his mouth and seemed to savor the flavor. Then, in what seemed to have taken an eternity, he looked at me, and then, at Dolly and then, back at me and said, "Mary, you have made something that is delicious."

If I could have, I would have jumped for joy. I had wanted this to be so good that it would help the farm. I had wanted to be recognized by these two as a person of value, a person who had a contribution to make…yes, if only for making a better cheese. From the reaction of both Dolly and Lucas, I had achieved my goal.

In all of the time that I spent at the Taddum Farm, I would always be able to focus on making my cheddar as a respite from the stresses in my young life. It was that important to me. But, now, it would be up to our clients at the Fair to determine if they would pay more for this than they do for our Farmer's cheese or any of the competitors' products. That was the real test.

The next Saturday, I took my aged cheddar to the Fair along with everything else that I normally sold there. I decided to cut off a chunk of the cheddar and break it into small bite size pieces and give them away for the tasting. Well, there are always takers for something that's free. The people stopped and grabbed one or two pieces of my cheddar. They were hooked. Almost all of the cheddar was sold out in less than two hours. And, the cheddar was sold at a much higher price than the Farmer's cheese.

Jack came over and tasted the cheddar. He thought that I had a winner. He left, going back to his nearby table, shaking his head up and down. I could see a big smile on his face even from the side. The head shaking only stopped when he got back to his table. I think that I impressed him.

Then, as I was packing up at the Fair, Jack came back over to talk with me. He had something other than cheddar cheese on his mind. He told me that he saw a poster for a barn dance that was coming up in a few weeks' time. It was for Wednesday night, the day before Thanksgiving. Then, he said, "Would you like to go to the dance with me?" Well, I froze. I couldn't answer. I wasn't trying to be deceptive or coy. I was shy. I just couldn't find an answer. That moment of silence seemed to take forever. All the while, Jack was looking into my eyes, waiting for my response. In my mind, I heard what Dolly had said to me about the worker bees and the queen. I broke out in a broad smile at the thought. Jack said, "What…what's so funny?" Then, I caught my breath and said to Jack, "But, I don't know how to dance!" I didn't tell him what I was really thinking about, those worker bees and that queen, that is. Well, it was also true that I didn't know how to dance; not The Charleston, whatever that is, or square dancing or waltzes or Foxtrot or any of those dances. I had never learned. I wondered if Jack knew how to dance. Jack said, "That's not a problem. I've never actually gone to a dance before and I certainly don't know how to dance. Look, we'll learn together. I'm certain that we will not be the only people there that do not know how to dance. But, Mary, you didn't answer the question. Would you like to go to the dance with me?" I took a deep breath and said, "Of course."

Sometimes, Lucas would spend Saturday afternoons at the kitchen table reading the paper as if he was studying for an exam. He wanted to be ready for Jim when the Clark family joined us for dinner. And, there was a lot going on during the last year of the "Roaring Twenties". Lucas shouted out to Dolly several times, reporting all that he had read. He said, "Hey, Dolly, there is excitement about what the papers are calling the Depression. They described people losing their money and actually jumping out of windows, killing themselves." He stopped and read several more minutes, then resumed his monologue, "The paper is talking about how people are on the move. More people, having strange names, are coming from Eastern Europe. Dolly, I don't see any of this stuff here in Muskogee. Whenever I go into town, I see the same people. I don't see anyone jumping out of windows. They couldn't hurt themselves even if they did. I don't think any of the buildings downtown are more than two stories tall. The paper must be talking about the big cities like New York and Chicago. They're certainly not writing about Muskogee, Oklahoma." Lucas seemed satisfied with all that he had learned and reported to Dolly.

Lucas' preparation for the dinner battle with Jim Clark was complete. As dinner was well underway, the battle of wits began. Lucas and Jim, although unaffected directly, were not pleased with what they read about those new people coming here with those strange names. They quickly forgot that their forebears were once immigrants themselves. They were intolerant of the new arrivals even though there was no scourge of immigrants in Muskogee. Jim and Lucas rarely agreed, but they did about immigrants. They thought that the army should be used to stop those people from coming. Jim was always seeking a higher ground so that he could speak down to Lucas. He said, "Even people in the East were intolerant of the new arrivals. The paper said that they use their lawyers to add land deed restrictions that prevent Jews, Negroes, Spanish and other 'less desirable people' from moving into their towns or neighborhoods. As I said, those lawyers back there are a pretty smart lot!"

There was a quiet time. Then, Lucas tried to regain his position by saying that he read a lot about Al Capone and others in Chicago, selling booze, violating the Prohibition against alcohol sale and use. Lucas ranted how they should just put those guys in jail. I listened, thinking how Lucas and Jim just couldn't relate what they were reading and ranting about with what they were doing themselves. Laws like Prohibition just didn't, couldn't, apply to Lucas or Jim, or any of the other local farmers who had secreted stills for the production of hard liquor alongside their beer fermentation.

I read the same stories but somehow I found myself interpreting what I read completely differently from these men. As for me, I had plenty to say, but said none of it. Women's opinions did not carry much weight in those rural farming communities of the 1920s. For me, it was worse. I had no social standing at the table. I was an observer. But, one who could readily see the dichotomy in their arguments. They were against immigration but were the children or grandchildren of immigrants themselves. They were in favor of raiding speakeasies and smashing drums of alcohol in Chicago but had no problem with their alcohol stills and the beer that they fermented. The facts of the matter be damned. It didn't matter. Those counter arguments were on the tip of my tongue and that is where they stayed. Anyway, I believe that Lucas and Jim mostly enjoyed arguing and competing. What they were arguing about didn't much matter.

After dinner, when Lucas and Jim went out to the barn to imbibe in some of those very illegal homemade spirits, Jack said, "Mom...Mrs. Taddum, I would like to take Mary to the Thanksgiving Barn Dance in three weeks. May we have your permission?" The two women just looked at each other. Dolly wasn't surprised. But, Helen was. Dolly didn't say anything. Helen said that she would have to talk it over with father. Nothing more was said. I was confused. Was Jack asking Dolly? I didn't know that I needed permission from Dolly or Lucas to go to a dance in my spare time. Or, was Jack asking his mother?

I thought about the scene some more. I realized that what just happened was that Jack knew something that was unspoken. It wasn't just him asking permission to take a young lady to a dance. No. For a young man with an impeccable reputation and manners like Jack, no mother would say that she needed to speak to her husband. No...no. There was more. There were many possibilities. But, I was focused upon only one of them. What happened was exactly what my grandfather had talked about for me. He said that my life would be very difficult because of what I was. I had hoped that he was wrong. But, I realized, once again, that he was right.

I was so upset that I just had to walk out of the house and get away from these "well-mannered" people. I held the tears back until I was far away, in the dark, so no one would see me cry.

Jack ran out of the house and found me near the root cellar. It was dark but I guess that he heard me sniffling. Jack said, "Mary, why are you crying? What did I do? What did I say?" It took a while for me to compose myself. I didn't quite know what to say to him. How could I tell him of my feelings about what just happened? Am I exaggerating? Was there nothing sinister involved? Am I about to open up a subject that would destroy our relationship, a relationship that I was beginning to feel so good about? What should I say? Should I just keep quiet?

But, my anger bubbled up. I took a deep breath and said, "Jack, I appreciate that you invited me to the dance. I really think that we would have had a good time together. But, asking for permission to go to the dance upset me. Why would we need permission? I am almost seventeen. You're older. Many girls of my age are married already. Yes, I work for Dolly and Lucas. That makes me their employee. But, I am not a slave…their slave. I don't need their permission to go to a dance. So, that leaves only a few possible reasons for asking for permission from your parents. Is it because I am just an employee of the Taddums? Or, is it because I am half Cherokee? Is it because I am a bastard child? What is it? Why do you need your parent's permission to take me to a dance?!" All of these things that never should have been said just came out of me as a catharsis of everything that was always in the back of my mind.

Jack was flabbergasted. It took him a minute to compose his response to my outburst. I started quivering with emotion. Jack grabbed me around in the still and darkness that was night. He held me tight. It was the very first time that I had been held like that. I felt his warmth. Jack said, "Yes, you work for Lucas and Dolly. But, Mary, I asked permission because I thought that it was the right thing to do. I didn't know what Lucas and Dolly would have thought about me taking you out. You're right. I didn't need to ask their permission but I thought that it was respectful of me to ask. And, Mary, before that incident at the Fair with the Cherokee women and the ceremony burying your grandfather's eagle feather, I didn't even know that you were Cherokee. And, until right now, I certainly didn't know anything about your parents. Yes, I knew that you were raised by your grandparents. But, you are not the only person in the world that was raised by their grandparents. And, yes, frankly, I also thought that Lucas and Dolly's 'approval' would go a long way with my parents. After all, I am only seventeen myself and I still feel that I need my parent's permission to go to a dance with a girl." I had thought of Jack as much older. Yet, I knew that there was more to it than that. Jack was not yet able to verbalize what the real issue was.

Jack reached out to me with his hand. I didn't take it this time. He said, "Come back to the house with me. Everything will be fine. I don't care what my parents or the Taddums say. I should have just told them that we were going to the dance together. I'm sorry for asking. That's all. Please, will you come to the dance with me?" Jack reached out his hand again. This time, I accepted the offer and squeezed his hand gently, but firmly. Jack said, "Wipe those tears out of your beautiful eyes." I picked up a piece of my sleeve and wiped my eyes. He said, "Now, they are as beautiful as they were before."

We walked, hand-in-hand, back to the farmhouse. Before we even got too close, we could hear them arguing. As we got nearer to the porch, we could hear what was being said. Jim Clark was the loudest. I could hear him say, "...I'm prejudiced? Really? Isn't everybody? Isn't everybody prejudiced against everyone else? Hell, the Catholics hate the Protestants and the Protestants hate the Catholics. Everyone hates the Jews and Negroes. Hell, even the Cherokee are prejudiced. Lucas interrupted Jim and said, "Wait a minute, isn't Dolly's doctor, your doctor, Doc David Held, a Jew? Didn't he help you when Betty was very ill? Isn't the owner of Tanner's General Store a Jew? Isaac's a fair guy. He's a nice guy. I never heard that you had any problems with him or the good doc. There are a few Jews who are farmers in the area. You've never had any problems with them...have you?" You're friendly with many of the Catholics in town. You're always talking with Bill McLaughlin, the owner at St. Marks. He's a Catholic. Why, the Cherokee people that I know are very nice. I have no problem with the Cherokee." Lucas was rambling. Jim was frustrated, always seeking the high ground in his battle with Lucas. "Lucas, did you know that the Cherokee had slaves themselves even before the white people came to this place. Did you know that they fought for the Confederacy during the Civil War? You see, prejudice is all over. I'm the same as everyone else." Lucas' spine stiffened. He'd had enough! He said, "First of all, 'no one's jeans are clean', period. My people came from Tennessee. That state was on the side of the Confederacy. I don't know if my people fought in the war or not. I don't know if they had any slaves or not. They might have. Dolly's family was from North Carolina. They fought for the south. They might have had slaves...I don't know! But, if you want to talk about the Cherokee, what about the Cherokee soldiers that fought in the Great War? Did you know that some American Cherokee soldiers used their language skills to help the Brits hide their communications from the Germans? There was an article in the newspaper just last week about what they did. But, ya know, Jim, I don't give a 'tinker's damn' about any of that because Mary was neither fighting for the Confederacy, nor was she one of the Cherokee fighters in the Great War. I don't want to talk about the Civil War or the Great War. Because, here is what I do know. I can tell you that Mary is so much more than just someone who works here. She's wonderful, taking care of Dolly as she does. She's smart. She's talented and creative. Dolly already thinks of her as a sister...as a daughter. I'm very fond of her, myself. And Jim, if you haven't noticed, she's beautiful! If I had a son that wanted to take that girl to a dance, I would be proud."

 With that, there was silence in the house. I wanted to run away, but Jack continued to hold my hand and every time that I wanted to pull away, he held me tight, using his other hand to stroke mine. Jack urged me to follow him back into the house. I was torn. But, I was also buoyed up by everything that Lucas had said about me...about me as a person, not a member of anything other than the nation of people. That is what I wanted to be, period.

 We walked into the house, hand-in-hand. Jack said, "We were standing on the porch." When Dolly saw me crying, she struggled to walk over and hug me. There was a silence with everyone's heads down wishing that they were not there at that moment, each for a different reason. Helen and Betty were uncomfortable having heard all of what Jim had said. Dolly and Lucas were embarrassed by what I heard. Looking at their faces, I thought that they might have wanted to distance themselves from

Jim. That would have required re-opening the discussion. They probably didn't want to continue all of that ugliness. Jack told me later that he had never heard his father say anything like that before. Maybe, his father revealed those feelings only to discussions that he had with his friends.

Jack had never disobeyed or disputed his father in his seventeen, almost eighteen years. But, he knew that he had only a moment before he would either ignore his father's rants and lose me, or dispute them and save his friendship with me. He had a difficult path to travel in just the next few seconds. Jack released my hand so that he could get closer to his father without dragging me into the fray. When he did, I said to him in a whisper, "Jack, please, don't fight with your parents over me…please." With that, I walked further into the background. I didn't want any part of this fight. I didn't want a fight, period. But, Jack would have to decide what he wanted to do. And he did!

Jack went up to his father and spoke as an equal in a clearly unequal relationship. "Dad, no one is perfect in that they don't have any prejudices. But, I do not want to suffer from that disease of the spirit. I do not want to pass down those prejudices that you live with. You may. I choose to look at people as they are. I look at their souls and the manner in which they treat others. I look at who they are, not what they are or who birthed them. We go to church every Sunday. What have you learned? Do you remember Pastor Berkley's sermon where he said 'the way that you treat or mistreat other people…is a reflection…of your own spirit and humanity.' I look at Mary and see a wonderful individual that has a history that is somewhat different from mine. But, maybe, just maybe, it is her history that makes her as wonderful as she is. Father, this is Mary as you see her before you. She came here to be a help and comfort to Dolly and a help to Lucas. But, she is so much more than that. You have heard her speak. You have watched her work. You know her value, her quality, her goodness. Father, I love you. But, I hope and pray that this is the last that I will ever hear from you on this subject."

Jack turned away from his father. But, then, quickly, turned back. "Father and mother, I tell you now that Mary and I will go to the Thanksgiving Barn Dance. That is, if she will still come with me. We may not be able to dance, but that is all right. She will see others and will be seen by those others. All of those people with big eyes and small minds can say what they want. I will be Mary's date for the dance. And hopefully, she will agree to go with me to other social events. And, that is all that you will hear from me about this matter."

  The looks on his parent's faces were priceless. Jack had been firm, but respectful. He was perfect. I admired the sense of composure that he had. I thought that I would not have had the courage, had I parents of my own, to be as forthright and to stand up to them as Jack did with his parents that Saturday night.

  I pivoted and walked out. Jack followed me into the darkness of the barnyard. He caught up with me. Jack was about to say something when I grabbed him around and kissed him as if we were husband and wife. "Jack", I said, "What you did tonight was so…brave. I don't know quite what to say. But, please, I don't want you to feel that you have to say anything more about your father to me. He is probably no different from many of the people in this community. Yet, somehow, you are different. I wonder how, given your father's strong opinions, his family leadership…" Jack started to talk. I placed my hand gently across his mouth and said, "Please, let me finish what I have to say to you. Jack, I heard every word that you said. This was not the first time that I have seen your goodness. But, I also know that much of our world is not of your spirit. Please understand, I don't want to come between you and your family. That is your world. I don't want to put you into an even more difficult position should your father tell you not to take me to the dance. I wouldn't want that. So, I want you to forget about taking me to the dance. I am releasing you from any obligation that you feel you have to take me to the Thanksgiving Barn Dance." This time, Jack placed his hand gently on my cheek and said, "Mary…Mary, please. I want to take you to the dance because I want to be with you. As far as my father is concerned, I will deal with him. He may still have the feelings, as you say, like so many others. But, those are his feelings. They are not my feelings."

I loved everything that Jack said and did. But, I thought that he was naïve. He lived under his father's roof, in his house. It was not fair to have him in this position. With that, he just looked into my eyes. We just stood there just looking at each other.

I wanted to just stand there and look into Jack's eyes forever, but I had to end the discussion. I told Jack that I had to go and tend to Dolly. I walked toward the house just as Jim, Helen and Betty were leaving. I slowed down just enough such that I wouldn't have to confront them. When I got to the porch of the house, I could hear Lucas and Dolly talking in whispers. When I walked through the door, they stopped. They smiled. Then, they both offered me their open arms and their love written from ear to ear. They both hugged me as I cried in their arms.

I didn't want to make it harder for Dolly and Lucas so I redirected the conversation, asking if I could make a cup of tea for them. They both accepted. So, I heated the water. The three of us settled at the kitchen table and had a nice cup of hot tea. As we finished drinking the tea, in almost absolute silence, Lucas said, "We should all get to bed. I really think that it will do us all some good. What do you think?" There was something ironic about what he just said about "doing us all some good". I laughed out loud just because it struck me in that way. Dolly started laughing and then, although he tried to suppress his laughter, Lucas joined in, well…a little. The tension was gone from the house. We all said good night while continuing to hold back laughter. It was good.

I settled into my straw bed. I was about to blow out the single remaining candle when Dolly asked me if I would sleep with her this one night. I was still stung by the evening's events. So, when her offer reached my ears, I was very happy. I quickly climbed into bed with her.

While I lay there trying to go to sleep, I thought about my own culture wars. The purpose of the Indian Schools that I had attended had nothing to do with being an "Indian". That was all about transforming "Indians" into Europeans by learning about one-sided histories of the founding of this country and about loving Jesus Christ. It was about denigrating our history, traditions and religious beliefs. But, even after the white people transformed us, they would never accept us as part of their community. And now, we have exhibit number one. Jack's father hated me, and people like me, even though I had adopted everything that I had been taught. I spoke English, dressed like everyone else and prayed to Jesus Christ. What more was required? But, here we are. Fortunately, one good thing came of all of this turmoil. Forced by Jim Clark's obvious prejudices, Dolly and Lucas welcomed me, even more, into their home. To them, I was just another human being. And that is what I wanted to be…just another human being who happens to be part Cherokee and part Scot-Irish!

      As I dropped off to sleep, Dolly draped her arm around my shoulders and gave me the smallest of hugs. There was nothing more that needed to be said. I felt her love. I hadn't had someone with whom to share my feelings and my emotions with since I left my grandmother's side and went off to school so many years ago. Now, I had someone that I could share with, someone who felt to me like a mother or a big sister. I know that I enjoyed being with her. We both slept well.

Chapter 10

Morning came quickly. Dolly seemed to be in good spirits and didn't seem to be in any real pain. I don't know if it was the yarrow patches or the willow bark tea that helped her. I didn't know enough about her illness to really understand when she would have pain and when she would be comfortable. As I got Dolly ready for church, she told me that I called out in my sleep. I asked her what I said. Her response was that I said, "Jack, oh, Jack!" How many shades or red are there in a blush? I think that she enjoyed telling me that. She wanted to see my reaction.

We headed off to church. This was to be the day after the night before. It was to be a time of tension, a time that could be pivotal in my relationship with everyone involved. I decided to remain still, quiet, and let it work its way out.

We walked into the chapel. Jack and his family were already seated. Lucas, Dolly and I sat two rows behind them. I guess that Lucas didn't want to be so close as to require anything more than a formal greeting. That is just what happened. The Clarks turned around as we entered the pew two behind them. Each of the Clarks except for Jim simply said, "Good morning all". Jack waited to be last. He turned to Lucas and said, "Good morning Mr. Taddum". Then, he turned ever so slightly in the direction of Dolly and said, "Good morning Mrs. Taddum". It was obvious, wasn't it? He could have just said, "Good morning all". But, that is not what he wanted to do. So, with everyone in those two pews holding their breath, Jack said, "Good morning Mary. How are you on this fine day?" The question required a quick answer. I didn't wait. I said, "Good morning Jack. It is a beautiful day. I am fine and I hope that you are, as well." I purposefully didn't want to end with yet another question hanging there in the air. The pastor harrumphed and greeted the congregation. "Good morning everyone".

Typical of most of the worship services at his church, the good pastor offered an opening prayer and then suggested that everyone greet their neighbors and wish them well. My heart skipped a beat. I said to myself, "Why couldn't we have sat on the other side of the isle or further back so that we would have to be so close to the Clarks?" That was certainly a question without an answer. So, I swallowed and waited until Lucas and Dolly had completed their greeting. Then, I reached my hand out to Helen who returned the favor. Betty was next. Then, I extended my hand to Jim Clark and looked right into his eyes. He took my hand, but it was like a honey bee lighting down on a blossom. Like the blossom, I was barely able to feel his touch although I saw his hand next to mine. I withdrew my stare and looked down at my hands as I felt the disdain of Jim Clark. I knew that nothing had changed in the hours since last night. I knew that everything that I was concerned about was well-reasoned. Finally, I reached out to Jack who took my hand in both of his and said, "Greetings, neighbor!" Our eyes connected for the briefest of moments. We all turned toward the pastor as he continued the service with scripture readings. Interestingly, he read from Ecclesiastes. He read the same prayer that he had during the memorial ceremony at the burial of my grandfather's feather. When he completed the reading, he looked straight at me. I knew...I knew. He did that for me.

Then, the pastor harrumphed again. It got our attention. Pastor Berkley began, "One of the lines from the third psalm of Ecclesiastes says that there is 'a time to tear down and a time to build'. We live among people of many descriptions. There are Catholics and Protestants of many denominations. There are white folk and there are people of the Cherokee Nation. In fact, this very land that we live in was once an Indian Territory that was combined with the Oklahoma Territory to become the State of Oklahoma. Up to now, the people of the Cherokee Nation have not been welcomed in this church. That ends now...today! Yes, we're all different...we're all different. But, the differences between us pale by comparison to the sameness of people of all kinds. If we are to be one with Christ, then we must be one with each other, with all of the people."

The pastor talked about the trials of the Cherokee with the English language, finding jobs and being accepted by the town's people. He asked that we include these people in our church and that we give them jobs when and where we can. He said, "Support their businesses. Buy local tribal wear at the Saturday Fair. Support them as they will support us." Finally, he said, "I am looking for volunteers to help our friends learn to read and write English. I will be here on Wednesday afternoons to lead the way. Please join us." Then, he reiterated, "Yes, we are all different. Let's celebrate our differences. Let's learn about each other and create an even greater community of faith. As it says in Ecclesiastes, let us build up. No more tearing down." The pastor folded his hands together and asked for a moment of silent prayer and meditation. After that moment, he looked up directly at me and offered a closing prayer to the congregation. Oh, my, how brave he was.

And, over some time, I was able to convince some of the Cherokee ladies that I knew from the Saturday Fair to attend those Wednesday afternoon English classes. And, as some of them grew more comfortable with their English, a few Cherokee families came to Sunday morning services. Of course, initially, there were those unmistakable looks coming from some people in the congregation. Or, as Jack would say, "those people with big eyes and small minds". And, yes, there were those, like Jim Clark, who didn't join in the welcome that the pastor sought and never would. But, with the pastor's encouragement, the Cherokee families were more and more accepted over time. What can I say?

As we left church that Sunday. I delayed ever so much to come closer to Jack. He smiled and asked, "Are we still going to the dance?" I shook my head and said, "I think so". He replied, "Really?" I was being playful and he was being playful back to me. "Yes, yes, of course, I want to go with you. I'll try to dance with you but you know that I don't know how." Then, I walked over to the pastor and thanked him, saying, "Your sermon came at just the right moment." I didn't explain.

I didn't know it but Dolly overheard my conversation with Jack. When we got back to the farm, she said, "Would you like to learn how to dance?" I said, "Yes, neither of us knows how. We haven't ever gone to a dance in our lives." Dolly responded,

"Tomorrow, after Jack finishes his chores here, ask him to stay for a moment, and then, come and get me. We will meet in the barn."

Monday came. I got up early to take care of Dolly, breakfast for everyone and then, I went to the barn. Jack was already there. I took care of collecting the eggs so I could move them into the root cellar for storage until next Saturday's fair. Then, I took one of the milking stools and sat just feet away from Jack. I said, "Good morning." He responded with a smile and a greeting. Then, there was some silence. I blurted out, "How would you like to learn how to dance?" Based upon the look on his face, he was surprised by my offer, saying, "Mary, I thought that you didn't know how to dance?" I told Jack that I don't know how but that Dolly offered to teach us. He said, "Sure, I'll try, but I don't know how well I'll do. I'm pretty clumsy, ya know."

After we finished milking the cows, I asked Jack to get one of the chairs from the kitchen. I left the barn to get Dolly. He rushed to get the chair back to the barn before I got there with her. We settled Dolly into the chair and brought up two milking stools and sat alongside her as she told us about the dances that were being done nowadays.

Dolly started by telling us the names of some of the new dances. She said, "The Charleston, the Shimmy, the Texas Tommy and some of the others bother some people because they seem to represent a lack of control. They are more passionate and just the opposite of the spiritual growth that Christians desire for their children. To some, they represent all that is wrong with the 'Roaring Twenties'. So..." She continued, "I think that you should learn only the more sedate dances, those that would not upset anyone." We agreed. There were enough issues with us going to the dance. We didn't want to add anything that would upset Jack's father even more.

Dolly began the arduous process of teaching two people how to do the basic box step of the waltz. At first, she had us stand side-by-side. She said, "Step forward with your left foot. Then, step forward and to the right with your right foot. Bring your left foot next to your right foot. Then, step backwards with your right foot, step to the side with your left foot and then bring your right foot next to your left foot." Dolly had us do these basic steps for several minutes to her cadence of one, two, three, one, two, and three... You can imagine that it wasn't as simple as it seems. Then, Dolly told us to face each other. She said, "The traditional dance position is for the man's left palm to hold the woman's right hand. Then, the man places his right hand on the woman's shoulder blade and the woman places her hand on top of the man's arm. I don't know if it was Jack or I that were more embarrassed at the thought of being so close. Then, we both started giggling. Dolly said, "Well, really, there is nothing to it. But, if you are going to be embarrassed, then I will start you off by myself." To our surprise, Dolly stood up right in front of Jack and said, "Jack, place your right hand on my shoulder just like I told you." Jack stood there like a deer, looking straight at Dolly, but did nothing. So, Dolly grabbed his right hand and lifted it up to her shoulder. Dolly said, "Good. Now, reach out with your hand and grab my palm." Jack did as he was told. His face was as red as a beet vegetable. Dolly told him to relax. Of course, he couldn't. Dolly asked Jack if he now understood how to hold his dance partner. He didn't say a word. He just shook his head. Dolly dropped her hand and sat back down. She said, "Mary, now it's your turn." She directed me into position in front of Jack and slightly to his right. Then, Dolly got up again and placed Jack's hand on my shoulder blade and raised my hand to his. The thrill of being held by Jack like that made my heart beat so fast and so hard that I thought that it would come out of my chest. With Dolly's count, we went through the steps, awkwardly and slowly. Dolly said, "Work together to be comfortable in each other's arms and practice again and again." After about twenty circles, Dolly snapped me out of my trance saying that she was tired and asked that we take her back to the house. I felt that we had accomplished something. Jack picked up the chair. I supported Dolly until we got to the porch. She asked to sit there for a minute. Dolly told us that not everyone will know how to dance. And, for many others, they only know how to waltz. Then, she asked us what we thought about dancing. Of course, I liked it. Of course, it was wonderful. But, I could only say that it was "very nice". Jack responded in the same way. Dolly said, "Jack, you had better be going along. I'm certain that you have a lot to do at home." Those wonderful few moments in my young life ended.

Two days later, Dolly asked me to fetch Jack and come into the house after he completed his chores. So, after milking alongside Jack, I told him that Dolly wants us in the house after we've washed up. So, that's what we did.

When we got close to the house I heard music. We looked at each other and continued through the door to find Dolly playing a record on her Victrola. When she saw us, she lifted the needle off of the record. Dolly said, "This is your second dance lesson. Do you remember what I taught you on Monday?" In unison, we said "Yes". "Well", said Dolly, "Now we are going to waltz to music. Are you ready?" Again, we both blushed. Dolly said, "Now, none of that. You have to get used to dancing with each other or other people...seriously." Dolly said, "Stand here in the middle of the room. Take up your position. Jack, hand on Mary's shoulder. Mary, your left hand on top of Jack's arm. Hold each other's hands in your palm. Yes, that's it. Now, the music." The label on the record said that it was "April Showers" sung by Al Jolson. Dolly wound up the Victrola and set the needle onto the record. She said, "I think that this will work. Now, Mary, remember that as Jack moves forward, you move backwards. You'll get it once you practice it a few times." Once the music started, we stumbled around for a minute or two. Then, we started to smooth it out just as Dolly had said. The record ran out. Dolly started it again. We danced and danced. After listening to the Jolson record a few times, we started to actually dance together. Dolly's enthusiasm was contagious. It fueled our efforts. After another few minutes of dancing, Dolly said, "OK, that's enough." As we separated, we realized how close we were for all of that time. Dolly told us that we should have two more practices prior to the barn dance. She added, "By then, you should be pretty good."

Chapter 11

The days grew colder as we headed toward winter. Snow, if there were to be any, wouldn't come until Christmastime or later. I had been at the Taddum Farm for five months or so. I had everything pretty well organized. I took care of the Saturday Fair and all of the foods that we sold there. I helped with the canning and storage in the root cellar. Since there was nothing to be done in the garden during this time of the year, I actually had some spare time. I used some of it to read the newspaper once Lucas and Dolly were done with it. I found myself able to contribute to the discussion at the dinner table. I was feeling less and less like that naïve schoolgirl.

One night, Dolly started to moan in her sleep more than I had heard before. I went over to her and listened to her breathing. She seemed fine but I was somewhat concerned about her. In the morning, I told her that she had seemed to be in pain during her sleep. She admitted that her pain had been increasing, especially, when lying in certain positions. Then, she started to smile. She said that I shouldn't worry about her. Of course, I worried about her. The next few nights were repeats of the same, some moaning overnight, then, seemingly nothing during the day. After a few more days of the same, I decided to speak to Lucas.

So, after the morning activities, I went out to the barn to find Lucas. I needed a few minutes alone with him. I didn't want to panic. But, I felt that I had to tell him about what I thought was Dolly's increasing pain. After all, I wasn't a nurse so I couldn't be certain whether she was just sleeping in a bad position in her bed or actually in pain from her illness. I explained to him that it might be nothing. I told him that I normally sleep very well but since that first night, hearing her moan, I stayed up as long as I could and if I did wake in the middle of the night, I tried to listen. I was cautious in what I said. I didn't want to yell "fire" if there was none. He listened carefully and then went into the house. He spoke with Dolly for a while. Then, he told me that Dolly admitted that she was experiencing some pain. He thanked me for being so caring. Lucas asked if there was anything that I needed from town since he was going there to speak with the doctor. There was only one doctor in town. I knew his name from the night of that terrible argument between Lucas and Jim Clark. It was Doctor David Held. But, I had never met him or seen him.

I didn't tell Jack anything about Dolly's "discomfort" or that Lucas had gone off to speak to the doctor in town. I didn't think that it was anyone's business but Dolly and Lucas. I didn't want to be that type of person telling tales that weren't mine to tell.

Since it was mid-November, the sunrise was near to eight o'clock. A few days later, as I walked out of the barn, I saw lights bounce up and down as a car drove up the road to the house.

I called out to Lucas that someone was coming. The doctor arrived in the dark. He was a tall, good looking gentleman in his mid-fifties. Lucas came out of the barn, greeted and thanked the doctor for coming out so quickly. Then, Lucas introduced me to him. I knew that it was time for me to step aside so that the two men could speak. They had a conversation that lasted about five minutes. Then, they went into the house. Lucas called out for me to come into the house. When I got there, he said that the doctor wanted me to help him with Dolly. I had never been to a doctor myself so I had no idea exactly what they do other than to "heal" people. At least that is what I thought. But, I was fairly confident that no doctor would ever be able to "heal" Dolly.

I walked into the bedroom. The doctor and Dolly were talking about her level of pain. He tried to have her compare her pain with things that commonly gave people pain like touching a hot tea kettle or stubbing your toe or a wood splinter. He kept looking for examples with which Dolly could compare her pain to. Finally, he said, "Did you ever stick yourself with a sewing needle?" She said, "Yes, it's like that, sharp like a needle, but not terrible."

Doctor Held asked Dolly, "I am going to have to examine your breast. Is that okay?" She shook her head. Then, the doctor asked me to help by removing Dolly's night shirt to expose her breast. He stopped and asked, "What is this?" With that, he removed the yarrow paste patch that I had prepared fresh every two days for Dolly. As he removed the patch, I explained everything to him. He responded quickly saying, "Ahhhh...some of my Cherokee patients have mentioned their traditional remedies including yarrow for healing sores and pain. Have you tried anything else? He seemed really interested. He wasn't being judgmental. So, I told him about the willow bark infused tea. He told me that he knew about that, as well, and believed that it had a true analgesic effect. I have to admit that I didn't know what "analgesic" meant. So, I asked him. I was embarrassed for not knowing. He apologized. Imagine that, he apologized to me! Doctor Held said, "Painkiller". I said, "Oh".

The doctor proceeded to examine Dolly's breast and he examined her other breast. Then, he asked her to point to where the pain was coming from. She indicated her one breast and her lower back. He took in a big breath and shook his head ever so slightly as if that was what he expected. Finally, he asked me to leave the room. I stood outside of the bedroom. I wasn't trying to eavesdrop but I heard him anyway. He asked her, "Dolly, do you have any bleeding from anywhere other than your monthly period?" I couldn't hear her answer.

After the examination was complete, I got Dolly dressed. The doctor took Lucas out to the porch. I stayed away. This was very personal. I figured that they would tell me what I had to know at the time that I had to know it. But, it was pretty clear that the news from the doctor wasn't good.

After speaking with Lucas, Doctor Held sat down on the settee and asked for me to get Dolly. I did. Dolly sat next to the doctor. Lucas pulled up a chair from the kitchen and sat across from Dolly holding her hands in his. The doctor spelled it out. He said, "Dolly, I am sorry to have to tell you that I believe that the cancer has spread. That is why you are feeling pain in your back. There could be other reasons, but really, I think that this is what is happening." He took a moment. He pursed his lips and gave a quick jerk of his head left and right. "Dolly, there is nothing that I can do for you. This cancer has spread and there is no way to stop it." He rested his hand on her knee. I saw a tear in his eye. Yes, in the doctor's eye. Then, the tear broke over and ran down his cheek and fell onto the floor. I think that said everything that we needed to know about Dolly's condition and Doctor Held, as well.

"Dolly", Doctor Held said, "I brought some medicine for you. It is called 'Laudanum'. It is somewhat bitter in taste but it is remarkable in relieving pain. It's here for you. Don't take it until you need it. But, then, you can use it up to six times a day. Each time, just pour out a teaspoon full of the elixir. Then, put it under the tongue. That's all. If you need more of the Laudanum, just have Lucas come into town. I will make sure that I have a supply there for you.

"Dolly, I don't know what to say other than I am sorry to bring you such news." Dolly gently squeezed his hands. She responded by saying, "Doctor Held, the news is what it is. It is not of your making. I guess that I can blame myself for letting it go too long. Although, as you have told me, that would not have been a guarantee that I would have had a cure. I know that. I feel sorry for Lucas and Mary. They will have the burden of taking care of me." Lucas stood there with tears streaming down his face. I couldn't stand there in the background. I moved toward Dolly and hugged her from her side as tightly as I could. I whispered to her that I would do everything that I could to take care of her no matter what it took. She thanked me. While in some ways I was still just a child. In other ways, I was already a woman.

Doctor Held rose to leave. I released Dolly so she could get up to say goodbye. Lucas grabbed Dolly and they both cried as the doctor was leaving. Seeing that, I walked him out. Once we were out of earshot of the house, the doctor told me a little more. He said, "The pain may increase to a point that the Laudanum will not be able to help her. If that happens, I can prescribe Morphine by injection. I would have to instruct both Lucas and you regarding injection of the Morphine. Then, if all else fails…Heroine. There is time to make those decisions later." Then, he sadly shook his head, climbed into his car and left.

When I walked back into the house, Lucas, Dolly and I filled the space. But, the house was empty if you know what I mean. The air was still and silent. There were no words possible.

Night followed that day. That night was even more uncomfortable than the day had been. I think that it was the silence that I found disquieting. Lying there, I was always anticipating Dolly to be in pain and any sound that she made, broke that silence that was night. My sleep was in parts, an hour here and there and then awake. Then, more sleep followed by more time just lying there in my bed. Then, I realized that I was actually waiting for Dolly to moan, to be in pain. It was almost like when I was in the dormitory at school. One of my girlfriends snored almost every night. If snoring bothers you, as it does me, then you lie there waiting for the next snore. Would it be louder than the ones before? Would it stop? From that day on, I learned to hate the nights because I was always waiting for Dolly's next moan resulting from the pain that she was suffering. I still hate the nights.

Being with Dolly from that point on was tense. I think that I was so sensitive to her having pain that I thought that I heard her moan even when she was perfectly comfortable. I had hoped that I could make her comfortable, to perform my job thoroughly and perfectly so that neither Dolly nor Lucas would have any stress beyond the obvious.

The next morning, Dolly was comfortable and apparently pain free. She smiled at me and said that she wanted to have a good day. She paused and then added, "Let's have many good days."

I went through the usual routine of getting Dolly ready for the new day. There was no discussion of the doctor's visit the day before. In fact, there was nothing that we talked about while I was dressing Dolly.

Jack continued to come by, every day, to help out. By this time, I was fully capable of doing all of Dolly's, now Jack's and my chores. But, I wasn't in a rush to tell Lucas that he didn't need to have Jack come over any more. I probably should have since Lucas was paying him. But, truth be told, having Jack come over to do these chores was a way that I could see him and I wanted to see him and to be with him.

Chapter 12

It was the day before Thanksgiving, the day of the Barn Dance. Jack walked into the Taddum house wearing a pair of pin striped slacks, a white shirt opened at the collar and suspenders. He certainly looked great. I said nothing. But, that didn't stop him. When he saw me, his eyes lit up. He said, "Mary...you are a sight to behold. You are beautiful!"

Jack had his father's truck. He drove us to the barn where the Thanksgiving Dance was held. It was just outside of Muskogee. When we arrived, Jack pulled up alongside the entrance. Then, he came around to my side of the truck. He opened the door and extended his hand out to help me climb down. I have to believe that didn't come naturally to him. Someone had to teach him about that courtesy. It had to be one of the women.

We walked toward the door of the barn. Low and behold, Pastor Berkley was at the door. He greeted us warmly. But, his being at the door wasn't only to greet us. There was a twenty-five cent cost to get into the dance. The pastor was there to collect tickets. Frankly, I hadn't thought about purchasing tickets. But, fortunately, Jack had. He handed two tickets over to the pastor. Pastor Berkley tore off about half of the ticket and gave Jack what was left. This was the first time in my life that any boy, or man, had ever bought me anything. Well...that wasn't quite true. When I first got to the farm, Lucas had purchased clothing for me. But, for sure, this was my first real date and this was the first time that anyone purchased anything for me like this.

We walked into the barn. It was electrified. The top of the barn was strung with lights, some were burned out. I had grown so accustomed to having no electricity since coming to the Taddum Farm that this was a treat.

The ceiling of the barn was crisscrossed with banners from one side to the other. The largest of the banners, strung from one corner to the other announced;

Thanksgiving Barn Dance
Muskogee, OK
1929

The lettering on the banner was huge. It was beautifully enhanced by flourishes. Some other banners filled three of the corners except where the bandstand was. The smaller banners advertised several of the stores in town. The largest of those was from the Ford automobile store just outside of town. It was quite an amazing sight.

As we walked in, Jack was greeted by several of the young men. He acknowledged them and made quick work of introducing me. As he left them, their gaze, their stare, was not on Jack, but was on me. I didn't know quite what to make of it until later when some of these same young men asked me to dance. Jack also greeted some of the young ladies. As he did, he introduced me to them telling me where they lived. I believe that he made those introductions hoping that I would build friendships with the other woman of my age from Muskogee. The only girl that I recognized was Aida Tanner. She was the daughter of Isaac, the General Store owner in town. But, when Jack introduced me to her, he said that her name was "Dolly". I didn't understand. Then, he told me that, "Her parents named her Aida. But, her nickname, and what we knew her by in school, was 'Dolly'. So, that is why I introduced her as 'Dolly'". Jack then introduced me to two other girls; Alice Hollings and Becky Smith. I said, "I'm certain that I have seen you at the Fair or maybe at church." They both said that they had visited my table at the Fair. They seemed nice enough.

Jack walked me around the barn to show me the band and the radio. We didn't have a radio for the students at the "Indian School". But, I knew that the headmaster had one. I saw it there when I was in his office as I was about to leave school. I believe that there was also one in the room where the teachers congregated before classes started. Of course, at the Taddum Farm, there was no electricity, so we didn't have a radio.

Then, someone got up on the bandstand and welcomed everyone saying, "Come one, come all, come up close so you can hear me…Ha, ha, Ha! No, you don't really need to come too close. I've got a big mouth and an even bigger voice. Ahhhh…so now, you are listening. I had to get your attention because I wanted to tell you what to expect tonight. First, we will have an invocation given to us by the good Pastor Berkley. Then, he is going to tell you young people what you can and cannot do. I think that you had better listen to him. He just might have some sway with your parents. And if he doesn't, then he knows another pastor or priest who does. Belieeeeve me! Then, after the pastor finishes, we will start with the music. We are going to start off with our own fiddlers. That's Billy McNeal and Joe Waters up there on the fiddles. Larry Billings on the base fiddle and Danny Page on the drums. And, oh, I almost forgot about someone. Yes, that's me, Ken Michaels. I'll be playing the piano and singing. Then, when we take a break, we will turn the radio on and listen to station 'WLS' out of Chicago. We'll listen to the host, George D. Hay and his fiddlers. Finally, we will say good night at about 10 o'clock so you have plenty of time to get back home and be ready for your work in the morning, especially you farmers. I know that tomorrow is Thanksgiving. But, you and I know that the cows don't take any time off, even for a holiday. With all of that said, I will turn the stage over to Pastor Berkley…pastor".

Pastor Berkley got up on the stage, thanked Ken Michaels for his introduction and started immediately with the Lord's Prayer, "Our Father, who art in heaven…" Many people joined in. Then, the pastor offered some words that he called advice on how to behave at the dance including not dancing too closely. He said, "This isn't New York or Chicago. Don't forget that." He cautioned about the use of alcohol and fighting. I thought that his approach was very smart. He kept his remarks to a minimum, making them more effective. Had he dwelled on anything too long, people would have gone into a trance. He left the stage and walked among the folks saying hello to as many people who offered a hand.

Ken Michaels got back up on the stage and said that he was going to start off the evening's music with a special request. And with that, he started to sing "April Showers" at a nice slow tempo. That was the song that Dolly had played on her Victrola for us to practice our dancing. That brought a smile to my face. Jack saw my smile and offered me his hand just like he had been taught to do by Dolly back at the house. I latched onto it for fear that if I let go then all of this magic would disappear in a puff of smoke. Jack wrapped his right hand around my back and I placed my hand on his arm just like Dolly taught us. And we danced around the floor of the barn just as if we knew what we were doing. I thought that we were really doing well until I saw some other couples literally dancing circles around us. But, I was okay with that.

When the song was over, Jack dropped his hands. Everyone clapped for the band. We stood there looking at each other completely satisfied that we hadn't made fools of ourselves. Then, I thanked Jack for having them sing that song, "April Showers". He said, "No, Mary, I didn't do that, honestly." Then, both of us said the same thing at the same time, "It must have been Dolly". Well, we knew that Dolly couldn't have done it directly but she could have asked Lucas to speak to the band leader. I said, "I'll ask Lucas and Dolly if they arranged for that song to be sung. And sung first."

With success under our belt, Jack asked if I wanted something to drink. He told me that they had apple cider or hot chocolate. I had never had hot chocolate so I asked him to get me a cup. Jack said that he would also get one for himself as he preferred hot chocolate to apple cider. When he walked away to get the drinks, several of the boys and men walked over to introduce themselves to me. I found that all very flattering. Just before Jack came back, one of them introduced himself and asked if I would like to dance with him. That was another first for me. All of this was so new to me. I didn't know the proper response but I knew that I wanted to be with Jack. So, I said, "Thank you very much but I am here with Jack Clark." With that, the gentleman thanked me and walked away. A minute later, another man came up to me with the same question in mind. And just like the first gentleman, I refused him too.

When Jack came back with the drinks, I told him what had happened. He looked a little nervous. But, when I told him how I refused their offers, that I was here with Jack Clark, he seemed more relaxed. I asked him if I was right to refuse the offer. That seemed to have pleased him even more. He could have laughed at my naiveté. But, if he wanted to laugh, he held it to himself.

Ken Michaels led his small band through some more upbeat songs. Some of the more experienced dancers did "The Charleston". It looked easy enough. But, the way these girls were dressed, and all of the shaking that they did, well, it was more than I was willing to do. So, when Jack asked whether I wanted to try it, I told him that I would rather not. I didn't explain my reasoning to him. There were several other dance numbers that seemed to be a bit more progressive than I was prepared for at that moment. But, then, they started playing music for doing square dances. Neither of us had any idea of what to do, but we joined in a square and copied the others. We tried to not step on anyone else's feet. We made mistakes, stopped, and then, started up again and laughed and laughed. But, I didn't worry about it. By the end of the night, we were doing pretty well, not as well as many of the others, but good enough not to be embarrassed.

In between sets of songs from the band stand, they turned on the radio. The band members got something to drink themselves, chatting during their time away from the bandstand with people around the barn. Jack introduced me to several more people as we walked around, enjoying the music and also enjoying talking with people. Then, a song by Fanny Brice came on the radio. I had never heard of her, but, oh my, did she have a wonderful voice. It resonated from the radio to every corner of the barn. The song was called, "My Man". Of course, I had never heard it before. But, it was perfect. I said to Jack, "Let's dance to this song." And we did. I didn't know, at the time, how prophetic the refrain lyrics would be in my life.

After some more songs from the bandstand, Ken Michaels, the band leader said that he would be playing the last song, "Who's Sorry Now". Ken sang and the fiddles strained. Jack and I danced more comfortably knowing that we had successfully navigated the Thanksgiving Barn Dance without any problems. Neither of us was embarrassed by our dancing or anything else that we did that evening. But, then, a chill ran through me as I thought about going back to the farm and Jack going back to his house where his father hated the idea of Jack taking me to the dance in the first place. I thought that there might be some words between Jack and Jim when he returned. I tried to ignore that feeling. When the song was over, Jack leaned over and whispered in my ear, "Thank you for a wonderful evening." I didn't say a word. I just smiled, closed my eyes and nodded my head.

Jack drove back to the Taddum Farm. We hit a few bumps in the road with the lights rising up, lighting the branches of the trees one moment and falling down highlighting the holes in the road the next. As we were going along with the truck lighting the way, I wondered how we would have made out in the dark if we just had a horse and buggy.

We got back to the farm without any problems. Jack jumped around to my side of the truck and opened the door in a true gentlemanly fashion. He walked me to the door. I faced him, gave him a kiss on the cheek. He responded in the same way and then we kissed on the lips. It wasn't the first time.

I ran inside. Jack left and I rushed into the bedroom to talk with Dolly. She was still awake as if she was waiting for me to come home. I was so excited. I had to tell her about every moment from when we left to when we came back. Dolly admitted that she and Lucas had arranged for Ken Michaels to sing "April Showers". She wanted for us to be comfortable dancing our first dance. I undressed in the dark so that Dolly could get some rest. Then, in the dark and still of the room, I said to Dolly, "Jack kissed me on the lips". She responded, "He did, did he..." Nothing more was said. Silence filled the air in that bedroom. Me, well, I couldn't sleep. I played the entire evening in my mind, over and over. I think that I was smiling in the dark. But, eventually, I did fall asleep.

The next day was Thanksgiving. This was my first Thanksgiving while living with the Taddums in their farmhouse. I was preparing dinner under Dolly's supervision when I noticed her wince several times as she shifted around on the chair that she sat on. I noticed, but couldn't say anything or ask about it. It was our unwritten agreement. She told me, "Otherwise, you will be asking me about it all of the time, every day, and that will make it worse for me. Please...Please". I was uncomfortable watching her in obvious pain. However, it was her wish to be left alone.

Dolly started giggling, with her hand in front of her face, at my displeasure as I was stuffing the turkey. When I was done, I wiped my brow and said, "There, I have done it!" We both laughed out loud. I continued cooking under Dolly's supervision, enjoying being with her, as always. From out of nowhere, Dolly asked me whether I had celebrated Thanksgiving when I was at home or in school. I laughed even louder, "At school, sure. But, at home, No, no, no, not at home with my grandparents. That's for sure. It was a sore subject with my grandfather." Dolly asked me why that was. I responded somewhat sheepishly, "Well, my grandfather didn't tell me why until I was older. One summer, I told him how we were taught that the holiday celebrated how a local tribe of 'Indians' provided food for the colonists during that first winter. They celebrated by breaking bread together and praying for a good harvest the next year. When I finished telling him what I had learned at school, he became angry. He almost never showed me that side of him. He wasn't angry at me. He was just frustrated with what I had learned. He started by saying to me, "Ahyoka, this is just another one of those truths that were ignored by the white people." Then, he told me that, yes, there were some good tidings between the original colonists and the local tribes. But, there was also conflict. He said that the holiday also celebrated a victory of those colonists and some of their 'Indian' allies over other 'Indians'. "Seven hundreds of that other tribe, those other 'Indians', were killed or taken into captivity in that Pequot War. The Pequot people were never more. So, I guess one person's celebration is just another's annihilation. Some celebration! And, so, I understood my grandfather's reluctance to celebrate this holiday." I stopped and covered my mouth. I had gone too far. I was worried that I had been too harsh. I wanted to lighten up our conversation. So, I added, "There are more roots to this holiday than has a weeping willow tree." Dolly laughed. She shook her head up and down for a while as if she understood the gravity of what I had told her. Then, she said that she liked my turn of phrase about the weeping willow tree. She hummed away as I continued cooking. All was good…I hoped.

The turkey, stuffing and mashed potatoes that I had prepared were well received by Dolly and Lucas. Then, for dessert, I offered some coffee and our now "well-known" apple pie. However, Thanksgiving dinner was quiet. It was without the Clarks and all of the posturing and competition that always had been the hallmark of dinners with them. These families, the Taddums and the Clarks, had been friendly neighbors for more than a generation. Now, there was a lot of bad blood between the families. And that bad blood was over me and Jack, but really, it was over me! I felt responsible for the falling out even though I did nothing wrong other than being me.

The quiet of that dinner table was broken by the sound of a car or truck approaching. I went to the door to see the Clarks' truck come to a stop. Jack and his mother, Helen, came into the house without even knocking. Helen said, rather rambunctiously, "No one will stop me from wishing my friends a happy holiday." She shouted out for all to hear, "Happy Thanksgiving!" Of course, yelling back, we responded in the same way. I was glad to see Jack. He didn't say much. He didn't need to. He looked at me with that look that could melt ice. And don't think that it wasn't noticed by Helen and Dolly.

I was so happy to see Helen together with Dolly. That relationship was important to Dolly and it could have been destroyed. Helen's coming over was a clear sign that there would be peace between these two women even if there wasn't peace between the two men.

Helen and Jack accepted Dolly's offer of coffee and apple pie. I served and was just about to clear the table when Helen said that it was time to go. I stopped what I was doing and joined in saying good night to our good friends. Jack shook my hand and looked into my eyes. After they left, both Lucas and Dolly commented regarding how brave Helen was to have come by herself. Dolly said, "Obviously, there will be a price to pay in their house for Helen and Jack coming here." Lucas just accepted Dolly's conclusion without a word. I said nothing!

Chapter 13

It happens every year. Once Thanksgiving is behind us, the remaining weeks of the year just fly by. Sometimes, I think of December as a two or three week month. That's how fast that I feel that it goes by.

There was to be another barn dance on New Year's Eve. I hoped that Jack would invite me. But, I knew that he and his father were barely speaking. Their relationship wasn't good. And, that made me wonder what would happen.

Christmas was coming soon too. I started to think about gifts for Dolly and Lucas and of course, a gift for Jack. I decided to get a needlework frame, fabric, thread and tools for Dolly. This would allow her to have something to do which didn't require much effort, something that she could do in a sitting or even from a reclining position. Dolly had asked me to help her by getting a gift for Lucas. She wanted to get a few pipes and a pipe stand for him. That gave me the idea of getting some nice smelling tobacco for Lucas to compliment the new pipes. Ahhhh, but for Jack, I had no idea. I had to think about that for a while.

I saw Jack the Friday morning after Thanksgiving as we worked alongside one another milking the cows. I asked him how his Thanksgiving dinner was and if there were any repercussions about their coming over to the Taddum Farm. His response was measured. He told me that it was okay. But, it would have been better if we were together for dinner. Then, after a few minutes of silence, he said that it wasn't okay. He confided in me that his family's Thanksgiving dinner was uncomfortable, to say the least. Jack said, "My father has been livid ever since we went to the dance together. It was even worse after we came back from visiting you, and Lucas and Dolly, last night. There was such a silence that you could cut it with a knife. Mary, I never knew my father to be that way. I never knew that he was that prejudiced. He, and our family, use Doctor Held. We purchase our goods from

Isaac at the General Store all of the time. Both of those people are Jews. He has never said a bad word about them. In fact, he has always thought of Doctor Held as being so good. I don't know if you had heard, but my sister, Betty, was very sick about two years ago. Doc Held treated her and she recovered. He was always there for us. As far as Isaac and his daughter Aida at the General Store, he has never said that they weren't nice to deal with. He deals with the Catholics, who happen to own St. Mark's Farm and Feed Store, all of the time. He buys all of his seed there. Many times, I have seen him sharing a cigarette and drinking out of the same bottle with Bill McLaughlin, the owner of St. Mark's. So, I just don't get it. When I asked him how he could hate Jews and Catholics at the same time as saying how nice these people are, he said that these are the exceptions. So, I asked him if there were Jews or Catholics that he didn't like talking to or working with. He didn't answer me. He just shrugged." With that, Jack shrugged his shoulders and continued milking.

    I stopped milking and asked Jack, "Does that mean that you will not invite me out again?" That was very aggressive of me but I wanted to hear the answer. I needed to hear the answer. When Jack heard that question, he turned toward me. He didn't pay attention to what he was doing. Warm milk squirted all over his coveralls as he rose up. He said, "Please...how could you think that of me?" He sat back down on the milking stool and continued, "It's true that I will have to deal with my father. It will take some time, but I plan on inviting you out as often as you will have me. We could go to a movie or celebrate New Year's Eve together. We can even go out to eat in Muskogee. What do you think?" All I could ask was, "What will your father do? What will he say?" Jack was quick to reply, "My father will sulk. He may even threaten me, but what can he really do? I am his only son. I work the farm along with my parents and sister and the hired help." He stopped and looked at me. You could see that he was struggling. "As far as my mother is concerned, she likes you a lot but doesn't have the courage to stand up to my father. Mary, they have a good marriage as long as my mother doesn't push back too much. She isn't as strong as he is. And, she isn't ready to push back now because my father is still very angry. But, what she did by visiting you all last night was an act of bravery on her part. And, I believe that she will get through to him...eventually. It will take a while. I am counting on it."

I found it all so very upsetting. "Jack, this isn't good. I don't want to cause a rift between you and your father and put your mother in such a difficult position." With that said, Jack ran around the back side of the cow that I was milking, his coveralls dripping with milk, he grabbed me up and kissed me on the lips, again! He said, "I have some work to do with my family, but nothing will stop me from seeing you. As long as you want to be with me, I will be there." I broke down, crying my heart out on his shoulder. He just held me tight and whispered, "It will be alright. I will find a way."

I went back to milking and my other chores in the barn. When I was done, I left the barn without saying another word to Jack. I walked back to the house in order to take care of Dolly. But, as soon as I walked into the house, I heard her moaning. The noises frightened me. I rushed in. She was rolling back and forth in bed. I woke her up. She was startled. I violated our unwritten agreement by asking if she was in pain. I had no choice. She cleared her head and said that she was alright. But, the look on her face belied her response. I asked her if she wanted to try some Laudanum. She shook her head. I ran to the root cellar to get it out. I took out a tea spoon from the kitchen, filled a glass with water and went back to Dolly. I sat her up in bed and asked again if she wanted the Laudanum. She said, "Yes, please." I handed her the glass of water and carefully poured some Laudanum into the tea spoon. She opened her mouth and I placed the spoon in her mouth, under her tongue, just like Doctor Held had said. She took the spoon from me so she could get all of the elixir and followed that with a sip of water. I reached out for the glass. But, before I could take it away, she grabbed it out of my hand and took a big gulp of the water saying, "Boy, Doctor Held was right. This stuff is very bitter". I helped her to lie back down in bed and sat in a chair alongside her until she dozed off. Then, I ran out to find Lucas. I told him what had happened. He said, "I'm not surprised. I knew this would happen, I just didn't know exactly when it would happen and then...how many days..." That frank statement was very upsetting. It is not as if I hadn't had the same thoughts, it was just that her husband stated it so matter-of-factly. Sometimes, I feel that until and unless something is said, it just isn't so. This was no longer just something off into the future with no context. With those words, Lucas made Dolly's fate a matter of fact that could not be denied.

Dolly dozed for about an hour. When she woke up, she was good. No pain. I didn't know how long Laudanum's pain relief would last. We would have to "play it by ear".

That Saturday, I told Lucas that I wanted to spend some time in the library in Muskogee after the Fair. I wanted to read up on recipes to make other types of cheese. I was looking for something that wasn't sold at the Fair, so I could increase the cheese business. After a while, I came to the idea of making fresh mozzarella. I took down some notes and left the library.

From the library, I went to the General Store to speak with Isaac. I told him that I needed to purchase Christmas gifts. He was very helpful. I got everything out of a catalog. I ordered the needlework frame, fabric, thread and tools for Dolly and the pipes, pipe stand and tobacco for Lucas. I was lost as to what to get for Jack. So, I said to Isaac, "What do you think I should get for Jack Clark?" He thought for a minute and yelled over to Aida who was folding some fabric that had been disheveled by customers. "Aida, what do you think that Mary should get Jack Clark for Christmas?" She didn't hesitate, yelling to her father, "Buy him some suspenders. It's not too personal and they're useful. I have some back here." Isaac said, "Mary, that's a good idea." He walked me over to Aida. She picked up a few pairs of suspenders and said, "Take a look at these. I think that you will like them. I know that Jack will like them." I asked Aida how she knew that Jack would like them. "Because he has been in the store a number of times looking at these two pairs. When he is here, he picks them up and holds them up to his shoulders. When I've walked over to him, asking him if I could help, he puts them down, and says, 'No, no, I'm okay. Thanks'." I looked at them and told Aida that I would buy the two pairs. I asked if she could wrap them as a gift for Christmas. She took them to the front of the store and wrapped them for me. I paid Aida. Isaac told me that he should have the other gifts in about two weeks. I went back to the farm and hid the suspenders.

When I returned, I told Lucas and Dolly what I had found about mozzarella. Of course, I didn't say anything about the Christmas gifts. They laughed at my entrepreneurship but it was in a celebratory manner. I didn't feel embarrassed. In fact, I laughed along with them. The next day, I experimented making some fresh mozzarella. I wrapped the balls of the "Mutz", as I called the mozzarella, in cheesecloth making the kneading and squeezing out the final amounts of milk whey ever so much easier. But, whatever we called it, mozzarella or just "Mutz", it was wonderful. At the next Fair, I offered free samples as I had done for my cheddar. In front of the plate with the new cheese, I put a piece of paper on which I wrote "Mutz - Free Samples". It was a big hit. Well, the free samples were a big hit. Next week, I will really know just how much my customers like the new cheese when they have to pay for it.

Jack came over. He saw the sign and tried some. He loved it. Of course. What would he say? I needed an objective opinion and his would not be one of those. Not, when it had anything to do with me.

When I returned to the farm, I suggested to Lucas that he get another cow or two so that we could have milk to make more cheese to meet what I perceived as the demand for the cheddar and, now, the "Mutz". I was serious. He laughed in a roar that probably could be heard for miles. But, then, he quickly turned serious when he looked at my face, flushed with embarrassment. He said, "Ok, ok, Mary, let's see how you do. Buying another cow is a big expense. I don't want to do it unless we are pretty darn sure that it will be a success." I let it drop. We never got another cow.

The next Saturday, Dolly seemed to be having more and more difficulty getting going in the morning. All of us have that problem, certainly, but it seemed like Dolly was having difficulty that she didn't want to talk about. I wanted to offer her some Laudanum, but that was a crutch for me as much as a pain relief for her. So, I resisted my natural inclination to offer it, waiting for a certain sign of her pain, or for her to ask directly for some. I didn't want it to be about me.

Jack drove Helen over to spend time with Dolly. Lucas and Jack helped load up my buckboard. When I left for the Fair, Jack went back to his farm to gather his own farm goods for sale. I arrived first and unloaded my buckboard. About a half hour later, Jack arrived. I smiled at him but didn't venture over to his tables. I had plenty of people coming up to my tables purchasing my eggs along with the chickens and cheddar that I had brought for sale. But, my greatest single success that day was the new "Mutz", the mozzarella cheese. It was sold out in less than an hour.

Some of the Cherokee women came over as usual. Some purchased goods from me but all of them just wanted to chat in their native language with someone outside of their immediate group. I have to say that I enjoyed it as well.

After a few hours, I began to pack up when Jack came over. He greeted me with a smile and asked how I was. I didn't think that he was talking about my sales at the Fair. Given my attraction to Jack and all that was going on with his father, I didn't want to be too forward. I was being cautious. Then, Jack asked if I wanted to go to the New Year's Eve Barn Dance with him. I had hoped that he would ask. In fact, I was thrilled that he did. But, I didn't want him getting in trouble with his father and told him so. He told me not to worry. I asked, "Jack, are you sure?" He shook his head. I said, "Of course."

When I got back to the farm, I unloaded, settled the horse, let him forage in a fenced area and then, I ran into the house. When I got there, I told Dolly and Helen about the success with the "Mutz". Helen didn't know anything about it so I explained. She had this curious smile on her face, somewhat between being proud of me, on one hand, and wondering where all of this would go, on the other. I explained how I was going to organize production of "my cheese". "I will be making the 'Mutz' only on Thursdays and Fridays to ensure that the 'Mutz' is never more than two days old when we sell it at the Fair." I told her that "Mutz", especially, had to be very fresh. I ran through the litany of production days for the cheddar, butter and raw milk. Both women said that I was very well organized. They wished me good luck. Then, they laughed. I blushed.

I used all of that talk about cheese, to segue about what I really wanted to talk about with Helen. It was time. I said, "Mrs. Clark, Helen, Jack just asked me out for New Year's Eve. There is another barn dance." Dolly seemed pleased, while not surprised. Helen's response was flat. So, I asked her straight out and with as much emphasis as I could, "Helen, do you have a problem with me seeing Jack?! If you do, I'll refuse and I will stop seeing him!" She answered, "Mary, I like you an awful lot, but my husband, Jim, has not changed. It's not as if he doesn't like you, Mary. It's just that he would rather have Jack get together with..." I stopped her, "You mean someone who is not half Cherokee...someone who is not a bastard." I was angry. "Helen, let me tell you who I am. I am the person who is taking care of your best friend. I am the one that Jack believes is special enough to invite out." I stopped. I wanted to run away. What have I done? What did I say? Why couldn't I just keep my mouth shut? But, once again, my temper had taken over. There was silence again. It made me so uncomfortable. Then, Dolly cleared her throat and said it felt like rain. Talk about changing subjects.

Helen didn't take the bait to change subjects. She said, "Mary, everything that you have said is correct. I can't account for Jim's feelings. But, look, I can understand a part of it. No, not his prejudice for God's sake. But, I do believe that everyone would like to see their children be with someone who shares their same background. For example, if Jack dated a Catholic girl, I might say that the girl is lovely, but I wish that she were a Methodist. I don't know, does that make me the same as Jim? Does that make me prejudiced? Am I awful?" Dolly answered for me, "Helen, no, that doesn't make you prejudiced against anyone. I guess that it just means that you have a 'preference', not a prejudice, for someone or something. I think that's different. Frankly, your feelings are not much different from most people. I never met Mary's grandparents. You know that. And I can't know what their thoughts would be. But, I imagine that their thoughts wouldn't be much different from yours except that they would be from their particular point of view. Do you understand what I am trying to say?" Helen, chimed in one more time on the subject. "Mary, on the subject of prejudice and preference, I have one more thing to add". Oh...I wondered what she was going to say. "Mary, I am prejudiced...in my own way. I will repeat what I said before to Dolly. I like you...I like you a lot! Period. But, you must understand that these other issues do exist. And, no, I don't have any problem with Jack dating you in spite of my 'preference'. No problem at all. Again, I cannot speak for my husband, Jim. I said that before."

With that, we heard Jack driving up to the house. Helen said her goodbyes. She gave me a small hug and a smile. I was okay with what she said even given the sensitivity of such a subject. On the way out, close enough to Jack for him to hear, Helen said in the loudest of voices, "I'll say hello to Jack for you Mary." There was more to that than just saying hello. I had seen Jack just a little while ago. I think that it was another way of Helen telling me that it was okay with her for Jack and me to date even given what she had just said about her preferences.

I walked Helen to the door and onto the porch using that courtesy as an excuse to see Jack. As Helen walked off of the porch, I retreated to the doorway and gave Jack the smallest of waves. I don't believe that my hand got above my shoulder. I smiled at him as he smiled at me. That was all that needed to be done.

I would have loved to have been that proverbial fly in the truck during their ride back to the Clark Farm. What would Helen have said to Jack? What would Jack have said back? Would there have been silence? Maybe, some things are better off not being known.

I turned on my heel and faced Dolly. She was frank with me saying, without any introduction or reservation, "Jack's father will be difficult. He may interfere in your relationship with Jack. Helen will remain mum. She may like you a lot, but she is married to Jim Clark. You cannot forget that for a moment." I had nothing to say. I just shook my head. I thought that I really can't disagree with what the ladies had said. In this case, you are either a "fish" or a "fowl". The Clarks were fish and I was a fowl. In Jim Clark's eyes, I could never be a fish. Helen made that clear.

I asked Dolly how she was feeling just to have something to say after all that was discussed. I know, I know…. I said that I wouldn't do that, but I did it. But, now, I needed to talk about anything other than Jack and Helen and Jim Clark.

Dolly said that she wanted to take a nap. I didn't know if she was really tired or just wanted to avoid all of the obvious issues that were right there in front of us. Maybe, it was the stress of the discussion that tired her out.

Chapter 14

The early days of December passed quickly. There had been some good weather days during the early part of the month when the warmth of the sun brought back memories of the preceding summer and fall. Then, winter weather started to make itself known. There were cold snaps bringing the temperatures to below freezing. Toward the middle of the month, the sun was obscured by clouds, providing a gray overcast, day after day. That overcast was becoming depressing due to both its grayness and its sameness. Night came sooner than I would have liked. The cold temperatures of the night lingered throughout the morning. Some nights there was a chill in the house even with the fire roaring in the fireplace. When I was in school, there was heating in the dormitories. Here, the fireplace was cold by morning. So was I. It would only get worse.

The chores in the barn and in preparation for the Fair became more and more routine. The new cheeses at the Fair were a big hit. Every week, there was a line of folks queuing up to buy my cheeses. No one else had a line in front of their table. Overall, dollar sales for the cheeses were more than 25% higher than when I arrived. I was pleased that I had made a contribution.

Dolly was experiencing more and more painful moments that required Laudanum for relief. I still felt comfortable taking care of her even with her degrading condition. Taking her to the outhouse in the cold, combined with snow and ice in January and February, was going to become a problem. I remembered that I had asked Lucas to buy a honey bucket. Of course, I used it for making cheese before I got the opportunity to use it for anything else. But, a honey bucket for Dolly would make her life easier. I spoke to Lucas. He was very handy with his tools. And, within a few days, Lucas had crafted an indoor toilet using a new bucket, with a liner of straw, placed below a chair. Lucas had cut out the middle of the chair seat and padded the edge around the hole. What he made may have been crude, but it worked. I thought that it was pretty ingenious. When Dolly saw what Lucas had done, she laughed and laughed. It was so good to hear that joyful laugh of hers. Dolly no longer had to go to the outhouse in the bad weather.

Life went on. I enjoyed seeing Jack, every day, even if it was only as we were sitting nearby milking the cows. We didn't need to talk. The fresh warm milk, right from the cows utters, would steam off in the cold air. Looking back, it was like a picture that you would see in a museum. One morning, Jack started to talk about this and that. That was unusual as most mornings few words were shared. I had a sense that there was more coming. I was right. He asked me if I would like to go to a movie. I had never been to a movie. I didn't even really know what a movie was. We certainly didn't have any movies at school. Of course, I said, "Yes".

Jack told me about the movie called "The Jazz Singer". He added that it was the first "talkie". He had to explain that to me. Many times, I felt that I was so unsophisticated, so lacking in knowledge of anything in the real world. Yes, I did very well in school, but that was what they taught and there is so much more to the world, to life, that I didn't know about. Probably, even more importantly, there were so many things that I didn't even know existed.

I spoke to Lucas and Dolly about going to the movie with Jack. Which meant, of course, that I wouldn't be there to take care of Dolly. I wasn't looking for their permission. I was hoping that Lucas would be able to look after Dolly for a few hours. Lucas immediately told me not to worry, that he would take care of Dolly for the evening. So, without any fanfare or discussion with his parents, Jack picked me up the following Saturday evening in his truck and we drove into Muskogee. For the first time in my life, I went to the movies. Once I sat down in the theater, Jack got up to buy a bag of popcorn for me. He knew that I liked it from when I had some at my first Fair. Jack and I shared the bag. We finished the popcorn before the movie began.

I was mesmerized by "The Jazz Singer". And, once we left the theater, Jack and I talked about the movie until we arrived back at the farm. Of course, as we reached the farmhouse, he was very courteous, as always, opening the truck door for me and then, the door to the house. With Dolly and Lucas sitting there by the fireplace, I extended my hand and thanked him. He told me in a most respectful manner how much he enjoyed taking me to the movies. What can I say? He and I both knew that the audience of this particular drama was sitting right there in front of the fireplace. We had to be very careful as Lucas and Dolly would interpret our every move. And then, there would be a report to Helen.

After Jack left, I told Lucas and Dolly about the remarkable movie theater and the even more remarkable movie I had just seen. I shared with them my amazement about seeing and hearing moving pictures on a screen as big as their house. I described the movie theater itself as I had never seen one or been in one before in my life.

I also told them all about the movie itself since I knew that with Dolly's condition, they would not be able to see it. "The star of the 'Jazz Singer' was Al Jolson. Dolly that is the same person who sang 'April Showers' on the record that you played for Jack and me when we were learning to dance…you remember, don't you?" Dolly nodded. "Oh, could he sing and dance. But…" I told Dolly and Lucas, "The movie was more than just about Al Jolson's singing and dancing. It was about his struggles, how he was torn between his career and his loyalty to his father and their Jewish religion. It was about how his parents wanted him to sing at the Jewish 'church', called a 'synagogue', just like his father. But, he chose to sing at Jazz clubs instead. When his father was near death, he wanted his son to take his place on the night of the most important of the Jewish holidays. It was also the night that Jolson was to debut on a Broadway stage. In a turn of heart, and risking his career, he honored his father, his tradition, and sang that night in the synagogue. His debut on Broadway was delayed. And he reconciled with his father just before his death. It was wonderful. I was so happy that he sang and made up with his father. I cried."

Then, before Lucas and Dolly could say anything, I asked them, "Do you think that Jack and his father could ever reconcile if Jack and I stay together, I mean, as a couple?" Dolly responded, saying, "Not everything works out in life as well as it does in books, or now, in the movies. Life has a tendency of getting in the way." Dolly always had a way of saying things that rang true. While Dolly's response shattered my hopes, I said, "Dolly, you are amazing. I learn from you every day." Lucas pulled the pipe out of his mouth and just shook his head up and down in agreement. He said, "I do too." He continued shaking his head.

As I almost always did, I thought about the day's activities just before falling asleep. I played the Jazz Singer over again in my mind. But, now, I wasn't just thinking about a family in turmoil. It brought to mind the conflict of traditional values being pushed aside by modern life. I wasn't the child of a Jewish father whose traditional values were being discarded by his son. I was the daughter of the Cherokee Nation whose life no longer included those traditions and values. They were memories that were fast fading unless I chose to hold them dear. I wondered if there had been more to the movie, whether Jake, the Jazz Singer, would have maintained those values, those of his father, or whether his singing that night, in the synagogue, was just to satisfy a dying man's wish. Was there any continuation of that man's traditions in his life or would he just be another modern man? Of course, I was really thinking of myself. Would I keep those values and traditions that my grandfather and grandmother had taught me? Would I pass them on to my children as grandfather asked…some day? Or, would all of those stories and lessons be lost as I became just another modern woman? I always felt that the "Jazz Singer" was a metaphor for my life.

I also thought about all of the things in the movie that I'd never seen before; jazz clubs, professional singers, music, big cities like New York and San Francisco. Again, so many things that I didn't know even existed and had certainly never experienced.

Then, in the quietude that was, Dolly woke and called out to me. She was in pain. I jumped up and found the Laudanum, a teaspoon and some water. Dolly took the medicine and after a time, seemed more relaxed. These episodes seemed to be happening more frequently. I wasn't surprised.

The days rolled on, one into the other. Christmas was just around the corner. Lucas had cut a white pine tree from the nearby woods and set it up opposite the fireplace. Dolly asked me to retrieve a box of ornaments that was stored in the barn. When I brought them into the house, we had a great time dressing the tree. Dolly and I got along so well that it was as if we were friends for years. No matter what we were doing, we would be talking and laughing.

The next Saturday, just after I finished my work at the Saturday Fair, I stopped by Tanner's General Store and sought out Isaac. I found him stocking some shelves in the back of the store. I knew where he was because I could hear him humming away. I tried to figure out what song he was humming, but I couldn't.

I interrupted him when I said, "Hello, Isaac". He responded, "Hello, Mary. I think that I know exactly why you are here. Just give me a minute." He went into the back storage room and came back to me with his hands filled with packages. He said, "Here you are Mary." Isaac handed over a large and a medium size and a smallish package. The large box was pretty heavy. I struggled keeping everything that he handed over from toppling out of my hands. I put them down. Isaac told me that the large package was the needlework frame and the rest for Dolly. Then, he asked me to smell the smallest package. I did. "Mmmmm", I said, "That must be the tobacco." Isaac smiled and shook his head. The medium package held pipes and a pipe stand that Dolly was going to give to Lucas. I thanked Isaac and settled up. Now, the problem was how to keep these gifts, along with the suspenders that I had bought for Jack, from being found by Lucas or Dolly.

Christmas Eve came to the Lucas Farm as it did at the Clark Farm and everywhere else. Typical of the weather around Christmas time, winter hadn't completely taken over yet. Chores didn't take the day off either. I was able to prepare Christmas Eve dinner; roasted chicken, potatoes and beets from the root cellar and fresh bread. Of course, there was dessert and coffee. I prepared rice pudding based upon a recipe that Dolly had from her mother. It was quite a feast. After cleanup, I got Dolly settled and waited for her to drift off to sleep. Once she was snoring, and Lucas was out of sight, I got up and moved all of the presents from under Dolly's bed to the base of the Christmas tree. The only thing that I forgot to do was to label the packages so that Dolly would know which package was what. By the time that I got to the Christmas tree, there were already two small packages there. I wondered if either of them were for me. I knew that Dolly couldn't have put anything there since I was with her all of the time. Ahhh, but, Lucas....

Christmas morning activities were the same for Dolly and me. Since she was still asleep, I went into the barn to begin taking care of the cows, chickens and eggs. Jack wasn't there being that it was Christmas. At least, that was what I thought. Once I took care of the chores in the barn, I came back to the house to get Dolly prepared for the day and I made breakfast. When breakfast was nearly finished, Lucas said that it was time to open our Christmas gifts. I told him that I had to clean up first. He said, "Not today. Today, Mary, you are our guest. And, guests do not clean up the dishes, at least not on the day that they are a guest." He laughed so hard that I thought that he would turn blue. Dolly joined in. So, I helped Dolly to the settee across from a blazing fire and next to the beautiful Christmas tree, now adorned with gifts. I sat next to her. Lucas did the honors, picking up one of the small gifts and handing it to Dolly. She opened the box and then unwrapped layer upon layer of paper. When she got down to a purple felt pouch and opened the draw string, she found a necklace. She was surprised by its beauty and Lucas' generosity. She said to Lucas that the necklace was so beautiful that she was embarrassed. With that, Dolly began to cry. Lucas said, "Here, here, Dolly, there is no need for that. I am glad that I was able to find something that would make you happy. Smile for me, would you?" Lucas helped her put on the necklace. She just kept touching it. Her tears turned into a big smile.

As Dolly composed herself, I reached down and picked up two packages. I knew which package held the tobacco from the odor. The other one had to be the pipes and the pipe stand. I handed that one to Dolly who handed it to Lucas. She said, "Merry Christmas Lucas". He opened the package and was very pleased, saying that he was going to smoke one of the new pipes right away. He placed the pipe stand on the fireplace mantle lining up his new pipes. I picked up the package with the tobacco and extended it toward Lucas, saying, "Merry Christmas Lucas". This will go with your new pipes." He brought his nose down and took in a deep breath saying, "I think that I know what this is". As he opened the package containing the tobacco, he took another deep breath and said, "Ladies, thank you so much for my gifts. I am going to make use of them right now." And with that, he took some tobacco, tamped it down into one of the new pipes from the stand and struck a match. As he inhaled, he thanked us again.

I reached under the tree and brought out the needlepoint work that I had purchased for Dolly. I handed it to her and said, "Merry Christmas Dolly". When she unwrapped the needlepoint frame she was excited. She said, "This will give me something to help pass my time. This is great!" That was exactly why I had picked that for her. Dolly looked at all of the parts and pieces. She was fascinated by it all. Then, she looked up and said, "Mary, your gift is in our bedroom." Lucas rose and supported Dolly as they both preceded me into the bedroom. There, where my straw bed had been for these months, was a brand new bed, standing off of the ground, with new bedding, and a new pillow, all made up perfectly. I didn't know what to say because I was so surprised, so pleased. I told them so. I walked over to the bed, sat down and gently bounced up and down and smiled. I said, "Lucas...Dolly, this is wonderful! I don't know how to thank you." Then, I said, "Lucas, how did you get this bed in here? When did you do it? How could it have happened so quickly?" Dolly told me that it will all become clear in a moment.

Then, Dolly said, "Mary, you have one more gift but you need to wait a moment." She smiled and nodded toward Lucas. He walked out of the house. A few moments later he came back with Jack in tow. Seeing Jack immediately answered the "how and when" about the new bed. Obviously, while I was making breakfast, Lucas and Jack were busy bringing in the bed from their hiding place somewhere in the barn. How did I miss it? But, that wasn't all.

As Jack came into the house with Lucas, he walked over to the tree and retrieved the last small gift. He extended his arm and hand toward me, bringing the gift into view. He said, "Merry

Christmas Mary". But, I didn't take the package from his outstretched arm. I said, "Wait one minute." I went into the bedroom and reached under Dolly's bed. My gift to Jack was still where I had left it. I scooped it up and almost ran back. I extended my arm and hand toward Jack. He quickly copied my motions. We both took the gift from each other. I brought my gift back with me to Dolly sitting next to her on the settee. I quickly opened the package and found the most wonderful, beautiful, elegant, porcelain cameo brooch. Jack opened his gift of two pairs of suspenders. I said to him, "My gift is humble and your gift is beautiful and so generous." Jack just smiled. Then, he said that my gift meant the world to him. He asked if I liked the brooch. I told him that I was "over the moon". I had difficulty trying to take apart the clasp and put it on. Seeing the trouble that I was having, Dolly grabbed it from me and said, "Here, here, I can help you with that." She pinned it to my outfit. Since I had been milking cows, candling fresh eggs and making breakfast, the brooch was way too much for me to wear with what I had on. But, I was serious about putting it on so Jack could see how much I appreciated his gift. When Dolly had secured it to my shirt, I rose and faced Jack saying, "I couldn't be happier". He had already put on one of the pairs of suspenders. He wrapped his thumbs underneath and snapped the suspenders with a smile saying that they fit just right and they were exactly the best colors for him. Jack said, "I had been looking at suspenders at the General Store. These look the same as the ones that I had tried on." I laughed and said, "Jack, oh my, of course. They are the ones that you have been trying on at Tanner's General Store. Aida Tanner told me how you would go to the back of their store, try on these two pairs of suspenders and then take them off, leaving the store without purchasing them." We all laughed. Jack blushed. I repeated that I thought that the cameo was so beautiful. It was.

   Then, Jack said, "Mary, did you know that mistletoe is the floral emblem of the state of Oklahoma, our state?" He was having his fun. I ignored him but my face was probably red with embarrassment. He was being bold, especially with Dolly and Lucas right there. "You know, that mistletoe is usually hung near a doorway. And, if two young people find themselves under it, they kiss." Oh my, that minor blush was now full blown. I must have turned three shades of red. Lucas and Dolly looked at each other. Then, I decided to have a little fun myself. I said to Jack, looking straight into his eyes from less than a foot away, "Well...I guess that you are out of luck, today, Jack, because we do not have any mistletoe." With that, I did a little curtsy. Dolly and Lucas, watching this drama, broke out in laughter. Jack broke out in a huge and wonderful smile. He shook his head up and down. I thought that I had delivered the final blow! But, at that moment, Jack reached into his pocket and pulled out a small piece of mistletoe. He raised it into the air above us. He said, "Well, I guess, Mary that I am in good luck. May I?" Oh, my...I turned to look at Dolly. I said, "Yes." I believe that both Dolly and Lucas held their breath as Jack kissed me.

The exchange of gifts and good tidings was over. Jack said that he had a lot to do and bid Lucas and Dolly goodbye. He turned to me and said, "Thank you for the lovely gift. It is a good day." As Jack was leaving the house, Lucas called out to him thanking him for his help with the bed. Then, Lucas added, "Jack, remember, I will not be needing you in the mornings after the end of the year." Jack responded by waving without turning around. I didn't want to say it. But, not seeing Jack after this week, every morning, would be a great loss to me.

I plopped down on the settee, smiling both outside and inside. Dolly looked at me and smiled. Lucas came over, repeating the notion, "It's been a good day". Nothing more needed to be said.

That afternoon, after Lucas disappeared, Dolly asked me to sit with her near the fireplace. She asked me to make some tea, reminding me that the water for tea must be boiled for at least one minute. I didn't know why, but her saying it was sufficient for me to follow those directions exactly. She asked for a little sugar. I brought the tea and a biscuit for each of us back to the fireplace. I have to admit it, the tea was better with well-boiled water.

Dolly started off, "You know, Mary, you are not a child". With that as an opening, apprehension had to be written all across my face. She added, "There is nothing to worry about here. But, after seeing Jack kiss you and knowing how you are enjoying each other's company, I just want you to be aware of certain facts.

I wasn't totally naïve but I wouldn't say that I was knowledgeable either. I thought that if Dolly was going to spend the time to tell me, I was going to spend the time listening. And I did. It was terribly embarrassing but it was important to know. Once she had talked through everything with me, she asked me if I had any questions. Questions? How could I have asked any questions about such a matter? In truth, I learned a lot from Dolly. What my friends at school had told me was a mere fraction of what Dolly explained to me that day. Also, as I learned, a lot of what my friends told me in school was wrong.

Then, as we were almost done, Dolly finished this very difficult conversation by saying some things that stuck with me more than most anything else that she ever said to me. "Remember, Mary, never let anyone force you to do anything that you don't feel comfortable doing. The choices that you make must always be your choice, not that of someone else." Then, she stopped and thought for a moment. "I don't mean to be harsh, but you remember about choices and consequences?" I said, "Yes." She had a very serious look on her face. She finished by saying, "In this case, the consequence could be getting pregnant when you don't want to become pregnant. Do you understand me?!" "Yes, Dolly." I shook my head. I smiled. In spite of the harsh words at the end, I loved every minute with her, every word from her, anything and everything that she ever said or did.

That night was a different experience. It had been months since I had slept in a real bed. Indeed, it was a good day.

The next days between Christmas and New Year's maintained that warm Christmas feeling. There wasn't that much work to be done in the fields so I saw more and more of Lucas. And he spent more time with Dolly as winter arrived.

Chapter 15

New Year's Eve and the Barn Dance were here. I looked forward to being with Jack and having him hold me as we danced. That was all that I could think about as I went about my work.

When Jack came to pick me up to take me to the dance, he looked stressed. But, once he saw me, he smiled and said, "Mary, every time that I see you, whether in your coveralls, or now, in your beautiful blue dress, you are more beautiful than the time before...if that is even possible. The color of the broach goes perfectly with your dress." Even with his wonderful greeting, I could see the sadness in his eyes. I responded in the softest of voices, not wanting to spoil the mood, saying "Jack, the broach that you bought for me for Christmas will always be a favorite of mine because it is so pretty. But, more importantly, it will be special to me because it came from you. And...I...." I had to change the mood. "I love that you are wearing the suspenders." At that, he tucked his thumbs behind the suspenders and snapped them against his chest just like he did Christmas morning.

After Jack greeted Dolly and Lucas, he told them that he would bring me back at about 12:30 since we wanted to stay past midnight, through to the New Year of 1930. They had nothing more to say to us other than to wish Jack and I Happy New Year and to have a good time.

Jack said, "Happy New Year to you both from my mom, and of course, from me." Obviously, absent from the greetings and well wishes was Jim Clark.

I realized that I would not be there at midnight so I added my New Year's greetings to Dolly and Lucas. I kissed Dolly on the cheek and turned to Lucas and extended my hand. He took it but then gave me a kiss on the cheek and responded sincerely, "Happy New Year Mary". Jack kissed Dolly on the cheek and shook Lucas' hand. Then, he escorted me out to the truck. As we drove away from the house, I noticed that Jack was very quiet. His silence added to his appearance when he first came into the house, telling me in no uncertain terms that there was trouble in Jack's life. I asked him if there was a problem and he said that he was just being reflective of the year. I let it go but I didn't believe him. I just couldn't pry, at least, not at that moment.

When we got to the dance, Jack remained quiet. Then, I decided that I couldn't let it go. So, I asked him once more, if everything was OK. This time, he shook his head rapidly back and forth and pursed his lips as he looked down at the floor. "My father and I had a terrible fight before I left. I just don't understand his..." I placed my hand on his face, caressing his cheek. He stopped talking. I told him to forget about what happened and try to have a good time, if just for this evening. I added that tomorrow will be time enough to deal with such issues. He smiled. But, I could see that his pain would not go away that easily. And, of course, I knew that Jack's fight with his father was all about me and our relationship. But, we had to let it go, at least for now, at least for tonight.

When we entered the barn, I noticed that it was just like the Thanksgiving dance except the decorations were slightly different, reflective of the time. Now, the banners and other decorations exclaimed,

HAPPY NEW YEAR 1930

Just like at Thanksgiving, the sign was beautifully enhanced by colorful flourishes. There were many other banners and signs in the barn. As the barn filled with revelers, Ken Michaels took to the bandstand and yelled out, "Belieeeeve me!" That seemed to be his trademark opening. Everyone quieted down waiting for him to say what he had to say. He introduced the band and talked about listening to the New Year's broadcast on the radio. Then, he introduced the good Pastor Berkley who immediately started off with the "Lord's Prayer" as he did on Thanksgiving. Then, he gave the "Do's" and "Don'ts" of what was expected. He repeated the same thing that he had said on Thanksgiving, reminding us that "this isn't New York or Chicago. We have our own standards to live up to here in Oklahoma." Finally, he wished everyone a good New Year, praying for good health and an abundance of crops come the spring. Applause filled the barn. The pastor walked off of the bandstand and Ken Michaels took over asking the audience, "Are ya ready to have a good time? If ya are, let me know by shouting back, 'Yes, we are'." And, of course, everyone shouted back, "Yes we are!" With that, Michaels started playing some of my favorites.

Jack and I danced the waltz and the Foxtrot. I no longer felt embarrassed thinking that we stood out like a "sore thumb" because of our poor dance technique. We were actually pretty good together. And, being held by Jack and looking into his eyes made it all the more enjoyable. We tried a square dance, again, looking at our own feet so as not to step on anyone else's. We even tried The Charleston, having watched others from near and far. And, like at the Thanksgiving dance, whenever Jack left my side, other boys and men came over to me and asked me to dance. That attention should have made me feel good, but, by this time, I only had eyes for Jack. Anyway, it would have been rude to go off and dance with someone else even if I didn't like Jack so much.

After dancing for a while, we sat in a corner along with so many other people who didn't dare to get out on the dance floor, fearing, as I had, that they would make fools of themselves. Some of those men came alone, not having the courage to ask a girl to the dance. I understood that angst, as well. The fear of rejection can be overpowering.

I was deep in thought about these other people, these "wall flowers", lining the walls of the barn when Jack brought some lemonade back to where I was sitting. Then, Aida Tanner came over with a guy that I had never seen before. She greeted me and then turned to her date and introduced him. "Mary, this is

Benjamin, Ben Held. He is Doctor Held's son." Then, she added, pointing toward Jack and said, "Ben, this is Jack and this is Mary." Handshakes were exchanged all around. Aida then told us that Ben was home for the holidays. "Mary and Jack, Ben is in medical school at New York University in New York City. He is following in his father's footsteps." I thought that he was nice looking. He seemed quiet. I asked Ben how long he would be home. Before he could answer me, I excitedly asked him what New York was like. I think that part of the reason for me jumping on Ben Held's answer was that I was just upset about Jack and his father and letting that affect my normally good manners.

Ben told us that he would be home for about a month. Then, he said, "New York is unlike anything that I had ever experienced even when I was a student at the University of Oklahoma in Norman. New York has more people in one neighborhood than Norman has in the entire town. There are more people in New York City than in all of the state of Oklahoma. You could probably throw in the state of Kansas, and some others, too. New York City would still have more people. It has live theater and movies and museums everywhere you go. It has more restaurants than there are people in Muskogee." He laughed. "There is so much to do. But, the most remarkable thing about New York is its subway and trolleys." I asked, "What are those?" He responded that, "A subway is an underground railroad that comes out of the ground here and there and then goes back underground again. It's remarkable." He explained about trolleys as well. I was amazed. I looked at Aida, "I have to be the least knowledgeable person in all of Muskogee, maybe in the entire world. I have never even heard of a subway or a trolley." Ben said something to try to remove my embarrassment. "But, I spend most of my time studying so I don't go to those live theater productions and I rarely go to the movies." I didn't want to add that I had never seen live theater, I had never seen a museum and I had gone to the movies exactly one time in my life. I didn't want to seem to be a girl from Nowhere, Oklahoma. But, that was what I felt like. Aida broke my mood by saying, "We should go out together for dinner." Jack and I both said, "Sure" at the same time, but we really didn't mean much by our response. Aida and Ben left us wishing us a good year. Handshakes were exchanged and I gave Aida a big hug. I liked her.

After they left, Jack asked me quietly if I would want him to spike my drink with some alcoholic spirits. I immediately thought of Dolly's prescription, "Your decision...your consequences". I didn't want to lose control so I said that I would pass for now, "Jack, no thank you. Maybe, a little later". I noted that Jack took out a flask and spiked his own drink. He wasn't the only one. Despite Pastor Berkley's specific prohibition, people throughout the dance floor and the surrounding "wall flowers" were spiking their drinks. This was not unique to Muskogee or to this dance. Prohibition was actually part of the Oklahoma state constitution. But, most farmers were like Lucas or Jim Clark. They made their own and didn't give a "fig" about that law. It certainly wasn't written about them. And, the town people were the same. They just purchased their spirits from people like Lucas. No one thought that it was wrong, at all.

As the evening progressed, Jack seemed to be relieved of some of the tension. Possibly, it was the alcohol that untied the knot in his stomach. But, all along, I knew that the subject of Jim Clark and Mary Ahyoka Awiakta was not closed. That discussion was only postponed. I tried to avoid thinking about the consequences, but it never left me. Those thoughts prevented me from having a really great New Year's celebration.

Right before midnight, the radio was turned on. They were playing a new song exclaiming that "Happy Days are Here Again!" Little did we know that those 'Happy Days' would soon be just a fading memory. But, for now, people were joyous.

When it came to be midnight, ending the year 1929 and beginning 1930, Jack and I kissed just as many of the other couples did. It was loving and warm. It felt so good to be kissing Jack. Then, we went around to people that we knew, wishing them a Happy New Year. But, some of the men were terribly inebriated. When I extended my hand out to one of Jack's friends, he grabbed it and brought me into his embrace and kissed me. I didn't like that and Jack immediately pulled him away saying, "Hey, no...not that. Keep your distance!" He was clearly annoyed by his friend. Then, Jack said that we should go. We said goodbye to people that we knew as we headed toward the exit and into the truck.

The party was over for us and reality had set in once again. The ride back from the dance to the Taddum Farm was silent. It was amazing how "loud" that silence was. I didn't know quite what to say to Jack. There was nothing that I could possibly have said that would have helped.

The ride home seemed both too short and too long. It was too short in that I wanted to be with Jack. Once he brought me back to the Taddum Farm, the night would be over. It was also too long in that there was nothing but that silence, nothing but tension that filled the air. There were just so many unsaid words. Those words could only be hurtful. I wanted to cry but I knew that would make it even worse for Jack. He would be even more torn in his feelings for me and for his family, his father. I began to understand that I was going to have to think about our relationship, that of Jack and me, as part of a triangle with the third leg being that of his father. In a way, it was a love triangle, but not of the sort that you read about in books.

When Jack pulled up to the house, he smiled at me, saying all of the right things about what a wonderful time he had and how he wanted to take me out again, "Maybe, next time, we could go out for dinner at one of those nice restaurants in Muskogee. Maybe, we could get in touch with Aida and Ben and go out together. What do you think?" I told him that I had never been to a restaurant in my life, sharing yet another part of my sheltered life's experience with him. He looked surprised, saying, "Well, then we have to make it a special event." I wanted to say that any time together with him would be special, but it wasn't the right time for such a comment. So, I just shook my head and said that it would be nice. I thought that if I smiled, my cheeks would crack because I felt so stressed.

Jack walked around the truck to open the door for me. He extended his hand to help me down. As I reached the ground, Jack grabbed me around, kissed me and said, "We don't need to go to any fancy restaurants for it to be special. Every time that we're together it's special." He said exactly what I was thinking. I kissed him again. I broke down crying. It was all too much. I ran into the house passing by Lucas as he sat near to the fireplace smoking his pipe. I ran right into the bedroom. Dolly was asleep so I didn't light the single candle near to my bed. I changed into my nightgown, in the dark, as quietly as I could. I really didn't want to talk with Dolly.

As I lie awake, I thought of the worst scenario. Tears rolled down my face in silence. Eventually, I fell asleep. It didn't seem to be but mere minutes when I had to get up. It was morning. I dressed and took care of my personal needs. Then, I crossed the barnyard to take care of my daily chores that I now knew so well; feeding the animals, the eggs, and then, to milk the cows. By the time that I set my milking stool up, I would have thought that Jack would be there milking the cow next to me. But, he wasn't. So, I began milking the cows myself one at a time. Lucas showed up and pulled up a stool and began milking next to me. I greeted him with a warm Happy New Year. He responded in kind. He didn't ask about the dance.

There was silence for a few minutes. Then, Lucas said, "I told Jack not to come over any more in the morning. Didn't I tell you?" I responded softly, "Yes, Lucas, you did." I think that he ignored what I had said. "Well, I thought that I did…well, anyway, I told Jack about a week ago." He didn't say any more. The truth was that we hadn't needed Jack there to help me for many months. I should have told Lucas a long time ago that Jack wasn't needed any more, but I didn't. Lucas must have known that. I was being selfish. I just enjoyed having Jack there next to me every morning.

As I left the barn, I told Lucas that I would have breakfast ready shortly after I took care of Dolly. But, he knew that. It was my daily ritual. But, I needed something to say. That's what I did.

I was upset. I needed to compose myself prior to speaking with Dolly. I was already feeling, thinking, that there had been some discussion about Jack and me by Lucas and Dolly, maybe involving the Clarks. I knew that I was walking into a trap of sorts. I could see it happening to me. Yet, I could do nothing about it.

I wished Dolly a Happy New Year. She responded in kind and asked me how the dance was. I told her about the dancing that we did; the reliable waltz and Foxtrot and now some square dancing and even The Charleston. She said that she was proud of me and of Jack for being so adventurous. Then, Dolly said, "What else happened?" I told her about the guy who grabbed me and kissed me and Jack's reaction. But, I knew, that was not what she was asking about. She wanted me to tell her about Jack, and his fight with his father, but didn't want to ask directly about it. So, impatiently, I decided to be more direct myself. "Dolly, please ask me exactly what you want to know." She didn't ask. She took a deep breath and told me. "Shortly, after Jack and you left for the dance, Helen came over with Betty. Imagine, Helen drove the buckboard, in the dark, with only one oil lamp to light the way. I thought that was courageous. But, that's not the point. Helen was very, very upset. She told me that Jim and Jack's argument got so heated that they almost came to blows. Helen said to me, 'Dolly, frankly, I was very scared. Jim told Jack that he must break off his relationship with Mary after tonight. He told Jack that, if he continued seeing Mary, he would cut him off. Imagine, for a father to say something like that to his son. I argued with Jim for hours. I told him that he should never, and I mean never, say that to my son again. I told him that I would leave him if he ever threatened Jack again. Dolly, I meant what I said. But, I don't know what to do. There is a war going on in my house. It was the worst New Year's eve.' At that point, Betty started crying. Helen grabbed her around and soothed her, but the tears kept flowing down Betty's pale cheeks." Dolly took a deep, deep breath and then continued, "Well, then, they went back home. Mary, I don't know what to say other than, I am truly sorry. I mean it. How did this become such an awful rift in their family?" That question had to be rhetorical because I certainly didn't have an answer for it. But, truth be told, everyone knew what the rift was about!

I excused myself and walked out onto the porch to get some air. The cold didn't bother me. There was a lot more to bother me than cold air. For these past five or six weeks, from

Thanksgiving to New Year, I thought that Jim Clark's feelings would moderate, that things would be better. I thought that his objections about me would fade as he got to know me. I hoped that it would work out, that he would be more accepting. I thought that he would, at least, put a smile on his face while still hurting inside. Now, not even a false façade. For the first time, I began to understand how serious, how visceral, Jim Clark's objection was to me and Jack, as a couple. His objections would not be overcome by who I was. They were only based upon what I was.

I was bitter and thought just how vile Jim Clark was for what he said, for his prejudice, for what he was doing to his own family, to his son. In my life, I had never had such an experience, one that affected me so directly. Once again, I was so naïve.

I sat there on the porch in the cold and thought and thought, essentially ignoring Dolly and my responsibilities on the other side of that door. But, then, after a few minutes, I came to realize that there were few alternatives. Jack and I could continue seeing each other. We might even become very serious. And, after some time, we might even marry. But, then, what would our situation be? Jack and I would be on our own. He probably would never speak to his father again and his family would be destroyed. He might never be allowed to see his mother or sister again. The more that I thought about that alternative, the alternative that includes Jack and me as a couple, the more that I knew that I had to break it off. Truth be told, I think that I knew it last night when Jack told me about his fight with his father.

As I thought more about it, I also knew that I couldn't break off from Jack in a way that would further polarize him and his family. I would have to do it quietly, gradually, without fanfare. Jack would have to accept it. Maybe, I would have to see other boys or men. Maybe, if Jack thought that he had lost me to someone else, rather than just breaking off with him because of his family feud, that he would be more accepting. Oh, what a terrible thought. I will just let it play out by refusing to see Jack other than our casual meetings.

With Lucas no longer hiring Jack to help out in the barn in the mornings, the only times that I would see him would be at the

Saturday Fair and Sunday church services. I could handle that. I would just say hello and, hopefully, that would be it. Oh, God help me!

I wiped my eyes on my apron and went back into the house to tend to Dolly. I told her, "Dolly, there is no happy ending for Jack and Mary." With that, neither one of us could say anything for a moment. Dolly looked as sad as I felt, saying, "Mary, what are you saying? Are you saying that you will stop dating him…that you will give up Jack?" I said, "Yes. I don't believe that anything will change Jim Clark's mind about me. Jack's family is being destroyed. I can't let that happen." I explained my thinking to Dolly, "But, I have to be smart about this. If Jack thinks that it is only about the feud, then he will fight with his father and continue the drama. So, I have to do this gradually so as not to imply that it was all about Jim's reaction, his prejudice, and his fight with Jack. It had to be about me wanting to move on, away from Jack, for my own reasons. He has to think that I am interested in dating other men." Dolly shook her head knowingly. "And, if you speak to Helen about it, you have to make her believe that it is about me and not about them. Dolly, I was once told that if you say something often enough, and with enough conviction, that people will start to believe you, even if it is a lie. That is what I must do. But, whether Helen believes it or not, that is what we must tell her. At least, then, she would have a means to bring her family back together. And, that is what I want. That is what I want! If we continue as it is now, any relationship that I might have had with Jack would always have the specter of a ruined family. It would always be there. It would always be about me. I couldn't live with that." There was a constant stream of tears rolling down my cheeks. I couldn't stop them.

Dolly just sat there with an amazed look on her face. She shook her head and opened her arms beckoning me to draw near. She held me around my shoulders, looked into my eyes and said, "Mary, you constantly surprise me. You are seventeen years old but have the maturity of a much older person. Giving up Jack has to be the hardest thing that you have done in your young life." That was all that I needed to hear. I fell into her lap. After a while, she asked me if there was any way that she could help. "No, there is nothing that you can do. I must do it." Dolly stroked my hair and held her hand on my cheek for a moment. Looking down at me, she said, "I can't believe how brave and selfless you are!"

    Since there was little to do in the fields or in the garden during the winter, timing for breakfast was now more relaxed. Then, we had a small snack at about 2:00 with a cup of coffee. Dinner was usually about 6:00. I prepared the afternoon snack for Dolly and Lucas. I rang the bell and Lucas appeared. We sat together. After eating, Lucas helped with the cleanup. After everything was away, I excused myself and went to the barn. It was good to be by myself. It was cold but I didn't let it bother me. I felt that the discomfort that I experienced around my ears and fingertips was a punishment of sorts for what happened to Jack's family. Maybe, it was a sort of penance for all of the harm that I had caused. I know that didn't make any sense, but the pain from the cold air was almost liberating from the emotional pain that I was suffering.

    Lucas walked into the barn and came over to my work table. He said, "Mary, I know that this isn't a good time for you. Why don't you go for a long walk? I'll do the work here." I knew immediately from the look on his face that Dolly had filled him in with my plan. Then, Lucas echoed Dolly's sentiments, "Mary, what you are planning is… I don't know if many people would be willing to give up so much." His head went back and forth in agreement with his own sentiments. Then, he took a deep breath, almost in a sigh.

    Lucas was being so considerate. I believe that his offer to do the work was sincere. I thanked him. "Lucas, I would rather be alone. In fact, the more work that I do, the faster the time goes by and the less that I think about the mess that I am in. But, again, thank you for offering." Lucas left without saying a word. I thought that he was being wonderfully sensitive to my plight.

    When I was done making cheddar cheese, I went back into the house to see Dolly and Lucas sitting comfortably near the fireplace. I told them that I would soon be making dinner. But, before I could finish the sentence, Lucas asked me to join them. I sat there with them for a little while without a word being shared. The heat from the fireplace warmed my frosty fingers.

The next few days passed without much more being said. With Jack no longer being needed in the mornings, my life was a little less complicated. But, now, it was Saturday, Fair day, and I would be seeing Jack. It would be the first time since New Year's Eve.

As Lucas was helping me pack up the buckboard, I realized that Jack had not brought Helen over to be with Dolly. Lucas said that Helen might be too embarrassed to come over with everything that was going on. I felt badly for both of them.

I was off to the Fair thinking about how it would work out. What would I say to Jack, what would my face say to Jack? What would he say? Would he ask me out? Gee, I hope....NO!!! Don't hope for that.

By the time that I reached the Fair and unpacked, Jack hadn't shown up. So, I was my smiley self, selling as much as I could, enjoying speaking with the Cherokee ladies, explaining mozzarella, "Mutz", to anyone who came by. Then, Jack came to the Fair. He unloaded his truck. Fortunately, he had some customers as soon as set up. During a lull, he smiled at me. I returned the smile. I whispered under my breath to myself, "I have to remember...nothing too abrupt, nothing to make him believe that my refusal to go out with him was about the feud that he was having with his father. Gradual...gradual."

My sales of chickens, eggs, butter, cheddar and Mutz were strong. And, within about two plus hours I was almost completely sold out. My business slowed. Jack's business slowed at the same time. I probably hadn't noticed before, but, everyone's business at the Fair slowed at about the same time. It never mattered before. But, now, there was Jack and there was me. What I feared was about to happen.

Jack walked over. He said hello and I responded with "How are you?" He told me that he missed being with me in the morning. Then, he said, "Do you miss me in the mornings?" I told him that I did. I told Jack that there was a lot to do back at the farm and that I needed to get back. "I'll see you at church tomorrow or at the Fair next week." He didn't object or ask me for a date. I was glad and sad at the same time. He was probably going through some of the same angst about his family and how we could have a relationship given his father's prejudice. I cried on the way home realizing that I had set a course that would take Jack away from me forever.

When I returned to the farm, I immediately turned over the receipts to Lucas as I always did. Dolly asked me about the sales. It was a safe question for her to ask. I told her that the sales were good, that everything was just about sold out. Then, I told her about Jack. She said, "Mary, it is for the best. You will find someone."

There was more than eight inches of snow the next day that prevented us from going to church. I wasn't unhappy.

The next week's Fair was on the 12th of January. When all of the work was done, I tried to clean up as quickly as I could to minimize the time that I might have to be with Jack. But, as night follows day, he came over and greeted me warmly. I responded saying, "It's nice to see you". I tried to control the discussion. I said to him, "We haven't seen Helen this week or last. I know that Dolly would love to see her." Truly, Dolly never mentioned missing Helen. In fact, she tried valiantly to keep our discussions flat, neutral, with no mention of the Clark family, at all. But, I also felt that Dolly needed a friend and, after all, Helen had been her best friend ever since Dolly first arrived at the Taddum Farm. Jack said, "I will speak with my mother. But, I think that she is a little ill at ease after the discussion that she and Dolly had on New Year's Eve. She doesn't know if she would be welcomed." Softly, I said, "I understand. But, they are the best of friends." Jack said hopefully, "I think that if my mother knew that Dolly wanted to see her, she would be there." I didn't know for sure, but I said, "Dolly would love to see Helen." After a momentary pause, he added, "Tell Dolly that mom will be there next Saturday." I shook my head and thanked him.

Then, what I feared would happen, did happen. Jack asked me out to dinner the next Saturday. He said that we could go out with Ben and Aida, if I liked. I knew that this would come up since I had made my decision. I had no choice. So, I lied. I told him that I had a date for Saturday and that I couldn't possibly ask Lucas for more time off. He asked for the following week and I lied again, saying that I couldn't plan that far in advance with Dolly's health starting to decline. I said, "Jack, thank you for asking. I would like to go out with you but Dolly's condition is really worsening. She asks for Laudanum, the painkiller, daily, and sometimes more than once per day. I know that Lucas can watch her for a few hours, but I feel guilty about leaving her too often. I just don't know what the future holds."

Well, there you go. I had set up the ruse for all of the other lies that I would have to make up in order to stay away from Jack. I thought that I was prepared for this, but clearly, I was not. Now, I knew that I was in trouble, the type of trouble that results when one lie compounds another; a lie that I would have to live with forever.

In my grandfather's letter to me, dictated to Waya just before he died, he said, "The truth will never fail you." How true that is. How smart he was. Lies, on the other hand, will always fail you, they will always screw you up. And, in this case, the person that was most affected by the lying, the most screwed up, was me.

The weeks seemed to be punctuated by Saturdays and Sundays when I got to see Jack. He had spoken with his mother about her visiting Dolly. And each Saturday, weather permitting, Jack drove Helen over to the house to be with Dolly. So, I ended up seeing him twice, and sometimes, three times on Saturdays; when he dropped Helen off, at the Fair and then, and when he picked Helen up. On Sundays, I would see him in church. Although I tried to make myself scarce when his truck came up our driveway, some days, it was just impossible to avoid contact. Occasionally, we spent some time together on the porch. One of those times, he asked to go out together, again. And, once again,

I made my excuses, my lies. But, he kept coming by with Helen and asked to speak with me. We did. We shared pleasantries while sitting on the porch. I hoped that he felt rejected enough to stop asking me to go on a date.

The winter weather was settling in and would be all around us for several months. The chores were becoming drudgery. The days were sad. The nights were long. The routine that had started as something foreign, then grew into something enjoyable, was no longer that. Dolly was getting worse. There were days when Dolly needed the Laudanum several times a day. I was using the great invention that Lucas had created, a chair with a hole in the middle over a bucket filled with straw rather than taking her out to the outhouse. At first, it was just when it snowed out or was very cold. But, increasingly, it was the norm rather than the exception. I used the same set up to bathe her by exchanging the bucket below the chair for a larger wash tub.

Increasingly, Dolly's moaning at night woke me up. If she was awake, I offered her some Laudanum. If she was still asleep, I just listened, not knowing what to do. Waiting for her next moan was just like when I had waited for the next snore from my high school girlfriend. It was almost impossible to sleep.

During the days, Dolly remained stoic, saying that the pain in her back was not so bad. But, when Lucas was out of earshot, many times, she asked me for the Laudanum.

Everything that I had said to Jack earlier, about Dolly's worsening condition, first just a lie, then an exaggeration, was now becoming reality. Maybe, it was inevitable. Or, could it be that I was being punished? Could my lying about Dolly's condition have caused it to happen even faster than it would have? I felt even guiltier about my lies than I had before.

Then, one Saturday in February, I was sitting on the porch, half expecting Jack to join me there for a quick chat. Instead, he walked right by me, brought Helen into the house and left without a word. He barely acknowledged me. Again, I thought of my discomfort from the cold February air as penance for what I was doing to Jack. After he left, I sat on the porch by myself, with tears running down my cheeks, as the two friends talked inside, just on the other side of the door.

Apparently, our cooling relationship was not lost on Helen. Her voice came across the doorway to the porch as a whisper. I didn't want to hear what they were saying. I should have gone further away so I couldn't hear them talking. I should have already left for the Fair. But, they were talking about me and about Jack. So, I couldn't help myself. I would be late for the Fair.

I heard Dolly say in a very angry voice, "Helen, you were the one that told us all about Jim's reaction to Mary and Jack dating. We all know about the fight that the two of them had on New Year's Eve. After you told us, we heard about it again from Mary when she came home from the barn dance. She told us how distraught Jack was." Helen shouted back, "Dolly...it was awful. Thankfully, Jim and Jack are speaking again. But, there is certainly tension in their relationship. I feel like I am in the middle of a tornado because I'm being turned around so much. I love my husband and I love my son. Nothing good can come of it. And, I believe that Jack loves Mary. Oh, my, what a horrible situation." Then, Dolly told Helen everything that I asked her to keep to herself. "I'm not supposed to tell you this. But, I believe that it is important for you to know. But, you, Helen Clark, must not tell anyone, period. OK?" Helen agreed. Dolly asked again, "Are you sure that you can keep this to yourself?" There was a pause. Helen said, "I promise". Dolly continued, "OK, then...I think that you should know that Mary is very fond of Jack. I believe that she is in love with Jack. But, it doesn't matter now. Mary sees no future with him. She sees what is happening to your family and doesn't want to destroy Jack by continuing to date him. She has decided to turn down any proposals to go out with him, period. She will not see him anymore. Helen, Mary is doing this, making this great sacrifice, for Jack and you and for Betty. She sees only pain for your family and pain for herself if she continues to see Jack. Yet, she doesn't want Jack to think that it is because of the fighting going on in your house. She believes that would make it even worse for him. Mary wants Jack to believe that she has just lost interest in him and is looking forward to dating other men. She wants your family to heal. Helen, Mary cries all of the time. She thinks that I don't hear her in bed, but I do. She is about as unhappy as a person can be."

Helen said, "Dolly! Oh my! I feel horrible." Helen added, "What a brave young woman. Jack would be lucky to find such a wonderful person. And yet, Mary is right. There cannot be any relationship between them if Jack expects to still have a relationship with his father. And, as much as it pains me, I have to stand by my husband. He is my husband. You understand, don't you? Oh, what a terrible situation!" Dolly finished by saying, "Helen, again, you cannot repeat any of this to a soul. If Jack finds out what Mary is doing, what she is lying about, why she doesn't want to go out with him, he will push until she agrees and then, the entire situation with Jim will blow up again."

Hearing all of that, I ran off of the porch and into the barn. I had to get away. I climbed up into the hay loft. I heard someone yell out. It was Lucas. He yelled, "Who's up there?" I told him in a shaky voice, filled with dread, that it was just me. Hearing my voice, he called up to me in a kind and gentle voice, "I thought that I heard someone rooting around in the hayloft. Mary, please come down." After a few moments, I did. We sat together on two milking stools. Lucas asked me what was wrong. Of course, he knew about my plan. I told him what I overheard. He said, "I'm sorry that you heard all of that. What can I do to help?" Lucas said all of the right things. He finished with, "Mary, Jack is a great guy, but sometimes, we can't control everything the way that we would like." In a way, hearing that from Lucas was like an echo. That was one of my favorite sentiments, letting go of those things that you can't control. But, again, it works much better in theory than it does in practice. Here, letting go meant losing Jack. That was exactly what I was doing and it was killing me.

I walked out of the barn, climbed aboard the buckboard and fled to the Fair.

Chapter 16

By the middle of February, the miserable weather was reaching out from the gray skies. The tree branches were bending down, heavy with snow and ice, making them seem even sadder than I had become. The winter wheat stood in the fields as a beacon of hope for the future. The problem was that I didn't feel that beacon of hope for Dolly and for me.

I spent a lot of those short winter days and longer winter nights, thinking about my future. I know that it was very selfish of me. After all, my concerns paled as compared to Dolly's condition and her future. But, Dolly's certain demise was the core of my problem. Yes, I know...how can I compare? But, I knew that sooner or later, Dolly would pass away and I would have to leave the Taddum Farm. Where I would go, and what I would do, were my primary concerns to ponder as I lie awake at night or even while milking the cows during the day. The solutions that I considered would take me further from Jack. And, that would spell the end of Jack and Mary forever. Yes, you are right. If I really wanted for Jack's family to heal, then, going farther away would be a good outcome. However, that thought made me cry all over again.

I felt the need to talk with someone about my future. Whenever I had a problem in the past, I would always talk it over with Dolly. Obviously, I couldn't talk about this problem with Dolly or Lucas. So, I decided to reach out to Pastor Berkley and his wife Sally.

The next week, I asked Lucas if I could take care of some "personal matters" in town after the Fair. He looked at me sort of cross-wise when I said "personal matters". That made him clearly uncomfortable. That put him into a position where he had no choice but to say, "Of course, Mary, take what time you need. I'll look after Dolly. Just be careful of all of the snow and ice. The ruts in the road can be a problem for the horse and the buckboard." Of course, I knew that. But, I think that he was uncomfortable with this conversation and needed something to talk about other than "personal matters".

Just before I was ready to close my table at the Fair, Aida Tanner came by. I was happy to see her. We chit-chatted away about a variety of things and people...mostly people. As time went on, I found her to be a better friend than Becky or Alice. She was someone who would listen without judging. Someone, who would listen to my woes without falsely minimizing them. But, as I listened to her talk about her future, her future, I came to realize that Aida and I lived in two different worlds. You'll see what I mean.

Aida told me that she was pretty smitten with Ben Held. I didn't know him well, but from my limited exposure to him, he seemed fine. So, I couldn't blame her. Then, she told me about her college applications. She said, "I applied to three schools. Two of them are back east; Princeton in New Jersey and NYU in New York City. I have already been accepted to the University of Oklahoma in Norman. It's much less expensive to go to school in Oklahoma. But, my father said that I should go where I could get the best education." After Aida finished, I told her that I thought it was great to be applying to such wonderful and far away schools. I smiled as I told her how excited I was for her. Aida went off and I continued cleaning up my table at the Fair.

While I congratulated Aida, I have to admit that I was more than a little jealous of her. She has parents and they are supportive. She will end up with a great education and she will be secure. Me, well, I would never even graduate from high school and, certainly, I would never be applying to any colleges. She will end up with Ben. I will push Jack into someone else's arms. Truly, my jealousy, when I compared my situation to hers, blighted any good feelings that I had for her successes. Yes, I should be ashamed of my feelings, but sometimes, I just can't help myself. I'm not perfect. But, in spite of my jealousy, I still liked Aida. I just wished that my future held as much promise as hers.

After everything was taken care of at the Fair, I walked over to the church and looked for Pastor Berkley. I came upon him in the chapel just straightening up. Sally Berkley and two parishioners were there, as well, cleaning in preparation for church services the next day. I walked up to him and asked if we could speak. He said, "Of course, why don't we sit over there." He led me to the back benches so we could be out of earshot of the others. He was upbeat. He had a smile on his face, probably thinking that I had something simple to talk about, something that he could easily resolve for me. It wouldn't be that easy.

I spent the next several minutes explaining everything to him about Jack and his father, Jim. "...and pastor, if Jack thinks that I am doing this because of his father, it will start another war between them. I am trying to separate from Jack so that his family heals." The pastor shook his head saying, "OK, Mary, I understand. I am so sorry for you. You are giving up everything for Jack and yet, he will never even know about it." The good pastor thought for a moment and then said, "What if I talk in my next sermon about tolerance and prejudice?" I told him that was a good idea but that he must steer clear of the relationship between Jack and myself or Jack and Jim. He agreed. I was grateful. But, I didn't hold out much hope. If it were that easy, then Jack's straightforward talk with his father on that fateful night before the Thanksgiving Barn Dance would have done it. It was never going to be that easy. Life just isn't that way.

Then, I asked the pastor if he had any more time. He said, "Of course". I said, "I have another problem to discuss." While I was reluctant to talk about it with anyone, I told the pastor about Dolly's declining condition. Of course, he knew. But, he didn't put that fact together with my situation. So, I shared my thoughts. I had to be frank. "Pastor, when Dolly passes away, I will be left in the house, alone, with a widower. Even if Lucas wanted to keep me on to work on the farm, I couldn't stay there. Don't get me wrong. Lucas has been very respectful. He has been very good to me. But, I can't be there after Dolly passes." The pastor shook his head in agreement. He still didn't understand my situation completely.

I was frustrated. I needed to get him to understand. My voice was not as nice as it should have been. "Pastor, Dolly will die and I will be out of a job. My grandparents are gone and I am out of a place to live! I'm sorry to be so cold-hearted about all of this, but that is my reality!" I softened my tone of voice and added in almost a whisper, "And, that reality is coming toward me very quickly." Based upon the look on his face, I think that I finally got through to him. His head dipped down as he looked at the floor. He said, "Mary, none of us thought about what would happen after Dolly dies. None of us thought of what would happen to you. There wasn't a 'you'." The pastor was clearly uncomfortable. I was embarrassed by his thoughtful admission. But, I was right. I felt a little better knowing that my concerns were real. They, Lucas, Pastor Berkley and Pastor Smyth, just never gave a thought about the young girl that would become emotionally attached to a dying woman. They never thought about a human being at the end of the road with nowhere to go! The pastor shook his head back and forth. He thought for a moment and then called over to his wife. "Sally, we need to talk."

When Sally Berkley came over, the pastor summarized our discussion about Jack in a few words. He was able to do it because he did not have the emotional involvement that I had. Then, he told her about our discussion regarding what will happen to me after Dolly dies. That situation was clearly easier for the pastor, a man, to deal with than my relationship with Jack Clark. Here, he was analytical. "Sally, we will help Mary. After Dolly passes, and I hope that it doesn't happen all too soon, Mary will live with us for a while. We will work to get her settled. And, once she is settled with a good job, we will help her find a good, clean and safe place to live. What do you say?" Sally agreed immediately. I had no idea that they would have welcomed me into their home. I didn't know what to say in response, but I said, "That is so nice of you both…thank you."

Sally Berkley was much more attuned to my drama with Jack Clark. She grabbed me around the shoulders and whispered since there were listening ears in the chapel. "Mary, are you certain that you are willing to give up on Jack? Is there no other way?" I said, "Not unless the pastor's sermon magically changes Jim Clark's opinion of me. I appreciate what the pastor is willing to do, but no, I don't think that anything will change Jim Clark." Then, after a momentary pause, I concluded, "No. There is no other way." "Then, I'm sorry to say this to you my darling. If you are really serious about giving up on Jack, you can't give him up only a little or mostly. If you are serious, then, you have to give up on Jack completely. And, the only way that Jack will understand that your relationship is over is for you to date other men." She was adamant. "You can't just talk about it. You have to do it." Although her words were piercing through my heart, I knew that she was right. Seeing Jack at the Fair and at the house when he brought Helen over, or at church, was just a tease to him and to me. Sally's voice broke through my thoughts. She repeated herself, "Mary, you have to date other men. That is the only way that Jack will get a clear message. That is the only way that you can accomplish what you set out to do." I took a deep breath and gathered myself, "Yes, but the thought of it hurts. I love Jack. I'm sure of it. That's the only reason that I want to do it. I don't want to destroy the person that I love and his family." Sally said, "I sensed that. And, frankly, if you didn't love Jack, all of this would be easy. But…" She was like a dog with a bone, not willing to let go. "…are you willing to go out with other men?" I reiterated that Dolly's condition was starting to go downhill. I told her that I had to be with her. I was dodging the question. Sally offered, "The Pastor said that we will help you. We will. When you have a date, he and I will look after Dolly. I'll arrange it." What could I say? Jokingly, I said to Sally, "OK, okay, now, all I need is a date". I thought that I had made a joke. But, Sally wasn't done. There was that bone in her mouth, again. She asked, "Who are your friends in town?" I responded, "There's Alice and Becky, both of whom I know from the fairgrounds and there is Aida, Isaac Tanner's daughter. Sally said, "Good. Now, go and talk with them and let them know that you are available. You don't need to tell them anything about Jack and all of that. They might have friends that would be willing to go out with you. You need the message to get back to Jack that you are seeing other people, just not seeing him."

  Sally Berkley's thinking was crystal clear. She had no problem with pressing me to move forward. Now, I have involved the pastor's wife in my charade. Even Sally was helping me perpetuate the lie. How would I face Jack if he ever found out? What would he think of me? Ugggh!

I had told Sally Berkley that I would follow her advice. I did. I marched right over to Tanner's General Store. I knew that Aida would be there. Despite what Sally had said, I spent at least a half hour with Aida telling her the entire story including the ugliness between Jim and Lucas and Jim and Jack. I always referred to that night prior to the Thanksgiving Barn Dance as "the ugliness". I needed to share it with one person and Aida was the one person that I knew would understand. Aida was saddened to hear of Jim Clark's reaction, his prejudice. She said, "As Jews, we experience prejudice like that a lot." I didn't know that. I guess that was yet another part of my naiveté. But, before I had met the Tanners, Isaac and Aida, and Doctor Held and his son Ben, I had never met a Jew. I had only heard about them from the church pulpit while I was at school in Tahlequah. And, what the pastor said there at Easter time was not very complimentary.

Aida Tanner told me that the only boy that she had dated was Ben Held. And, she didn't know many boys or men for me to date. Aida recommended that I speak with Alice and Becky. Then, Aida said, "I understand how painful this is for you. If you are uncomfortable, I can speak with them for you." I agreed. But, I told her not to say anything about the drama between Jack and Jim Clark. "Aida, do you promise?" She told me not to worry. She put her fingers across her mouth, twisting her lips, feigning locking a secret inside. When she did that with her lips, it reminded me of an old adage that my grandfather would say to me, "Ahyoka, the only secret kept is one that is shared with no one." I hoped that Aida would keep this one secret to herself. I left town and went back to the farm.

The next day, Sunday, the pastor talked about the evil of prejudice and how Jesus would welcome all comers into his kingdom. I gently shook my head as he spoke. I think that the pastor saw me and smiled. I smiled. He did what he said that he was going to do without making it about Jim and Jack. If Jim got the message, then good. Maybe there is hope...yet. Somehow, I doubt it. I think that Jim Clark, like many people, separate the piety and the lessons of a Sunday morning sermon from their life all of the other six plus days of the week. Yet, they would never consider missing church services; a contradiction that is shared by people of many faiths. I guess that they just don't understand.

After the church service, outside in the brisk air, Jack approached me. He asked me out for next Saturday night. He did it within earshot of his parents. I wondered if that was purposeful given what the pastor had just talked about. Of course, I told him that I was busy and couldn't go out with him. But, I thanked him. He started to respond, probably to ask for a different week, but I put my hand up, half way between us and toward his face, in a fashion that indicated that he should stop. He seemed shocked. I had rudely shut him down from asking me again by raising my hand. What I had just done to Jack killed me inside. Especially that hand in his face. It was cruel and mean-spirited. Apparently, that is what I had become. Shame on me!

I think that I can rationalize what I did to Jack only one way. It is the thought of what would have happened if I had accepted his offer to go out on a date with him right there in front of his father. The sermon be damned. All hell would have broken loose and I don't mean the kind of hell in the Bible. That thought made it even more obvious to me that this was the only path that I could travel. I have to keep remembering that. Okay, I got through this confrontation without crying right in front of him. I would just have to reserve my tears for when I am alone.

I never considered all of the damage that I would be doing. But, I guess that if Jack was really disgusted with me, his interest in me as a girlfriend would just fade away. That is what I bought into, and that is what I must accept…as much as it hurts me. On the way back to the farm, I told Dolly and Lucas what had happened. Dolly repeated how brave I was. I told Dolly I don't know about being brave. I just know that my heart is broken. Then, that was it. I guess that I couldn't wait until I was alone. My tears sprang forth like a waterfall from my eyes right in front of Dolly and Lucas.

The next day was Monday. While I was milking the cows in the barn alongside Lucas, Jack walked in. Clearly, from the way that he was walking, he had a purpose. He said, "Lucas, do you mind if I speak with Mary alone?" Lucas said, "Of course. Mary,

I'll take care of the cows this morning." So, I walked outside into the cold air with Jack. I knew that this would not be pleasant. I thought that he would reproach me for how I had treated him outside of church, in front of everybody. But, that wasn't why he came. As soon as we were far enough away from the barn for our conversation not to reach Lucas' ears, Jack said, "Mary, I don't know what to say. But, I want for you to know how I feel about you and I thought you felt about me." He reached out to me. "I am falling in love with you…" However, tempted, I withdrew from his arms. He said, "Did I do something to hurt your feelings? Just let me know and I will apologize. I will make it right." I needed to let him finish. I just couldn't hurt him any more than I absolutely had to, any more than I already had. But, then, he said, "Was it about New Year's Eve and the fight that I had with my father? Because if that has anything to do with it, please let me know and I will leave my father's house and get a job in town. I'll do whatever I need to do to make you happy." Now, I had to be a very good actress. I took a deep breath and told Jack the biggest lie of my life. "Jack, it has nothing whatsoever to do with you and your father. It has to do with me. I thought that I liked you…and I do. But, there are other men that I might be more interested in. For now, I want to meet other men and see how it goes. I don't want to be just with you." Jack's shoulders slunk down like that of a dog that was being reprimanded. I placed my hand on the side of his face and said, "Jack, please understand." He left without another word. Oh, my God, what a liar. God should strike me down dead!

    I went back to milking the cows. Lucas was still there. He asked if I was alright. What sort of answer could I give him? I told him that everything was good. I didn't want to go into details.

    The next Saturday, as usual, Jack brought Helen over to spend the day. He barely acknowledged me. And, then as he left, he told Helen that he would be back to pick her up at somewhere around 12:00 PM. Helen said, "Fine. Please don't be late." Helen and Dolly chatted away as always. I heard some of it. They were talking about Jack and me. Helen told Dolly how I had succeeded. Jack was terribly disappointed.

I left for the Fair. It was cold outside when I arrived. That morning seemed to take forever. It was to be the beginning of a very difficult day. I was this close to the man that I loved, the man that told me that he was falling in love with me, the same man that should hate me now. I had accomplished what I set out to do. The only saving grace was that there would be peace in the Clark family.

After the Fair, I returned to the farm and looked in on Dolly. Helen was still there. I left without a word and walked over to the barn to do my chores. I didn't want to speak with anyone.

A few weeks later, I stood behind the table at the Saturday Fair serving customers, as always. It always surprised me how I could feel Jack's presence even though he was fifty feet away.

Toward the end of the morning, Becky came over to my table with a guy in tow. Becky and I greeted each other. She introduced me to Harry Miller. He said, "Hello". We chatted for a while. Harry was a student at the University of Oklahoma in Tulsa. He told me about life on campus, about his courses and about what he wanted to do after graduation. He seemed interesting. I told him a little about my life at the Taddum Farm. After a while, Becky dragged him away. I finished up the day's business and began to pack up when Jack wandered over. Of course, he asked about Becky and her friend. He might have thought that Harry was a potential suitor. I had nothing to tell him. Jack and I bid each other goodbye. How awful I felt. Jack certainly didn't deserve to be treated in that way. I loaded up the buckboard and returned to the farm.

The next week at the Fair, Becky's friend, Harry, came over to me as I was unpacking my goods for sale. He offered to help. I accepted. We chatted all along while we were working together. He sampled my cheeses and complimented me on the flavor. I believed that this was just a means of "buttering me up". I was right. He asked if I would go to dinner with him next Saturday night. Then, he asked if I would be willing to drive with him to Tulsa. When I agreed, he said that we would have to leave early because it is a long drive. I explained to him how my primary responsibility was to watch over Dolly and that I could only go out if I had adequate backup for her. I told Harry that I would have to arrange with the pastor before I could be sure that it would be okay. He understood. I suggested that we meet at noon at the church. He agreed and left the Fair.

After I cleaned up my tables, I went to the pastor's house and spoke with Sally Berkley. She agreed that they would be available the following Saturday afternoon and evening. She said, "This is what you have to do!"

I quickly went to the church and waited for Harry. We set the time for our dinner date. When I told them, Dolly and Lucas said that they were happy to have the pastor and Sally Berkley come over for a visit. All set.

I got ready for my dinner date with Harry Miller. I wore my blue dress, fixed my hair up in a bun, and added a little lipstick. I was ready to go. I walked from the bedroom into the main room. When Helen saw me, her eyes widened. "Mary, how beautiful you are. Dolly told me that you are going out." I said, "Helen, yes, I am going out on a date." I was ready to explode. "You don't have to worry about me and Jack anymore…Jack and I are no more. Your family could be whole again." She shook her head in agreement as she started crying. "Mary, oh, Mary. I am so sad." I ignored what she said. I told her that it was for the best. My response to her was somewhat rude but I had no patience for any of this. You see, I was angry. I thought, "Why do I have to make this sacrifice? Why can't it be Jim Clark?"

I needed to change the direction of our discussion. I said, "Dolly, the Pastor Berkley and Sally should be here a little later." Just then, Harry drove up and knocked at the door. I greeted him and introduced him to Dolly and Helen. Dolly asked, "Where are you taking our Mary?" He told her that we would be going out to a place in Tulsa, adding that the restaurants in Tulsa were much better than those in Muskogee. Then, he said that it was a long ride but he would have me back by 9:00 PM, the latest.

As we were about to walk out, Jack drove up. He was there to pick up Helen. His timing couldn't have been more perfect. God... He walked over and introduced himself to Harry. I greeted him as well. I was probably rude by saying, "Jack, we have to go. We're driving all of the way to Tulsa. It's a long ride". And that was that. I felt as if I was going to throw up. But, I had to keep myself together. If Harry saw anything in my eyes or heard anything in my voice, he would wonder if he was being played for a fool and that I was going out with him only to make Jack jealous. What I was really doing was just the opposite. I was thoroughly ruining my relationship with Jack. If everything that I had done up to that point wasn't enough, seeing me with Harry, going to dinner in Tulsa of all places, should have been the final blow to my relationship with Jack.

Harry had a wonderful car. I think that it was a Packard but I can't be certain. As we took the long ride to Tulsa, I was somewhat apprehensive. Here, I was, alone with a virtual stranger on these terribly lonely roads, going to a large city.

Since Harry was going to school there, he knew the restaurants in Tulsa very well. We reached "Mel's Chili House" on East 11th Street at about 04:30 PM. That was his favorite spot to eat. Eating chili was yet another new experience for me.

After dinner, Harry asked me if I would like to see the campus of the university. Yes, another something that I had never done or seen before. I guess that I looked hesitant. He said, "It's actually on the way back to Muskogee." I said, "Sure. I had thought about continuing my education after high school but life got in the way." I laughed and laughed. He didn't completely understand my sarcastic comment. But, he smiled. We drove the fifteen minutes from the Chili House to the university in silence. When we got to the school, we walked around for a while as he told me about the different halls of learning; science, arts, etc. It was fascinating. I let myself dream that maybe, someday, I might be able to continue my education at a place like this. Then, he brought me back to reality as he pointed out his dormitory. I would never be going to a college.

He asked me if I would like to go up to his room. "Ahh, no thank you...you really wouldn't like me if I said 'yes', would you?" He smiled and then, laughed. "No, I think that you are right. Let's get you back home."

The return to the Taddum Farm from the university was uneventful. We didn't say much but some things didn't need to be said. He tried to get me up to his dorm room and failed. He can't be blamed for trying. He is a young man and has needs and desires just like a woman. I had learned that much from Dolly. But, this woman understood now, today, more than ever, what Dolly had meant when she said "your decision...your consequences". My decision was not to suffer the consequences that could result from a few moments of pleasure. That would have to wait for the right time and right place and with the right man. I can dream, can't I?

Harry returned me to the farm and walked me up to the door. Then, he asked if he could see me again. To my surprise, I said, "Yes". He said that he would come by the Fair next Saturday to plan it out.

Once he had finished his chores, Lucas had told the pastor and Sally that they could leave early since he was able to look after Dolly. As I walked into the house, Lucas told me that Dolly was in bed. I said goodnight to Lucas and went into the bedroom. Of course, Dolly asked me how the date went. I told her everything. She said again how brave that I was. I had nothing to say in return.

I blew the candle out. Dolly moaned in her sleep as she did on many of the nights. I slept very few hours that night. I was feeling increasingly vulnerable. I was thoroughly confused about my life. Here I was, sleeping in the bedroom of a dying woman who I was growing to love and I was going out with a new guy to end the relationship with the man that I do love. And, I am a woman with seemingly no future. How pathetic am I? I thought that I have to focus. I have to think about my future beyond more than a few days or weeks or months. What do I really want to do with my life? How will I achieve what I want?

The week went by. The winter weather was firmly in control. Mid-February through mid-March usually has some of the coldest temperatures and certainly, the most snow. This year was no different.

Saturday came again. Lucas helped me load up the buckboard for the Fair. I didn't know what Jack's reaction was going to be after last week. I was rude to him when Harry came to pick me up to go to Tulsa. He might not speak with me. He might be nasty. I didn't know what to expect. I told myself to just take a deep breath and continue on the path that I had chosen. I did.

When I got to the Fair, there was a covering of snow on the tables. I brushed it off and unloaded my goods; cheeses, butter, milk, eggs and chickens. Jack called over saying "Good morning, Mary. How are you today?" I responded in a flat voice, "Good morning, Jack". Then, I thought, "Given all of the insults that I had hurled at him, why couldn't he just be nasty or not even say hello. Why does he have to be so nice after the way that I treated him?"

About an hour later, Harry walked up and greeted me with a big smile. He really was nice. He asked me if we could go out to the movies. Once again, I told him that I would have to see if the pastor and his wife could be with Dolly. And, once again, I asked him to come to the church later to wait for me to be able to respond.

As I had done before, I went to the Pastor's house and spoke with Sally Berkley. She agreed to the following Saturday night. I quickly went to the church and waited for Harry. We set the date and time for the movie. I went back to the farm and told Dolly all about what was going on.

Church services the next day were uneventful. Jack was cordial, saying hello to me. Betty and Helen Clark did as well. Jim Clark just ignored me but said hello to Dolly and Lucas. The pastor talked about the "cancer" of prejudice. He said that prejudice had to be cut out of your soul just like a cancerous tumor needed to be cut out of your flesh. Not a sound came out of the assembly. That probably meant that the congregation either believed in what he was saying or just couldn't wait for it to be over and done. I wondered what Jim Clark thought of it. Probably, he was happy when it was over and done.

The next Saturday night, Harry took me to the movies. This was the second movie that I had gone to in my life. As we got back to the farm, Harry asked me to go out the next week. He said, "I know that you will have to arrange with Pastor Berkley, so give me your answer when you can. I shook my head. Harry walked me to the door and said good night. I kissed him on the cheek without saying anything.

With Dolly settled for the night, the pastor and Sally had already left. Lucas was smoking his pipe by the fireplace. I greeted him and then walked into the bedroom. In spite of my trying not to wake Dolly, she rolled over as I walked in. She said, "So, how was your date? How was the movie?" So, I told her about the movie. "The movie was called 'The Crowd'. Again, I was greatly affected by it. The movie was complex and very sad. John has a quite ordinary job. He falls in love with Mary and offers to marry. She agrees. They live a life of ups and downs; he winning a $500 prize, coupled with the tragedy of the loss of a child. That tragedy adds to John's failure at work and stress on the marriage. John even contemplates suicide."

Then, Dolly asked if I liked Harry. I told her that he seemed very nice. "He is good looking and smart…and I went on listing Harry's many attributes." She stopped me, "But, he's not Jack. Mary, once you started to list Harry's attributes, I knew that you could not feel about Harry as you do about Jack. That's because you've never listed Jack's attributes. You have just told me that you love him. Because, when you love someone, you just know it. You don't have to list anything. It's not like a scale at the grocers where you weigh a guy's attributes to see if he has enough." Dolly chuckled and reached out to me. I grabbed her hand and sobbed quietly. Then, Dolly said something to me that I already knew. She said, "Mary you are doing the right thing. Maybe, Harry isn't the right guy. Maybe, he is. Maybe, you will never find the guy to replace Jack. Sometimes, you just have to accept a situation that isn't ideal. Look at me. I was basically a "mail order bride". I could list Lucas' attributes that I recognized once I met him. But, I don't need to do it because I fell in love with him, period." I shook my head understanding what she told me.

With Harry asking me out for a third date, I went back to Sally Berkley, thinking that I was doing just what she prescribed to separate from Jack. Then, Sally said to me, "You know, Mary, while what you are doing to separate from Jack is best, I wonder if you know what you are doing to Harry. You are leading him on by agreeing to go out, yet again. I hope that by doing such a noble thing regarding the Clark family, that you are not hurting Harry. I believe that if you continue going down the path that you are on with Harry, you will find yourself in yet another very difficult position."

Sally added, "You know, Mary, you are very easy to fall in love with. Harry may have fallen in love with you already." Sally asked me if I loved Harry or thought that I would fall in love with him. I told her, "Oh, I like him well enough, but it isn't love. When I think of Harry, I think of him as a friend." Then, she was adamant. "Mary, you have to see a lot of different men, but none too often." More advice. My head was spinning. Ughhhh.

The pastor joined us, reviewing the conundrum that I had created. I knew that my lies and deception would only make my life worse. It violated everything that grandfather had taught me about the truth. Well, now, I was going to hurt Harry. I told Sally Berkley, "I understand what you said and I know what I have to do."

The pastor added, "OK, I think that Mrs. Berkley and I will not be available to stay with Dolly for the foreseeable future. Ahhh, or until you find someone else to date." Now, even the pastor was telling a lie. Well, maybe not a real lie. But, it was the cover that I needed with Harry.

When I met with Harry, I told him that it would be a while before I would be available to go out. He was disappointed, but told me that he understood. He offered to come by to say hello at the Fair. I told him that would be nice. Frankly, I didn't know what else to say. Doing this with Jack and now with Harry was torture. My lies were hurtful to both men and not serving me at all. There had to be more than one way to "skin the cat" but I was pursuing the most devious and hurtful way of all. It wasn't that I was just telling lies. I began to think of myself as a liar. That was worse. Shame on me.

I determined to not accept any offers to go out for a while. I had to figure all of this out. After all, I had to take care of Dolly and that is all I needed to say.

I still saw Jack at the Saturday Country Fair, when he came to bring and to pick up Helen on Saturdays, and at church on Sundays. We were cordial, but that was it. Harry came by the Fair a few times to help and talk.

Then, one Saturday, my friend Becky came by and said that she wanted to speak with me. I pulled back from the table and said, "Hi, what did you want to talk about?" She was seemingly angry with me. She was straight forward, "What about Harry?" I responded, "What do you mean 'what about Harry'?". She almost shouted. **"I MEAN...you know exactly what I mean.** Why have you stopped going out with him?" What could I say? This plot, aimed to push off Jack, was going to kill me. "Look, Becky, I think that Harry is a very nice guy. But, I'm just seventeen. I am not ready for a major commitment and I feel that if I keep saying yes to his offers to go out, it will get to that point quickly. I don't want to mislead him". For the first time in a while, I had been very truthful, although my motives were much more complex. But, Becky didn't need to be part of my canard. Becky said, "I understand. Harry was worried that he did something wrong, that he angered you." "No...NO!" I responded. "Let me assure you that Harry has been a perfect gentleman. He will make some lucky girl a wonderful husband someday." Becky said, "Ahhhh, but not you". I had to tie this off as gently as I could. "Well...not me, not now. I don't know about later." I repeated myself, "Becky, I'm only seventeen." Becky said, "Well, some girls do get married at seventeen." I knew that. But, I responded, "Well, not me." Becky understood and left me to my business. It was obvious to me from Becky's comments that Sally Berkley was correct about Harry. His interest in me was serious. I didn't see Harry for a while.

Chapter 17

The weeks passed. The sun was rising earlier and setting later. The winter wheat was standing up like soldiers. But, it would not be ready for harvesting until mid-May. At that time, Lucas would be hiring more workers to help. I was hoping in my heart that he would also ask Jack to help in the barn while he was in the fields with the harvest, just like before. Then, I came back to reality...what's the use?

And, with the passing of those weeks, Dolly's condition, her pain, increased to the point that she was using Laudanum more often, sometimes several times each day. And, she was sleeping more and more. Her pain was also eating away at Lucas. You could read it in his face and in the way that he walked, with a slouch. But, even with the stress of seeing his wife's decline, Lucas didn't shy away from being with her. He spent nearly all of his free time with Dolly.

Dolly was stoic. Even given the inevitability of what was approaching, she maintained her spirits. She continued to advise me about my social life, although, honestly, I hadn't had much of a social life over the last many weeks. But, as always, I just enjoyed her company. I thought only of how to make her more comfortable.

This disease, Dolly's cancer, was much stronger than anything that my traditional Cherokee remedies could fend off. It was unstoppable. Regardless, every day, I said my prayers that the God above would remove this terrible cancer from her body. My prayers may have been merely a means of offsetting the helpless feeling that I had when I heard Dolly moan from pain. While I didn't really think that my paltry prayers would do the job, it made me feel just a little better. Frankly, there was nothing else that I could even think of doing.

Dolly hadn't gone out to use the outhouse in weeks. Between the cold and the exertion to get dressed and walk that far, she preferred to use the contraption that Lucas had made for her. His contraption was just the beginning of my exposure to Lucas' talents. He was very handy with the engines in his truck and tractor. He never had to call in a mechanic to help out. He seemed to know just what needed to be done and where to get replacement parts. And, he seemed to enjoy doing it.

By mid-March, Aida came to me at the fairgrounds. She was so excited. She exclaimed, "Ben Held is in town." I settled her down and asked her what she expected. I was trying to support her. She said, "That is a good question. I don't think that I know the answer. I hope that he asks me out to dinner or to a movie. I don't know." Then, Aida perked up. She said, "Oh, my. I didn't tell you…did I? No, no, I couldn't have." I said, "Tell me already." "Ok. I received my letters from those universities that I applied to for the fall. I was accepted by the University of Oklahoma, you knew that already. And, I was also accepted by New York University, NYU. But, I was rejected by Princeton University. Their letter that I got was very complimentary. That was what they said in the first paragraph. But, the second paragraph started with the word, "Unfortunately". I knew right away that there was not to be an acceptance. They said that they don't accept girls at Princeton. My teacher never told me that Princeton doesn't accept girls. Well, the hell with them!" Aida burst out in a gaggle of laughs.

I told Aida that I had been to the Tulsa campus of the University of Oklahoma with Harry. She asked me what I was doing there. Then, the memory of that evening came back to me. "Harry showed me the campus and then asked me to come up to his dormitory room." Aida giggled and said, "Well, you know that would have come to no good." I shook my head, "Well, you can't be angry at him for trying." Then, I told her about Dolly's adage, "You decision…your consequences, especially the part about becoming pregnant." Aida loved it. She told me that she will always remember it. We both shook our heads knowing exactly what each other was thinking.

Then, a light went off in my head. "Did you say, New York University?" Aida said, "Yes". I said, "Well, now, I am impressed! It isn't enough that you were accepted by these wonderful schools. You could have applied to any school in the country, no, in the world. But, you chose New York University as one of your three possibilities. Now, tell me again, where does Ben Held go to medical school?" Aida blushed. I said, "You are much smarter than just your grades. I give you full credit for being so...what should I say...let's say, crafty. Yes, that is a good word." Aida covered her face. She tried to complain saying, "It's a really good school with a great reputation..." Then, shyly, she asked me if it was that obvious. I told her, "It's obvious to everyone with the exception of the dead." Aida said, "You know Mary, you can be very funny if you try?" I just smiled. That was all that was called for. I told Aida that Ben Held would have picked up on her choice of schools immediately. But, I added, "Just maybe, Ben wants it that way".

I realized that I wasn't the only schemer. But, in the case of the brilliant Miss Tanner, her objective was to get together and build a relationship with Ben Held. In my case, my objective was just the opposite. It was to pull asunder my relationship with Jack Clark. And, apparently, I have been very successful in my endeavor...damn it!

"Ok, Aida, I'm impressed. You can go now and smile all of the way back home." As Aida left, Jack's curiosity couldn't be contained. He walked over and asked me what was up with Aida. I think that he was just looking for an excuse to come over and talk with me. I told him about the acceptances to New York University and the University of Oklahoma, but I left out the most important part of the story, the part about Aida going to the same school as Ben Held. I didn't want to open that can of worms. Jack said, "That's great! Please congratulate Aida for me." I think that he was looking for something more from me. But, it wasn't forthcoming. After a very uncomfortable moment, he walked back to his table and began the task of cleaning up. Neither of us looked in the other's direction. But, even from that distance, I could still "feel" Jack. I could always "feel" his presence. I lingered at the table just enough to have Jack leave before me. I didn't want to add to the tension that would have resulted if we both left the Fair at the same time.

When I got back to the farm, I excitedly told Dolly and Helen about Aida's acceptances to wonderful schools. I mentioned that she would be going to school very close to Ben Held. I said, "I think that they will end up together." As I said that, I walked toward the fireplace to prevent these women from seeing my face as I came close to breaking down. Then, Helen said, "Oh, my girl, I am so sad for you." Helen came up to me from behind and held me for a moment. She said, "I have to tell you that Jack and Jim are getting together again." Nothing more was said. A little later, Jack came to pick up Helen as was their routine. I made myself scarce, working in the kitchen to get dinner preparations underway. There was no better time to be hidden from view. Jack came, and left, without a word to me. As I said, there was nothing more!

Going to church was becoming more and more difficult for Dolly. She hadn't gone once over the last three or four weeks. But, that Sunday, Easter Sunday, she told us that she wanted to be there. So, Lucas and I did what we had to do to get her there. I dressed her in her most beautiful dress and shoes. But, when we walked into the church, people were whispering. As we walked down the aisle to our seats, I could hear some of the comments about how poorly she looked. The comments about Dolly's appearance upset me. I had been with Dolly every day for the last ten months. To me, she just looked like Dolly, the same Dolly that I was with and took care of each and every day. But, some of these people hadn't seen Dolly in a while and they were able to notice the change in her appearance which I did not. As we sat down together I took a closer look at Dolly and understood what they were observing. Dolly's face was more drawn. She looked older.

The pastor's sermon had to do with Christ's passion and resurrection. The subjects of Easter's sermons were always about the same biblical passages.

When we got back to the farm, I helped Dolly into some more comfortable clothing. After lunch, Lucas went out to take care of his chores in the barn. I was also about to leave myself when Dolly said, "Mary, don't go off to your chores just yet. I need someone to talk to." I didn't know what was coming. But, in retrospect, it shouldn't have been a great surprise given the subject of the pastor's sermon and the essence of this Easter holiday; Jesus' resurrection after death.

Dolly said, "I just can't talk like this with Lucas. It would be too difficult for him. I know that he loves me. And I know that he is greatly upset when he sees me in pain. He doesn't know what to say to me. He doesn't know how to feel and how to act when he sees me like this. Work is a relief for him. He gets lost in it. It allows him to get away from me. I don't mean that he doesn't want to be with me. It's just that it is too painful for him. He needs the relief. That's why it is so helpful for you to be here."

She stopped and took an uneven breath. I had some concern that she was in pain. But, upon looking at the concern, she told me that she was okay, that she just needed to collect her thoughts. "Mary, I need you to let me talk freely without you telling me that everything will be alright. Do you understand?" I shook my head. I knew that this was another case of when "less is more". She was asking me to allow her to speak about all of her fears about her future. She knew that her demise wasn't that far in the future.

Then, Dolly expressed herself in a way that was almost analytical. It was as if she were talking about someone else. "Before I felt that lump in my breast, I didn't think much about my mortality. I'm young and young people don't think about such things. So, I spent my days working and my nights worrying about living. I never worried about dying, not in my darkest dreams. Now, the hardest part of my day is waking up and thinking that this may be the last day, not just another Sunday or Monday. Then, I try to counter my fears by thinking, after all, none of us gets out of this world alive. Everyone has died or will die. So, really, what I am going through is not different from anyone else. It's not any different than what you will experience. It's just that I know what you don't. I know what I will die of.

Mary, I don't know how much time I have left. No, I don't know exactly. No one knows when it will happen, but for me it isn't very long. I know that I will not enjoy another Christmas. Maybe, I will see the warmth of the summer sun. Maybe not." Her head dropped down and she closed her eyes. Silence filled the room.

Dolly had always been a sounding board for me in my travails with Jack. Now, it was my turn to help her. She went on. "I don't know how difficult it will be going forward. So far, the pain has been mostly tolerable. More recently, it has been more consistent, although still tolerable. I wonder, will the pain be great in the future? Will I suffer without relief? Yes, I know that you and Lucas and Doctor Held will do everything that you can to help me, to relieve my pain, but what I fear is that it will not be enough." She put up her hand when I tried to say that she shouldn't worry. "Mary, I know that you will do your best". She stopped. I waited for her to continue. But, for a minute there was nothing. Then, taking a deep breath, she shifted the discussion. She said, "I don't know what happens to people after they die. Is there really a heaven and a hell? Have I been a good enough person to go to heaven? Mary, I know that I am rambling. I know that there are no answers to my questions. But, I needed to talk."

Once I heard everything she said, it was clear how she was thinking. First, pain and death, and now, questions about afterlife. I held Dolly's hand and tried to think of something smart to say, something philosophical, such as taking a quote from a biblical psalm. But, my mind was blank. I had only seconds to respond before Dolly would think that I was uncomfortable, which, of course, I was. After all, I was seventeen years old. I was not someone with great experience in life, let alone death.

"Dolly, I don't have many answers for you. If I was more experienced in life, maybe, I could say something that would be meaningful. I don't have that experience. But, here is what I do know. The Cherokee people believe that after dying, our souls continue to live on as a spirit. Some of those spirits are unseen, while others live on in the living bodies of people or animals. Christian beliefs vary. You probably know them better than I. In school, we had no choice but to read the Bible and go to church every Sunday. So, some of the things that I was taught stuck in my head. One of the biblical sayings that has stayed with me is from Genesis, '...*for dust you are and to dust you will return.*' That isn't very hopeful. But, beyond that from Genesis, most Christians believe that death is not the end of existence and that we will see the face of God after we die. We believe that there will be a day of judgment where every soul will have to account for their living thoughts and deeds. I guess that this simple view, that there is something beyond death, is the same whether I am a Cherokee or a Christian. I am both. So, I am comforted knowing that I could believe in both traditions without conflict. Both views help the living at the time of their grief. But, Dolly, I don't know…I don't know what is right and what is wrong. I can't say which one or what part of these traditions is real or not." I stopped as silent tears rolled down my cheeks. Dolly squeezed my hand as tight as she could. She realized that she needed to give me comfort. "I don't know about the Cherokee tradition but it sounds similar to the Christian beliefs." Through my tears I let out a stifled laugh. "Yes, I guess that they are both right and true, or…both are just good guesses." Then, I hugged her and we both had a good cry. Through our tears, Dolly said, "I guess that I will find out soon enough." We both looked into each other's eyes and burst out laughing through those tears.

It was quiet for a few minutes as Dolly composed herself. Then, she continued, "Mary, I will need your help even more in the future, whatever future that I have. I will be less and less able to take care of myself. I understand that you are a wonderful young lady and that we are putting this tremendous burden on you while only considering ourselves." "Dolly, it's true that I didn't understand exactly what my life would be like when I first came here. And, truly, I still don't know what the future holds for me as the days of your life wither. But, it was almost as soon as I came here that I felt so close to you. I committed to myself a long time ago that I would do everything that I can to make your journey as comfortable and safe as God gives me the power. I am committed to minimizing your pain and making your days as positive as I can. And, when that last day does arrive, I swear to God, that you will feel no pain. I will do anything and everything to keep that promise." What I said was certainly my wish. But, I had made a promise that I had no right to make. Dolly hugged me without saying another word.

It was a good segue to talk about pain, Dolly's pain. "But, Dolly, I need for you to be honest with me about your pain. I hear you moan in your sleep and I feel that you try to hide your discomfort during the daytime so as not to cause Lucas distress. But, I have to know the truth. Doctor Held told me when he was here last that he had medicines that are even stronger than Laudanum. I need to know when to ask him for them. Only you can guide me. I don't want to use them too soon if their effect would be reduced through overuse. Now, we have the Laudanum. Then, maybe morphine. Each in its own turn. So, please, tell me..." "Mary, I will tell you the truth. My pain is mostly in my breast and in my lower back. Sometimes, when I sleep on my chest, the pain is very sharp. It is interesting to me that when I lie on my back, the pain in my back doesn't change, it is no worse. So, I try my best to sleep on my back. During the day, well, when Lucas is around, I try to hide my pain. You knew the truth without me telling you. I won't hide it from you anymore. I promise." I shook my head up and down. I didn't need to chastise Dolly for hiding something that is so personal. She's had to deal with all of this in her own way. I drew in a big breath. "Dolly, with what you just told me, I need to speak with Doctor Held in order to get his guidance. This Saturday, I will try to sell out early at the Fair and go to Doctor Held's office, review with him how you are feeling and where and when you are experiencing pain. He might have to come to the farm."

So, that is what I did. That next Saturday, I hawked my goods at the Fair as aggressively as I could, pushing more and more to my usual customers. A few of them laughed at me. One of them said to me, "Mary, what's going on? I've never seen you like this before." I told him that it was his imagination. I didn't need to give him my reasons.

Jack came over to talk. He asked how I was. All of the while I gave him bland answers, my insides were killing me. I thanked him for bringing his mother over each week to visit with Dolly. I told him how much it means to her. He shook his head and said that he was glad to do it. Then, he smiled at me and said, "Anyway, it gives me a chance to see you." I smiled. If I said anything at all in response to what he said, I would have lost control and I couldn't do that. So, I changed subjects and asked him how his sales were going. He told me. But, I barely listened. Then, I abruptly told him that I had to finish up and rush back. It wasn't entirely true but I didn't want to get into the discussion about my going over to see Doctor Held. Jack left and went back to his own tables. I sold out, cleaned up and departed the fairgrounds.

I left all of my baskets and other containers on the buckboard and went to Doctor Held's office. I walked in and explained everything to his nurse. She asked if I could wait until he finished up with his patient. I said, "Of course". As I responded, I saw Ben Held out of the corner of my eye. I turned as he was walking over to me. "Ben...I didn't know that you were home." Ben explained how it was spring break at school. Then, I thought about the conversation that I had with Aida. "Ben, did you get to see Aida?" He timidly responded, "Yes" "Did she tell you that she was accepted by New York University, entering in the fall? Isn't that great! That means that you will be able to see her in New York." He shook his head and smiled. "Yes, I would like that." That was enough. I didn't want to torment the poor guy right in his father's office. So, I changed the subject. "How long will you be in Muskogee?" The time flew by as we talked about nothing of consequence. The nurse came out of the inner office. She said, "The doctor will see you now."

I waved as I left Ben and walked into the inner office. Doctor Held asked me how I knew his son, Ben. I told him that Aida introduced me to Ben at the New Year's Eve Barn Dance. Then, I told Doctor Held about my discussion with Dolly. His first reaction was that this was quite a burden for someone so young. I said, "When I arrived at the farm, I thought only about the chores that I would have, do this…do that. I did not take into account the strong feelings that I have developed toward Dolly. I really like her. I guess that we just don't know anything about the future and even less about ourselves." The doctor said, "Ben told me how impressive you are. Now, I understand…" He stopped himself. "Mary, based upon what you told me, I believe that the end of Dolly's life will probably be in only a few months. Our job is to make her as comfortable as we can. Then, I told him that, "She doesn't ask for the Laudanum when Lucas is around. She is willing to suffer more than she is willing to let Lucas know about her pain." Doctor Held just shook his head. "Dolly is very brave, but she needs to be relieved of both the physical pain and the emotional guilt that she suffers. We must help her."

"It's already Saturday afternoon. I will come out to the Taddum Farm soon. I will check my schedule. I will bring some more Laudanum with me. I don't want you to be without it. I will also be bringing morphine. It is much stronger than the Laudanum. It is most effective if it is injected using a hypodermic needle. But, I only want you to give it to Dolly when the Laudanum no longer works. Mary, that is important. We want the morphine to be effective when she needs it most. If we use it too soon, its pain relief may not be as effective later. We don't want that to happen."

The doctor told me to wait as he opened a safe behind his desk. It was there, in the safe, that he kept the morphine. When he took out a box of vials, he said, "Mary, I will keep this with me and give it to you when I come out to see Dolly." Then, he called out, "Ben, what do I have scheduled for Monday or Tuesday of next week?" Ben responded, "Give me a minute." Then, he walked into the inner office and said, "You are fully booked on Monday but you have nothing scheduled Tuesday morning, so far." "OK, block out all of Tuesday morning. I'm going to the Taddum Farm. "Sure dad…I got it."

"When I come out to the farm, I will go over everything that I have told you today again with Dolly and Lucas. Mary, I trust that this powerful drug will only be used to relieve Dolly's pain and only when absolutely necessary. There are a lot of people that abuse morphine, cocaine and heroin. They would do anything to steal this from you. You must guard Dolly's morphine supply. Do you understand?" I said I did although there were so many thoughts floating around in my head. I had thought that this is something that I was prepared for, but was I? I had told Dolly that I would keep her comfortable. But, would I be able to accomplish that sacred goal? Now, there was a greater sense of what it meant to keep her "comfortable" and pain free.

Then, Doctor Held called out to his nurse to come in and to bring a rubber ball that was on her desk. He never called his nurse by her name. I wondered why? His voice broke into my thoughts. "Mary, I want to show you how to give an injection." The doctor then showed me how to crack the glass vial of morphine with a file, to use a hypodermic syringe to suck up the morphine solution, push out any air and then, plunge the syringe into the rubber ball. After I followed his instructions exactly, he said, "Well done! Remember to keep the needle pointed up to expel the air from the syringe."

The doctor escorted me out. He reminded me that I should tell Lucas and Dolly that he would be out to see her on Tuesday morning by ten o'clock. Then, he said goodbye. Ben was there. I said, "Ben...say hello to Aida for me". A little push. A little levity was just what I needed to push fears of the coming horror out of my head. Ben smiled back at me.

I went back to the farm. Helen was still visiting with Dolly so I couldn't tell her about my talk with Doctor Held. That would have to wait. I took the opportunity to do my work in the barn. About a half hour later, I heard Jack's truck pull up. Then, Jack came rushing into the barn. He didn't stop rushing in until he grabbed me around. I was in overalls and an apron. I was dirty. That didn't seem to matter. He hugged me tightly and kissed me on the lips. I kissed him back, but then, I pulled away. "Jack, what is this all about?" I pulled away further. Jack said, "Mary, I like you so much....I love you." I was shaking. "Jack, you are very nice. I like you, I...like you, as well." I was that close to telling him the truth, that I loved him, too. I had to stop myself. "But, I am not in a position to have a relationship with you. There's Dolly." Jack said, "I know about Dolly," "No Jack", I stuttered, "No, Jack, you don't know about Dolly. And you don't know about me and you don't know about my future." Jack pursued, "Mary. I'll know it if you tell me." I decided that it wasn't the time to continue this discussion. I couldn't let Jack into my thoughts, about Dolly's prognosis and all of the rest. "Jack. It's not a good time. I can't continue this conversation." Jack looked devastated. "But, Mary..." He hadn't given up on me. I put my hand over his mouth and said, "Jack, not now." He looked at me in a most beautiful way, smiling just so, and then, his smile faded and he left the barn. How awful I was!

It wasn't more than about five minutes after Jack left the barn that I heard Jack and Helen drive away. Once I heard that they were gone, I walked over to the house. Lucas was still out in the fields so I was able to sit with Dolly. It was the right time. I told her about my visit to Doctor Held. I told her everything. It wasn't easy. I asked Dolly if she wanted to speak with Lucas now or if she wanted to defer until the doctor came to the farm. She said, "I will just tell Lucas that I asked you to arrange for the doctor to come out to give me an examination. I don't want him to spend these few days concerned with what the doctor may find or say. You and I know pretty much what he will say. The only question that remains is when and how. With that, I started shaking and crying. I apologized. "Dolly, I'm sorry. I have to be here for you. I can't be the one that needs emotional support." Dolly squeezed my two hands and said, "Mary, if you didn't have emotions, as you do, if you didn't react, as you do, you wouldn't be Mary…you wouldn't be human. This has to be very difficult for you."

Sunday came. Dolly was able to go to church but it took the Laudanum to get her through all of the dressing, climbing into Lucas' truck and all of the rest. At church, many of the women came over to her to say hello and then, they would say, "How are you feeling dear? Are you alright?" These women, who never came to visit Dolly as she lived, were going to mourn her dying and death. It would give these bored women something to talk about. How phony…how crass. What little humanity they had as they asked her how she was feeling. How can anyone be if they are suffering from cancer that would soon take their life? I stopped myself from thinking that way. I don't know, maybe, I was just feeling low and taking it out on these women in my mind.

I got out of my funk as the pastor was giving his well thought out sermon. I looked around. I saw Jack. He told me that he loved me. Oh, my God! But, Jim Clark still hated the idea of Jack getting together with me. Nothing had changed. Stop yourself! The emotions of everything were taking its toll on my well-being. I had to take hold of myself.

Tuesday came. Doctor Held came out to the farm as promised. He asked Lucas if it were alright for him to examine

Dolly. I helped Dolly into a loose fitting gown. Lucas said that he would wait outside. I stayed. The doctor examined her breasts and her back. When he pressed on her breasts she let out an audible moan. She sat up and he pressed on various places in her back. You could see from her facial expressions that she was uncomfortable. He felt around under her arms and around her neck. Then, he asked Dolly if she was experiencing menstruation, her period. She told him that she hadn't recently. He asked whether she saw blood in her urine or whether she had any blood in her bowel movement. She said "No, I hadn't seen any." He seemed pleased. Then, he asked questions about Dolly's appetite and whether she had recently lost weight. Dolly indicated that she wouldn't know if she had lost any weight. He inquired about whether she had any fever or broke out into sweats at night. Dolly replied that she didn't think that she had any fever but occasionally did break out in sweats. Then, she added, "Since it's still cold, I don't mind." He smiled at her joke, shaking his head at her sense of humor.

      The doctor asked me to call Lucas back in. I did. Doctor Held said, Dolly, the tumor in your right breast has grown. While that is not unexpected, it isn't good. I can't feel anything in your back, although the pain that you have described to Mary is an indication that the cancer is spreading. The lymph nodes beneath your arms are swollen indicating that the disease has spread there, as well. The fact that you haven't seen any blood in your urine or feces is a good sign. The lack of a fever is a good sign, although having these night sweats is not good. As I am saying this to you, I realize that we have spoken about your prognosis before. It isn't good." Dolly was ready for this all. But, based upon the pallor of Lucas' face, it was clear that this was still very upsetting. The doctor asked if Dolly had any questions. She shook her head and asked simply, and bravely, "How long?" Doctor Held knew that this was the question that had to be asked. He hesitated. She asked again, "How long?" His face saddened as he shook his head side to side, "Dolly, only God knows that for certain. I don't. Mary told me that you do not think that you will see another Christmas and I agree with that. But, beyond that, I just can't say. But, I believe that it is months, not years." Now, his head moved slowly up and down giving an indication that he was satisfied with his answer. He gave a small and slight smile. Dolly said, "OK. Thank you doctor. I know that you are doing the best that you can. You have been wonderful." Lucas appeared to be stunned even though everything that the doctor had said had been known with as much certainty the last time that he was here. Some things are known with certainty. Dolly would not be alive for the next Christmas. Some others are just not knowable. No one knew what month or week or day that Dolly would die.

"Now, can we speak openly about your pain level?" And, that is what Doctor Held did for the next five to ten minutes going through the same litany of medicine use that he had with me three days earlier. He emphasized two things as he had with me; do not start using the morphine until the Laudanum no longer worked. Secondly, guard the morphine. He explained to Lucas, as he had to me, how people are becoming increasingly addicted to morphine, cocaine and heroin. It was funny how the four of us plotted about where to store the morphine. We ended up agreeing that it should be kept in the root cellar, far back, among the onions in a brown paper bag.

Doctor Held told Lucas that he had trained me in the way to inject the morphine. But, the doctor asked for someone to come and get him when Dolly required morphine for the first time. He would come out, night or day, and help oversee the first morphine injection and then he would stay for a while to see if there was any adverse reaction.

Then, it was quiet. The doctor got up and bid us goodbye. As he was about to walk out the door, he reiterated that he was available any time of day for us. He left. The doctor was a dear man. It was clear that Dolly would be well taken care of.

The week went by like all of the rest. Saturday's Fair gave me another opportunity to see Jack, if only from a distance. Aida came by to say hello. She wanted to know if Ben said anything about her when I met him at his father's office. I smiled. "He didn't say anything other than he was pleased that you will be going to NYU and he was glad that he would get to see you in New York. His father didn't know before, but he does now." Aida said, "Wow, you really...well, if I ever need help, I'll know where to go." I told her that it was my pleasure to help out. Then, in a rush, I realized that she might have been saying those things cynically. At that, I giggled. Aida laughed. I said, "Aida, what is Doctor Held's nurse's name. He never introduced me to her and he always just called her 'nurse'." "That is the doctor's wife, Grace. She is his nurse. But, he always maintains a professional standard in the office. That's just the way that he is." "Oh!"

Jack looked across at me at the sounds of giggling. He started to walk over. Aida said, "I'm sorry if my coming here put you in a bad position." As he drew close, Jack asked, "What is going on ladies?" We told him that we were talking about how Aida would be going to school back east and how much fun that it would be to live in New York City." Jack congratulated Aida on being accepted by such a great school. Then, Jack asked an interesting question. "Who will be taking your place at the General Store once you leave for college?" Aida said, "You know, I hadn't thought about it. I'll have to discuss it with my father. But, there's no rush, I won't be leaving Muskogee until sometime in August." I also thought that it was an interesting question. Then, as I stood there, I grew embarrassed thinking about it as a possibility for me in the future. Jack said goodbye to Aida and congratulated her again.

I was daydreaming, thinking about the kiss in the barn. But, as Jack walked away, he looked at me with a penetrating stare that cut through me like a knife. Aida left, but not before she gave me that knowing look as she glanced over toward Jack. She didn't know what had happened last week in the barn.

Chapter 18

I have to admit it. I was thinking more and more about my life after Dolly's death. I know that I shouldn't have but how could I not. The pastor and his wife Sally had told me that I could stay with them after Dolly's passing until I got settled. Settled meant getting a job and a place to stay. How can I think about things like that? Oh, how awful.

Weeks passed. It was mid-May and the harvest of the winter wheat was underway. Lucas hired a combine and several other workers to help. With the wheat harvest followed by tilling to prepare for planting the soybean crop, Lucas had no time to breathe. This was one of the two busiest times for him every year.

I was spending most of my days with Dolly as her mobility was more and more limited. Keeping her pain free, fed and clean was my main objective, every day and every night. Her use of the Laudanum was increasing. But, there was no need, not yet, to use morphine.

It was also time to plant the vegetable garden. I explained to Lucas that with taking care of Dolly and my chores in the barn and the Fair, I didn't have enough time to plant the garden. With all that he had to do, I knew that Lucas couldn't help. So, he agreed to hire some additional workers. And, later that day, he told me that he had help for me. He just asked me to direct the planting. I agreed to do that.

The next day, two day laborers came to the farm in an old rickety truck. Dolly filled my head with instructions. I could barely remember them all. While the workers tilled the ground, I took the buckboard and went into town to purchase seed and other supplies at St Mark's Farm & Feed Store. When I got back, I checked on Dolly and then spoke to the workers, explaining how I wanted everything arranged. Of course, that was the way that Dolly wanted everything arranged. They planted snap beans, corn, beets, peppers, tomatoes, potatoes, squash, peas and melons. The patch of asparagus was well established.

The emotional intensity of caring for Dolly was difficult to sustain. So, when I could, I did spend some time in the garden, in the dirt. Similar to working in the barn, gardening gave me a respite, a time to relax.

The harvest of the winter wheat was trucked to the local grain elevator. It was done. When he returned to the farm, Lucas found me in the kitchen and told me that the winter crop was bountiful and the bushel price was modestly higher than last year. And with that, Lucas handed me an envelope. I opened it in front of him. It held a one hundred dollar bill. I had never seen one before. It had a picture of Benjamin Franklin on the front. I had no idea who Benjamin Franklin was or why he was on the front of a hundred dollar bill. "Lucas…I cannot accept this…it is so much." He was insistent, "Mary, this is a gift for all that you do for Dolly and for me. It is the least that I can do…that we can do for you. There is no other way that I can thank you." There was nothing more to be said. I thanked him and put the hundred dollar bill into my overalls. When I had a moment, I added it to all of the rest that I had saved. I thought that before too long, I would need it.

Once the new soybean crop was planted, Lucas had more time to spend with Dolly. At that point, the only thing that the soybeans required was rain and sunshine and good luck. That did not require any help from either of us. And, within a few weeks, you could see the little seedlings, breaking through the ground, seeking sunshine.

The weeks went by. Dolly's disease was taking its toll. More and more, she was missing church because she just didn't have the strength to travel. So, one Saturday, after the Fair, I went to speak to the pastor. "Pastor Berkley, Dolly tries to come to church services every Sunday. She wants to come. But, it is getting more and more difficult for her to travel. I just wanted you to know how much it hurts her when she isn't at church." The pastor shook his head upon hearing what I had told him. He thought for a moment or two, and then called over his wife Sally. He said, "Hey, Sally, we are going to the Taddum Farm after services tomorrow and we are going to have another service right there for Dolly. It won't be the length of a regular service. I know just what I want to do. Sally, we'll get a few of the congregants to come with us. We'll fill up the truck!" Then, the pastor turned to me. "Mary, who is Dolly's best friend?" He didn't wait for an answer. "Isn't it Helen Clark? Does she still come over to visit with Dolly on Saturdays? Mary, please speak to Helen when you get back to the farm but don't tell Dolly. I want it to be a complete surprise. Remember, tomorrow, at about three in the afternoon." I broke out in a big smile. I couldn't believe what he was about to do. I was so excited! "Pastor Berkley, what a wonderful idea. How very thoughtful of you." This was yet another example of Pastor Berkley being everything that you could ever want in a religious leader…or in anyone for that matter.

When I got back to the farm, I pulled Lucas aside and told him about my discussion with Pastor Berkley. Lucas couldn't believe what the pastor planned. He said, "Oh, my…what a wonderful thing for him to do for Dolly." A few minutes later, when I was able, I pulled Helen aside to tell her. With a big smile on her face, she said, "Dolly will be absolutely thrilled." Later in the afternoon, Jack came by to pick up Helen. I said hello but that was it. I didn't want to get caught alone with him.

The next day, Sunday, Dolly told me that she didn't feel well enough to go to church. I shrugged my shoulders and told her, "Well…maybe, next week". I suggested that she get dressed anyway and sit with me on the porch. That was the way for me to have Dolly looking good when the pastor and the other parishioners arrived in the afternoon. I didn't want her to be embarrassed if she were in her bed clothing.

I made some coffee and brought it out for us as we sat on the porch. The warmth of the May morning sunshine was palpable. Usually, we spoke all of the time. But, there was an unusual quiet as we sat there together. Dolly seemed to be lost in thought. Then, out of nowhere at all, she asked me, "Mary, have you thought about what you will do when I'm gone?" I always found my discussions with Dolly to be so fulfilling, so warm, and so comfortable. But, this one…this one? I took a deep breath. I knew that I had to respect her question and give her an honest answer. "Dolly, I don't know. I have to admit that I have thought about it. I know that I cannot stay here at the farm. That wouldn't be right." She said, "Of course". Then, she asked me where I would go and what I would do. She had not gone off topic. "Dolly, I don't know exactly what I will do. I have discussed my situation with the pastor and his wife. They have offered to have me stay with them for a while…until I get settled. They also offered to help me find a job in Muskogee. How wonderful they are! I will have enough money to hold me for a while, several months, without working. I hope that it doesn't come to that." Dolly seemed pleased. She said, "There will be other issues." She chuckled. I responded, "I guess if I knew what those issues will be, then I could better prepare for them. But, Dolly, here is the one thing that I do know. You have been a light in my life, giving me warmth and comfort just like the morning sun on my cheek. I feel that you are the mother to me that I never had, a sister that I would have wanted very much." Nothing more was said. I looked into her eyes and I saw happiness. I laid my head on her shoulder. She stroked my hair. We stayed just like that for quite a while. Then, Dolly said that she was tired and would like to rest. I helped her into bed.

  With Dolly napping, I sought out Lucas and asked him to put up some chairs in the main room of the house for the church service. I didn't know how many people would be attending. So, I guessed and prepared ten cups and a large pot of coffee. Then, I set out to bake two apple pies with the apples from last fall that were still left in the root cellar. When the work was done, I left the pies to cool on a couple of trays in the kitchen.

  At 2:30 in the afternoon, the pastor and his wife showed up at the house. We asked them to be quiet as they walked in. I told them that Dolly was still asleep. The pastor was excited. He said that he had told the congregation in the morning what he was planning. He said, "Everyone thought that it was a wonderful idea. So many people offered to come. Sally and I had to pick out about a dozen people, including us." I said, "Lucas, did you hear that?" Lucas, being the practical guy that he was, said, "We only have six chairs." The pastor responded quickly. "Lucas, don't worry. I told them to bring their own chairs." Lucas and I said together, "Great!"

At just before three o'clock, ten more people came into the house, a few at a time, struggling with their chairs. Lucas shushed them as they entered. Of course, there was Jack and his mother Helen, and…Jim Clark. I was surprised. But, I guess, given the circumstances, he thought it was something that he had to do…or…more than likely, Helen ordered his presence. Helen and Jack came over to me to say hello. Jim hugged the wall just like a shadow. All of the people brought cake or cookies. There was enough food to feed a small army.

I woke Dolly telling her that if she slept all day that she wouldn't sleep at night. I took a basin of water and washed her hands and face. I ran a brush through her hair. Then, I opened the door and helped Dolly into the main room of the house. She was shocked as all of these people quietly gathered around her and smothered her with love. I didn't think that it would impact me quite the way that it did. I felt the good wishes of the congregation. I was all smiles. I realized that I had been less than generous in my previous assessment of some of the folks at church.

As everyone settled down, the pastor said to Dolly, "We would like to hold a Sunday service right here. Would you like that?" I held her around as she shook her head slowly and said, "Pastor, I would love it! Please, please, go ahead." With that, the pastor called the "congregation" to order.

The pastor led an amended service that took only about 30 minutes. Toward the end of the service Pastor Berkley sat next to Dolly and asked her to read together with him. Together, they read from Isaiah 26:19 as the "congregation" listened intently...

> *Your dead will live; their bodies will rise. Awake and sing, you who dwell in the dust! For your dew is like the dew of the morning, and the earth will bring forth her dead.*

And then, the pastor and Dolly concluded the service with John 3:16...

> *For God so loved the world, that he gave his only Son, that whoever believes in him should not perish but have eternal life.*

The service was over. All of the people came over to Dolly, once again, to wish her peace. Dolly thanked each person for coming. She seemed very happy. The two concluding prayers were what she needed. I was so grateful. It was a wonderful day for Dolly, Lucas and me. Pastor Berkley got it just right. He always did!

I helped Dolly into the kitchen, and then, invited the parishioners to join us for a cup of coffee and to share my apple pies and everything else that they had brought. The congregation quickly devoured the sweets just like the proverbial return of the locust. I helped. I think that I had a taste of everything that the folks brought. Jack came over to talk. There was nothing to it but I was uncomfortable with Jim Clark lurking just feet away.

Then, the congregants bid Dolly and Lucas goodbye. They left with their chairs dragging behind. The pastor and his wife lingered. Once everyone was gone, the pastor asked if he could spend some time with Dolly alone. Lucas responded immediately, "Of course". I asked if he could wait just a few minutes so that I could get her into more comfortable clothing. I brought her into the bedroom and helped her change. Once she was settled into bed, I went out of the bedroom and nodded toward the pastor.

While the pastor was talking privately with Dolly, I took care of cleaning up the dishes. Lucas helped. Sally Berkley sat in the kitchen as we cleaned up around her. We reviewed the day. There was a feeling of great satisfaction in the room. Pastor Berkley spent about fifteen minutes alone with Dolly. I never asked, and Dolly never told me what that discussion was about.

As he left, the pastor said to Lucas that he would come every week with a different group of parishioners. He did. And, every time, the pastor asked Dolly to recite the same prayers with him. I believe that he wanted her to be confident that there was a life after death.

That first Sunday was special. It was one of those days that you remember all of your life.

By the end of June, with high school graduation underway, there were loud celebrations all over town. The graduates came to the Saturday Country Fair just to have fun, to blow off steam. I didn't think that they actually came to purchase food for their homes. Not likely. But, I was an expert at sweet-talking people into buying my cheddar and I did. Then, they left, prancing around as the boys do when joyous, slapping each other on the back. The girls hugged as if they actually liked each other. Most of them will not even remember the names of most of these "friends" in ten years. Was I being jealous? Yes! They had two things that I didn't. I didn't graduate from high school. And, college was never even a possibility for someone like me. But, it would have been nice to at least graduate from high school. The other thing that I questioned in my mind were girls that I could call "friends". Maybe, it was just me but I had always struggled with exactly what that word, "friend", meant. Oh, well. I admit it. I was jealous! These graduates could see their futures. I was…well, you know. I didn't even know where to look for mine.

By the time that I got back to the farm that day in June, I noticed a change in Dolly's condition. It was that sudden. She was clearly struggling. I could tell by the look on Helen's face that she had observed the same thing. Right in front of Helen, I asked Dolly if she wanted more Laudanum. Then, Lucas walked in and surprised me by saying that he had just given it to her. I always assumed that when she wanted the Laudanum that I was the only one giving it to her. But, apparently, recently, when I wasn't there, she had Lucas give it to her, asking that he not reveal it to me. She was taking it in ever increasing amounts hiding that fact from both of us. Why didn't I notice that? I could have. I should have been more circumspect. Then, Dolly said, "I have been taking Laudanum about four or five times a day for the last several days. I don't think that it is working very well for me anymore." The alarms in my head went off. I said to Lucas, "I am going to ride into Muskogee. I need to speak to Doctor Held." He said, "OK, but, look, Jack is coming over shortly to pick up Helen. He can drive you into town and back. It will be faster. I'll stay with Dolly."

Jack, understanding the seriousness of our mission, kept our discussion related only to Dolly's condition. Fortunately, when we got to Doctor Held's office, he was still there tidying up before leaving for the day. I related to Doctor Held what Dolly had told us. He wasn't surprised. He had prepared us for what was about to happen, and now, it was happening. As he had said, the day will come when the Laudanum would not be adequate. He said, "Go back to the farm. I will be along shortly."

Jack drove me back. He hadn't heard the details about Dolly's condition before and was thunderstruck. I thanked him for helping out. When we got to the house, I pulled Lucas aside and suggested that Helen go back with Jack…now…Now!

Shortly after Jack and Helen left, Doctor Held arrived. He asked to be left alone with Dolly and we agreed. Lucas and I walked into the kitchen and had some coffee. I prepared enough in the pot to have a cup or two ready for the doctor. After about fifteen minutes, we were asked to come into the bedroom. The doctor had his box of morphine vials there. Without any discussion, he asked me to give Dolly an injection. He cautioned me, again, about removing the air and then, to inject the morphine into muscle. My only concern was that I didn't want to hurt Dolly by giving her a "needle". While I was apprehensive, it really was easy. "There", I said, "How was that?" Dolly said, "Not bad...not bad. Maybe you should consider becoming a nurse. You did well." The doctor shook his head in agreement. Lucas said, "Mary, I don't think that I could have done what you just did."

The doctor told us that he wanted to wait around for a while in case Dolly had a reaction to the morphine. He said, "I'll have that cup of coffee now." I told him, "I can match the coffee with a piece of cake." He smiled and said, "Let's see what you have."

Dolly dozed off. The doctor checked her pulse and respiration looking for a reaction. After another half hour and another check, he said, "Everything is OK. Do not give her another injection unless the Laudanum does not work. Remember to keep these vials secure. But, always keep one or two vials, the syringes and the file nearby at all times. Over time, Dolly will need more and more of it. My hope and expectation is that it will work right through to the end. The doctor reiterated that if the morphine doesn't work, we can use other pain relief medicines. Let's hope that we don't have to use anything else. I will come out every few days to look after her. At first, twice a week, then, depending upon her condition, I will come out more often. But, really, pain relief is all that we can do."

June morphed into July. Despite my commitment not to ask Dolly about her pain, I asked her once or twice each day. And, I reminded Dolly of her commitment to me that she would be honest about her pain so that I could do my best to help in its relief. Overall, while there were a few moments when she winced, she seemed to be fairly comfortable. So far, it was a battle which we were winning. Thanks to God!

Then, one day in mid-July, Dolly said that she wanted to speak with Lucas and me together. We sat in chairs around her bed. As always, Dolly was straightforward. She said, "I want to discuss my funeral and burial". With that, Lucas buried his head in his hands. I just sat there with tears rolling down my cheeks unabated. Death was a part of life that I was not prepared for.

Dolly continued, "Look. This is not going to be easy. But, it is important to me, so please let me speak." She actually yelled at us. "Help me!" We both took in a deep breath. The first thing that Dolly said was that she wanted the funeral service to be right here in the house, not in the church. She said, "I have enjoyed the services that Pastor Berkley and the parishioners have held right here in our house so much. I couldn't think of any other place that I would want to do this." Lucas asked, "Dolly, are you certain that it would be better here than at the church? There are more seats there. We can only have about a dozen or so people here. And, with your casket up front, maybe not that many." Dolly laughed, "Lucas, now you're in the spirit." He laughed through his nervousness. Dolly added, "It doesn't really matter how many people attend the funeral. A funeral is really just a means for the pastor to finalize what is already final, and for friends to attend to the grieving. After all, the dead are dead. And, if you have just a few friends, that is all that you need. The others...they don't really help anyway." Lucas responded, "Dolly, maybe you are right and maybe you are wrong. But, I believe that the dead are not dead. They have eternal life. The Bible says that, *'For God so loved the world, that he gave his only Son, that whoever believes in him should not perish but have eternal life.'* Dolly, the pastor is right. The bodies go to dust but the souls of the departed live on just like the Bible says." Dolly and Lucas seemed satisfied with that compromise. It was interesting to me that Dolly felt so strongly about the value of a "friend" as compared to just acquaintances. She sounded just like I felt. Or, maybe, that was yet another "something" that I learned from her.

Dolly told us that she wanted a joyous service. She didn't want anything depressing or dour. She wanted a celebration of life. Through a giggle that she tried to suppress, she asked if someone could tell a joke or something funny about her. Maybe, two funny things. We laughed. There probably weren't two funny things about Dolly.

Another of Dolly's wishes was to have the four Clark's; Helen, Jim, Jack and Betty, be pallbearers along with Lucas and me. She wanted Lucas and me at the front of the casket. The six of us would carry the casket for burial. I didn't know how that would work given Jim Clark's feelings toward me. I didn't know what Dolly's motive was to have him and me so close. Maybe, she was having her last little bit of fun at his expense. Mine too!

Then, Dolly asked me to give the main eulogy. She implied that the burden on Lucas would be too great. Dolly said that I would be more organized. For sure, that is what I was…organized. At that moment, she looked right at Lucas. "Lucas, you will say what you will say, but only if you want to speak. You don't have to. Is that okay?" Lucas shook his head. He wasn't insulted. I think that he was relieved. I told her that it would be my honor.

Obviously, I had never done anything like that before in my life. I knew the importance of getting it right. So, for the remaining weeks of her life, I thought about what I would say upon her death. I thought about it every day, and almost all of the time.

Finally, Dolly wanted to discuss where she was to be buried. She turned to me and said, "Mary, would you mind if I were buried right next to your grandfather's memorial?" I said to her that it is a wonderful place. Lucas agreed that it was the best place. With that, the plan for Dolly's funeral was in place.

Dolly seemed satisfied that she was able to get us through this discussion. Surprisingly, well, maybe not surprisingly, it was much more difficult for us than it was for her. But, I thought, now, we can be certain that Dolly will be pleased as she looks down upon us from heaven.

The entire discussion about Dolly's funeral and burial was so analytical. It was as if we were talking about someone else or something else. Maybe…there is no other way to do it. If we had been slaves to our emotions, we certainly couldn't have gotten through this conversation. But, Dolly was so under control, so secure and so stable. Being by her bedside was always a learning experience for me.

As Dolly experienced more and more discomfort, I gave her more morphine. The doctor came out to visit with her every other day. It was a relief to have him there. There was nothing that he could do. But, his presence gave Lucas and me confidence that we were doing the very best that we could.

Helen came over frequently with Jack. She spent some time each visit alone with Dolly. All Helen did when she walked out was cry. She was about to lose her best friend. Jack held his mother around on the porch until she had spent her last tear. Then, they left. I took the opportunity of having Helen there with Dolly to tend to my chores in the barn. It also gave me a way of steering clear of Jack.

Lucas sat next to Dolly's bed most of the day. I tried to leave him alone with her as much as possible so he could share her last days without me being there. I watched over her all night, falling asleep only occasionally. Towards the end, her speaking became less and less coherent. I used wet cloths to cool her body in the heat of the day. There was little else that I could do.

As I administered more and more morphine, Dolly slept more and more. Most days, toward the end, she slept more than twenty hours. Dolly spoke with us when she was awake. And, as the days slipped by, she ate and drank less. It was all as the doctor told us it would be.

Dolly's last days were not as bad as I had feared they would be. There was no horror. She died on a Wednesday in August of 1930. Doctor Held was there with us. He declared Dolly dead at 10:15 in the morning. It was sunny and warm, a good day. I had fulfilled my sacred oath to keep her pain free and comfortable. Dolly would not suffer. I was at rest in my own way.

Over the preceding weeks, Lucas was on a mission, actually two missions. He purchased lumber for a casket. He hand built it himself. He also dug a grave right next to grandfather's memorial. He was prepared. I believe that he did this all by himself as there was no other choice for him. It was a measure of his love for Dolly. It was a measure of his worth. For farmers, good work, meaningful work, was a measure of a man's value in this world. Everyone knew what Lucas had done for Dolly in life. He, now, had performed this final tribute to Dolly in death. Lucas had fulfilled his need to honor Dolly in his own way.

Lucas told the pastor that according to Dolly's wishes he wanted to invite only those people from the congregation that had attended the services that he conducted in the Taddum home. I asked him if Doctor Held could attend. He said, "Oh, my, I should have included him. Is there anyone else that you would like to attend?" I asked if Aida Tanner and Becky Smith could be there for me. Lucas said that would be fine. The pastor agreed. All told, there were about 35 people who met the criteria. Many of the people would have to be outside on the porch. With the door open, they would be able to hear what was being said.

Helen Clark was wonderful. She stayed with me at the Taddum house so that we could prepare Dolly for burial, dressing her in her finest dress. For those difficult days, Helen slept there in Dolly's bed. I slept in the same bed that I had slept in since the preceding Christmas.

The weather was hot and humid. And, two days after Dolly passed away, we held the funeral at the Taddum Farmhouse as per her wishes.

All of the parishioners from the church services at the farmhouse were there. Pastor Berkley started the funeral service reciting the usual prayers. Then, it was my turn. I stood next to Dolly's coffin. I decided to begin with Dolly's history which was likely largely unknown to her friends and co-congregants.

"Dolly was born and brought up in Asheville, North Carolina. Her early life was very different from the farming life that she loved so much here in Muskogee. Her father died suddenly, when she was a teenager, leaving her mother and Dolly essentially destitute. She was a high school graduate and had a job, but her mother didn't work and their life was hanging on by a thread. Her mother was taken in by her aunt but there was no room for Dolly.

"She met Lucas via letters which, as you know, is quite common. They formed a union, a bond as a couple, just like many of you. She grew to be Lucas' life partner and love.

"Now, I want to tell you about the Dolly that I knew. When I came here more than a year ago, I had no idea what to expect. I didn't know how I would be treated. I knew that there would be hard work. I was well educated. But, I was not learned. I was not knowledgeable. I had few skills.

"But, from the first day that I came here, Dolly and Lucas welcomed me as part of the family. Dolly taught me everything that I needed to know to be a part of this farm. Dolly and I became intimate in ways that were required for me to take care of her. She made something that could have been so difficult, so easy.

She was patient with me, never being critical when I made mistakes. She didn't lecture me. But, she made it clear that as I move through life that decisions have consequences. That is not guidance that many young people can accept. She would always say to me, 'your choice...your consequences'. It says everything that a young girl needs to know in order to survive growing up.

"Dolly told me that some of the boys in her high school, back in Asheville, could be overheard saying that she was 'plain', 'plain as homemade pie'. But, I want for

you to know that she was anything but 'plain'. She was beautiful both inside and out.

Dolly became the mother to me that I never had, even though she wasn't that much older. She was the sister that I could have only hoped for. She was my friend. She was there for me when I needed to share or confide in someone. She did this without judgment. She was wonderful in every way that I can think of. 'Plain'...not in any way. She was a wonderful person. I will miss her terribly.

Rest in peace, dear friend."

I walked back to my chair and sat down. The pastor thanked me for my comments. Aida and Becky came over to me, hugged me and held my hands tightly. Lucas got up to speak. I hadn't thought that he would speak as it was not his nature to do such things.

"As Mary said, Dolly first came here because she liked what she read in my letters. I liked what I read in her letters. Doesn't sound like much, but you can tell a lot about a person's manners and personality from their letters. And after a while, with the help of Pastor Berkley and his wife, Sally, we met and found ourselves in a relationship that developed over time. Many people marry after falling in love. Dolly and I married and then we fell in love. Many people find themselves falling out of love after they marry. We found ourselves falling more and more deeply in love with time."

Lucas hesitated as if he had more to say. But, then, he sat down holding his hand in front of his face as if shedding a tear was something to be embarrassed about. The pastor asked if anyone else would like to say something. He told the congregation that Dolly wanted someone to tell a joke about her at the funeral services. Helen started to get up. But, then, she sat down too overwhelmed by emotion. Standing in front of their seats, a few people commented about how they liked Dolly. But, no one could come up with a joke.

Then, there were no more comments. So, after a few moments of silence, with his hands folded in front of him, the pastor said to Lucas, "Shall we go up the hill?" And with that, the six of us escorted Dolly up the hill, above the root cellar and under the beautiful oak tree, near to my grandfather's memorial. All of the other parishioners followed us up the hill.

With Dolly's coffin resting just above her grave, Pastor Berkley completed the ceremony by repeating the same two prayers that he read during the church services at the Taddum home; Isaiah 26:19 followed by John 3:16. All of the parishioners joined in with him. He finished with …

"We pray that our friend Dolly rests in peace and may her memory be a blessing to Lucas and to all of us."

Lucas and several of the other men, including Jim and Jack Clark, lowered Dolly's coffin into the ground. The Pastor handed the shovel to Lucas. He gently placed the first shovel full of dirt on top of Dolly's coffin. He offered the shovel to me. I did the same and then, passed the shovel to Helen. All of the parishioners helped fill in the grave, one shovel full at a time.

We never asked him, but Jack had prepared a head stone as he had for my grandfather. This one was a little bigger than grandfather's. I thought that was appropriate. After the grave was filled in, Jack and Lucas set the new head stone. It said simply,

Dolly Taddum
1906-1930

And, then, it was over. I left the hill that day feeling sad. But, Dolly had given me permission to not feel guilty. And, so it was.

Helen had been wonderful, being there for Lucas and for me. She had helped prepare Dolly for burial and also helped with the cleaning associated with the funeral services. All of that work that had to be done would have been difficult or impossible for Lucas. And, without Helen, I couldn't have stayed at the farmhouse alone to do it myself. No one in our community would have thought it appropriate. I didn't think that it would have been appropriate. So, I was especially grateful to Helen.

Lucas said that he would like to contribute all of Dolly's clothing to the church. He said, "She didn't have much. But, there are plenty of people in the community who have little or nothing. For them, her clothing would be a treasure." But, Lucas never got to contribute Dolly's clothing to the church. He found that he just couldn't do it. It was too painful.

After we completed all of the work that had to be done, Lucas and Helen helped me pack up my few belongings. I still had the school uniforms that I had kept from Sequoyah High School and all of the clothing that Lucas had purchased for me. So, I had enough clothing to keep me for quite a while. I took out the brooch that Jack had given to me as a Christmas present and put it on. I just couldn't put it into the bag along with my clothing.

But, now, it was time to go, time to leave the Taddum Farm. It was time to say goodbye to Lucas. He faced me, saying how much he appreciated what I had done. Then, he gave me a big hug. I didn't expect it but I was OK with it. I had grown fond of Lucas. Then, he released me and took a small bag out of his front pocket. He said, "Dolly told me that I should give this to you. It's her jewelry." He opened the bag and spilled the contents into my hands. There were five pieces. There were two earrings, a necklace and two bracelets. Lucas had given Dolly the necklace just last Christmas. Lucas said, "I think that the bracelets are called 'bangle bracelets'. Dolly bought them the last time that we were in Tulsa at a jewelry store there. None of the jewelry is expensive but it is pretty. You know that I would have bought her the real thing but she said that she was just a plain woman and anything very expensive would look phony on her. She would always say that in spite of me telling her that she was a special person. She never really believed me. Then, Lucas started to cry. I held him around. Helen joined in a circle to help him through the moment. He collected himself and went on. Lucas picked the necklace up out of my hand and said, "Dolly said that this is 'art deco'. I don't know what that means exactly. I guess that it is just a style. I like to think of it as just 'costume jewelry'…it finishes a costume. Anyway, I hope that it will remind you of Dolly." I thanked him and placed all of the jewelry back into the bag. Affirming what he had just said, I told Lucas that the jewelry would always remind me of a very special person in my life. I said, "Goodbye Lucas." He kissed me on the cheek and walked away.

Jack pulled up in front of the house to collect Helen and me. It was time to go. Helen asked Jack to take me to the pastor's house in Muskogee.

As the Taddum Farm faded from view, my eyes were wet with tears. I thought about Dolly and the loss of innocence that I had experienced there in that farm house. Helen held me around my shoulder and gently stroked my hair. There was silence. Jack didn't even look in my direction. I don't think that he saw that I was wearing the brooch that he had given to me for Christmas.

As I left the truck, Helen got out and gave me a big hug and kiss. She whispered in my ear, "I know how much you have done for my family. I can only say thank you." She got back into the truck. From Jack, there was just a simple goodbye. That hurt me. I guess that everything had already been said.

As Jack dropped me off, I wondered whether I would see him or her again.

I had been at the Taddum Farm for fifteen months or so. When I arrived, I was a sixteen year old school girl. When I left, I was a seventeen year old. But, now, I was no longer that girl. I was now a woman. Everything before going to the Taddums and taking care of Dolly, was already fading from my memory despite desperately wanting to hold onto everything, the traditions and the stories, that my grandparents had told me. But, for now, the only thing that I thought of were the conversations with Dolly and the time that I spent with Jack.

Chapter 19

I knocked on the door of the pastor's house. Sally came to the door and welcomed me warmly. She showed me to my room and helped with my small bag. After a few minutes of chit chat, I told her that I wanted to take a walk around town. I said, "I need to get busy with my new future."

I spent a while walking around, talking with store owners, trying to gauge whether I would like working there. Then, I went to visit Aida Tanner. I had spoken with Aida prior to Dolly's passing. She knew that I would be looking for a job. She told me, "Look, I will be leaving for New York in only a few days' time. Let's go talk with my father." And so, we went together to Tanner's General Store. Isaac was at the front helping a customer. Once he had completed the sale, Aida said, "Dad, do you remember that I told you that Mary would be looking for a job. I think that it would be just perfect for her to take my place here. She is already a great saleswoman. And, she has a great relationship with the Cherokee women. That alone will certainly bring new business to the store." Isaac smiled, "Mary, Aida speaks so highly of you and your work ethic. Frankly, you have made quite an impression on her." Then, with a twinkle in his eyes, looking at his daughter, he said, "And, since Aida is totally immersed in packing and getting ready to move to New York City, I don't see much of her around the store any more. I think that she is anxious to get out of her responsibilities here." Isaac looked at Aida with a sort of smirk on his face. "And, I…I can certainly use the help. So, when do you think that you can start? How many days a week do you want to work?" I responded that I could work six days a week. Isaac said that he would pay me sixteen-fifty for five days and if he needed me for a sixth day, he would pay me four dollars more. Then, he added, "And, if you bring in a lot of new business, I will give you a bonus, but you will have to trust me about that." I reached my hand out and said quite formally, "Thank you, Mr. Tanner. I am grateful for the opportunity. What time should I come to the store on Monday?" He was probably taken aback by my formality, calling him by his last name after calling him Isaac all of this time and offering my hand to seal the deal with a handshake. But, after a brief hesitation, he reached out to shake my hand and let out a huge roaring laugh. Aida said, "See dad, I told you that she was one of a kind." Isaac told me to be at the store at eight o'clock on Monday. Then, he said to Aida, "You, my daughter, have to be here on Monday, at eight o'clock, as well. I want you to train Mary." As Aida and I walked away from Isaac, I thanked her. But, Aida was adamant. She said, "It is my father that will be lucky to have you work at the store. Dad couldn't have a better person. I know that you will do just fine." I said, "Thank you for your confidence in me. I hope that I don't disappoint you or your father." And with that my career in retail began. And, once a month, Isaac did give me that bonus that he mentioned. It was a crisp, new, five dollar bill. Sometimes, he gave me a new ten dollar bill.

    I went back to see Sally and told her what had happened since I left her. She was very pleased. She said, "Let's have you work at Isaac's store for a couple of weeks, save up your salary, and then we will find a place for you to live. I'm certain that you don't want to live with us old people for too long. If you do, you may become old yourself...before your time". She laughed. Changing subjects completely, Sally said, "Well, tomorrow is Sunday and we need to prepare the church for tomorrow...today. Are you ready to help?" I responded by asking Sally if I could just go off to the Fair first, just for a little while, and then come back to the church to help clean up. Her face brightened up in a knowing smile. I said, "No, I am not going there to be with Jack, although I will say hello to him. I just want to speak to some of the Cherokee women who have been good customers of mine at the Fair. I want to let them know that I will be working at Tanner's General Store. You see, I am already trying to add to Mr. Tanner's business." Sally said, "OK. Enjoy your time at the Fair. I'll get started on the cleaning. Join me when you can."

    I walked over to the Saturday Fair. I knew that Lucas would be there. People are born and people die but nothing changes at the farm. Farmers don't take time off even for grieving. So, I went to the table that I had worked at for more than a year. I told Lucas about my new job. He was surprised that I got a job so quickly. I told him that I had discussed the possibility with Aida Tanner a while ago, knowing that she would be leaving for New York City. He said that he was happy for me. I talked with him for a while and snacked on some of "my cheddar". I said to Lucas, "You know…this is pretty good cheese." He smiled. Throughout my life, some places and activities elicited my memories of listening to Dolly's sage advice. Eating cheddar always brought my life on the Taddum Farm to my mind. And, of course, that brought "my Dolly" to mind.

As the Cherokee women came by, I told them of Dolly's passing. They offered their condolences to Lucas and to me. For most of them, it was too complicated of a traditional sentiment for them to express in English, so I translated for Lucas. I also told them that I was no longer going to be at the Fair but that they should continue to purchase their groceries from Lucas. Then, I told them about my new job. I asked them to come by to see the types of goods that Mr. Tanner had in his store. Many of them had already been shopping there. But, there were some, especially those that didn't speak English very well, that were enthusiastic about me working at the store.

All of the while that I was speaking with Lucas and these women, I had felt Jack's presence. It was like the intense feeling that you have when the sun is very strong on your face. The time had come. I walked over to Jack and said hello. I told him how much Lucas and I appreciated the headstone that he had carved for Dolly. I followed by telling him about my new job at Isaac's. He was happy for me. He said that he goes to the store quite often and would be happy to see me there. That was it. It still hurt every time that I was so close to him, yet so far away. He respected my position. My heart was still torn. I almost wish that he would grab me up in his arms and carry me away. But, that wasn't to be. That would always be just a dream. I had done too good of a job of dissuading him.

I walked away from the Fair and went to the church to help Sally. As we were cleaning, Sally went on, and on, saying that no one wants to sit in a pew if the floor under their feet was dirty. No one wants to sing in a place where they could see dust on the windows. Before she mentioned it, I wouldn't have given those things a thought. But, once she said it, I knew that she was right. We worked together, making the place spotlessly clean. When she was satisfied that everything was ready for church services the next day, we went back to her home with the brooms and mops dangling over our shoulders.

The next day was Sunday. For the first time, I really didn't know where to sit in church. So, I sat with Sally. After the services, I went over to talk with Helen Clark. She was pleased about my new job and said, "I'll buy something from you even if I don't need it." We both laughed heartily. She was so nice.

Monday came. Aida trained me. But, there really wasn't much to it. I quickly learned what I needed to know about the store's products and, more importantly, building relationships with customers. Oh, yes, it's also about being able to stand on your feet all day. But, I found that working at Tanner's General Store was easy, much easier, than all of the work that I did at the Taddum Farm. This new experience gave me a comparison, allowing me to understand just how physically demanding farm life is.

Many of the men that came into the store would never feel comfortable being served by a woman of any background, just as the white or Cherokee women would rather be served by a woman than a man. That was just the way that it was. Of course, I had a head start with the Cherokee women. And, just as they said at the Saturday Fair, they came to buy from me because it gave them an opportunity to speak in their language. Of course, they also did it because of what I was, part Cherokee.

When I thought about it, I came to understand that my background, instead of being the forever impediment that my grandparents had thought it would become, could be used to my advantage. Well, maybe not the bastard part, but being able to speak both languages and being half Cherokee certainly gave me a unique opportunity that I took full advantage of during the time that I spent working for Isaac. I finally came to understand that I was much more than the sum of my parts and pieces that I had thought would plague me my entire life. Both Dolly and Helen had told me that. More and more, I had come to believe it and to believe in myself.

I had grown comfortable living with the Pastor Berkley and Sally, going to work and then eating dinner with them. It had been a little more than two weeks since I started working at the General Store when Sally came to me and said that with my success at the General Store, it was time to "spread my wings". That is what she said. I truly believe that she meant more than one thing with the expression that she had used. The obvious meaning was for me to find a place to live. It would be the first time in my life that I would be living alone. But, I also believed that she meant to spread my wings, socially, to be with teenagers instead of older people all of the time. Well, first things first.

Unbeknownst to me, Sally had already begun the process of looking for a place for me to live. She sat me down to explain the choices that were available. "Mary, we can try to find someone who is willing to let out a room in their house. The problem with this type of living arrangement is that you might not like the family that you boarded with. And, once you are there, you might be reluctant to move, you know, and then you would be unhappy. I don't recommend this for you or for anyone else for that matter. You could really get stuck.

"Another choice is to rent a room at a boarding house. There, you can just rent a room. That would be basic. Or, you could rent a room that has a bath. Finally, you can choose whether you want to eat at the boarding house or to eat out. Some places offer just breakfast. That would be called 'half-board'. Other places offer breakfast and dinner or even all three meals. If you take all three meals at the house, that is called 'full-board'. The more that you add to the room, the more expensive it is. Socially, of course, you would not be allowed to have any of your friends in your room. So, what do you think?" I responded, "I really hadn't thought about it. But, I would like a bath included or at least a bath in the hall nearby like I had at school. Meals? Well, breakfast included sounds right since I always thought that it was good to start off the day with something. I don't eat much lunch. If I did get hungry, I would just walk down the street from the store to a local luncheonette and get something lite. Sally, I think that I would like to eat dinner out. It would give me an opportunity to meet with people. Maybe, I could go to a movie at night. Maybe, some guy would ask me out to eat." My face exploded with a big smile. Sally understood the humor in what I had said. Sally said that my thinking made sense. She told me that she knew of a few places that we should look at. Over the next few hours we did visit a few of the boarding houses that Sally had picked out for me. And, after some discussion, I asked the question, "How much?" Mrs. Ambrose told me that the room with a bath on the hallway was twenty dollars a month. A simple breakfast, seven days a week, was another ten dollars. That's what I took. All told, thirty dollars per month. That would leave me with over thirty dollars a month to spend on suppers, for clothing and to save for a future that I couldn't even envision.

So, the next day, after work, Sally and the pastor helped me pack up my things and drove me to the Ambrose Boarding House where I moved into a room on the second floor with a bath down the hall. There was a sink in the room with running water and electricity for the solitary light in the middle of the room. It was a lot more than I had at the Taddum Farm where I shared a room with Dolly, using candles for lighting, or, at school where I had to share a dormitory room with many other girls. It was luxury; a new stage of my life.

Over the next weeks, the leaves on the trees were starting to turn to a beautiful yellow-orange. I lived in my little room with breakfast served downstairs. The other residents were all women, much older women. They were very friendly, always looking for someone to talk with.

I went out for dinner every night. That was a new experience for me, for sure. I didn't eat lavishly. I was on a budget. But, I found that it was also very isolating. I was amazed how boring the time can be from when you arrive at the restaurant until you order dinner and then, after you order until your dinner arrives. Sometimes, it is only minutes and then, at other times, if they are really busy serving other customers, it could be more than twenty minutes. Regardless, each of those minutes seems much longer when you are alone. At times, I thought that I should have taken dinners at the boarding house. I guess that I could have changed if I got too lonely eating by myself. But, after a while, I found a way to satisfy myself. Most of the restaurants where I ate had newspapers for use while dining. So, I was able to fill the time that I spent at dinner reading. It was a new education and a very good use of my time. Sometimes, the newspapers weren't enough, so I borrowed books from the library and brought them with me to dinner. I seemed to gravitate to books that described tragic love stories. Unfortunately, it seemed all too familiar. I think that someone could have written a book about Jack and me.

Occasionally, someone would come over and ask to join me for dinner. They were as lonely as I. One would believe that having company for dinner was better. Frankly, the times that I ate with these strangers, I was uncomfortable. These people just had to fill the quiet with inane comments about things that they had no interest in themselves. Sometimes, I wanted to say, "Stop, there is no need to just keep talking. Rest for a while!" But, I didn't. I just sat there and listened, trying to seem interested. So, dining with strangers was not an improvement over sitting by myself.

One day, Alice Hollings and Becky Smith came by the General Store. We chatted a while and then, Alice asked if they could go out with me for dinner. So, we agreed to go out the next Tuesday and that is what we did. At dinner, we caught up with each other. Alice was working at the nearby restaurant as a waitress. Becky had a job as a telephone operator. While I knew about telephones, I had never used one. And, I didn't have any understanding of what a telephone operator did. She had to explain it to me. Then, out of nowhere, Becky asked me if I would be interested in seeing Harry Miller again. It was quite a surprise. But, at that moment, I knew why these girls wanted to go out to dinner with me. They were Harry's envoys. Obviously, he didn't want to ask me directly for fear of being rejected. This was easier for him.

I had stopped seeing Harry because I didn't want to get serious with him. I didn't want him to have the wrong impression. I didn't want to hurt him. Also, I didn't believe that Harry was the guy for me. But, over time, I grew to accept just how hopeless any relationship with Jack would be. So, I decided to give Harry another chance to impress me. I accepted the offer. I told Becky to get the message back to Harry that I would be interested in going out with him.

So, over the next weeks, I began to see Harry. At dinner, he told me that he had graduated from the University of Oklahoma the preceding June with a degree in civil engineering. He said, "But, there isn't that much work. I couldn't get a job as a civil engineer. So, I took a position as a surveyor." When he told me about his difficulty in getting a job as an engineer, we started to discuss the Depression which had begun with the stock market crash the preceding October. Yes, I had read about it in the newspapers, but I still didn't understand how it could impact us here in Muskogee, so far from New York City or Chicago. That is when Harry explained the implications of the business reversals on everyone in the country. "Stocks had lost almost half of their value and that is how some of the people lost their money. But, for people that didn't even own stocks, they get scared and stop buying things because they worry about losing their job and not having any money. Then, after a while, the factories no longer need to make those things because fewer people are buying them. And, then, some of the people that work at the factories don't have jobs and their money runs out so they can't buy anything and so on. People lose confidence…they panic."

The way that Harry had described it to me was like a line of dominos placed on their edge near to one another. Once one falls, it takes down all of the others. I asked Harry, "Does it also affect the farms?" Harry shook his head and told me, "Sooner or later, some people can't even afford to buy food to eat. Then, they have to get on a bread line. Some starve." That statement frightened the heck out of me. I told Harry that he was being overly dramatic, pessimistic. He responded, "I hope that you're right!" He told me that I was lucky that I still had my job. He said, "Haven't you noticed that fewer people were coming into the General Store?" I told him, "No, I hadn't noticed it so far." He continued, "Well, don't be surprised if business slows down and possibly grinds to a halt." Now, I was really frightened. I said again, "You're being a pessimist". Again, he said, "Maybe, but I don't think so." My immediate reaction was that Harry's inability to get a job as an engineer had really affected his thinking.

I had not thought about the stock market crash affecting my life or anyone else's here in Muskogee. But, with what he said so far, I asked Harry, "Will Isaac have to fire me?" Harry said, "I certainly hope not, but he may have to cut down on your hours or your salary if things don't go too well."

I felt badly for Harry for not getting a job as a civil engineer. Now, he was working as a surveyor, making a fraction of what he would have made as an engineer. So, when the check came for dinner, I offered to pay for half. He wouldn't hear of it. I didn't make a big deal of it because I didn't want him to feel badly. But, I honestly felt a little guilty after all of the talk of the Depression and Harry not getting the good job that he went to college for. I thanked him for dinner.

After dinner, we took a walk through the streets. Frankly, everything seemed normal. I don't know what I was expecting. But, from what I saw in the newspapers, both headlines and pictures, and from what Harry told me at dinner, I guess that I was expecting to see unemployed men, just appearing out of nowhere, lining up for a job or for a meal like they were in the big cities. I had let my imagination run wild. That's when I said to Harry, "How come we don't have lines of the unemployed here? How come there are no bread lines?" He said that as a farming community, food was the very last thing to be affected. But, it might happen later. Farms may fail." I thought, again, that he was being overly pessimistic.

That dinner's discussion with Harry was upsetting. But, it was also good for me to hear. It wasn't the first time in my life that I thought in terms of my own security. It was a constant refrain only interrupted occasionally by good times. But, now, I started to think about what would happen to me if I did lose my job at Isaac's. It boiled down to a simple view of the world, my world, that is. If I lost my job, I would have to find a new job. And, if things got really bad, there may not be another job. Then, I would have to rely upon my savings. And, when my savings ran out, I would become homeless and be one of those people that I had read about standing on a bread line. I said to myself, "Dominos anyone?" It was quite a sobering thought.

Harry walked me to my place at Ambrose and said good night. He didn't try to kiss me but he did ask if he could see me again. I said, "Yes". He said that he would get in touch with me to set a date and left.

I went up to my room and counted my hidden money. I had about three hundred and eighty-nine dollars and that included the twenty-nine dollars that grandfather had given to me. I calculated how much that I needed to live on if I didn't have a job; how long would my savings last. All told, I figured that I needed about fifty-five dollars or more a month. And that included very inexpensive dinners. I calculated that my money would only last about seven months. The only way to improve upon that is to find another girl or two to share the room with me. That would save at least ten dollars a month. That would add, maybe, two months. But, in the end, unless I increased my savings, I might be on the street in less than a year. Even though I knew that I was being a pessimist, frightened by what Harry had told me, those thoughts were now always in the back of my mind. Becky or Alice had families to move in with if they were fired and out of work. I didn't.

When I was in the Indian School, everything was determined for me. Even the beatings at the school were controlled by someone else. Once I got the job at the Taddum Farm, my activities were proscribed by Dolly's needs, compounded by the cows' needs to be milked or to cook the meals. But, now, I was by myself, on my own and, now, I felt even less secure than I had ever felt in my life. I needed to have more security. And that meant more money in my pocket. I had to do something.

An idea came into my head. I wasn't working on Saturdays. So, I was going to ask Lucas if I could help out at the Fair. The next Sunday at church, I walked over to him to say hello. Then, I asked him if I could speak with him privately. He said, "Mary, is everything OK?" "Of course", I said. Then, I proceeded to ask him, "Lucas, do you need help selling your goods at the Fair? I could certainly help with the Cherokee women." He thought for a moment and said, "Mary, I think that the Cherokee women would feel more comfortable with you being there. In fact, I believe that would be true for the white woman, as well. You were so well liked here. Everyone keeps asking about you." He chuckled. He asked me how much I would want. I told him that I would be happy with two dollars for the four hours. "So, okay, you have the job. But, here is what I want. I need you at the Fair by eight o'clock. That is when I will come to the Fair with all of the goods. I will leave the truck near the stand and you will unload it, sell all of the goods and then, re-load anything that is left. I will use the time to shop in town for all of the things that I need for the week. We will give it a try. And, I will pay you two-fifty. Can you start next week?" I said, "Lucas, I'll see you bright and early next Saturday." I walked away. It wasn't a lot, but it made me feel better that I was trying to do something to build a little larger nest egg. The extra two-fifty meant that I would be able to save another ten to twelve-fifty a month. I knew that I had to help myself and this was better than doing nothing. Anyway, I had nothing to do on Saturdays. This would keep me busy.

I told Isaac about taking the job with Lucas and that I would not be available to work in the General Store on Saturdays. He thought that it was good for me to do. He told me that with reduced business recently, he didn't expect that he would need me on Saturdays anyway. I was uncomfortable about how quickly he agreed. Then, I realized that I hadn't seen a bonus from Isaac in a few weeks. I felt that his comment about not needing me on Saturdays, and not getting a bonus in a while, all foreshadowed trouble for the future.

I quickly changed the subject. I asked him, "How is Aida doing in New York?" He filled me in with her course work, but that was not what I was really interested in. I said, "Does she see much of Ben Held?" I was being a romantic, if not for me and Jack, then, at least for Aida and Ben. Isaac could only tell me that they saw each other occasionally. I didn't want to ask him if they were serious. I was just having some fun. I said goodbye to Isaac.

The next Saturday, I worked at the Fair. It was good to see my old customers. I came to understand that the goods that

I sold weren't important. It wasn't even so much about making the extra money, although that was important. What gave me the greatest joy was chatting with the people, enjoying their company, if only for a few minutes at a time.

While Lucas had told me that he would do his shopping while I attended to his tables, he did that for only a small portion of the time that he was away from the Fair. The rest of the time, he spent with some of the other small farmers from the area, gossiping in front of St. Mark's Farm and Feed Store. They were as bad as young girls. Knowing that he didn't really need the time to shop, I felt as if he gave me the job only to help me out.

I walked over to Jack and asked him how he was doing. We gossiped and then, he asked me directly, "Are you seeing anyone". I told him that I had seen Harry Miller several times and was planning on seeing him again. I realized that what I was saying to Jack had to be very hurtful, but I had to be honest. I turned the discussion around by asking if he was seeing anyone. He told me that he had dated several women but nothing that was terribly serious. As we were talking, three women came over to Jack's table and asked him some questions about something or other. As I was waiting for the women to finish and leave, I thought to myself..."I think I still dream about Jack because he is unobtainable. Maybe, it would be better if I continued to date him and found out that he is nowhere near as perfect for me as I thought."...the women were still talking to him. I grew impatient. I wanted to say to them, "Why can't you just be quiet? Why must you interrupt this time that I am having with Jack...Quiet!" But, I shouldn't be so selfish. The world isn't just about me.

Then, Jack's voice penetrated the women's chatter. He said, "Mary, would you go out to dinner with me?" I should have realized beforehand that being together with Jack could lead to something like that. The shadow of Jack's father, Jim, came over me and darkened my mood. How was I to answer? After all, there was no longer an excuse to be made about my not being able to go out because I was caring for Dolly. I didn't answer. But, I slowly shook my head gently, subtly, left and right, and closed my eyes. I thought that he had already gotten the message but I was wrong. Jack started to say something and then thought better of it. Then, he seemed to recharge his thinking and said with some insistence, "Mary, I don't know what I did to turn you against me so. I wish that you would tell me. If there is anything that I could do..." His voice trailed off. This was not the first time he asked those simple questions. I didn't respond. I was killing him and I should rot in hell just like my teachers said I would. What could I say? I realized that I had to distance myself from Jack or this sort of drama would happen again and possibly, yet, again. I have to remember why I am doing this. I walked away from Jack with a sadness in my heart. It hurt so much! God, I love him!

I finished cleaning up Lucas' stand, put the supplies back into his truck and waited for him to return. When Lucas returned from "shopping", I gave him a report of the sales and all of the money. He thanked me and paid me the two-fifty.

My new life, my room at Ambrose, my jobs, all felt good. But, in the back of my mind, always, I was thinking of my security. The extra work at the Fair, working for Lucas, was just not enough. So, I tried to minimize my spending on dinners and anything else that I deemed as unnecessary. I thought that I would stop eating lunch completely. Clothing, everything else, would have to wait. I needed to build my nest egg. I was one of those dominos that I thought about, just ready to fall if I wasn't prepared.

Every week, I continued to be impressed with Pastor Berkley. He seems to sense all of the dynamics and disagreements of the congregants; who takes sides with whom and who can't keep their opinions to themselves. Then, he takes all of the information, out of the cauldron of his congregation, and prepares his sermon. Almost every week, while listening to him, I understood how he determined what he was going to speak about and which congregants he was trying to influence with his sermon. Sort of like when he talked about prejudice trying to influence people like Jim Clark. A lot of good that did!

As I bid goodbye to the pastor and his wife, Harry drove up in his car. Harry and I had planned on going out for a ride into the country. Everyone at church saw me get into his car, including

Jack. The day was brisk, but, clear and sunny. It was a good late fall day for a ride.

I still didn't think of Harry in terms of a husband and lover. I thought of him as more of a good friend. He was the person that I enjoyed talking with about serious matters of our age, like the Depression. I guess that was because he had a broader knowledge of the outside world having gone to college. So, as we rode out into the countryside, I peppered him with more questions. I focused our discussion upon the farm economy and the potential that I linked that economy with losing my little job at Tanner's General Store or even my Saturday job, helping Lucas out at the Saturday Fair. Yes, I was insignificant in the big picture, but I...I was all that I had. I said, "Harry, honestly, while I feel badly about what is happening in the factories at places like New York, Chicago and Cleveland, I am most concerned about people here in Muskogee, people like you or me." He shook his head. I don't think that he found my statement to be a character flaw.

"Harry, all that I read about in the newspaper is how the Depression is starting to reach us here in Muskogee even though there is no stock market or factories nearby. We're a farming community. We make food or we support those that make the food with supplies and sometimes, a good time. After all, people have to eat, otherwise, they will starve." Then, I remembered that Harry had said just that..."then, they starve". Harry said, "Look, Mary, what is becoming apparent to me is that although people have to eat, they don't have to eat, as well. And, there are those people, here, and especially in Europe, that don't have the money to purchase our wheat and soybeans. And, when people stop buying our wheat and soybeans, even a little bit, the prices that our farmers get for their harvest drops. Then, the farmers don't have as much money. And, that is what has been happening here. So, Mary, you see, we aren't affected as badly as those people in the big cities, but we are affected and it is only going to get worse for us here." I sighed. That interrupted his train of thought. He might have thought that I was tired of hearing all about it, that I was not able to absorb everything that he had to say, but the opposite was true. My sigh was reflective of my fear, my frustration, of not being in control of my future. I had to find a way of controlling it. I gave Harry a small smile, "Harry, this is frightening. But, please go on." Harry shook his head up and down and continued almost in a way of summarizing everything that we had talked about, "Mary, no one can predict the future. There have been depressions before in the history of the United States. I learned about that in college. We seemed to get out of it after a while and have gone on for quite a long time before the next one. But, I can tell you that the Depression that we have now is much worse than those of the past. As I told you, there just isn't work for young civil engineers, or now, even a surveyor." Of course, he was referring to himself. I didn't want to ask him if he had lost his job as a surveyor or feared losing it. "I don't see a quick way out. This may get a lot worse before it gets better. This may go on for years." I sighed again. The beauty of the countryside that we were driving through was overshadowed by that cloud, the Depression, which was now coming our way.

Once we got back to town, Harry asked me if I would like to go for an early dinner. I had to quickly understand that would possibly lead to other things after dinner. I was not prepared to go to the next step with Harry, or anyone else for that matter. Maybe later. Then, I thought to myself, "What the heck?" So, I said yes to Harry. We went to dinner. Then, when Harry walked me to the front door of the Ambrose Boarding House, I kissed him on the lips and let him walk me upstairs to my room even though it was forbidden by the rules of the house. We kissed for a while and he started to put his hands where no other man had ever gone before. I let him do that for a few moments and then, I smiled and said, "Good night, Harry. I think that you should go home now." I said it nicely. I didn't want him to think that he had done anything wrong. He hadn't. Harry gave me one more kiss on the lips and then said, "Good night, Mary. I will call on you again if that is okay." I shook my head. Had he not left at that moment, I would have declined any further invitations to date. I always remembered Dolly's lesson, the choices that you make with your body must always be your choice, not those of someone else.

I have to say that I did enjoy the time that I spent with Harry that night. Going out with him had been interesting, mainly because of our discussions about life in the Depression era. We dated several more times. Each time, he got a little more adventurous. And each time, I let his wandering go only so far. I had to maintain control of the situation. Unfortunately, there just wasn't any passion with Harry even after we did go further than just that first kiss.

Chapter 20

The weeks, and then, the months, passed by. Somehow, it was the summer of 1931. The girls that I occasionally dined with at night were mostly from the local shops along the street where Tanner's General Store was located. We would get together and talk about nothing interesting, just gossip. Mostly, they had negative things to say about everyone else. I hope that I didn't contribute to all of that negativity.

Other than Harry, the dates that I went on were with no one special. I can't even remember their names. Maybe, I had become too serious, too introspective, and too critical, and maybe too fearful. I just was in a different place. Frankly. I was settling into a rut.

I needed someone to talk to, if only to hear my complaints about myself, my disappointments. Without Dolly, I felt that there was no one that I could open up my heart to. Alice was more of an acquaintance than a friend. Becky was a friend but also a friend of Harry Miller's. So, I couldn't share my feelings about dating Harry or anything else with her, for sure. Anything that I would say about Harry would certainly get back to him. Lucy is still a little standoffish. It's hard to get her into a discussion about personal matters. Maybe after I get to know her a little better, she will warm up.

The only girl of my age that I felt that I could confide in was Aida Tanner. I know that we were in a different place in our lives; she…stuck like glue to Ben Held, and me…just stuck. Although she had all of the security in life that I didn't, I still felt her to be a friend who I could speak to without being judged. I guess, once you feel that someone's a friend, you don't necessarily understand why you feel that way. It's like love in a way. It's all of the intangibles.

I only saw Aida on some holidays and a few weeks of her summer break. After a while, I decided to write to her. I got her address in New York City from Isaac and wrote about what was happening in Muskogee. I brought her up to date regarding my dating with Harry and others. I told her about my personal disappointments and finally, I wrote about my concerns about the Depression. I didn't tell her about my fears of losing my job at her father's store. I couldn't broach that subject with Aida. After all, what could she say? Finally, I asked her about Ben Held. Her relationship with Ben was far more interesting to me than anything that she could have told me about New York or the university.

A few weeks later, I got a response from Aida. She started off by telling me how happy she was to have heard from me. That made me smile. She did describe how the Depression was affecting life in New York City telling me about bread lines and the unemployment lines. She said that people in the big cities, unlike folks back in Muskogee, cannot grow food themselves. They don't have any place to do it. So, they have to rely upon handouts when they are out of work. She told me that, unlike Muskogee, the Depression was everywhere in New York.

The next thing that she wrote was that I was being unduly harsh on myself. She tried to buoy up my spirits by listing all of the qualities of my being that she appreciated. Then, she filled me in with all of the gossip about her life. She told me that Ben would be graduating from medical school in June of 1933. Then, he will have a year of internship and two years of residency at one of the hospitals in New York. Almost at the end of the letter, she wrote, "Ben and I are seeing each other very seriously. I can't say more about it but I will complete my college education at the same time that Ben completes his internship…you will just have to figure out the rest for yourself." She signed it, "Your friend, Aida Tanner" and then she wrote a postscript. "PS; You didn't mention Jack Clark. I didn't hear anything about him getting married. Do you see him at all? Are you still terribly in love with him?" She signed it again. This time she just wrote "Dolly". I had completely forgotten that Aida had used "Dolly" as her middle or her nickname forever. Seeing that in her hand made me think about "my Dolly" all over.

I wrote her back immediately, peppering her with questions and possibilities about her and Ben getting married. I knew that she would ignore those questions. I would have. But, the one question that I thought would be revealing was about where she would be living after graduation, "Aida, will you be coming back to Muskogee after you graduate?" I thought that if I had the answer to that question, I would know a lot more about her plans with Ben. I thought that I could tie that in with whether those two were getting married right away. After all, I didn't think that she would be moving to another place by herself or staying in New York unless she were married.

When I got Aida's response, about two weeks later, the first thing that she said was, "Aren't you just the smartest...trying to use my living plans after graduating as a way to find out about Ben and me.... Well, 'smarty pants', you'll just have to keep guessing." Then, she burned another stake in my heart. She asked again about Jack. I had thought that I could control the dialogue with Aida, but she was insistent. I felt that I didn't have a choice. So, I wrote back to her that nothing was going on with Jack. I reminded her that nothing could happen with Jack. "Jack is just a myth, a dream by night and day, one that would never become my reality. I have moved on completely." Liar! Ugggh.

Lucas and my relationship was completely different than it had been when I worked at the Taddum Farm, caring for Dolly. When I saw him at the Fair I found him much more open to talk with. He was always joking around. I guess that when we were at the farm together, Dolly's illness cast a shadow over everything.

One Saturday, at the Fair, as Lucas was about to leave, he asked me to have dinner with him. "Hey, Mary, let's catch up. How about dinner?" It had been nearly a year since Dolly had passed away. I responded, "Sure that would be nice. When do you have in mind?" He said, "Are you busy next Saturday night?" That is what we agreed upon. I asked him if he knew where I was living. Of course, he did. Yet, I felt the need to ask. It was clumsy of me. I said, "Lucas, I leave it to you to pick a nice restaurant." I mean, would he pick a restaurant that wasn't nice? Are there really that many choices in Muskogee?

That next Saturday night, Lucas waited at the boarding house front door while one of the residents came to get me. I walked downstairs and said hello. Then, Lucas said, with a smile on his face, "I picked out a 'nice restaurant'." He was having fun with what I had said a week before. I guess that I deserved it. I kept forgetting his wry sense of humor.

Once we were at the restaurant, Lucas pulled out the chair for me and helped me settle in. Then, once he sat down, he said, "Mary, I see you coming and going at the Fair every Saturday, but we never talk. How are you doing?" So, I told him about my friends and some of the guys that I had dated. It was probably wrong to talk about the guys that I had dated, but why not. I viewed Lucas as an old friend.

Then, Lucas said, "You know, you meant so much to Dolly and me." Then, there was a long period of silence as we began to eat our dinner. I didn't mind. Apparently, Lucas didn't mind either. Then, he broke the silence and said, "As I was thinking about meeting you for dinner, I came to realize that in all of the time that you spend with us at the farm, I never told you much about me and about my people. You had shared so much about yourself. You knew all about Dolly's history. I don't know why I never told you about mine." I told him that I would love to hear about it.

Lucas went on with his story, "My family, on both sides, came to Tennessee from somewhere in either Scotland or Ireland. No one really knew exactly where they were from. But, from what my mother had told me, the family that settled back in Tennessee were a close knit group. She also told me that there were a lot of marriages of close cousins. Many of the children from those marriages weren't 'quite right', if you know what I mean." I told Lucas that I didn't know what that meant. He said, "My mother told me that some of them were mean, while others were just plain stupid. That always scared me a bit, ya know.

"So, you see, both of us have some Scot or Irish in our blood. But, unlike your grandparents telling you about their Cherokee family history, my grandparents didn't seem to know too much about theirs. It was already so bad that my grandfather didn't even know his own grandfather's name. My mother told me that not knowing much about their families had bothered my grandmother. She felt that unless something were done about it, the loss of our family history would continue forever. So, my grandmother started to keep a diary so that her children and their children, throughout time, would know about her and her kin. She began by writing down everything that she knew of her parents and grandparents and the little that they knew of my grandfather's family, as well. It wasn't much. But, there is enough there that I know where my family came from, when they came here to Oklahoma and why.

"My mother continued the writing, keeping a diary as soon as she was able to read and write. Mostly, she wrote of their lives here on the farm. I inherited those diaries. Someday, if you like, you can read them." I stopped him. "Lucas, what about you? Do you keep a diary?" He said, "Well, I am a little embarrassed. When I was a child, I had a diary that my mother had bought for me. But, I felt that it wasn't something that a boy should do. I didn't. But, once Dolly came here, I told her all that I knew about my childhood. She took over the job of writing it down. And, then, with Dolly's passing, I began to write in the diary myself. I don't do it too often but I do it when something strikes me." A light flashed in my head. "Lucas, what a great idea! You have absolutely inspired me. I need to begin writing down my own story. I think that I will start by writing all of the stories about the Cherokee that grandfather told me and all of the natural cures that my grandmother had taught me about, like the yarrow and willow bark that I used for Dolly. They were never written down. But, I must...I must write everything down before I forget what they had told me. Then, I will add my story on top of that." I added, "I don't know why it never occurred to me until this very moment." I was excited about the prospect of starting my own family diary. Lucas said, "Well, I'm glad! You should. You know, you have a lot to write down."

After a pause to eat, Lucas continued, "In her diary, my grandmother wrote that farmers like my great-grandparents were able to come to Oklahoma and obtain legal title to the land after five years of farming and building a permanent home on the site. That was the deal. Like so many of the other white settlers, my family came here when they heard about the land 'giveaway'. That's what she called it. It sounded so good to them. But, after hearing about your great-grandfather's history, I began to understand that the government 'giveaway', which my family took advantage of, was a 'takeaway' from your people. But, that was what it was." Lucas repeated himself, "The 'giveaway' to my people was a 'takeaway' from your people. I came to realize that the wrongs that the white men did to your people resulted in my being here." I had to stop him. I said, "Lucas, neither of us can relive our family's history. We are not responsible for what has happened in the past." Lucas said, "Thank you for that."

Lucas always had a knack of reducing complex issues, sometimes throwing away so much in the process. I was a little uncomfortable with Lucas talking about the collision of our families but this was another case of when saying "less is more". That's what I did. I listened. So, I just shook my head.

"Mary, the rest of my grandmother and mother's story was pretty much about births and deaths. I can barely remember my grandparents. I was young when they died. As far as my parents are concerned, well, I was only around fifteen when both of my parents passed away from disease in the same year, probably the pox. I was their only child. I inherited the farm. That is the home that you lived in with Dolly and me. And you know everything else."

The rest of the evening was comfortable. We ate and talked a little here and there. There was no need to keep up the chit chat. We had history on the farm of being together without much said like when we would milk the cows next to one another.

Initially, I had my concerns when Lucas had asked me out. I didn't totally understand his motive. But, we spent a completely enjoyable evening together. Lucas didn't ask me out for another "date". At least, not soon thereafter.

Weeks, and then months, passed by. There were more dinners with the girls. There were more dates with boys and a few with men. It is truly amazing how these boys, young and old, only wanted to talk about themselves and brag about their accomplishments. It was as if they were trying to put themselves up for sale and I was the buyer. But, a man of interest to me would be someone who viewed me as an equal, who wanted to know about me as much as I would like to know about them. My relationship with Harry or Lucas and of course, Jack, was like that. That was not true with so many of the others that I dated.

Instead of the economic conditions brightening, they got worse…much worse by late 1931. This Depression, unlike the others that Harry and I discussed, would last a long time. Harry had predicted that it would. It was increasingly difficult to enjoy dinner while reading about all the many horrible things that were happening in our country and in Europe. The newspapers said that President Hoover wasn't doing anything to help. That was frustrating. I realized why they called it a "Depression". I found it all very "depressing".

My insecurity grew as the Depression took hold of more and more of our small farming community. Now, it was clearly affecting business at Tanner's General Store. I didn't think that the business at Isaac's was strong enough to keep me on, but he did. It was very generous of him. However, I wasn't convinced that it would last very long. And, at some point, Isaac would have to pull in the reins and cut costs. I was one of the "costs" that he would have to cut. I have to say that I would do it if I were in his place.

I was invited to go to the New Year's Eve Barn Dance celebrating 1932 by a guy by the name of Frank Jackson. The invite came via Alice Hollings. She told me that Frank had spoken with me at the Saturday Fair and bought some goods at the General Store. I didn't remember. Not much of a recommendation, I guess. Before I responded to Alice, I thought about it for a moment or two. Then, I realized that there could be nothing worse than sitting, all by myself, in my little room in Ambrose's Boarding House on this New Year's Eve as I had the New Year's Eve of 1931. I also thought that this may be the only invitation that I would get. Harry had just about given up on me. I believe that he saw little future in our relationship other than as friends. I felt the same way but I did enjoy talking with him. Also, although he never said so, I had heard from Becky that he had lost his job as a surveyor and was out of work. I felt awful about it. Harry was now one of those falling dominos.

So, I told Alice to say "yes" to Frank for me…I accepted.

As I listened to myself respond to Alice, I had thoughts of the last date that I had for New Year's Eve. It was with Jack, two years earlier, New Year's Eve of 1930. Certainly, he wouldn't ask me given my reaction to him every time that he approached me. But, in my dreams, night or day, he is still there, trying to court me. And some nights, when it is very dark and very quiet in my room, I dream of him making love to me. The reality is quite different. When I see Jack on Saturdays at the Fair, and on Sundays in church, he's pleasant enough, but quite withdrawn. A thought struck me. "I wonder whether he will be there at the New Year's Eve Barn Dance." I continued daydreaming. "I wonder who he would be going with if he did go to the Barn Dance. Ahhhh, stop it!"

New Year's Eve came. Frank picked me up at the boarding house. He was nicely dressed and I have to say, he wasn't bad looking. When we got to the Barn, I said hello to all of the people that I knew. I introduced Frank. And, Frank said hello to people he knew and introduced me to his friends, as well.

Then, Ken Michaels took to the bandstand and said, "Belieeeeve me!" It was just the same opening that he had when I was at the Thanksgiving and New Year's Eve dances in 1929 and 1930. I even think that Pastor Berkley's speech was identical with the one he gave us back then. Even the "Dos and Don'ts" were the same. So, after the usual introductions and the talk by Pastor Berkley, the music started. Really, nothing had changed except that I wasn't there with Jack.

Although it had been a while since I had danced, it came back to me quickly as Frank wheeled me around the dance floor. And, then…there was Jack. He was dancing just as Dolly had taught us. I could even see his lips move as he was counting in time with the music. He was dancing with this breathtaking blond. I didn't know her. But, I had helped her at the General Store buying this and that. I also think that I had seen her at Lucas' table at the Saturday Fair. But, then again, it's a small town. You see everyone at the Saturday Fair.

And then, Jack looked my way. I couldn't help but to lock eyes with him until Frank swept me off in another direction. I almost felt weak. I told myself, "Buck up. This is what you signed on for." I always said that to myself when I had a moment of weakness.

After a few dances, Frank left me sitting along the wall when he went to get lemonade for us. And, as Frank returned with drinks, Jack walked over with his date. He introduced her to me as Claudia Dunellen. He said, "Claudia, this is my good friend, Mary." Oh, can't you just die? That's it, just a good old friend? I introduced Frank. We chatted for a while and told each other to enjoy the dance. And then, Jack and Claudia walked away with her arm tucked neatly into his. But, before he was too far away, he turned and said, "I really like that brooch. It's very pretty. Happy New Year, Mary". I didn't even realize that I was wearing the cameo brooch that Jack had given me on Christmas day of 1929. Did I turn red enough for all to see? But, that was when I knew that he still had feelings for me. I saw it in his eyes. I didn't know if Claudia or Frank caught on. I responded, "Happy New Year, Jack and Claudia". I emphasized the word "and". I don't know if I felt better or worse. I started to wonder if I would ever find anyone to replace Jack in my heart. I remembered the warmth of being next to him, even as we just milked the cows or any of the other chores around the Taddum Farm, or eating popcorn together in the movie theater or dancing, so close, or kissing. Yes…everything!

The New Year came. Just like that it was 1932. Frank kissed me at the stroke of midnight as the announcement came over the radio. His kiss was on the lips. I kissed him back. After all, he did nothing wrong. He just picked the wrong girl to take to the dance. That wasn't his fault. But, all that I could think about when he was kissing me was when Jack and I were together at the New Years of 1930. I said to Frank, "I was here two years ago. It is hard to believe how quickly time flies by." Frank said that he had never been to this dance before. Then, after a pause, he asked, "Who did you go with back then? Was it anyone that I know?" I responded, "Well, you know him now. It was Jack Clark who you just met." That was a big, I repeat, a big mistake. It was rude, pure and simple. I had treated Frank poorly. Boy, why did I do that? There was silence. Frank probably had many questions, but was polite enough to know not to ask. He took me back to the boarding house. There was nothing more to it. There just wasn't any chemistry between us. He didn't ask me out again and I was not unhappy with that outcome.

A few weeks later, at the Saturday Fair, there was Jack, as always, just fifty feet away. I greeted him and I turned away to finish organizing the goods on Lucas' tables. When I turned back to Jack, there she was, Miss Claudia Dunellen. They seemed to be having a great time, laughing and bumping into one another. After that, I had to see this week after week. It was like a preverbal dagger in my heart. There was a moment that I was ready to tell Lucas that I could no longer work the Saturday Fair for him. It was just too painful. But, I guess that I was willing to torture myself. I stuck it out.

Chapter 21

I enjoyed going to church. It was a respite of sorts. I always just sat there quietly listening to Pastor Berkley's sermons even though I had heard them, or sermons just like them, many times before. I enjoyed saying hello to the other parishioners that I had gotten to know and like over the years. It was warm. But, then, every week, I would see Jack. But, I also saw Jack's father, Jim. Poof...that ended that daydream in a flash.

As we left church one Sunday in April of 1932, Lucas walked over to me just outside of the chapel. He said hello. Then, he asked me, "How long has it been since you were at the farm." Of course, the last time that I was at his farm was just after Dolly's funeral in August of 1930. But, he knew that. Then, he said, "Mary, would you like to come out to the farm? If you like, we could visit Dolly's grave and the memorial to your grandfather." I don't know why, but the thought of my being back at the farm was comforting. At the least, it would give me a chance to get away from the monotony that my life had become. Sundays, after church, were the worst. I had nothing to do; no work, no Fair, a little reading, but, mostly, nothing. I hesitated a bit but then said, "Yes, that would be nice." But, then I added, "Lucas, I would like to be back before nightfall". He told me that would be no problem.

We got into his truck and drove out to the farm. On the way out, I started to think about what I was doing. Was my acceptance to go to the farm more than just a friendly gesture? Would it be construed by Lucas to be anything more than that?

As we drove out, Lucas talked about how "Someday...someday", he repeated himself as he pointed his finger into the air. He told me how some of the guys down at the St. Mark's Farm & Feed Store talked about the newly obtained electric power, allowing them to modernize their farms. He talked excitedly about these electrical pumps that can move water to a water tower, so you could have water whenever and wherever you wanted it, even in the house. "Someday, I hope to have electricity at the farm." Of course, we had water towers and piping providing water to the houses on our street in town already so I was familiar with what he was saying. Lucas kept going on about lights and refrigerators and radios. He said that he had already seen a Kelvinator refrigerator at the farm house of one of his friends from St. Marks. He was so excited by the possibility. I responded by telling him how much of a luxury I thought it was having electric lights in my room at the boarding house, at Isaac's store and at the restaurants where I ate dinner. I agreed with him that it would be wonderful to have electricity at the farm. As I talked with Lucas, I remembered using oil lamps and candle lights for everything during my time at the farm with Dolly, only having the root cellar to keep foodstuffs cool so that they wouldn't spoil. Electricity would make all of that so much easier.

    I asked Lucas which of his friends had electricity. He mentioned a few names. I knew some of them from church. Their farms were located much closer to the Muskogee town limits than the Taddum Farm. So, I said, "But, Lucas, those farms are close to town. It is not a surprise that they would get electric service sooner than at your farm." He responded, "I guess you're right. But, I sure would like to get it. It sure would make my life much easier!" Unfortunately, electric power would not come to the Taddum Farm for some time.

    As we continued driving out to the farm, I reached back into my many good memories of my time with Dolly. Those wonderful talks that I had with her and the lifelong advice that she gave me. I couldn't avoid thinking about some bad times toward the end of her life, as well. The bad times just left me with some sadness. But, overall, I had a smile on my face. Lucas saw it and asked, "What are you smiling about?" I told him about my memories of Dolly. He just shook his head with a knowing smile. Then, after a few moments, he said, "Mary, you know, I guess, that when Dolly came here to the farm, she didn't really know me. She only knew me from my letters and a brief encounter. She certainly didn't love me. How could she? But, ya know, that changed over some time. We fell in love and had a warm and comfortable relationship. It was good." I remained silent. I knew everything that he said. I didn't know why he was bringing it up.

As soon as we got to the farm, I told Lucas that I first wanted to pay my respects to Dolly's grave and my grandfather's memorial. But, I told him that I also wanted to see how he was keeping up with the manufacture of cheddar. I always felt that the cheddar was "my baby". He laughed.

Lucas and I walked up the hill to the oak tree that shaded both Dolly's grave and my grandfather's memorial. When we got there, it was clear that Lucas had well-tended both. The headstones were clean and there were no weeds. I looked at the inscriptions on the stones that Jack had made and shed a few tears. I cried for the loss of my childhood that my grandfather and my grandmother represented to me. I cried about my loss of innocence that Dolly helped me through as I grew to be a woman in her house. Then, I said something to Lucas that I had never thought about before, "I think that Dolly would have liked talking with my grandfather. They both imparted life lessons to me that were not easily learned without a lot of pain and suffering." Lucas shook his head. And I cried as I thought about Jack who carved the stones that I was looking down upon. Here, underneath the oak tree, I was reminded of the loss of all three; grandfather and his wisdom, Dolly and her life lessons, and my unrequited love for Jack.

As we stood there, I said to Lucas, "Before I came here, I was too young to understand how it feels to be without a place to live and food on my plate. Although they treated us poorly at the "Indian School", I had that roof and food to eat. When I was living here with you and Dolly, I felt warmth and security. I had a place to sleep and food to eat. Now, with the Depression, I worry about the loss of my job and just how long my savings would last if I couldn't find other employment. For other girls of my age, if they fail, they have family to live with, family to rely upon. Not me! Maybe I worry more than I should. But, sometimes, I think about nothing else. It is always at the forefront of my thinking."

We walked down the hill. The root cellar was almost exactly beneath these memorials. We walked through the root cellar together lit by a single oil lamp. Lucas had a full house of cheddar, all with the dates when they were made on the cheesecloth covering. I was pleased. I said to him, "But, you know Lucas, the refrigerator that you talk about getting will be small compared to all of the things that you need to keep cool. It will be nice to have once you get electricity but it will only be big enough for meat and produce for the week. That's all. You would still need to maintain the root cellar for everything else." Lucas said, "You're right. But, I want one anyhow." He chuckled. I said, "Sometimes, wanting something is good enough. Not everything that we do has to be for a purpose. I would want one also."

As we drove back to Muskogee, I started up a conversation with Lucas about the impact of the Depression. After a few moments of silence, he said, "Mary, I have to admit that I don't understand the Depression, especially in the big cities, the factories and everything else. Here, in farming communities, like Muskogee, prices have been falling and that hurts the farm. We survive. We do talk about it at St. Marks, but no one really understands it. But, I have read enough in the newspaper and heard enough to appreciate that it could"…he hesitated, "…no…it will impact me more. I just don't know when, or how, or how much. Sometimes, I ask myself, 'What should I do about it?' I do know that as long as I pay my taxes and make payments against the loan that I have taken out, I should be alright. That, and some food. If nothing else changes, I can survive. I think it is that simple for me." He paused for a moment and then repeated himself, "It is that simple…so far, everything is okay." He was being confident. He was always like that. Then, there was silence. Well, maybe he was right. Maybe, it is that simple.

We got back to town, Lucas escorted me to the door of the boarding house. Then, as he was about to leave, with some hesitancy, he asked me if I would like to go to dinner with him. He said, "Well, it's almost dinner time…okay, it's a bit early. But, would you like to go to dinner?" I said, "Yes, that would be nice." This would be the second time that I accepted a dinner invitation from Lucas.

Dinner with Lucas was comfortable. The food was good. And, not surprisingly, Lucas asked me about my work at the General Store. I told him about how well Isaac had treated me. Then, he wanted to know about my friends. I told him about Aida and Ben and Alice and Betty and Lucy and all of the rest. He told me that he found it amusing how I dwelled upon other people's social relationships, especially Aida and Ben. I explained that girls enjoy sharing gossip much more than men. But, then, I remembered how Lucas spent Saturday mornings after he dropped off his goods for me to sell. He always went to the St Mark's Farm and Feed Store gossiping with his friends there. I said, "Well, Lucas, maybe it isn't just girls. Isn't it the same thing that you do with your friends at St. Mark's Saturday mornings?" He actually blushed. He said, "I don't like to think of what I do there as gossip, but it sounds just like what you do with your girlfriends." I felt victorious!

Then, to my surprise, our discussion changed back from the frivolous to the more serious. He started talking about the Depression, again. This was a continuation of our discussion that we had in the truck on the way back to Muskogee. He said, "Ya know, Mary, farming is always a challenge. It's always been that way. I told you how wheat prices have fallen. The lower prices that I get for my crops now makes it more and more difficult every year. I know that it is no different for me and my farm than it is for all of the rest of the farmers here in Oklahoma or Kansas or Texas." All of us are experiencing the same thing." Then, after a moment, he said, thoughtfully, "Boy, I hope that the wheat prices stop dropping." We went back and forth, talking about the farm economy. Before, I thought that Lucas was a man in a world of his own, focused only on today. Now, I found him to be well read about everything that might impact his farm going forward. He was even up to date with some of the more newsworthy current events. I was more impressed with Lucas than I had been in the past. I thought to myself that it was good for me to have brought the newspaper back to his farm when I was living there. It opened up the world to Lucas.

The Depression continued to darken our lives; all of our lives. In early 1933, I read about how thousands of banks across the country, small and large, had already failed, leaving their depositors near penniless. I had never contemplated putting my four hundred dollars in the bank. Thank God, my money was literally under my mattress or in my underwear. It was as safe as it could be. But, for all of those poor people that had their money in the bank, even here in Muskogee, they panicked and pulled all of their money out of the bank. Their withdrawals pushed a few of the banks in town into bankruptcy. Then, in March of 1933, I read that the president declared a "Bank Holiday", literally shutting down the nation's banks. In the end, it helped stop the "bleeding", but reading about it just added to my fear, my insecurity. What was next for those poor people who lost their money? They were just like those dominos teetering on the brink of falling, on the brink of ruin.

Over the next months, I started dating Harry, yet again, and several other men. I had thought that Harry had lost all interest in me but I guess that he was still hopeful. I never asked him whether he had a job or not. And, I also saw Lucas. I never found that flame for any of them which I had in me for Jack. And, Jack was seeing Claudia Dunellen. And, why not? She is very pretty. I heard that she is smart. I also heard that her family is well off. Putting all of her attributes together, I thought that Jack would be lucky to be together with her. Why would he still be interested in me? Obviously, Jack must have come to the same conclusion. For, after a while, Jack and Claudia even started to sit together at church, separate from their parents. I wished that Jack would do something or say something that would make me not like him, not love him, but that never occurred. Damn him!

After a dinner that we had in late May of 1933, Lucas asked if we could speak. So, I invited him into the parlor of my boarding house. We sat there talking for a while. It is obvious to me, now, that he had planned this all out when he said, "Mary, I know that you still hold out the hope that you will get together with Jack and...maybe that could happen. But, I want for you to know that I love you and want to marry you. I know that you do not love me right now. I would hope that...if you did marry me, you could learn to love me. I think that we could have a good life together on the farm." Then, he got down on one knee right in the middle of the parlor. The people that were passing by came to a complete halt, just as if they were posing for a photograph. Down on his knee, in the middle of all of these people, he formally asked me to marry him, repeating that he loved me.

I wasn't totally shocked. Lucas had been paying more and more attention to me over the last year or so. Yet, through those dinner dates, our time together at the Saturday Fair and even now with him kneeling in front of me, he had never tried to kiss me. I wondered why. How could he want to marry me, saying that he loved me, yet, never kissing me? So, I leaned over and asked him, quietly, in a whisper so no one could hear, "Lucas, why haven't you ever tried to kiss me?" His response was honest. He said, "I was always scared. I didn't want to lose you because of some clumsy attempt to court you. I was afraid that you would reject me even before you really knew me. And, then, I wouldn't have a chance. But, I would love to kiss you right now." I said, "Then, do it and we'll talk."

So, Lucas got up and picked me out of the chair and kissed me passionately on the lips and I kissed him back. He held me tightly. We stood there for several minutes before he stopped kissing me. Then, he held me by the shoulders. He looked intensely into my eyes and said, "Mary, I would be so very happy if you would marry me."

All the while, the people around us were enjoying seeing this drama play out before their eyes. I think that they all held their breath.

While I liked Lucas, I didn't love him and he knew it. He was about twenty-seven. I was just twenty years old. I'd dated many of the eligible boys and men in town and it's not like I would be traveling to the big cities to find others or writing letters to men in other towns. And, I thought that the farm would give me the security that I sought. So, I decided. I said, "Lucas, I want you to know that everything that you said was correct. I still have feelings for Jack. Often, I think that my feelings for Jack may have been more of a school girl type of crush. I just don't know any more. At the same time, I know that he and I will never be together. You know the reasons. Lucas, I will marry you and hope that everything that you and Dolly had could happen to us. That was magic. Lucas knowingly shook his head. He said, "Mary, I will do everything that I can to make you both happy and secure. In fact, if it will make you more comfortable, more secure, I will change the deed to the Taddum Farm to include you as half owner." I thanked him for the offer but told him that it was unnecessary. I never asked him to do it. As he looked into my eyes, I removed the cameo pin that Jack had given me. Now that I was about to marry Lucas, I would never wear that brooch. My life was about to take another path, another future.

I agreed to marry Lucas, not because I loved him, but because it was a "good arrangement". I know that it sounds predatory, even greedy, cold, and loveless. Okay, maybe, I am guilty of all of those adjectives. But, I really hoped that we could duplicate what Lucas and Dolly had as lovers.

Monday, I told Isaac that I would no longer be able to work at the store. "Isaac, I will be marrying Lucas and working at the farm." He appeared surprised, but seemed to be suppressing his feelings, knowing that his face, his reaction, might be hurtful to me. But, I was prepared for that reaction from Isaac and frankly, from most of the people that knew me. Isaac immediately recovered and told me that he was happy for me. He was looking for something to say. "Boy, I will miss you. You have been a great asset to the store bringing in new business...the Cherokee women, white women and even some of the Cherokee men. You did great right from the start." Then, Isaac hesitated, "Mary, more than any business that you brought in, I just enjoyed being in the store with you. I always enjoyed talking with you." But, then, after another longer hesitation, he said, "I have to ask...I'm sorry for being so nosey. Aida told me all about your 'friendship'...is that the proper word...with Jack?" Obviously, Aida had not locked away my secret as well as I thought and Isaac couldn't control his curiosity. I raised my hand indicating that he should stop talking. Given what he said so far, I thought that he knew most of it. So, I explained everything to Isaac. Then, he took a big breath, "Mary, I wish you and Lucas the very best of luck and happiness." I gave Isaac a big hug. With a huge smile on his face, he said, "Ok, ok, but for today, now, go back to work".

  I had been writing regularly to Aida and was awaiting her latest letter from New York. However, now, I decided not to wait. So, I wrote to her about the news. But, before I even got to the post office with the letter, I heard that Aida and Ben had just returned from New York after their spring semester. I ran over to her house to see her. We both hugged and laughed. We enjoyed seeing each other again. Then, once I told her, she asked me the obvious question, "Why Lucas?" I said, "What a question?" I tilted my head to one side. "...But a good one. Aida, people face their future based upon all different types of life experiences. My life is much more precarious than yours. I have a job with your father in the middle of the most severe Depression that has ever been. Your father has treated me generously, but there may come a time when his generosity will be constrained by his business...and he can't control what happens in the country. So, there you are. How would I be if I didn't have a job, a girl with no family, a girl with four hundred dollars to her name? What would happen? Well, maybe I would be able to compete for another job. Maybe, I could be a waitress in one of the Muskogee restaurants. But...those jobs are filled and business is noticeably slowing in all of the town's restaurants. If I were out of work, I would be able to live on my savings for what...maybe eight months, maybe even a year if I were very frugal. But, then, what? For you and Ben, and others who have families with some resources, you and they would be safe. But, for me, if this Depression continues to bring down everything in its path...I just don't know." Aida stopped me. She said, "Mary, I never even thought...you're right. I am lucky." She repeated herself as she looked down to the ground. "I never thought of the issues that you have lived with. I am very lucky."

I continued, "Aida, look, over the last year or so, I have gotten to know Lucas in an entirely different light. He has been kind and gentle. He has been sweet. And yes, he knows all about my feelings for Jack. And, yes, he knows that I do not love him. But, I do like him. I knew that Dolly loved Lucas. You know their story. Lucas is hoping that I will fall in love with him, over time, as did Dolly. About Jack, well...for me...Jack has become a mirage, like I have read about. You know, like in the desert where you see water off in the distance. But, as you get closer to the water, it vanishes. Jack isn't there now. Maybe, he never was! There is no Jack. There never could be. All there was, and all that could be, is just a faded dream. Anyway, Jack is seeing Claudia Dunellen. They seem to be serious. I don't know if you know her but she is quite the good looker." I came back to me. "Aida, I have woken up. This is my reality now." Aida could say nothing. Then, in order to break the tension in the room, I reached out to hold her hand and said with a brief smile, "Aida, I am not angry with you for asking. Everyone is asking or thinking the same thoughts." I smiled but my lips were taut from the stress of the conversation. Aida came back to Claudia, "Oh, my God. Mary, don't tell me that Claudia is a good looker. Do you have any idea how beautiful you are? There is no one in this town that is as good looking as you are, period. But, much more importantly, you are so smart and filled with such goodness. I know Claudia Dunellen. This Claudia has nothing on you. Frankly, I don't see Jack ever staying with her. She is just a fling, maybe even someone that he is seeing to make you jealous". "Enough! Aida, please...Enough!" I settled down and apologized. "Gee, Aida, I am sorry for being so rude. What did Dolly always tell me about 'your decision...your consequences'? Well, now, it is my decision to marry Lucas and I think that I know the consequences! Now, tell me about you and Ben."

We spent the next half hour or so talking about the plans that Ben and Aida had for the future. She repeated to me that she would finish college in May of 1934, the very next year, and Ben would complete his internship at almost the same time. Then, she said, "Who knows." She was being coy, but I thought that they were planning on getting married as soon as they both came back from New York.

In the following days, Lucas and I met for dinner in town and talked about our wedding. We both agreed that Pastor Berkley would perform the rituals. That was easy. Lucas said that I should have anyone at the ceremony that I wanted. I think that he was probably curious as to whether I would invite Jack or not. Of course, that could never happen. I did invite Alice Hollings and Becky Smith. I invited Aida Tanner and Ben Held. I also invited Aida's father, Isaac, and his wife, Eva. I barely knew Eva Tanner but couldn't see inviting Isaac without his wife. I also invited several of the Cherokee women that I had gotten to know over the years. Lucas invited several of his friends, the guys that he met with regularly at St. Mark's Farm and Feed Store. Lucas also took on an all too difficult task. He spoke with Helen Clark. Lucas told Helen that for obvious reasons, it would be difficult for him to invite her husband, Jim.

As soon as Isaac received the invitation, he placed a notice in the window of his store saying that the store would be closed for a half-day so that he could attend our wedding.

Lucas told me that Helen would be coming to the wedding without Jim. Lucas said nothing about Jack. He would not be invited by either of us. But, as I stood there, looking at Lucas, I began to think, to fantasize. I always knew that if it weren't for Jim, Helen would have welcomed me with open arms into her family, having no problem with me and Jack as a couple. My life would have been so different. But, that was not my fate. This is my fate!

I said to Lucas, that I was happy that Helen was coming.

Lucas and I were married by Pastor Berkley at the end of June in the year 1933. Sally Berkley was our witness. Besides the people that we had invited, many of the regular Sunday parishioners attended the ceremony, wanting to wish us well. The ceremony was short and sweet. Pastor Berkley's sermon that day was about how people grow together after marriage and how the love that develops over time is more enduring than anything that exists or existed prior to the formal marriage ceremony. It was obvious that he was talking directly to Lucas and me. It was OK. Everyone knew of the arrangement. Up to the time of the ceremony, I had thought that I <u>could</u> make it work. Now, with the marriage ceremony concluded, I told myself that I had made my decision and now, I <u>would</u> make my marriage to Lucas work.

As we left the church, everyone greeted us with smiles and congratulations. Isaac and his wife Eva begged off after the church ceremony saying that they had to re-open the General Store. Isaac pulled me aside and told me that Eva would be taking my place in the store. Then, he added with a smile on his face, "I don't believe that she could ever be as good a saleswoman as you." I had heard that his wife had never worked. But, with business down due to the Depression, having Eva work there meant that he would not have to pay anyone outside of his family. It made sense. I thanked Isaac for his comment. But, I added, "Your wife will do great. Once she gets to know the goods and is open and friendly with the shoppers, it will work out just fine." My comments were the same as when someone tastes your apple pie. "Of course, it is wonderful...of course, Eva Tanner will do just fine." That type of comment really doesn't mean much. Then, Isaac placed an envelope in my hands holding my two hands in his and wished me good luck. His sincerity was obvious and warm. The envelope held a hand written note wishing us the best of luck for the future. Isaac's handwriting was beautiful. Each letter was adorned with loops and other embellishments. It looked so professional, as if he were a calligrapher. Also, included in the envelope was a very generous gift certificate for purchase of anything at his store that we wanted.

After the ceremony, we all marched off for a luncheon at Hanover's Rib Restaurant in Muskogee. Curiously, it was one of the places that Harry had taken me for dinner. I had also eaten there by myself. It wasn't surprising that Lucas chose this restaurant. There are not many decent restaurants on the strip in Muskogee and Hanover's was just a walk away from the church.

As everyone sat in their chairs and quieted down. Pastor Berkley got up and started with the invocation. Then, he lifted a glass of water and offered a toast to the new bride and groom. Everyone raised their glass along with the pastor. "I have known Lucas since he was a young child. And, I have known Mary for just these few years. I feel like I have known her forever. I like both of them very much." He finished with offering his and his wife's best wishes, "Peace and a long married life." I felt afterwards that the pastor didn't have his heart in what he said. Maybe, it was just my imagination.

The restaurant served a prefix luncheon of grilled ribs, baked potatoes and a salad. Of course, with Prohibition, alcohol was still illegal. So, the bar at the restaurant was formally closed as it had been for years. But, by the time of our wedding, in mid-1933, Prohibition was gasping its last breath, finally ending in December of that year, just months later. Everyone knew that

Prohibition was soon to end, so no one worried about people enjoying the locally produced moonshine, even drinking it out in the open. To satisfy that thirst, Lucas brought a couple of jugs of his own making to the luncheon and passed them around to anyone who wanted to imbibe. This is what the men of the area had done all throughout the years of Prohibition anyway, so I was OK with this violation of law. I had some myself.

I walked around the room where we held the luncheon to thank each of the people for coming to our wedding. I spent a few minutes with each of them. Several of the guests gave us small gifts to adorn the house. Of course, I thanked them, gratefully. Then, I took a deep breath. I couldn't avoid it any more without it being obvious and rude. So, finally, I stopped to speak with Helen Clark. The first thing that she said was, "Jack asked me to congratulate you and Lucas". I told her to thank Jack for us. Then, we spent a few moments reminiscing about Dolly. And, that was it.

After lunch, Lucas settled the bill and sat down across the table from me. He said, "Well, Mrs. Taddum, what are your thoughts about the wedding ceremony and the luncheon?" That was one thing that I had learned to like about Lucas. He asked my opinion about things, big or small. It made me feel like an equal in the relationship. I told Lucas, "I thought that Pastor Berkley was perfect as he always has been." I added, "He always has a way of saying just the right thing, at the right time." I don't know if I meant it this time. I didn't share that with Lucas. Then, I added, "I enjoyed the luncheon. The food was great. Everyone seemed to enjoy the time." Lucas just shook his head up and down with a gentle smile on his face.

When everything was done, Lucas said, "Shall we go or do we have other business in town that we should take care of now?" I could have thought about a million things to do in town, but it was time to be Lucas' wife. "I have a few things to pick up at the Ambrose Boarding House, and then, I think that it is time to go to the farm". I couldn't quite say home. I didn't feel that it would be home for a while. Lucas drove me over to the boarding house. He asked if I needed help to gather my things. I told him just to wait in the truck. All of my things fit into that one bag. I tucked the money that I had saved into my underwear. I would not discuss that money with Lucas. It would be my money...just in case. In case of what, I wasn't sure. But, that four hundred dollar stash would always be mine, not ours, for a "rainy day" that I hoped would never come. I said goodbye to Mrs. Ambrose and walked out the front door.

  We drove to the farm. Lucas started off our conversation in the truck by talking about how pricing for wheat was rising with the election of a new President. Then, he said, "If it weren't for the dry spell that we're in, the wheat crop would have been much larger and the farm would have made much more money." I was impressed. But, uncomfortably, I said, "Well, OK, that's good. Let's hope that the prices stay high and we get more rain." Until that moment, I just didn't think about how much farmers relied upon regular rainfall to survive. But, farmers thought about it all of the time.

  I always felt that when people needed to jabber about absolutely nothing of consequence that it was out of nervousness. Now, it was my turn to fill the silence. I said, "Lucas, what should I do to help out on the farm? Should I do what I did when I was there with you and Dolly? Are there other things that I should do?' Lucas just shook his head, "Yes that will be fine. But, don't be concerned. We'll work it out. You will see what needs to be done just like you did before." There was silence for the rest of the trip.

  When we arrived at the farm, Lucas smiled and asked if he could carry me across the threshold. I said, "Thank you. That would be nice." It was the same doorway that I had walked through hundreds of times by myself. But, I thought he was being very romantic.

  I was now a married woman, not that girl that had come to the farm and walked through that same doorway a little more than four years earlier. Lucas gently placed me near the fireplace and sat directly across from me. He just stared at me with a slight smile on his face. Then, he said, "I have a difficult subject to discuss. Is that OK?" I just shook my head. "After Dolly's funeral, I had said that I was going to give away all of her clothing. But, it didn't happen. There was just never a good day to do it. I couldn't. I couldn't do it. So, yesterday, I took all of Dolly's things out of our bedroom and put them in the other room. If you like, you can go through it. Maybe, you will find something to keep as a reminder of her. Maybe, you will want to give it all to charity. Or, maybe, you would want for me to throw everything away and not have to deal with it. Whatever you want is fine with me." I knew that Dolly would be present in the house for a long time to come. Lucas said, nervously, repeating himself, "Mary, look, if you want, I will throw it all out and then, you would not have to deal with it. I just thought that there might be something of sentimental value to you. Really, I don't want you to feel funny about any of this." I said, "Lucas, please don't worry. I feel Dolly's presence in the house and in my heart. There is room here for both of us." With that, there was nothing more said about Dolly's clothing.

Lucas asked me if I wanted a cup of tea. I thought that was considerate. I told him that I would put my things away and then join him in the kitchen. I went into the bedroom that I had shared with Dolly for more than a year while tending to her. The bed that I had slept in was still there. It was immaculately clean. I put away my few things and joined Lucas. After we finished our tea, there was really nothing more to be done other than to consummate our marriage. I was nervous. He was clearly not comfortable as he slowly undressed me. But, he was gentle and respectful. We did what needed to be done. Enough said about that.

Over the next few days, I got into the rhythm of the farm. There was nothing new that I had to learn. So, the day after my marriage to Lucas, I began with milking the cows, feeding the chickens, collecting and candling the eggs, butter and cheese, and preparing all of the meals. Without Dolly to be taken care of, I had enough time to take care of everything that I did before and the vegetable garden. Lucas had already planted most of the spring vegetables. Shortly, I would be harvesting and canning what I could gather. Then, I would be adding other vegetables for the summer.

Our time together on the farm was like it was before except Lucas was much more attentive. In the time that I was gone from the farm, Lucas told me that he never missed a week without reading the newspaper that he got at the Saturday Fair. We spent time together after dinner talking about current events. I was surprised to see how quickly everything worked between us. I was pleased.

Lucas suggested that I learn to drive so I could take the truck rather than the buckboard to the Saturday Fair. I was looking forward to driving. It was important to me. Lucas gave me a few lessons but I wasn't quite ready yet. So, that first Saturday, after we were married, I took the buckboard and filled it with the goods for sale. That was to be the last Saturday Fair that I used the buckboard, and, my first Fair as Mrs. Taddum, not just Mary.

I left for the Fair that morning with great apprehension. As Lucas said goodbye, I looked into his eyes and knew that he was stressed. He wasn't particularly worried about my safety. That goes without saying. I believe that he was stressed because he knew that I would be just fifty feet from Jack. I told him that I would be OK by myself. Then, I added, "Lucas…everything will be alright!" I kissed him on the cheek.

When I got to the Fair, I set up as always. Then, Jack arrived and waived. I think that I blushed even though I wasn't close to him. We both went about selling our goods. At about nine in the morning, Jack's girlfriend, Claudia, came by. They seemed very happy to see each other, laughing and bumping into one another, as always. She waved to me. By ten o'clock, she was gone. By eleven, as business slowed, Jack came over. He congratulated me on my marriage to Lucas. Then, he hesitated, looking at me with the most sincerity that his two eyes could muster. He grabbed my hands and said, "I shouldn't be talking like this to a married woman, but I just have to say what I have in my heart." I withdrew my hands. He went on. "Mary, I have been in love with you from the first time that I saw you four years ago." I stopped him by placing a hand gently on his cheek. He said, "Please don't stop me. I have to say what I want to say. Every time that I tried to approach you or ask you out or just be with you, you rejected me. Could you tell me, now, please tell me why?"

I thought about what to say but I decided to be frank. After all, there could be nothing more between us. It was over. I was married to Lucas. "Jack, I never could have had a future with you. In your family, to your father, I would always have been Cherokee, a half-breed, a bastard. There was never a way for the two of us to be a couple. Never!

He interrupted me, saying, "Mary, I would have left home. We would have married. We could have gone anywhere. You know that." My insides were aching. "Yes, and your family would have been destroyed. You and your father would never have spoken. Very likely, you would not have been able to speak with your mother or your sister. You know that. You know what your mother was going through back then. How could I have allowed that to happen? How?" Jack just looked at me without saying a word.

"Jack, listen to me… Lucas and I are married. He's good to me. He says that he is in love with me. Lucas knows that I am not in love with him. He knows that I have had feelings for you. That must be over. Lucas and I both hope that I will fall in love with him as did Dolly. My greatest wish is for it to become true. No, I will work at it to make it so. And, Lucas and I will have a family. And we will love our children together." Jack tried to say something but couldn't. He just looked into my eyes with tears flowing from his.

"Jack, that's the way that my life has been. It seems that it has always been controlled by someone or something other than myself. Our futures cannot be known with any certainty. You think that you will go down one path and you end up going down another. As far as Jack and Mary, well, life got between us. I don't know what else to say." I took a deep breath. He reached out to me again with his hand. I didn't take it. I said angrily, "What more do you need to know!!??" I turned away. I didn't want Jack to see the tears in my eyes…but he did. Then, in almost an act of defiance, of courage, I turned back toward him, wanting to appear strong, even with the tears streaming down my cheeks. I saw his tears, his sadness. I saw Jack's shoulders slumped, once again. After a moment, he turned away and walked back to his tables. There was nothing more that could be said. It's not easy to stop loving someone just because you have to make other choices. I thought that I would always love Jack.

I finished selling our goods. Listen to me, "our goods". Well, I guess that they were no longer just "Lucas' goods". I needed to get Jack out of my head. So, I decided to take a walk around the Fairgrounds, saying hello to some of the ladies that I knew. As I walked around, I spied a copy of the "Farm Journal" on one of the tables. Since I had a few minutes, I asked the lady at the table if I could take a look at it. There were several articles that focused upon women's interests as mothers, cooks, seamstresses, and home decorators. None of the articles referred to women as contributors, as people who earned money to support their farm family. But, when I glanced at the ads for a feed company, I noticed that they pictured women feeding the chickens. I laughed and said to myself, "At least those companies recognized that most of the poultry on the farm is tended to by women folk, like me. They know more of the truth of a farm wife's days than the so-called "experts" that wrote those articles." I felt recognized. I returned the magazine.

I packed up, loading the empty baskets onto the buckboard and traveled back to the farm. When I got back, Lucas was waiting at the house. He asked if everything went well. I gave him the money with a smile and told him about the sales. He showed me where he kept money and said, "This is our money now. Do with it what you need to do. You never have to tell me what…or why…or how much. It is yours as much as it is mine." That was another surprise. Somehow, Lucas was a modern man, respecting me as a person, not just some baggage or an appendage as many men of his generation treated their wives.

Lucas asked me if anything special happened at the Fair; was there any gossip that I had to share. He laughed when he said, "gossip". We had this discussion many times about women versus men gossiping. But, this time, I knew what he was seeking. I told him about the many people at the Fair that came up to me to congratulate me, us, upon our marriage. Lucas seemed happy. Then, I realized that I had to tell him, I couldn't lie to him by omitting what had happened with Jack. I said, "Lucas, there was more…Jack came over." I saw Lucas' face collapse. He was probably in fear of what I might say. "Lucas, I told him that I was married to you. And, that I would have a family with you and make a life with you and love you." Lucas said, "Mary, I knew that today would be difficult for you. You are wonderfully strong." He added nothing more. He understood that nothing that he could have said would have any meaning after all that I had revealed, after I had bared my soul. I raised my hand and stroked Lucas' rugged sun-dried face and said nothing more.

Saturday afternoon chores needed to be attended to. Both of us worked until I prepared dinner. I found it wonderfully comforting to be in the kitchen. As I made dinner, there were moments that Dolly came to mind. I would have thought that thinking of her, here, in her house should have bothered me. But, I didn't view her memory as a threat of any kind. In fact, it gave me a feeling of warmth. I used her special pan and her recipe to make a roast chicken and added beans and muffins for dinner.

And, over the weeks, I did tend to Dolly's clothing, packing them up to be given to charity in town. I did keep a few items that

I wanted as remembrances. I probably wouldn't wear them, but I couldn't just give them away. I came across the needlepoint that I had bought Dolly for the Christmas of 1929. I kept it. I thought that I might want to work on it someday. There was nothing else left of Dolly in the house other than wonderful memories.

    The days flowed from one to another. My life, settled into a comfortable routine. At church, the Pastor and his wife were warm and always asked how life was going for us at the farm. Their inquiries into our life weren't prying, they were more casual than sinister. Helen Clark was always warm and friendly, always giving me a slight hug and smile when we met. Jack stayed away. Some Sundays, Claudia, Jack's girlfriend, sat with his family. Sometimes, they both sat together by themselves. I thought that the best thing for Jack, and for me, would be for Jack to marry Claudia. I thought that would put an end to it.

Chapter 22

The months passed. By 1934, electrical service was coming to our farm. Lucas traveled into town to attend a meeting with the electric company and a local electrician. He found out that the electric company would take care of the line from the main road to our house and the barn. They would end their work with an electrical meter so they can charge us for the amount of electricity that we use. The farmer would be responsible for the cost to run the wires into the house. Modernization of the farm would come at a cost to us.

Lucas and I discussed what we would want. Of course, what we might have wanted may not have been exactly what we could afford. We would add lights with switches in the kitchen over the table and the sink, in the middle of each of the two bedrooms and the main room in the ceiling with a switch near to the door. We planned on having outlets installed in the same rooms, especially the kitchen, to add things that we wanted later. We would also add a line into the barn for a switched string of overhead lights and a few outlets. Then, I said to Lucas, "Should this dry spell continue, we might want a water tower and a water pump to make certain that we would have a supply of water. It would be very expensive but at least we would have water for the house and maybe enough for the vegetable garden." You see, at the time, I didn't know that what I repeatedly called a "dry spell" later would be called a "drought" and that drought would last for the rest of the decade and change the landscape and lives of the people in the Midwest.

"Lucas, I don't consider a water tower to be a luxury." Lucas hesitated, pondering what I had just said. Then, he said, "Mary, I think it is a good idea." Then, he asked, "What about the Kelvinator refrigerator and a radio?" I think that he thought that I was substituting a water tower for his desire to have a refrigerator and radio. I said, "I called them luxuries before. I still think that they are luxuries. But, I agree that they would be nice to have. Let's see if we can do it."

Since it was winter, Lucas had plenty of time to do some shopping. So, we went into town and visited with Isaac Tanner. Lucas asked him if he knew anything about refrigerators and radios. He smiled. "Of course, I do. Let me take out my catalogs." He reached underneath his front counter. He had a stack of them. The first catalog that he took out was from Sears, Roebuck & Company. I had looked through that catalog with customers many times when I worked for Isaac. I knew that it was filled with so many wonderful things that we would want but couldn't afford. But, as he pulled out the catalog from beneath the counter, my first focus was on the beautiful cover. It was as if I had never seen that cover before. But, you see, the cover had something else that I wanted very badly, but didn't have so far. The catalog cover had the picture of a wonderfully beautiful girl of about three years. She had blond hair and dark eyes. Looking at the picture, I thought that if I had a daughter, she probably wouldn't have blond hair if she were to look anything like me. But, maybe, Lucas' Scot-Irish heritage would give her colorful hair. I thought of a "her" as if there was a baby, or as if I was pregnant. There wasn't...I wasn't. I wished that I were.

I snapped out of my dream. Isaac opened the catalog to the pages that described refrigerators. Lucas had his heart set on a Kelvinator but once I saw the advertisement for the General Electric refrigerator, I was in awe. It had a separate freezer compartment to make ice. The box was made of something called stainless steel which the ad said will not rust. I knew about rust. It said that it was quiet and uses less "current". I asked Lucas what is "current". He shook his head. Isaac said, "It means that it will take less electricity and cost less to use." I hadn't even thought about the cost for electricity. Lucas looked at me and said to Isaac, "We'll buy one. Can you get it for us at a good price?" Isaac turned to me and said, "For your Mary, I will sell it to you for what it cost me." I thought that was very generous. But, nothing surprised me when it came to Isaac. Lucas thanked him. Isaac told us that it would take as much as six weeks for it to come in. We both laughed. We told him that we hadn't had one for all of these years and that six weeks more shouldn't be a problem. After all, we didn't have the electrical service to our house yet.

Then, we looked at radios. Getting a radio would be a luxury, for sure. But, it was something that both of us wanted very badly. We could listen to music. We looked at several models starting with the Silvertone 7130. In the end, Isaac recommended the radio that he had recently purchased for his own home. It was an RCA Table Model 128, also called the "Magic Brain". Isaac said that it worked really well. And, that was good enough for us. I gave Isaac back the gift certificate that he had given to us at our wedding ceremony. I asked if it would be enough for a down payment. He said, "Certainly". Isaac broke out in a big smile and laughed as he always did when he was happy. He rapped Lucas on the back in a congratulatory way and said that he will let us know when they come in.

After we ordered our "luxuries", Lucas went off and spoke to some contractors. The first contractor that he spoke with had already recommended a package deal to several of the local farmers in our area. It included a 750-gallon water tower, electric water pump and piping. While he was there speaking about water towers, I walked around town looking in the windows. I didn't really need anything but I always enjoyed looking.

I met Lucas back at Isaacs. He reported back to me about what he found out about adding piping from the water tower to several spigots in the barn and in the kitchen. He told me that, "We could get away with just a windmill to pump the water up to the tower, but most of the other farmers that I spoke with are buying an electrical pump." I told him that I was impressed with all that he had learned. We agreed to go with the electric pump.

Once we got quotes for all of the construction, electrical and plumbing work and the refrigerator and radio, we went back home. Lucas and I sat at the kitchen table and added everything up. The cost for modernizing the farm was much more than I had ever thought it would be. But, I didn't think that we had a choice.

I sat with Lucas that afternoon and asked him to go over all of the farm finances with me. He did so willingly. Up to that point in time, I didn't really understand how much money it took to run the farm or what we could afford. First, he told me how much money we had in the bank. He commented that it was enough to keep us in seed for the several seasons and to cover our other expenses, but not much more. Our problem was that the recent dry years were now becoming a drain on the modest reserves that we had in the bank. We weren't any different than any of the small farmers in our area. So, as he went into detail, I thought that we needed a larger reserve of money to cover these years of little rain, of the drought that had already begun. I thought that was the key.

Lucas had taken out a loan in 1932 for the McCormick-Deering TD-40 Crawler and tilling equipment. Now, we would have to take out yet another bank loan for all of the modernization and the refrigerator and radio that we planned. With the deepening Depression, we knew that it would be even more difficult to get the money than his previous loan. But, we didn't really have a choice.

We went into town and made our case to the banker, asking for enough money to cover everything that we were planning to do and some more for that larger reserve of money in the bank that I wanted.

From the banker, I learned a great deal more about finances. It was an education of another kind. I learned all about the word, "collateral". You see, when you buy a new tractor or tiller, those are the "collateral". If you don't pay off the loan, the bankers could "call the loan" for failure to make payment. Then, we would lose the equipment, the tractor or tiller, but that would be all. But, electric lines and pipes are not much collateral except they increase the value of the farm. So, in order to get the money, the banker required us to take out a "mortgage" on our farm, our home and land. That would mean that if we didn't make payment on the mortgage, the bank could take our house, our farm. And, that frightened the heck out of me. But, Lucas said that the drought, which I had been calling a "dry spell", couldn't last forever. And, as long as we had crops to sell, we would be able to meet our obligations. He said, "Mary, don't worry. We'll be OK."

As we were finalizing the paperwork at the bank, Lucas asked me to sign the mortgage application alongside his name. I didn't understand. I looked at him. "Why do I have to sign?" He said, "Well, Mary, the farm is half yours so you will need to sign the mortgage papers along with me." Lucas reminded me of the time when he proposed to marry me. He had said that he would include me on the deed as half owner. Now, I understood. I gave him a big hug and kiss. Then, I signed the mortgage application on the line that said, co-owner;

Mary Ahyoka Awiakta Taddum

We got the money.

By March of 1934, the main electrical power line was completed on the road past our farm. Construction began on the lines from the road to the house and barn. By late April of 1934, everything was completed except the water tower and water pump.

We had the stainless steel refrigerator to hold some milk, butter, cheese and poultry. We also had that radio, our first, in our kitchen. The radio opened up a world of entertainment to us. We listened intently to the adventures of "The Lone Ranger" with his sidekick, Tonto. At least that "Indian", Tonto, was portrayed favorably as being very helpful to the Lone Ranger, a white man. We also enjoyed "The Green Hornet" and "The Shadow". We listened to music of all kinds from country to opera. At the time, I didn't know that this new world of entertainment also included talk programming. Later, that talk programming would change our lives. But, not in a good way.

When I lived in the Ambrose Boarding House, I had water when I needed it. I just turned on the spigot and out it came. I didn't think about where the water came from. It wasn't even a thought. Now, it was my business. The dry spell, which I now knew was a drought, continued without fanfare, without a whisper. I didn't appreciate, I did not understand, just how dry was dry, and how devastating the drought had become. But, here, on the farm, the impact was obvious. Here, it was a matter of success or failure. And, throughout the spring of 1934, the heavens did not produce much rain, not enough for our crop. Our winter wheat crop, which had been planted in the fall of 1933, faltered. A good yield of wheat was about 50 bushels an acre. But, without much rain, the yield could be half or less of that. That is pretty much what we were left with. The income from the crop was about half of what we expected.

The construction of the water tower, a new electric water well pump and all of the piping was completed in June. I was looking forward to that water tower for more than just having water in my kitchen, although that would be a great luxury. The watering of the vegetable garden was what was important to me so we could be sure that we would have vegetables for the next year.

Then, late in June, to add to our difficulties, there was a dust storm. It lasted for days, the likes of which even the old people around here had never seen in their lives. Certainly, I had never seen anything like it in my young life. One day, the sky turned so black from those dust clouds that you couldn't tell day from night. It reminded me of the Biblical story in the Book of Exodus where the Lord visited plagues upon the Egyptians. Maybe, there were no "boils", "hail", "locusts" or "flies" or "lice". But, there was "darkness", lots of it!

The dust storms made the news. It was reported in the newspaper and on the radio. The radio reporter said that massive amounts of our top soil, the soil that nourishes our crops and vegetables, was lost to the wind. Until I heard that, I didn't appreciate that the dust storm was actually our soil. Now, that I look back on it, I guess that it had to be someone's soil. Lucas and I talked about it at dinner. Lucas told me, "It wasn't the very first dust storm that I had heard about. There had been one the past November. But, that one didn't affect us here in Muskogee. That one reportedly affected areas south and west of here, extending from Texas in the south, to Nebraska in the west. But, Mary, you see, it isn't that dust storm that affected our wheat crop. It's the God-damned drought that did it. It is the God-damned drought that is allowing the soil to dry up and be swept up in the winds. That's why we are getting these dust storms." I don't think that I had ever heard the term "God-damned" before. I certainly hadn't heard Lucas take the Lord's name in vain. With the poor crop yields, he was angry. But, there wasn't anything that he could have done about it. I wished that there was a prayer specifically for rain that I could say. It might make me feel just a little bit better.

We listened to the news on the radio most nights while we ate dinner. A few days after the dust storm, the newsman reported that the dust from that one storm blew our topsoil all of the way to Chicago. Then, a few days later, we heard that the dust cloud had reached the eastern cities of Cleveland, New York, and Washington, D. C. Between the drought stunting our crop and the dust storms robbing us of our top soil, that terrible feeling of insecurity penetrated my consciousness, once again. Did it ever leave me? I started to feel as if all of this was somehow God's retribution for the sins that I had committed. Maybe it was because I married Lucas when I loved Jack. Maybe, it was because of all of my lies. All of these thoughts swirled around in my head and would not stop. I think that it was all of my insecurity that was driving my crazy thoughts.

One day, Lucas was reading the paper at the kitchen table. He said, "Do you believe this?" I said, "Believe what?" He said that the experts said that the dust was our own fault, that we created the whole mess by over-cultivating the great prairie lands. They said that the tall prairie grasses that were here before the white men tilled the land held the top soil in place." He stopped reading for a moment, "I just don't believe it!" Then, he read silently and said, "I just don't know." I could see his lips move but nothing was coming out of his mouth. Then, after a few minutes, he read more to me from the newspaper, "'The drought made it worse by not wetting down the topsoil.' Now, that part, I believe. You don't need to be a genius to know that one." He turned the page to where the article continued. Then, Lucas looked up and said, simplifying life as he always did, "Well, I don't know whose fault it was, or is, but I do know that without the top soil, the crops wouldn't get the nutrition they need." He looked down again, continuing to read the article. He said, "Look at this." He mumbled, "Then and then...look at this." He was pointing his finger at the page of the newspaper in front of him. "The article keeps adding other things that we did wrong to the list." I guess that I got frustrated by the newspaper story that he was reading. I said, "Lucas, if they were so darn smart to tell us, now, what we did wrong, why didn't they tell us before when we could have done something about it. It's always afterwards that people tell you what you did wrong. Why don't they all save us the inconvenience of being wrong and tell us earlier?" Lucas looked at me with a big smile on his face. Lifting and shaking the newspaper in his two hands, he started chuckling. "Mary, you always have the right way of saying things." In retrospect, I think that I was just looking for someone to blame other than ourselves.

Nothing changed. The dust storms, the drought and the Depression had become relentless. The newspapers reported that some of the snow that fell in northern New England was actually red, a result of those dust storms in the Midwest. Can you imagine? I thought to myself that those people should collect the soil that came out of the sky, with the snow, and send it back to us. We need it. I was being silly. I was becoming increasingly frustrated.

Yet, Lucas felt confident that everything would work out over time. But, his confidence belied the conditions that the Midwest suffered during those years; years of drought and dust storms, and a whole host of woes that resulted from the Depression, the forever Depression.

Of course, the biggest unknown and unknowable was, and remained, whether there would be enough rain throughout this coming year. And, if it didn't rain and rain enough, the crop that Lucas was about to plant would dry up and go the way that the dust had gone last year. Most of our wheat would end up in the east as part of a dust cloud, not in some loaf of bread on their store shelves.

Once again, life was getting in the way of my happiness.

It was the fall of 1934. I wanted to go along with Lucas the first day that he began tilling the soil for the winter wheat crop. I needed to feel useful. Also, I wanted to get a better idea of the condition of our fields after all of the dust storms. I wanted to learn and this was a good place to start.

I watched Lucas set up his McCormick-Deering TD-40 Crawler. He added the gang plow which did the actual tilling. As he was setting up to do the work, he said, "I purchased this larger tractor at the end of 1932 as wheat prices were beginning to improve. It is much more efficient than the one I had when you were here before. It made a lot of sense, then, but now we have a loan to pay off." He shook his head angrily. It wasn't that his decision back then was wrong to buy the better equipment. It was just that the loan was still there, another something that needed to be paid off.

Lucas held out his hand and helped me get up onto the bench of the Crawler. The bench was really just an oversized single seater but we were able to fit. Lucas began the work of preparing the soil. Back and forth...back and forth. He would be doing this day after day, tilling only about 25 acres each day. Truly, farming is mostly about doing the same thing tomorrow that you have done today and yesterday. There was nothing too exciting about what we were doing. But, on the other hand, if you don't do it well, you could lose your crop. The same was true for the livestock. They rely upon regularity, your regularity. That is their security.

Bang! The tiller blades uncovered a rock, no, a boulder, and a big one at that. The force was so great that the tiller on the back rose up in the air. Lucas stopped the tractor and got out to look at what had happened. "Boy! How can a boulder like that even exist in a field that had been tilled so many, many times in the past? Did it grow there?" I know that there was no answer to that silly question. It was a mystery to me how something so large could first be dug up now. But Lucas thought it through. He shook his finger into the air and said, "I guess that in the past that very boulder was lying right beneath the tiller blades and remained safely just out of reach, buried under the rich topsoil that covered our farm. But..." He stopped to think, "Yupp, I think that the soil that covered the boulder was swept up in those nasty dust clouds. So much soil had been lost that we had finally unearthed this boulder." I thought for a moment and told Lucas that he probably had the right answer.

Lucas helped me down and we examined the new uncovered part of our farm. When we got a closer look, we realized that we had only partially unearthed it. It was in the middle of the field and would always be there unless we did something about it. We had to move it. So, Lucas lassoed it with heavy chains that he always carried on the tractor, tied it off and attached it to the tail end of the tiller. Once everything was in order, he started up the tractor and tried to move the boulder. It resisted. But, after a minute of tugging back and forth, it popped out of the ground like the cork out of a Champagne bottle. Then, he drove off the field with this huge boulder dragging behind, creating a burrow as it bounced up and down. Once we were off the main field, Lucas unhooked the boulder. I took one last look at it with all of its intricacies created by Mother Nature over many millions of years. I started thinking about the history of this boulder and its having always been part of the farm long before it was the Taddum Farm. It was here forever, yet, it was just uncovered and brought to the light of day today.

Somewhat later, I felt that that boulder was another metaphor for our lives, for our future. The boulder, with all of its natural intricacies, now cut up by the tiller blades and all, was uncovered by those terrible conditions of drought and dust that we suffered during the years of the mid to late 1930s. And, in the same way, there were flaws in Lucas' character that were yet to be uncovered, revealed by these same terrible conditions that unearthed the boulder and were affecting our ability to survive on the farm.

The winter wheat that we planted that fall grew about four to five inches prior to being stunted by the cold winter weather of 1934-1935. We hoped and prayed for rain so that its growth would continue in the spring. Once again, the only thing that we could turn to was prayer.

Sometimes, winter in the farming communities can be a slow time, at least it could be a slow time for the men. So, Lucas shared the work in the barn, milking the cows, feeding the chickens and candling the eggs. But, I insisted on making all of the cheese. I felt that this was one part of the farm that was mine and mine alone. Probably more important to me, making the cheddar was a time for me to focus on something that I truly enjoyed doing. That focus relieved all of my tensions that resulted from the Depression, drought and dust. But, those conditions just never went away.

During many of those quiet winter nights of early 1935, we listened to the whistling wind and felt that wind pushing the dust into our home. The darkness, coupled with the wind, overwhelmed me. It depressed me. Every day, day after day, that dust permeated everything, covering the floor, the table and our bed. There wasn't a surface that wasn't covered with the very fine portion of the dust that fought its way through the cracks in the doorway and windows and even through the chinks in the walls. We swept it up, I washed the linens and I wiped down all of the surfaces only for it to happen all over again. If it would only snow. If it would only rain. Some rain would change everything.

The drought continued the following spring. The dust storms continued, as well. On April 14 of 1935, the dust storm lifted up the soil, the dust, just like snow in a blizzard. The winds that day help push the dust up against our barn and our house in huge piles. The radio announcer said that three million tons of top soil was lifted up, thousands of feet, into the air. I had no idea how much that was. But, it was enough that the guy on the radio called it a "black blizzard". I had always enjoyed waking up in the morning after a big snowfall, a "blizzard", looking out at the purity of the white driven snow. That was not the case with the dust, the "black blizzard". It gave snowfall and blizzards bad names.

As bad as conditions had been for us farmers that owned our land, it was even worse for the sharecroppers and other tenant farmers. It was a time of poor crop yields and wonderful new and efficient equipment in the field. It was wonderful for the landowners but not so for those sharecroppers and tenant farmers. Historically, they had lived and died on their forty acres. They had their mule to pull the plow to till the fields. For those people there was little money left during normal times after the landowners took their share. But, with the drought and the dust, there was little left even to eat, period. And, the landowners knew that they could consolidate those small farms, buy more of those large and efficient tractors and hire more tractor operators at $3.50 per day to till, seed the land and harvest the crops. Evictions increased. And, as soon as these people left the land, the landowners came by the very next day and plowed the fences right into the houses and all of it right into the dust. In just minutes, there was nothing left to show of the decades of hard work, of their homes and hearth, of raising their families and just living.

That farm consolidation increased greatly during those years. I'd seen these people leaving in droves. The first that you knew of them leaving was when they would say goodbye to the other parishioners and Pastor Berkley at church. Then, some days, on the roads nearby, the departing looked just like scurrying insects trying to get away from a mysterious threat. But, these people were not scurrying insects. They were our neighbors, folks that I knew from town, the Saturday Fair and from church. Some came to our wedding. I knew that I would never see them again.

Many of the evicted went to California. They had read newspaper stories and fliers which talked about good jobs and good wages out there. But, the more that people went to California, the lower the wages became due to the competition for the work. For some, it took a family a full day's labor to earn enough money for food. Yet, even knowing this, more and more people went out west to work the farms, fields and fruit orchards there. From what we heard and read, the people there treated the folks from hereabouts as second class citizens. The Californians wanted the Okies gone after the fruit picking season was done. The Okies, our friends and neighbors, lost their spirit. Families were breaking up. All of it, the evictions, the Depression, the drought and the dust were tearing at the very fabric of the Plains. It was beginning to tear apart the fabric of our small family, as well. The tension and fear for our future was palpable.

One day, a reporter on the radio called what we were experiencing and living in "The "Dust Bowl". I always felt that the guy who coined that name didn't really care much about what the dust storms meant to us and so many other small farmers. To him, it was just a catchy phrase. He didn't come to our farm to talk with the people that were living it. He should have picked a name that better represented all of the devastation and all of the rest. Maybe, I shouldn't be so mad at that newspaperman. The only knowledge that he had of the dust was that little bit of the cloud of our top soil that reached wherever he lived. Maybe he was in New York. I read that one of those dust clouds from the Plains actually reached the east coast, coating the Statue of Liberty. But, here, you can see it. Here, you can taste it. And, the dust resulted in children, of all ages, getting pneumonia. Many of them were dying. It was a real plague upon our people as devastating as any you would know of in the bible.

The winter wheat harvested in the spring of 1935 was another failure, again, yielding only about 35 bushels of wheat per acre. The summer crop harvested in the fall of 1935 was even worse. People all around us were losing their farms as their crops failed and they ran out of money. We were a little better off because of the extra money that we had when we took out the mortgage to modernize the farm. But, if the drought didn't end, and end soon, we were possibly going to become one of those farmers. We were struggling. I was angry at that "Dust Bowl" newspaperman. I needed to be angry at someone. I was bitter. I was fearful of becoming one of those dominos. I admit it!

Chapter 23

During those cold and dreary months of the winter of 1935 into 1936, we listened to some wonderful music broadcasts from the big cities, adventure series of all kinds and talk shows. Listening to the radio had been a blessing during those bleak months. But, some of those radio talk shows quickly became a focus of Lucas' world. Over some time, listening and watching Lucas' reaction to what was being said began to worry me. Increasingly, the radio was becoming a curse.

Lucas always listened to radio broadcasts from a Father Coughlin. In fact, we knew a lot of people in our area that listened to Father Coughlin. At first, Father Coughlin's broadcasts on the radio were about religion, about Jesus and about the resurrection and the second coming. I had learned about all of those things in school and I heard about them when Lucas and I went to church on Sundays. So, there was nothing new. But, then, the radio talk was more about things other than religion. In fact, after a while, the program had little to do with religion, Jesus, resurrection or anything else that we heard about in church. It was about politics.

Prior to listening to this show, Lucas had rarely expressed political preferences or opinions. Of course, there had been some discussion of politics when Jim Clark and his family had come over for dinner. It's not that we were against discussing politics. It was just that, honestly, we weren't knowledgeable. So, listening to talk about politics was like listening to someone speaking a foreign language. At first, we listened in the hope that we could get an education. I thought that we were learning. But, then, I began to realize that it really wasn't learning. It was just listening and repeating. You know what they say about repetition. If you say something often enough, people will start believing that you really know what you are talking about.

Coughlin was very good at what he did. He was smart. But, he was evil. I came to understand that sometimes Coughlin's political positions and the truth were coincidental. And, when he was truthful, it made him much easier to believe, even when he was lying. Many millions of people listened to him and mimicked what he said. Lucas became one of them.

As our concerns about the farm grew, Lucas was more and more vocal about the things that he heard on the radio. All of the problems on the farm were making him susceptible to the nonsense. He needed someone or something to blame for our situation and those radio shows gave him something to latch onto. And, slowly and surely he was being captured by it.

Sometimes Coughlin's dogma and our opinion were in step. Initially, it seemed that Father Coughlin supported President Roosevelt. I know that we did. I know that Lucas went and voted for him. So, we agreed with him on that. Coughlin initially seemed to like Roosevelt's New Deal. So, we thought, well, this Father Coughlin really knows what he is talking about. He even said that "the New Deal" is "Christ's Deal". For most of the people in our area, saying anything that has Christ as an advocate, made it something that we should support. Coughlin said that God was directing Roosevelt's work. Imagine that. God directing a President? I believed and still believe in God. But, how did Coughlin know? How could he know what God supported and what he didn't? I wondered who gave Coughlin the right to invoke the Lord's name and support of what he was spouting. I knew one thing, for certain. For Coughlin to presume to know what God wants or doesn't want, is just plain nonsense. I've heard someone say that "Some people are liars, they hide the truth. Others, don't know what the truth is, and if they did, they didn't know where they put it." I came to realize that was Coughlin. All of it!

As the months marched on, Coughlin began to talk against Roosevelt with the same "vim and vigor" or energy that he had previously supported him with. Given the large radio audience that he had, he could have really swayed the voters against FDR.

One day, Lucas said, "Coughlin is in favor of nationalizing major industries such as utilities, railroads and other industries. He said that these industrialists were making themselves rich while our people, the little people, like us, were hurting. Coughlin is in favor of supporting labor unions. He is against socialism and communism." I was getting sick and tired of hearing all of these things that Lucas was mimicking. First, I asked Lucas what "nationalizing" meant. He didn't have an idea. Then, my frustration spilled out. I said, "Lucas, I don't understand what he is saying. I don't think that you understand either. On one hand, Coughlin is in favor of the little people, like us. He is in favor of unions, against rich people and banks. Isn't that what the communists say? Aren't they against capitalists, people that have a lot of money? So, what's the difference? Again, Lucas didn't have an idea. Then, I thought about it a little and said, "You know why, Lucas. I'll tell you why Coughlin doesn't like the communists. First, because he, Coughlin, supports the fascists in Europe like Hitler and Mussolini and they are against the communists. But, maybe even more importantly, because the communists are atheists. They claim that they don't believe in God. And that is something that Father Coughlin cannot forgive." Lucas was dumbfounded by what I had said. I just didn't understand how he could listen to what was being said without thinking for himself. Then, I added, "Why do you even listen to that guy?"

But, truth be told, neither one of us really understood the nuances of communism, socialism, capitalism or any of the other "isms". But, that didn't change Lucas' feelings about what Coughlin preached. Whatever Coughlin said, Lucas believed in it as if it came from Jesus Christ himself. He seemed to be mesmerized by whatever that angry priest said on his radio program. And if Coughlin said it, Lucas repeated it over and over again to me and to his cronies. Lucas had become a follower, a believer, of Coughlin. In a very short span of time, Lucas was falling into a dark hole.

I was increasingly unhappy about what was happening to Lucas. He was a gentle, good and simple person. Now, he was becoming a changed man. Fear does that even to a good man. Lucas was afraid of losing his farm, a farm that was embedded in his soul. That possibility was tearing him apart. You could see it in his face which was aging from all of the stress.

Lucas listened and listened. He parroted Coughlin no matter what he said. Repeating Coughlin, Lucas said to me, "The bankers were all Jews and they were evil." I said to him, "But, the bankers in town are people just like you and me. The president of the bank where you got our loan and our new mortgage, is not Jewish. He goes to our church. He is a Methodist just like us." I didn't know the specifics of what Methodists believe regarding money and banking. I said to Lucas, "The bankers are not Jews, they're Christians." When I told him that, Lucas said, "That doesn't matter. They're all Jews in their hearts". Then, I said, "What about the Tanners and the Helds. They're Jews. Didn't Doctor Held take great and compassionate care of Dolly? Wasn't he here all of the time to help us? Didn't Isaac Tanner keep me on, working in his store, when his business was down? Didn't he sell us our new refrigerator and radio at his cost? These are people that I like!" Lucas just said, "Psft", a noise that reflected his disdain. When I heard that, I felt that it was no different from Jim Clark's prejudice against my Cherokee roots. No different! I tried a different approach with him. "Lucas, do you remember the pastor's sermons when he talked about how we must treat all other people with dignity and good will." Lucas didn't seem to be listening.

Sometimes, these farm men, like Lucas, would meet up in front of St. Mark's Farm & Feed Store and repeat the same vile trash to one another. As I said, if you repeat something often enough and loud enough, others begin to believe that you know what you are talking about. That was how bad it had become.

Occasionally, Lucas had these friends of his come over to our house for a drink. This was quite common during the winter season since there wasn't as much work to be done in the fields. They all sat around our kitchen table, drinking from the same jug of spirits and talking about these theories as if they had all gone to college. They sat around shaking their heads in unison, up and down when one of them said something that they thought they should agree with, and side to side with their face to the floor when they talked about how bad things had gotten. They all took turns being the "sage" of the moment with the others listening and believing whatever was said. But, really, they were all just parroting Coughlin's radio broadcast.

One night, I'd had enough. I didn't like what Coughlin was preaching and what Lucas and his friends were saying when they met at our house. So, I shouted at the men at our table. "Oh, my! I'm getting dizzy just listening to all of this! Do you know how disgusting that man is? Do you know that he is the devil?" I stormed out of the kitchen. Then, I just walked back around, walked back into the kitchen and said, "Most of what that priest is saying is just not true. The truth be damned! His 'truth' is just some political lie that he wants you to believe. The only time that he preaches the truth is when it suits his own agenda. But, you men just mimic what you hear, true or not. You have no idea. I don't think that you folks can separate the 'grain from the chaff'. For me, Coughlin and the others are just windbags who like to hear themselves talk. He is un-American. And, you are sounding like him, more and more, every day. He is evil. And, if you keep listening to him and repeating what he is saying, you too will become evil! And, you, Lucas, talking about our friends like that. You should be ashamed of yourself!"

Then, I walked out, again. I just didn't care what they thought about what I had said or how I had said it. I didn't care if I had embarrassed Lucas. I was angry. In fact, I found myself angry a lot of the time. It didn't take a genius to figure it out. My anger was the result of many threats to our security, our very survival here on the farm. Now, I included that windbag and his effect upon Lucas as a threat along with the dust storms and the drought and the Depression. There was certainly enough to make me angry and fearful at the same time.

Lucas continued listening to the radio. His comments about many of our friends were worrying to me. Then, Lucas told me that he, along with some of his friends, had joined a secret society. He never named it. These friends that he joined with had to be the same friends that he had over our house, all followers of Coughlin. At first, I thought that it might be good for Lucas to get out of the house given all of the strains of our situation on the farm. But, when I asked him questions about the meetings, he always said that the meetings were secret and that he was sworn to keep it that way. Well, with everything else going on, I didn't need to fight with him over this. However, with time, he went to more and more of these meetings, staying out late at night. Then, there were days and nights that he stayed out until morning. I didn't know what to think. For a while, I thought that he may have had a girl in town. But, I didn't give that serious consideration. That wasn't Lucas. That wasn't the Lucas that I thought that I knew. Anyway, with all of his friends going together, they would all have to be doing the same thing and that would have gotten out at the Saturday Fair rumor mill. I didn't hear any rumors. Yet, it troubled me greatly. I just didn't know what to do about it.

Then…then, as he was about to leave for one of those meetings, I saw him put a gun in his pocket. I was shocked. When I asked him about it, he said that I shouldn't worry. He said, "With all of the troubles in the world, it is for our protection. Don't worry." I said, "What troubles? What protection do we need?" He repeated himself, "Just don't worry. It's for our protection." I yelled at him, "What are you doing to us?!" He walked out.

I had always worried about my security, but I never meant my physical security for which a gun was required. We had rifles. We had shotguns. A handgun is used for people, only to hurt or kill people. I was even more frightened.

I didn't really know what to do but I knew that I had to do something. Between Lucas' now carrying a gun and speaking about some of our neighbors and friends…I don't know. He hated more and more. He railed about immigrants, Jews, Negroes, anyone that he could blame for our situation. The new people, the immigrants that he was railing about were coming from eastern and southern Europe. And, there were the Negroes coming from the southeast, leaving their poverty, trying to get a job. Most of these folks, white and Black alike, didn't stay in Muskogee. When they couldn't get a job here, they moved onto places like Cleveland and Detroit and Chicago. So, I just didn't understand why he would be upset about immigrants. Regardless, I was worried that he would do something stupid.

One day, after the Saturday Fair, I decided to go to the only person that I thought might have an influence on the direction that Lucas was heading. That was Pastor Berkley. So, I started to pack up my table early. As I started packing up, Jack walked over, "Mary, why are you pulling out so early." I didn't stop what I was doing, "Jack, I don't want to discuss it." He said, "Is it that you don't want to discuss it, or is it that you don't want to talk with me?" I wanted to say, go back to Claudia and go get married already. I didn't. But, I must have had a scowl on my face based upon his reaction. "Jack, please, please, just leave me alone." He sulked away. I continued packing up. OK, ok, maybe I shouldn't have reacted to Jack in that way. But, I was at my wits end. Our problems, Lucas and my problems, were of our own making. It had nothing to do with Jack. He didn't deserve to be treated that way. Jack, well…that train had left the station.

When everything was secured in the truck, I walked over to the church seeking the pastor. He wasn't there but Sally Berkley was. She told me that the Pastor was at home. I didn't like the idea of going to his home without Sally being there but I needed to speak with him. I knocked on their door and asked if he could take a walk with me.

As we walked, we began discussing typical pleasantries. Then, I said, "Pastor Berkley. I have a problem." This wasn't the first time that I had said that to him. I must have sounded like a broken record. But, the pastor was always there for me. And, so, I told him about our troubles beginning with the financial issues and finishing with Lucas' change. I told him how Lucas listened and mimicked the ignorant and misleading comments of that ugly priest and all of the others. I told him how these guys bait each other into a frenzy about "immigrants" that they called "foreigners". I told him about the awful things that he said about our Jewish friends and neighbors. Finally, I told him about the secret organization with a name that I didn't know. Embarrassed as I was, I told him about the gun. The pastor was very upset. I think that he knew or had heard something about these secret organizations. But, the pastor was aghast when I told him about the gun. He was shocked that Lucas was involved in all of that. He said, "Lucas? I am so surprised…that is so upsetting. That doesn't sound like the Lucas that I know." I said, "Pastor, that is not the Lucas that I knew either. But, it is the Lucas that he has become."

We spoke for a while longer describing some of the things that Lucas had said. Then, the pastor said, "Make certain that you and Lucas come to church tomorrow. I will have something to say." I felt a sense of relief. I knew that whenever the good pastor gave a sermon that he hit the nail right on the head. I knew that his sermons have had an impact upon some of the congregants in the past. I just hoped and prayed that Lucas would listen and be one of those affected.

Sunday came and the sermon that I was hoping for was about to begin. I said a silent prayer. "Lord, please open Lucas' heart to the truth." The pastor began...

"Have any of you seen the Statue of Liberty?" No one responded. "It's probably the greatest symbol of America that there is. Does anyone know what it says on the base of the statue?" Again, no one responded. "I'm going to tell you. There is a poem on the base of the Statue of Liberty. It was written by a woman by the name of Emma Lazarus. It says, 'Give me your ...your huddled masses yearning to breathe free...Send these, the homeless, tempest-tossed to me, I lift my lamp beside the golden door!' The poem talks about welcoming people to America. That is what America is.

"We all came here from somewhere else and each group of people that came here was the target of prejudice by the group that was here before them. But, that is not what is written on the bottom of the Statue. It says, *give me your huddled masses*. It says that we should welcome them here in America. It doesn't say for us to stop them from coming here or hurt them when they are here.

"All of you...all of you...All of us, came from somewhere else." He looked in my direction. "Raise your hand if your people came from England or Ireland or Scotland". Many people, including Lucas, raised their hands. "Well, when the Irish came here, many of them landed in the city of Boston. And do you know that the people who lived there before the new immigrants came put up signs in the windows of the stores and businesses that said, 'Help Wanted; No Irish Need Apply' meaning that they would not hire any of the new immigrants that were Irish. Those were your people. Do you understand? Was that American? No, but those people thought that they were Americans and that the new Irish immigrants were not. You Irish, Scot and English of this congregation are the children and grandchildren of those very immigrants that were not welcomed. Yet, some of you look at other people that come here, now, from other places, and say that they cannot be Americans like me. How sad.

"Some immigrants came here because they were persecuted, hunted down, beaten, and raped. Many of the Irish came here because of famine in Ireland. Each group of immigrants has their own story. Your grandparents and great-grandparents were those people. Their coming here was, and is, very American. The attitude of people, like you, of not welcoming them to our community is NOT...Not American. It is not Christian. Welcome these new immigrants to your America. They are the new Americans just like your grandparents were the new Americans when they came here!" The pastor seemed angry.

There was a lot of murmuring and then, a hush fell over the congregation. I looked at Lucas to see if he had been affected by the sermon. I couldn't tell if he was. After a few more prayers, the service ended. I walked over to the pastor and thanked him in a hush of words that only he could hear.

I was so focused upon Lucas' response to Pastor Berkley's sermon that I didn't notice Jack and Claudia. But, I certainly did notice them walking toward the back door of the chapel, arm and arm. Then, I saw it. Claudia had an engagement ring on her finger. As my heart sank, I chuckled to myself. Jack probably heard my thoughts when we last spoke. I had said to myself, at the time, "...go back to Claudia and get married already." Well, I got what I wished for...didn't I? I had stared so hard at the ring that I had no choice. "Oh, my, what a beautiful, beautiful ring. Is that an engagement ring?" I knew that it was. Claudia meekly shook her head. "Best wishes, Claudia...Congratulations, Jack! That's wonderful! Do you have a date for your wedding?" They both said at the same time, "No, not yet". As I walked away, with pain in my heart, I wished them the very best of luck! Somehow, I had accomplished my goal. Who am I kidding!

As Lucas and I drove back to the farm, I asked him what he thought of Pastor Berkley's sermon. He grunted. I said, "Didn't you hear the pastor?" He ignored my question. Obviously, the sermon didn't impact Lucas in the way that I desired. My prayers had not been answered.

Before, the old Lucas would have had some favorable comments to make about the sermon as we would drive home. Then, he would ask me what I thought of it. That modern man had always asked me what I thought about things, large and small. But, this new Lucas had no interest in anything other than the venom that he heard on the radio.

It was not a good day! Not good at all. It was then that I realized one other thing. That despite all of our togetherness and my trying to create and live the relationship that Dolly had with Lucas…that I would never love him. I could never love the Lucas that he had become. And, then, there was Jack. Claudia and Jack's engagement was the 'period' at the end of a very long sentence of anguish for me. I was now living, if you could call it that, robbed of hope in a world without any color. I gave up Jack and somehow, I lost Lucas.

During the years that she was away, Aida and I wrote to each other regularly. She wrote of all of the exciting shows and museums of New York City. She wrote of Ben and his successes. She was having a great time. While she was in New York, it was easier to communicate with her because I could better control the narrative in writing than I could have face-to-face. So, I wrote to her about nothing in particular. From that distance, I was able to just ignore some of her questions. I didn't want to share some of the more difficult issues that I was confronting.

As for my other friends, Alice, Becky and Lucy, they were so very self-centered that I never had to tell them anything about myself. Their interests were confined to the next date or the new guy who moved into town or a new hat in a storefront window. They had no interest in the size of our wheat crop or the current price of a bushel of wheat or soybeans or how sales were going at the Saturday Fair. But, in this one case, I found that their lack of interest in me or Lucas or the farm was exactly what I wanted. I didn't want to have to explain to them about our failing farm or our failing marriage.

After graduation from NYU, Aida had gone back to school studying to be a nurse so that she could support Ben in his practice just like Ben's mother Grace supported her husband. It took her another two years to complete her degree in nursing. Just after Aida graduated from nursing school, and Ben had completed his residency in medicine, Ben moved to Tulsa to set up his practice and Aida came back to Muskogee.

It was a Saturday in May of 1936 when Aida found me at the Fair to tell me that she and Ben were getting married. That was inevitable, for sure. Yet, I was thrilled for her. As I was telling her how wonderful her life would be in Tulsa, working alongside Ben, she looked at me as if she could see right through to my soul. There, despite the façade that I had hidden behind, she saw my unhappiness. She pressed for a response. There was no use in hiding it, so I told her about our difficulties making ends meet on the farm. But, I didn't tell her about the meetings or the gun or my husband's newly found prejudices. That all would have been too embarrassing. I was only willing to share that with the pastor.

Aida invited me and Lucas to attend her wedding ceremony on Sunday, June 28th at 3 PM in Tulsa. I thanked her and said that I would get back to her. When I got back from the Fair, I spoke to Lucas about going to Aida and Ben's wedding. Of all things, he said that he wouldn't go because Sunday was the Lord's Day of rest. I was furious. "What about all of the work that you do here on Sundays. The cows don't take a day off from needing to be milked, ya know. I won't stop making butter and cheese." He wouldn't go. I told Lucas that I was going with or without him.

After church the next day, I spoke with Pastor Berkley. He said that he was happy for Aida and Ben. He said, "She is a good friend. Of course, you should go even if Lucas won't go with you." After church, I found Aida at her house and told her that I would be delighted to go but that Lucas would have to stay behind at the farm to take care of the chores. I lied once again. My lie seemed to have satisfied her. I didn't feel that I had a choice.

So, after church that Sunday, the 28th of June, in 1936, I drove myself to Aida's wedding in Tulsa. Aida looked absolutely beautiful in her white dress and Ben was as handsome as ever in his blue suit. I saw Isaac and Eva Tanner. I waved from a distance. I said hello to Doctor David Held and his wife Grace. I hadn't seen the doctor since the day of Dolly's funeral. Grace looked lovely. I sat in the back. I stayed in the background. I just didn't want to get into conversation with anyone.

Ben and Aida were married under a canopy which I thought was very nice. I heard their Jewish prayers in a language that I didn't understand. But, I had that same experience when I had attended a Catholic Mass. They prayed in Latin. After the ceremony, and once everyone had said their congratulations, I went up to Aida and Ben to congratulate them. Of course, Aida asked if we could get together some time to go out to dinner. I gave a response that might be described as "a maybe". Then, I said, "Aida, what language was the priest speaking?" Aida explained to me how the Old Testament was originally written in the Hebrew language and the ceremony was chanted in that language. Then, I asked her about the canopy. She told me that it represents the home that the bridegroom, Ben, would take his bride to live in. I thanked her for the explanation. I thought that was lovely.

There was a dinner arranged after the ceremony. But, I didn't feel comfortable sitting with so many people, many of whom I didn't know. I didn't want to have to tell my story. I wanted to go home. So, I begged off, saying, "Aida, it is a long drive back to Muskogee. I am not comfortable driving once it gets dark. Please forgive me, but I will be leaving now." Aida and Ben hugged me and thanked me for coming. I gave them a small gift. The ride back took over two hours.

When I got back to the farm from the wedding, Lucas was sitting on the porch. When he saw me drive up, he just sat there. We had been talking less and less as of late.

After dinner, I was in a terrible mood. I had just come back from Aida and Ben's joyous wedding, back to the farm and everything that was threatening us. I asked, "Lucas, what is happening to us, to our world? So much has changed." While I asked Lucas, the question was rhetorical. I knew the answers. I had learned my lessons well. But, Lucas thought for a moment. "I think that you already know. It's the Depression, the drought and the dust. There's nothing else. That says it all." Then, Lucas said something that made me think better of him. But, at the same time, it also tore me up inside. He said, "Ya know, Mary, in a way, it's a good thing that we didn't have any children yet. It's not that I don't want them. I do…very much. I do want children. But, some families have lost children as they have died with swollen and empty stomachs. I couldn't take it, looking at a child of mine, of ours, in that condition, no, I couldn't. It would kill me." What Lucas said depressed me even more than I was, more than I ever could be. It wasn't only what he said about children dying from hunger. It was about me not becoming pregnant yet. It affected the very core of my being as a woman.

I had to flee. So, I lit an oil lamp and walked up the hill in the dark to visit Dolly's grave and my grandfather's memorial. I needed to talk with them. I needed their guidance. I needed their love that I still felt even after all of this time. I spent some time talking with them. Sometimes, just talking to a pleasant memory helps.

When I came back down the hill, Lucas said, "I hope that Dolly and your grandparents are watching over us because we need their help. Mary, if these crops continue to disappoint, we will have to make some decisions. And, look, from all that I have heard, going to California is not a good choice for us. I ain't going there with all that I heard. That's no life. So, for right now, we have to stay here and make a go of it. We have to fight."

I knew that Lucas' optimism was based upon blind faith. And, the face of confidence that he was showing to me, was fading. He was very worried about our future. And, that worry and the prevailing drought and Dust Bowl conditions and the God-damned Depression set the table for him to listen to guys like Coughlin and others of his kind. And, the more that I heard him regurgitate that vile nonsense, the more that I realized how frightened Lucas was under that veneer of confidence. He was looking for someone to blame for our failure. I believe that it is fear and embarrassment of failure that brings so many "good people", that Lucas was, and turn them into an angry and frightened person that Lucas had become. He was different. This wasn't the Lucas that I had married. He certainly wasn't the Lucas that Dolly had fallen in love with.

The cycle of crop failure continued. And, here we were, no different from those tens of thousands of small farmers remaining on the land just one step ahead of the bankers. And, those bankers were just like locusts. One payment missed and they were knocking on your door. Some folks sold off their farms just ahead of the bankers calling in their loans for failure to make payment, just in time to avoid bankruptcy. But, by now, any buyers that were out there knew that they could just wait and get the bankrupt farms at a bank auction for a mere pittance. Many farmers just had to walk away. We were determined to avoid their fate. We were just looking to survive. But, really, all of our determination, all of our dreams and desires were going to be dashed if it didn't rain enough. That was the only salvation that would prevent our failure. We needed the wheat crop that we planted during the fall of 1936 to be good when harvested and brought to market in the spring of 1937. Maybe, I just needed to pray harder for rain and a lot of it.

But, by early in 1937, we knew that the winter wheat crop that we planted the previous fall was going to be small. You could just see areas of "bald" spots in the fields indicating where the wheat plants had dried up and withered leaving the ground bare. In addition, the market price for the wheat was about the same as it was after the stock market crash at the beginning of the Depression in 1929. Between the smallish crop and the lower pricing for the wheat, the total amount of money that would be coming in was not enough. And, once again, we would have to dip into that reserve that we had taken when we applied for the mortgage. We knew that we couldn't continue like this. It was not sustainable.

During the spring of 1937, we planted summer wheat. By that time, more and more, Lucas and I lived our separate lives. He, barely talking to me and going to these meetings. Me, finding more and more solace in the barn, by myself, making my cheese. One day, after I had completed a batch of cheddar, I went to the house and told Lucas that I was going for a walk. He asked me where I was going. I told him that I just needed to get some fresh air. I didn't know exactly where I was going or for how long that I would be gone. So, I took an oil lamp and some matches with me.

I walked, literally, for hours along the furrows where the summer wheat was sprouting. I think that I spoke to every one of them…the sprouts. I asked each of them to grow big and strong. I also prayed for rain…again. I thought that if it would just rain so that we can just get back on our feet, financially, that I would get the old Lucas back and then, I could live my life, without love, but live my life.

By the time that I got back to the house, it was dark. That's how long that I walked. When I entered the house, I found that Lucas was gone. He left me a note saying that he had gone to a meeting. He also left a wet glass and a jug of spirits alongside it. Obviously, he had been drinking by himself. I wasn't merely just disappointed, I was devastated. I didn't have any idea of what I could do to change Lucas' direction.

My talking to the wheat sprouts was to no avail. Most disappointing of all, my prayers for rain were completely ignored by my God in Heaven! I was now praying for a rainmaker. I didn't care if he was a Christian or not. Rain is all that I thought about, every day, all day long. I was panicked. Unfortunately, the summer wheat crop of 1937 grew poorly. There were some of the same bald spots that had been revealed by the preceding winter crop.

We had known for a few months that unless the harvest of that summer wheat crop of 1937 was extremely good and the bushel pricing was higher than it had been, we would be draining our reserve, running out of our money to make loan and mortgage payments that following winter, by early in 1938. Neither rain nor the increase that we needed in pricing came to pass.

We had choices. None of them were good! We could continue and make payments until we were bankrupt. But, if we did that, we would be homeless and on a breadline somewhere.

We could try to sell the farm for more than we owed to the bank. Well, that would be good if you can find a buyer. But, by 1937, the economy had taken yet another downturn within that depression of downturns. There were few buyers. The final choice was to just abandon the farm. If we defaulted on our mortgage loan, the bank would take over the farm anyway. So, we decided to take the money from the summer crop harvest in late September, combine that with the little cash reserve that was left and immediately stop all loan and mortgage payments. Then, with the money in hand, we would have to go somewhere else to get a fresh start. We prepared to walk away from the farm that had been in Lucas' family for more than seventy-five years.

We debated, again, whether we should follow the mass migration of "Okies" to California. Unfortunately, we heard that things for our people out west were only getting worse. Since Lucas was very skilled with his hands, with mechanical things, we decided to go north to the big industrial cities where he hoped he would be able to get a job in a factory as a mechanic. We were looking for a means to survive…any means to survive.

We loaded up the truck with all of our belongings. I also loaded up the truck with as much cheddar as I could, filling the spaces between our few pieces of furniture and bags. I just couldn't leave it in the root cellar. I figured that I could sell it wherever we landed. I took one more trip up the hill to say goodbye to Dolly and to my grandfather. I stood there, crying and apologizing to Dolly for leaving her, for leaving the farm, her farm. From Dolly, in my mind, I heard the same refrain, "…your decision, your consequences." I said, "Yes, Dolly, I know that you are right." From my grandfather, I heard, "Don't ever forget who you are. You are a woman of the Cherokee Nation as well as the white people. You are ever more than what was created. You are greater than either. You are the totality of everything that you have said...of everything that you have done. That is who you are. That is the reflection of your life that will live on forever." I wasn't sure whether it was my grandfather's wisdom that I was hearing or the good Pastor Berkley or a combination of both. I walked down the hill. My sadness was as deep as the ocean.

We drove off, heading north and east toward Detroit. We were just like all of those sharecroppers, tenants and other small farmers that had already fled Oklahoma. We looked like one of those scurrying insects running away from some threat. We were one of those dominos that had been knocked over. Maybe, the only difference was that we had some money in our pockets from the recent crop and the reserves that we had left.

It was October of 1937 when we left. Seven days later, we arrived in Detroit.

Chapter 24

It was mid-September of 1939. I thought of the city as a sort of refuge where I wouldn't have to talk to or be with anyone. But, I didn't want to stay in Detroit any longer. There were too many bad memories there that just wouldn't go away. It was time to leave but I didn't know where to go. I didn't know of other cities or towns. Anyway, they would probably be just like Detroit. I would just be alone in a city filled with people. In the end, I couldn't think about anywhere to go other than back to Muskogee. I knew that it would be difficult. But, I wanted to go home. So, I quit my job, packed up my few things and drove back. I abandoned the furniture that we had taken with us. I just walked away from it. Seven days later, I crossed the Arkansas River and headed into Muskogee. It was about two years since we had left.

Frankly, I didn't know what to expect. I hadn't communicated with Aida or Becky or Alice or Lucy in all of the time that I was gone. I wondered, who was still there that I knew? What questions would they have for me? Well, I already knew the answer to that. I would ask those same questions. But, would they accept me back?

As I drove down Gibson and past St. Mark's Feed and Farm barn, there was a throng of men standing in front. I wondered whether Lucas' friends were among them. Then, I couldn't help but wonder whether Jack or Harry were one of those men standing there. I slowed down and looked and looked. There was no Jack. There was no Harry. Maybe, there was never a Jack. Maybe, Jack was really the mirage that I thought that he was. If he were real, then, for certain, he would be married by now to Claudia Dunellen, with at least one child, and maybe another on the way.

I parked near the Ambrose Boarding House. The single bag that I had with me contained the same clothing that I had left with, all of my worldly possessions. I had Dolly's jewelry and the brooch that Jack had given to me almost ten years ago. I took a deep breath. Ten years…

I knew that this would be only the first confrontation for me that would be so uncomfortable. I raised my head up straight to the heavens and went through the front door as if I had never left. I almost walked right into Mrs. Ambrose. She said, "Oh, my God. If it isn't Mary Taddum…Hello, Mary. How are you? How long has it been? Are you here for a visit? How is Lucas?" All too many questions from a person that I didn't want to share but only the smallest amount of information. That's what I did. I shook her hand and said with as big a smile on my face that I could muster, "It is good to see you, Mrs. Ambrose. Yes, everything is good. I'm here for a visit. Do you have any rooms available?" I had hoped that would suffice. She told me that she had a nice front facing room that she could let me have… She stopped herself and said, "How long would you be staying?" From the look on her face, I knew that she was beginning the probe. I had to be prepared for everyone doing the same thing. I told her that, "I would like to rent a room for a month, to be sure, but I don't know how long I would be staying." OK, I hoped that would work. She said, "OK, do you want breakfast as you did when you were here before?" I agreed to the room and breakfast, but no dinner. She said, "That room plus breakfast is thirty-five dollars for the month. It's a little more than you paid when you were here last time but it is a nicer room." I agreed. "I'm not sure how long I will be staying but I will pay you for a month in advance." I took thirty-five dollars out of my purse and handed it over to her. She thanked me and walked me up the stairs to the room. The room was much larger than the room that I had years earlier. Mrs. Ambrose said, "It is good to see you." She handed me the key and left me to be alone. That was nothing new. I had been alone for a long time.

    I put away my clothing and sat on the bed questioning myself why I came back to Muskogee when I knew that these questions would be asked, and asked, again and again, by people that I knew and people that I didn't want to know. Everyone wants to gossip about a juicy story. And, everyone wants to be a source, someone who spoke to the person. And, that person would be me. The answers would be difficult. But, I said to myself, "Here you are. No use in second guessing yourself." Anyway, I heard Dolly's voice in my head, "If you do not remember anything else that I have told you, remember this...the life choices that you make are yours to make. And, the consequences of your decisions are yours to endure. Your choices...your consequences." It is a life lesson that I had to learn, over and over and over, again. But, life really is that simple. I wished that Dolly was still here for me to rest my head on her shoulder.

I realized that I had to stop feeling sorry for myself. I had to pick myself up and get out of this room. So, I decided to take a walk over to the General Store. I figured that I would get a good reception from Isaac. I always got a good reception from him. He was a great guy. As I walked toward his store, I thought back to when I worked with him. I remembered how he liked to hum tunes when he was in the store, especially in the morning when he was stocking the shelves or straightening up. At first, I found it annoying because I couldn't figure out what he was humming. But, after a while, I stopped trying to figure it out. I never asked him. If I did, he might have stopped and I didn't want that. I knew that it was just the way that he was. And, I didn't want him to change. I liked him just the way that he was. I couldn't figure out why I did. I guess that there are some people that you just like, period.

When I was near the General Store, I hesitated, knowing that I would have to tell everyone eventually and this might be the place that I would start. I was nervous. I started walking again. I saw Isaac as soon as I entered the store. His eyes lit up upon recognizing me. He came toward me with a smile and open arms. He almost yelled, "Hello, Mary...my word, how long has it been since we've seen you?" I moved into his arms and gave him a big hug. Then, I lost control. He just let me cry myself out. Isaac was always so understanding. After some moments, I pulled away. He offered me a handkerchief to wipe my eyes. I accepted it and then, I looked down at the handkerchief in my hand. "I got this one really dirty." I chuckled. "I will have to wash it out before I return it to you." He grabbed the handkerchief out of my hand and motioned, flipping his hand up and down, indicating that I shouldn't worry about it. We stood apart. He looked at me with that fatherly look that meant that he wanted to comfort me. I made it easy for him. I said, "Isaac, it is so good to see you. Look, Isaac...there is so much to say, and to tell everyone, but I need to have some time first. I am not prepared to tell anyone what has happened over the last two years. So, please let me just enjoy seeing you." He replied, "OK, Mary, OK. I am here for you. Let me know how I can help you." He "opened the door". I asked, "Isaac, I just walked in out of nowhere and I know that this is very rude of me, but, I have to ask. Can you give me my old job back?" Isaac broke out in a smile and raised his right index finger into the air as he crossed his other arm and hand below his elbow. "Ahhhh...Yes, Mary, I said I would help and I will. When can you start?" "Oh, Isaac, you are so very sweet and dear to me. You always were." He said, "I have to be honest, Eva has other things that she would rather do. She would rather not be here." I didn't question what she would rather do. I wrapped my arms around him once again and said, "Thank you Isaac. You are wonderful!" We agreed that I would start the following Monday.

"Now, Isaac, tell me all about Aida and Ben." Isaac shook his head up and down. "OK, let's see, where can I start? Just before you left...when was that? Well, forget about my question. Stop me if you already know what I am about to tell you. I saw you at the wedding...right? So you know that they are married. Ben set up his practice in Tulsa. Aida has been his nurse in charge of the office and everything. He has been very successful. But, then...no." He hesitated. "I can't say anymore. I need Aida to tell you the rest. You need to speak to her. I'll get her on the phone." I took a deep breath. "Isaac, please, I don't know if I'm ready to see her". He said, "Mary, whatever happened, whatever you did or didn't do, Aida will be your friend. She will not judge you. You should see her." I agreed. Isaac got Aida on the phone. After some words that they shared, she told Isaac that she would be in Muskogee next week. She said that she would come to the store on Monday. Isaac handed me the phone. I said, "Hello Aida." She returned the greeting. I wanted to nip this in the bud, so I said, "Aida, there is so much to discuss. But, I am not prepared to talk about it...now. Please." Aida said that she understood and that she looked forward to seeing me next week. I returned the phone to Isaac. He hung up and stood there just smiling at me. I told him that I would be back on Monday.

I went back to the boarding house where I just sat, looking out of the window, watching life pass by on the street below. Every day and every night, I did what I had done for the many months before. I thought about how I had failed Lucas. How, I should have found a way to save him from his own fears and his embarrassment due to losing the farm. It had nothing to do with love, whether I loved Lucas or not. Lucas was a human being. He was my husband. I should have been there for him in a way that would have bent his trajectory, his path. This failure of mine would live with me every day of my entire life.

Toward evening, I walked down the street seeking a restaurant that had the fewest people. I didn't care about the quality of the food or service, I just didn't want to run into anyone that I knew. I sat down and picked up a paper from a table nearby. The last time that I had read a paper was in Detroit. The Detroit papers had talked about Lucas, page after page, picture after picture. I didn't want to read about that any more. I hadn't read a paper afterwards for all of these months. But, here, in this restaurant, I sought a newspaper so I could hide my face in it. I didn't want to be recognized.

The waiter came over and asked me if I had made a choice. I wasn't really hungry. I ordered some soup and bread. I picked up the newspaper again, and pulled it apart, leaving the front section on the table. I didn't want to read anything that was serious, talking about stores closing or the drought continuing or the damned Depression. I'd had enough negative news. I was already sad enough. I was more interested in local news. It was good to read the back section of the paper to catch up on the local gossip; about babies being born, weddings and happy events like that. I read on further, turning the pages, reading the "advice" columns and I tried my hand at the crossword puzzle. By the time that my soup and bread came, I had mastered the crossword puzzle. I put down the paper and sopped up the soup in the bread. It was good.

The waiter came over after I had finished and asked if I wanted a cup of coffee. I was comfortable and said, "Yes. Please." While waiting for the coffee, despite my feelings about negative news, I picked up the front section of the paper. It was shocking. But, it wasn't the news that I had dreaded or expected. The front section of the paper had nothing to do with Lucas or secret organizations. That news had probably never reached Muskogee. Anyway, that was a long time ago.

The pages of the front section of the Muskogee newspaper were filled with talk of war in Europe. Poland had just been overrun by the Germans, yet again. The Poles suffered the same fate in the Great War. The newspaper said that the British were going to defend the Poles. I said to myself, "...and it begins, again, just like at the beginning of the Great War in 1914. One country is invaded, another country comes to its aid, and then, everyone takes sides. Now, all of Europe is taking sides, preparing for the war to come."

I began to wonder if this war in Europe, like the Great War, would take our sons, as well. I got my answer, an answer that I didn't want. Because, once I turned to page two of the paper, I saw the answer to the question that I had asked myself. The United States Army was seeking new enlistees to expand the size of the army by 40%. They would only do that if the president thought that we too might eventually be at war. God Help Us! I said a silent prayer for the people of Europe. Then, I said the same prayer for the sons of our country.

I thumbed through the rest of the front section. On page four, there was an article about how there was now increased demand for wheat and soybeans coming from Europe because of the sabre rattling. The result was an increase in pricing for a bushel of wheat. I thought to myself, "God. Why couldn't that have happened three years ago? Why has my entire life been damned by my fate, a fate that was controlled by forces well beyond my own control?"

After I drained the cup of coffee, I went back to the boarding house and hid away there for several days, only going out to dinner at the same restaurant, eating the same soup and bread and yet another cup of coffee. And now, each night, I focused on the first section, the front page of the newspaper, reading about all of the horrors that were the reality for the people of the land of Poland.

Saturday came. I couldn't go to the Fair. There were too many memories. There were too many people that I just couldn't talk to, couldn't face, and couldn't respond to their questions, even though their questions were fair. So, I drove out to the countryside keeping away from any of the farms that I knew for the same reason. I didn't want to accidentally meet up with anyone that I knew on the road. So, I drove in the direction of Tulsa. When I got there, I found that same Mel's Chili House that Harry had taken me to so many years earlier. I ate lunch there and then started back to Muskogee. I just needed to fill time.

I thought about going to church on Sunday but I just didn't want the looks, the stares, the questions. Sunday morning, while others were in church, I took a walk around town looking into the windows of the various shops. I had avoided everyone for days since I came back. Now, I knew that it would have to come to an end. I couldn't hide forever. So, well after church services concluded, I walked over to Pastor Berkley's house. When Sally Berkley saw me at the door, she was shocked. I asked if I could come in. Of course, both Sally and the pastor were wonderful, inviting me in and asking if I would have a cup of tea with them. Neither of them asked any questions. I knew that they wouldn't. They were just pious, sincere and loving people that wouldn't say anything to upset anyone. Now, that anyone, that person, was me. They were waiting for me to tell them my story, the story of the last two years. I knew that they would not be judgmental. Even though, I found it hard to open up. But, if I couldn't speak to these wonderfully kind people, who could I speak to?

As we were sipping our tea, finding inane things to talk about, I said, "It is very difficult for me, but I want to tell you what has happened since the last time that you saw me." And, for the first time, I was going to tell the story of the last two years of my existence. I began…

"The Taddum Farm, like so many others, was struggling for several years. We thought that we could survive because we had a reserve of money that we got when we mortgaged the farm to modernize it, electrifying and adding a water tower to fight the drought. Well, it was OK for a while. Then, the drought, the dust and the Depression overwhelmed us, year after year, reducing our crop yield, compounded by low bushel pricing. When you add them together, our income was insufficient. And, every season, we had to dip into our reserve of money.

We never thought that any of it would last so long. Then, in October of 1937, we walked away from the farm, took what money we had and left Muskogee. Lucas and I, well, we had some difficult times. There was a dark side to Lucas that was uncovered by all of his fear of failure on the farm. Pastor, if you remember, we talked about that and you delivered that wonderful sermon about treating immigrants as we would any other Americans. Do you remember, you talked about that wonderful poem on the Statue of Liberty?" The pastor shook his head. I continued, "While I couldn't tell you at the time, I felt that our marriage, along with our farm, were failing…" I stopped to catch my breath. And, then, I continued telling the pastor and his wife everything that had happened as tears rolled down my cheeks. They were shocked by what I had told them. But, they just sat there without any comment or judgment. When I was done, they asked if there was anything that they could do to help me. I said, "I don't know if anyone can help me ever again."

I thanked them for the tea and for their listening to me. I left feeling a little better, because, at least, I had told someone about my travails since we had left Muskogee. I went back to the boarding house.

A little later, I wandered down the street to the same restaurant, eating the same thing that I had every night since I came back. While at dinner, I thought about beginning to work at Isaac's the next morning and how I would respond to the questions from people that wouldn't be as kind as Isaac and Aida or the pastor and his wife. My heart began to race. I needed distraction so I settled in, reading the "funnies" in the back of the Sunday newspaper. That made me laugh through it all.

I arrived at Isaac's on Monday morning a few minutes before 08:00. I certainly didn't want to be late on my first day. Isaac was there, outside of the store to greet me. I didn't know when Aida would arrive, but, I was more nervous to see her than I was to deal with the customers. I walked around the store waiting for my first customer. It surprised me to see the same goods in the same places as when I had worked there years before. Nothing had changed. A few customers wandered in. I took care of them. Thankfully, none of them looked familiar to me.

Then, Aida came into the store. She was pushing a baby carriage. I couldn't believe it. Aida is a mother. Aida saw me and grabbed me around. She said, "Good God, Mary, it's so good to see you. It's been so long. We all missed you. Where have you been? What has happened?" I was still flabbergasted by what I saw in front of me. Also, I was trying to deflect Aida's questions. I said, "Oh, my, Aida...you're a mother! When did that happen?" She was all smiles, "Well, after we got married, Ben set up his practice in Tulsa. I was his nurse and assistant. That was June of 1936. Wasn't the last time that I saw you...at our wedding?" I shook my head. Aida continued, "Then, in September 1937, we had Julie. I wanted to tell you. But, I was in Tulsa and you didn't have a phone at the farm. My father said that he rarely saw you in town. When did you leave?" "Oh, Aida, she is so cute. Where did she get that beautiful head of hair and those huge eyes?" I bent down to get a better look at the two year old. "Aida, she is absolutely beautiful. Who does she look like?" That's when Isaac chimed in. "Now, you know what other things that my wife Eva has to do other than working here. She just can't get enough of watching after Julie."

But, Aida was persistent, "What about Lucas? What happened to you? Why did you abandon the farm? Where did you go? What happened?" I said, "Aida, I am not ready to talk about Lucas or the farm or anything else that happened to me over the last two years. Please, for now, let's talk more about you. Aida looked exasperated. Really, she had every right to ask those questions. I would have. But, I just didn't have the strength to explain everything to her, not yet. I said, "Aida, please, be my friend and let it go." Aida shook her head in agreement. She asked, "OK, I understand. What can I do for you? Do you need any money?" I laughed. "No, I have a job…here…didn't you know?" She looked embarrassed, "OK, Miss Smarty Pants." She always called me that. I gave young Julie a kiss on the head. I said, "Aida, let me get settled. I need some time." We talked more about the old days. Aida was careful in her comments. She asked if we could go to lunch. I said that I would love to renew our friendship but I wasn't quite ready. I told her, "I will call you and we will get together. I want to see more of that gorgeous child of yours." We parted with a hug.

The rest of the day was good. Well, maybe not good, but better. It felt good to be back at Isaac's. He was literally falling all over himself doing everything that he could to make me comfortable. He kept asking me if I was alright. After a few more checks that he made, I told him that I was really okay and that he shouldn't worry. It was true. I certainly felt better working, interacting with the customers. It was always a joy for me whether it was at the Fair back in those days or here at Isaacs after Dolly passed away.

After work, I walked back to the boarding house. Mrs. Ambrose was there to greet me at the door. From the look on her face, I thought that her greeting was the preamble to pump me for gossip. She might have heard that I was working at the General Store. She might have thought that was inconsistent with just a visit. She would be right! But, I was prepared to deflect any questions that she might ask without being rude.

Supper was the same. The sleepless night was the same. The only thing that was good was working at Isaacs. He kept watching over me like a mother hen, humming away all the while. I didn't mind. I actually found it comforting because it was a part of Isaac.

I was working at Isaac's on that Wednesday when I felt his warmth. I always did. Then, from behind me, he said, "Do you have any suspenders?" I turned to see Jack, more handsome than ever. He wasn't more than two feet away from me. I said, "Let's go over there to the suspenders and see if there is anything that you might like." They were exactly where they were so many years ago when I bought him that Christmas present in 1929. When we got there, he said, "Aida told me that you were back. She also told me that I shouldn't ask you about Lucas or what has happened to you. I won't ask. Maybe, you'll tell me when you are ready." I thanked him...I knew that this meeting would come to pass. But, even with that anticipation, that preparation, I didn't know what to say to him. I was nervous. I wanted to hug him and cry on his shoulder. But, I maintained my dignity by just playing out the meeting.

    I had always disliked when people said something just to fill that nervous void of silence. Now, it was my turn to do the same, "We have a good selection of suspenders here. Have you looked recently?" "No, I haven't. Please, show them to me." I did. As he was trying them on, I still felt the need to talk. "Jack, how is Helen? I didn't ask about his father. He said, "My mom is good now. But, it has taken some time. It's only been about four months." "Jack, was she ill?" "Noooo...she's alright. Mary, didn't Aida or Isaac tell you?" "Jack, tell me what? What happened?" "Mary, my father died earlier this year. "Oh, Jack, I'm sorry. What happened?" "He had a heart attack out in the fields, tilling for the summer wheat crop. By the time anyone realized that he was out there, alone, it was too late. Doctor Held came out right away. But, there was nothing that could be done." "Jack, I'm so sorry for your loss. I really am. But, there's no secret that your father didn't like me. And, I guess that jaded me towards him, as well. But, I understand loss." I shook my head and looked down. "Believe me, Jack, I understand loss! It seems that my life has been touched by one loss after another." I realized that I had focused upon myself. I was feeling sorry for myself. So, I repeated, "I'm sorry, Jack." He looked at me and said, "I know, Mary. I know. Look, my relationship with my father had been like a roller coaster. I think that you know that. I both loved him and I hated him at the same time. I hated him for his prejudices. I hated him for what he did to us, to you. But, he was my father and I loved him." I shook my head in a knowing manner eager to let this discussion end. I certainly didn't want to go back into history and discuss all of that ugliness.

Trying to change the direction of our conversation, I said, "You know, sir, I spent a lot of time showing you our fine selection of suspenders. You had better buy a pair or I might just get fired." Jack knew that I was kidding with him. But, he said, "Mary, I know the exact pair that I want." Jack picked up a pair of suspenders and said that he would buy them. And, with that, he said, "Mary, there have been a lot of things that have not been said here today. The only thing that I do ask is that if there is anything that I can do for you, please don't hesitate to ask me. I mean that, Mary, don't hesitate. You have a lot of friends in Muskogee." Jack paid for the suspenders. As he was leaving, he asked if I would like to visit with his mother Helen. I should have thought of that. I had always liked Helen. Dolly loved her as a friend and sister. And, now, she was now a widow, just like me. "Jack, I would like to pay her a condolence call. Soon, but not today." I shook Jack's hand as he left the store with his package tucked under his arm. I didn't know what to make of the meeting. All I knew is that I had never stopped loving that man. But, it could never be more than that.

  I decided to go to the next Saturday Fair. Having seen Isaac, Aida and Jack, I was prepared to "be seen". I roamed around. I was greeted by some of the women that I knew. For any of those that asked anything about my whereabouts, I just told them that I had moved away but had come back for a visit. That seemed to satisfy them. But, there were looks from near and far. Most of those people weren't my friends but knew who I was. I guess that there were rumors in town about why I had come back, why I had taken a room in Mrs. Ambrose's Boarding House for a month and now, why I was working at Tanner's General Store. I was just going to have to accept the looks and the rumors.

  There was a lady behind the very table which I had always set up when we had lived here. I thought that she now owned the Taddum Farm. It made sense that the table would be taken over by the new owners. Of course, then, there was Jack where he had always been on Saturday mornings. When he saw me, he smiled and said, "Good morning, Mary. It's good to see you back at the Fair." We made some small talk with me asking what he had for sale. I knew. But, I just wanted to talk with him. Jack said,

"Well, I have the usual items for sale but I don't have any of that famous cheddar cheese that you had sold here." I smiled at him. Then, he said, "Mary, I told my mother that you were back in Muskogee. When I did, her face lit up. Ya know, my mom would love to see you. When can you come out to our farm?" He had asked me about meeting Helen, before, when we met at Isaac's. But, I wasn't ready and we didn't plan it out at the time. Now, I said, "Of course. I would love to see Helen." Jack said, "Are you busy this afternoon?" And, with that, I agreed to come out to the Clark Farm that afternoon at about 2 PM. Jack mused, "Hey, I just realized. I don't think that you have ever been to the farm." He was right. Jack had always come to the Taddum Farm to work or to bring and pick up Helen or me. I told Jack that he was correct. With that, he gave me instructions. We parted. I literally couldn't take seeing him and not being able to hold him, to kiss him. But, that was no longer possible with him being married to Claudia.

After a short time, I left the Fair and went back to my room at the boarding house. I put on one of the dresses that Lucas had bought for me when I first arrived at the Taddum Farm. I added Dolly's necklace that Lucas had given her for that Christmas, almost ten years before, and a little lipstick. I didn't put on the cameo that Jack had given me. I didn't think that it was appropriate. But, I did put it into my pocket.

I was ready to see Helen. The drive wasn't long, but was filled with apprehension. Once I got near to the former Taddum Farm, it was only a few turns more to get to the Clark Farm nearby. I knew the way well enough. Driving by my old farm was painful…so many memories, good and bad.

I expected that there would be a tension between Helen and me over Jim Clark's death. I hoped that we could get past that quickly. Also, I didn't want to see Claudia. That would just hurt too much. There it is. I saw their home from a distance. The Clark Farm was much larger than the Taddum Farm. The Clark home was much, much larger than what Lucas and I had on our farm. As I pulled up, Jack and his mother were standing out front to greet me. Helen waved at me. Jack stood by her side. Thankfully, Claudia was not there. She was probably inside not wanting to be part of this meeting between her husband and the girl that he had loved. I wouldn't blame her.

I parked near to Jack's truck, took a deep breath, put a smile on my face and walked over to Helen. I extended my hand. Helen took my hand and then released it as she opened up both of her arms as in an offering. I accepted and hugged her as she hugged me. We both shed tears without saying a word. Jack stood by with a smile on his face enjoying the good feelings that Helen and I had for each other.

I offered my sympathy for Jim's passing and asked her how she was doing. We spent a few minutes talking about her loss. I listened. Sometimes, that is the very best. Just listen. Then, Helen said, "Mary, I know all of the pain that Jim caused you in life. But, he was my husband. I had to be by his side." There was no reason to go over all of that once again. So, I smiled and responded, "Helen, I know well the role of a wife who has to stand by her husband." I left it at that for the time being.

When we were through that difficult discussion, Helen asked if I would like some tea and a piece of cake. I accepted. The three of us sat at Helen's kitchen table. By that point, it was obvious that Helen had been prepared by Jack to avoid asking me any prying questions. So, we talked about Dolly. It was a common subject that we all could enjoy. I pointed to the necklace that I was wearing. I told Helen that this was Dolly's. Helen picked up the necklace off of my neck and looked at it. She said, "Yes, I remember that necklace well. Dolly always felt that she was too plain to wear such a beautiful thing. That was so far from the truth." I said, "Yes, she was a wonderful woman, a woman that I loved. I always said that she was the mother to me that I never had. I wish that Dolly were still here for me to rest on her shoulder. She would soothe me even when she was in pain. She was selfless."

Then, Jack asked, "Mary...would you like to visit Dolly's grave and your grandfather's memorial?" I had abandoned both when Lucas and I left the farm. I hadn't thought that it was possible to go to the grave since someone else now owned the

Taddum Farm. "Jack, do you know the people that bought the Farm? Can you ask them if it is okay to visit?" He hesitated, looking toward Helen, and said, "Yes, I will speak with the people when we get there. It won't be a problem. Let me drive you there." I didn't understand the looks that were shared between Helen and Jack. I believed there had to have been some conversation between them about my sensitivity to going back to the Taddum Farm that we had abandoned and lost.

My emotions were conflicted as I got into Jack's truck. It was less than five minutes back to the house that I had lived in for many years, first as an employee and then as wife and owner. When we got there, someone walked out of the house…"my house". Jack walked over to him and they talked for a few minutes in whispers. I couldn't hear them but I assumed that Jack was getting permission for us to pay our respects to the grave and memorial. I stayed by the truck.

For me to speak with the new owners of the farm would have been devastating. I didn't want to meet them or know their name…nothing about them. And, I didn't want them to know me. Just seeing someone come out of "my house" was hurtful.

Jack came back to the truck and said, "Everything is OK. No problem. Let's walk up the hill." All of a sudden, a chill ran through me. What can I say to Dolly? How can I be a proud daughter of my grandfather after the way that I had screwed up my life? I said, "Jack, I can't go up there. I can't!! I'm embarrassed. I can't face them!! I can't face Dolly. Please, take me back to my truck. I don't. No…I can't go up there." Jack looked into my eyes. He said, "Mary, please, take my hand. Let's walk up there together and tell each other everything that stands between us." He repeated himself, "We will do it together." I took Jack's hand and walked together with him. Then, he released my hand and grabbed me around my shoulder, squeezing me, holding me tight next to him. I said, "Jack, you shouldn't." He said, "Shouldn't what?" "You shouldn't hold me around that closely. You're married." I realized at that moment that I didn't really know anything about Jack's marriage to Claudia. I didn't want to know. The last that I knew, he had given her a very nice engagement ring.

Then, I looked down at Jack's left hand. There was no wedding band. At that moment, Jack said, "It's true, Claudia and I were engaged for quite a while. But, no matter how much I tried, she saw right through me. She knew that I was in love with someone else. Oh, Claudia and I are still friends. But, I couldn't marry her. It would have been wrong. It wouldn't have been fair to her." I didn't know what to think. I didn't know how to react. We continued walking up the hill. My head was filled with wild imagining. Jack stopped, turned to me and said, "Claudia knew that I wasn't ready to give up on you, even though you were married to Lucas." I looked into his eyes. "How could you love me after all of the lies and deception, after I had hurt you so much?! I tried my best to get you to hate me!" Jack's stare penetrated my heart. He said, "Mary, I know why you did it. You told me right after you married Lucas. And, my mom told me what Dolly had told her. Mary, I loved you then, and I still love you now. I've never stopped loving you." "Jack, I always loved you. That has never changed. You knew it from my eyes. It's just that life has a habit of getting in our way. You know what I mean." We moved toward each other and kissed. I didn't want that moment to end. Now, I knew why I had traveled back to Muskogee; why I had subjected myself to people's looks and their rumors.

Jack grabbed my hand once again and we completed the journey to the top of the hill, under the oak tree. We reached the oak tree and were in front of the two headstones that Jack had hand carved so many years before. Once we got in front of Dolly's grave, I grabbed Jack's other hand and faced him. I told Dolly and Jack the story of the years that I was away.

"Jack, I'm ready to tell you everything." He just stared into my eyes.

"When we modernized the farm, added the water tower, the refrigerator and the radio, we took out a mortgage on our home and farm. At the time that we took the mortgage, we didn't think that the drought would continue forever as it has. But, we also thought that it would be better to have more of a reserve if the drought did continue. So, we took more money from the bank than what we needed to cover the improvements to the farm and the refrigerator and radio. Of course, it made the monthly mortgage payments larger. But, it was the right thing to do." Jack stood as still as a statue not wanting to interrupt and do anything to end the moment.

"By the early fall of 1937, the summer wheat crop was disappointing as was the selling price. The income from the crop was paltry. That followed two or more years of the same. With the drought, the dust and the Depression continuing, Lucas and I didn't see much hope for a better winter crop yield. We knew that the future wholesale prices for both wheat and soy the next year, in 1938, were projected to be even lower than in 1937.

"With our mortgage on top of the other loan that we had, and all of our other expenses, we were in a pinch. It was a perfect storm. Lucas and I had talked about our various options. We knew that if we kept on making payments against our mortgage and loan, repeating the same thing with that winter crop, we would be bankrupt. We had to learn from some other small farm owners who had gone down that path. How many people in the Midwest did that happen to?" It was a question without a meaningful answer. "We had to make a decision. The answer was really clear to us. We figured that we would be better off if we stopped paying the mortgage and loan and just abandoned the farm with some money in our pockets after the summer wheat crop was harvested. It was better than ending up on a bread line with no place to live.

"We took the money from selling our summer crop and what was left of our reserve just to live on after we left. So, as hard as it was, we abandoned the farm with the money that we had. I'm not proud of what we did. But, at the time, it was the best decision that we could have made." Jack said, "Mary, I didn't know that you and Lucas were at that point. I wish I would have known. I could have..." I shook my head and said, "No, you couldn't have. There's more."

I said to Jack, "I still don't understand why Lucas and I failed when others survived?" Jack was ready for this question. "Mary, I don't know about others, but the Clark Farm also took out a mortgage to pay for the modernization of our farm. We did exactly the same as you. But, the reason that we could afford to make the mortgage payments is just that the Clark Farm was more than four times the size of the Taddum Farm. We were bigger and made more money even though it wasn't what we had hoped for." It seemed so simple. I just shook my head in self-disgust. I looked down toward Dolly's grave. "Dolly, I'm sorry. I should have done better. I should have helped Lucas. Somehow. We would still own the farm, your farm. If I did better, we would own the ground that you are buried in. Dolly, I'm so sorry!" Jack grabbed me around until I settled down. Then, he released me, still holding hands, so I could continue telling him what happened.

I took an uneven deep breath. "So, we packed up the truck with our bedding and some furniture. You're going to laugh. We even filled every nook and cranny in the truck with wheels of my cheddar." We laughed. "Then, we drove northeast to Detroit. It took us seven days. We stopped at every rest stop along the way and sold the cheddar. It gave us a little more money. I have to admit that I kept a little cheddar for ourselves. After all, I really liked my cheddar. I thought, at least, we wouldn't starve.

"You would have thought that we would go to California like so many others. But, we read in the newspapers just how the 'Oakies' were treated in California. We didn't want that. Also, Lucas was very skilled with his hands. He had a great talent with machinery. So, he thought that he could get a good job in one of the many factories in the Detroit or Cleveland area.

"When we got to Detroit, we rented an apartment. Fortunately, Lucas got a job in just a few days. He worked at a shop that made parts for automobiles. A few weeks later, I got a job at a downtown dress shop. The shop owners were nice people. I really enjoyed working there."

"Jack, if that was all that there was, we could have lived our life in Detroit in peace. It wasn't. I told you that there was more. I don't think that you knew about how much Lucas had changed. He wasn't the same person that you knew when you worked for him. He was not as he appeared in church on Sundays." Jack stopped me, "Mary, did he hurt you?" "No, Jack, nothing like that. His change began right below us, here, on the farm."

"Let me go back to the beginning. At first, he was confident, thinking, believing that we could succeed. But, that confidence faded as the drought continued to hurt each crop of wheat or soybeans whether summer or winter. Lucas was terribly frustrated. He couldn't understand why he couldn't succeed, making a living on the farm that his parents and grandparents had lived on before him. It was embarrassing to him. And, like most men, he felt that he had failed if he couldn't provide for me. I kept telling him that we were in this together and that it wasn't his fault. Nothing that I said had any impact. He felt the failure. He lost that confidence that he always had. He was bitter and angry.

"The radio that we bought might have been the most dangerous thing that we ever owned. The damned radio opened up the world to Lucas. Yes, there were a lot of wonderful music programs and other shows like 'The Shadow". But, there were a lot of programs that twisted Lucas into knots. It opened up a world of hate, a world of prejudice, just at a time that he was most vulnerable. It allowed Lucas to find a reason for his failure here at the farm.

"Jack, have you ever heard of a Father Coughlin?" Jack said, "Yes, some priest that breathes fire, yelling about immigrants, Jews, Negroes, bankers and President Roosevelt, just to name a few. I've heard him speak a few times over the radio. No one should listen to him." I interrupted, "Well, Lucas bought into his vile nonsense, 'hook, line and sinker'. He would repeat what he heard on the radio to his friends. They would get together and repeat everything that they had heard in a volcanic chorus. They said some very terrible things about our friends here in Muskogee. It made me sick. I told him and his friends so. But, no matter what I said to Lucas, it didn't stop him from becoming a follower of Coughlin.

"I have looked back, trying to better understand what more I could have done to help him, to restore his confidence, to keep him away from the radio and from the others that also listened to that priest. I should have done more to stop him. At the very least, I should have thrown the radio on the ground and beat it with a hammer." Jack said, "Please Mary, stop berating yourself. There are limits to what you could have done." I raised my hand and said, "It was even worse, if that is even possible. What you didn't know about Lucas was that had joined a secret organization when we were here on the farm." Jack asked, "What secret organization!!!???" "I didn't know then. I never knew. At first, it was just an occasional meeting. At that time, frankly, I thought it to be a good idea for him to get out and away from the farm. I didn't object. No, I actually encouraged it. Again, I was naïve. I should have looked into it more to understand what Lucas was getting himself into. I didn't. Well, as time went on, his confidence about the farm melted into anger, anger about immigrants, even some of our friends, and all of the other things that Coughlin and people like him railed about, night after night. It wasn't logical. It didn't matter. And, as our finances got worse and worse at the farm, he grew angrier and angrier. He went to more and more meetings.

But, then, I saw it…he had a handgun. Then, I was really frightened. It was so bad for a while that I couldn't sleep. Any sleep that I had was so shallow and disturbed that it almost didn't pay to lie down. That was when I talked with Pastor Berkley. As a result, he gave a wonderful sermon about accepting immigrants that had come to America. He talked about the poem on the Statue of Liberty. You might remember the sermon." Jack shook his head. "The sermon was perfect. It was directed toward Lucas and people like him. I had hoped that the sermon would have changed Lucas' path. Unfortunately, he ignored it."

"We already owned a rifle and a shotgun at the farm. For some reason, I never worried about them." Jack said, "I have a few rifles and two shotguns of my own. We use them for wolves, foxes and coyotes." "Yes, Jack, but a handgun is not used on farms. It's used to hurt people. I didn't think that I was in danger myself. But, I was afraid that Lucas might do something to hurt someone else or commit a robbery. I mean, why else would you own a handgun on the farm.

"In Detroit, we settled into a new life. I didn't even think about secret organizations, Coughlin or the gun. Without his friends to spur him on, I thought that Lucas could get back to 'normal'. But, that wasn't the case. He began to associate with people in Detroit, who like in Muskogee, were also part of a secret organization. Jack, I don't even know whether that organization was the same as the one in Muskogee. He wouldn't talk to me about it.

"Lucas would get calls on our telephone in the evening. And then, he would leave, not coming home, sometimes, until the middle of the night or even in the morning.

"Then, I read in the Detroit newspapers where they reported about men going around and beating up immigrants. I came to the realization that Lucas might be involved in some of those terrible things. I confronted him. But, he denied it. Then, he wouldn't talk about it. Our life together, which had started out as one of mutual respect and companionship, if not love, continued to go downhill. We started to have fights about what he was doing. This went on for months. I told him that I would leave him if he didn't give up the secret organization and get rid of that handgun. He ignored my threats until one day when I started to pack my bag. Then, he knew I was serious. He swore to me that he would leave the organization. A few weeks later, I saw him getting more and more nervous. I asked him what was the matter. He told me that he had tried to leave, but they wouldn't hear of it. He told me of the threats that they made if he didn't show up at their 'meetings', including hurting me.

"I didn't want him or me to get hurt, so I backed off. We were in a trap of our own making. He continued going to the meetings. What can I say? But, we began talking about it more than we had in the past. One day, he admitted to me that he had wanted 'out' for a while. I just don't know what his reasoning was at the time. Maybe, he just didn't want to be involved in what they were doing because it was wrong. Maybe, because he didn't want to end up in jail. Maybe, he was afraid that I would leave him. I just don't know.

"Then, he began to ignore those nighttime phone calls. This went on for weeks. I thought that the calls would stop after a while. As he let the phone ring, I told him that I was proud of him. I thought that we could have a life. But, I didn't understand the danger that he, or I, were in. I had no idea who we were dealing with.

"Then, one day, Lucas didn't come home from work. He disappeared. I called the police. They didn't seem to be concerned. They told me, 'He'll show up. Don't worry.' They asked me if he had a girlfriend. Could you imagine? Lucas with a girlfriend? I called Lucas' boss and some of his co-workers. No one knew anything. However, I sensed something, in the voices of his co-workers, that told me more than their answers. I also went to several bars that Lucas liked to go to with his friends. I took a picture of Lucas that I had and passed it around. Again, no one knew anything. I called the police again and told them of my suspicion of his co-workers. I had no evidence. They didn't seem interested in my suspicions.

"Up to that point in time, I hadn't told the police about his membership in that secret organization or about his gun. I was too embarrassed. Then, I did. And, I told them that he had been trying to separate himself from the organization. Hearing that, they were more attentive. Then, finally, the police told me that there was good reason to be concerned. They suspected that Lucas was a member of either the Klu Klux Klan or the Black Legion. Both were known in Detroit. From reading the newspapers, I knew that both organizations were the type that would beat up immigrants or worse. From what the police said, I felt more and more that Lucas was involved in those horrible things that I had read about in the Detroit newspapers.

"About, two weeks later, I got a call from the police. They told me that a man matching Lucas' description was found in the woods, north of Warren, Michigan. The police told me that the man had no identification on him. But, a truck was found nearby. They tracked the license plates on the truck to Muskogee and the registration to Lucas. One smart detective put Lucas' name of Taddum together with my missing person's report."

Hysterically, I yelled at Jack, "Oh, God! Lucas had been hanged and left there to rot! They had painted the word 'traitor" across his chest! I had to go to the morgue to identify Lucas' body.

"Jack, the next day, Lucas' picture, hanging there from a tree, was all over the Detroit newspapers!! The only thing that they did right was to hide his face. The articles told how he was a member of one of those organizations that the police had talked about without naming names. But, everyone knew.

"Oh, Jack, do you know how awful that was? I was all alone."

Jack was in shock, "Oh, my God...Mary. How could you...how did you?" There was no response possible. Clearly, he didn't know what to say or think. Jack squeezed my hands even tighter if that was possible. Tears formed in his eyes.

I rubbed my forehead as if that might help me from feeling as I did. "The police interviewed me for hours. They took notes. They wanted to know what I knew about the secret organization that he belonged to. They thought that I must have known something; names, phone numbers, meeting locations, anything. I didn't blame them. I would have thought the same thing. God, I should have known more. Of course, I didn't really know anything about it since Lucas wouldn't share any of it with me. Such was the nature of these secret organizations.

The police wanted to know about the gun that Lucas had. Again, I knew that he had it in Muskogee, but that was all. They looked all around our apartment in Detroit but didn't find it."

I started crying. Jack grabbed me around with tears falling from his eyes. We stood that way for minutes. Then, I composed myself enough to continue. I placed my hand along the side of Jack's face. He stood back and just held tight to my hands.

"I arranged for Lucas' burial in a Detroit cemetery. Only a few of his friends came to the funeral. I believe that many people were frightened to show up with the police in attendance. Others were frightened knowing that Lucas had belonged to such an organization. Others may have been members of the organization. I never knew. I would never know.

"I had a lot of money left from the farm and from work to pay for the funeral and burial. And, I still had that lucky four hundred dollars that I had saved from when I worked for Lucas and Dolly and Isaac. That was my emergency money. It will always be my emergency money. I pin it to my underwear." Jack laughed. He said, "That is something that I never knew about you."

I smiled and took in a deep breath. "Jack, I didn't love Lucas, but I would have lived with him, for better or worse, for my lifetime. Do you understand that?" Jack shook his head. "Mary, one of the reasons that everyone loves you is for your sincerity, for your loyalty. I saw it with Dolly. I know that is a part of you that makes you who you are."

Jack stood mesmerized by my story. "Mary, I don't know what to say. You've taken the breath out of me. I'm so sorry. I liked Lucas. Well, I liked the guy that I knew when I worked for him."

It wasn't easy. When Jack said that he liked the Lucas that he knew, I almost fell apart. I bit my lip. I did all that I could do to control myself. I took in a big breath and exhaled slowly. "Ok", I continued, "I stayed in Detroit in the hope that the police would find who did it. I wanted to see the bastards exposed and prosecuted beginning with what they did to Lucas. The police were beginning to round up some of the members of those two organizations for various crimes, including another murder. But, they didn't have any evidence regarding what they did to Lucas.

"I kept calling the police detective who was in charge of the case. At first, he was very receptive to my calls. He spent a lot of time explaining everything that the police were doing to find Lucas' murderer. At the very least, I felt that I was doing something just calling him.

"After a few months, the newspapers forgot about Lucas. With the public interest waning, I sensed that the police weren't really interested in the case anymore.

"I worked, ate dinner and went back to the apartment. Every couple of days, I called the police to their distraction. And, after a while, they didn't even return my phone calls. I felt all alone. I was all alone.

"For quite a while, I was just frozen. I didn't want to stay and I didn't want to leave. I was lost in my own misery. Then, a few weeks ago, I decided to come back here."

Jack grabbed me around and held me tight. He said, "Sometimes, there are no words." He tentatively kissed me on the cheek. Then, he took out a handkerchief and wiped my eyes. He said, "Mary, no one should go through what you have experienced. No one. And, I am very sorry about Lucas." Jack, withdrew still holding my hands. And after a few minutes of silence, Jack said, "Mary, if you are finished here, let's walk down the hill." I turned to the graves one more time to say goodbye to both my grandfather and to Dolly, understanding that I would never be standing there again.

We walked down the hill and Jack guided me toward the house that I had called my own. I didn't want to go but he insisted. Jack knocked on the door and a young man walked out and said, "Hello, Mr. Clark". I was confused. Why would this guy address Jack so formally? "Mary, this is Bill Edwards. Bill is our farm manager. The other people who live in the house all work for Bill". I said, "Jack, I don't understand, who owns the farm?" "Mary, let's go for a walk." We said goodbye to Bill Edwards.

We walked in silence for a few minutes. Then, we stopped and Jack faced me. He said, "After you and Lucas abandoned your farm, the bank had to wait ninety days before foreclosing and seizing the property for lack of payment of the debt owed. That is what normally happens. After that, they tried to sell the farm. By the time that they put it up for sale, it was the early part of last year, 1938. Wholesale wheat and soy prices had hit the lowest point that they had been at since the early part of the Depression. I think that the bank knew they couldn't sell the Taddum Farm, but they had to try to get as much money for it that they could. Had they continued to own the farm, they would have had to pay taxes on it. They didn't want any part of that. They're not farmers, they're bankers. By that time, I believe they were happy to just recoup the mortgage money back. So, after a few months of trying to sell the farm, the bank placed an announcement in the newspaper that they would auction off the farm to the highest bidder. When I saw the advertisement, I spoke to my mother and father. I told them that I didn't want to see Dolly's grave and your grandfather's memorial plowed under or ignored. I told them that I wanted to buy the Taddum Farm. Immediately, my mother was in favor. My father hesitated. But, then, my mom spoke to him, no, she yelled at him. 'With how you destroyed Mary and Jack, you owe Jack and you owe Mary. Let him do this for her. It's only right.' "Jack, oh my, Helen wanted to do that for me?!" Jack just shook his head gently and smiled broadly. "Yes, she did. But, back to my mom. She settled down and tried to appeal to my father's business sense. She said, 'Jim, anyway, the cost for the farm and several others in the area that are at auction will be very attractive. We can expand our farm to over fifteen hundred acres. It will allow us to compete with the larger farms in the area. Jim, there are so many reasons that this makes sense. But, most importantly, you owe Jack so he can honor Dolly, Mary's grandfather and most of all, Mary.' My father still wasn't convinced. Then, my mother did something that I had never seen or heard her do before. She took the name of the Lord in vain. '**Jim, God Damn it!! Do it!!**' I had never seen my mother so adamant, so angry at him. Her face was beet red. My father knew what he had done to us, to me. He and I went to the auction. My dad gave me the high sign and I overbid the other two bidders that were there. I don't think that my father could have come back to our house if he didn't do it. My mother would have chased him out to the barn. Anyway, we bought the Taddum Farm for a fraction of its value. Later, that day, we bought two other farms that allowed us to connect our farm to the Taddum

Farm. Now, it's all part of the Clark Farm. Dolly's grave and your grandfather's memorial will always be taken care of. You will never have to worry."

Now, it was my turn to be overwhelmed. I had no words. I closed my eyes, put my hand over my mouth and shook my head back and forth. Once again, I cried for the many losses that I had suffered. I had cried for Lucas. I had cried for Dolly and my grandfather. This time, I cried for myself. For, I was the one that had lost them all.

Jack said, "Let's go back to my house. I have something that I want to give you. We drove back in silence. I didn't know what was going to happen. When we walked into the house, I said, "O, God, thank you, Helen. Jack just told me about your buying the Taddum Farm. I can't tell you just how good that makes me feel. Dolly will be able to rest in peace. My grandfather will know that he is remembered by friends." While I was glad that the farm was in safe hands, I still felt a sense of loss, a sadness of everything that was and would never be again. My face had to reflect that sadness.

Jack said to Helen, "Mom, I think that you have something that belongs to Mary." Helen said, "Mary, I do. Please wait right here." When she came back, Helen said, "We found this after we purchased your farm. We knew that this was important but we had no way of getting it to you." With that, Helen brought my black diary out from behind her back. "Mary, Jack found this in your house. He opened it to see what it was. Once he saw that it was your diary, he closed it and gave it to me for safekeeping. I hoped that you would come back some day so you could continue writing. Someday, maybe, you would be willing to share it with us."

Jack said, "Mom, Mary's Lucas has died. I will not go into the details. Maybe, Mary will tell you someday. But, for now, just know that he is gone." Helen said, "Mary, my dear, I am so sorry...Now, I better understand your comment about knowing loss. Oh, my, you have gone through so much loss and at such a young age." I thanked her.

Helen said, "It's been quite a long day. Would you like to stay for dinner? I remember your wonderful chicken and apple pie. Would you like to stay and join me in the kitchen? We can cook together." I couldn't think of anything that I would rather do. Once I agreed, a smile finally returned to my face.

Helen sent Jack out to get a chicken and prepare it for us. In the meantime, Helen and I prepared the apple pie and muffins that would go along with dinner. Once Jack had brought in the chicken, all plucked clean, Helen and I set out to make the chicken that Dolly had taught me to make so long ago. But, then, I stopped and reached back into my memory for the exact recipe. "Jack, is the kitchen still as it was at the Taddum farmhouse?" He said, "Yes, it should be exactly as you left it." I said, "Would you be willing to take me over there? I need to retrieve something from the kitchen." Jack said, "Of course. Let's go". I told Helen to just wait a few minutes until I came back. So, Jack drove me over to the house where I had spent so many of my formative years working and living. He introduced me to the men in the house and walked with me into the kitchen. Jack asked, "Mary, what are you looking for?" I told him about Dolly's favorite pan for making roast chicken and how she said that her roast chicken was wonderful because of the pan. I rooted around and found the pan almost immediately. I said, "Let's go back to your house, we have a chicken to roast."

When I got back, I told Helen about the pan and Dolly's insistence that the pan was what made her chicken so good. We worked together as Jack looked on, watching the two women that he loved, and that loved him so much, cook dinner.

The chicken came out delicious just like it did when I made it with Dolly. We ate in silence. Then, Jack turned to me and took my hand. He dropped down on one knee right there in the kitchen, in front of his mother. Jack said, "Mary, my Mary, I had no reason to ever expect that this day would ever come. But, I've waited for you, hope against hope. I've waited all of these years to say this to you and I don't want to wait even one more day or one minute more. So, here, in front of my mother, I ask you, Mary, will you marry me?" I repeated myself, not believing that Jack would actually want to marry me. "But, Jack, how could you still want to marry me after all that I did to you; after all of my lying and deceiving. I knew that I was hurting you and did it anyway. I hurt you time after time." He said, "I have never been as certain of anything in my entire life. Mary, please, please, marry me." I looked over to Helen. She was smiling. With her approval, given by that simple smile, I said, "Jack, you have been the one love in my life. For so long, life got in our way, but here we are and I couldn't be any happier. I love you. I will marry you." I kneeled down on the floor of the kitchen facing Jack. We kissed passionately right in front of Helen. She started to applaud. Yes, she actually clapped her hands. I rose up and gave her a hug and a kiss on the cheek.

Now, my tears were joyous. They were from a place that I had never been before, a place that I never expected to be. Jack said, "Mary, I wasn't expecting this. I don't have a ring. But, I will drive over to Tulsa tomorrow morning and buy an engagement ring. If you like, come with me and pick out any ring that you would like." I said, "Jack that is not necessary." I reached into my pocket and pulled out the cameo brooch that he had given to me for Christmas in 1929, almost ten years before. "Jack, please put this on me. It always meant so much to me because you gave it to me. There is no reason for anything else." Jack smiled and placed the pin right above my heart.

Maybe, the despair that I suffered was all fated. But, thank God, so is my life now that my man takes me into his arms. My world is bright, all right!

That is my fate now!

Epilogue

The short time between our engagement and wedding gave us an opportunity to tell our friends about Lucas and the last two years of my life. Our friends offered their condolences. And, after a short time, the questions and the stares stopped.

We were married by Pastor Berkley with his wife, Sally, as the witness. As always, the good pastor had just the right words to say. Aida Dolly Tanner Held was our matron of honor. Other friends, even some of Lucas' old friends, attended the ceremony. Lucy came up to me after the ceremony and said, "Thank God that you two are finally together." I just smiled.

Wheat prices, which had hit a recent low in 1938, began to rise significantly with the war in Europe having begun in September of 1939. At the same time, the drought which had plagued the Midwest for so many years was over, with precipitation returning to normal levels. With that, there were no more dust storms. The Depression, which began in October of 1929, was over with the advent of war. The plague of Depression, drought and dust, which had ruined so many lives throughout the country was over. It was that plague that destroyed Lucas, the Lucas that Dolly had loved. Unfortunately, that plague was to be replaced by global war and all of its horrors.

The Clark Farm was now over 1,500 acres in size and very successful. I took care of the same things that I had done before, responsible for the barn, the garden and the kitchen. And, of course, I made the cheddar. With the Clark Farm being so much larger, there were farm hands that helped. We expanded the production of garden vegetables to meet a renewed demand at the Fair. Jack and I always attended to the Fair as it gave us more time to be together. And his look of love, no longer from fifty feet away, melted my heart every day of the rest of my life. I found myself more in love with Jack than I had ever been.

In December of 1940, I gave birth to a baby girl. Jack asked that she be named Dolly Awiakta Clark. At the time of the baptism,

Pastor Berkley suggested that the ceremony be held on the hill top, under the oak tree, near to Dolly's grave and grandfather's memorial. I asked Helen if she would hold her granddaughter during the baptism. Helen was thrilled.

Just about a year later, on December 1st of 1941, I gave birth to a second child, a boy that we named Jack Awiakta Clark, Jr.

Unfortunately, war came to our shores just days later on December 7th. Jack went to enlist shortly after Pearl Harbor. But, given the size of his farm, his application was rejected. They told him that with so many of the nation's farm workforce going into the military, there would be few workers left to man the fields. His job was deemed essential to the war effort. Over time, he was contacted by the War Production Board and asked to produce different crops in their effort to ensure an adequate food supply for both the military and civilian populations. Each year, the request changed and the farm managed to produce what was needed. Of course, Jack, like all of the other farmers, willingly complied.

In March of 1941, Jack's sister, Betty, was married to Bill Mathews. Once the war started, Bill enlisted in the Marines. He was stationed in the Pacific, fighting his way to Tokyo. Betty gave birth to a son that they named Jimmy after her father. She and Jimmy lived in the Clark House along with Helen and our family waiting for Bill to return. There was room for all. Bill came home at the end of 1945 with shrapnel injuries that resulted in a limp. But, he came home alive and whole.

Doctor Ben Held enlisted in the Navy. He was assigned to the USS Enterprise where he served as a physician. From his letters, he told Aida about the Battle of Midway which turned out to be decisive in the war in the Pacific Ocean. When Ben left for service in the Navy, Aida closed his medical practice in Tulsa. Then, she and her daughter, Julie, moved back to Muskogee to live with her parents, Isaac and Eva, for the duration of the war. Ben was released from service at the beginning of 1946. After Ben returned from the war, David Held retired and Ben took over his father's medical practice in Muskogee. Ben and Aida had three more children, a boy named Daniel, a girl named

Allyson and another boy that they named Keith. Aida and I remained fast friends for our entire lives.

Many times, Helen and I would cook together. Our favorite was always that roasted chicken, made in that special pan, that Dolly had always said was the key to how well her chicken tasted. She was right. For dessert, rice pudding, again, from a recipe given to Dolly by her mother. Tea was always made with water that had been boiled for at least one minute, as per Dolly's prescription. We talked about Dolly all of the time, about her goodness, about her wisdom. She was always in our hearts.

Beginning in 1943, and for many years thereafter, I watched as Jack got on the floor with our children in front of the fireplace. He would act out the Cherokee hunt for buffalo just like my grandfather had done, for me, so many years before. Jack would prance around on the floor, on his hands and knees, mimicking a buffalo, scraping at the floor with his "hoof". Then, he would draw back on an imaginary bow and arrow just as I had written about in my diary describing memories of my grandfather and my childhood. Our children, Dolly and Jack, Jr., laughed at their father while I reveled in this act of Jack's great kindness. I watched the scene, reliving my own childhood and enjoying my culture, now, our culture, being told and reenacted by my loving husband, Jack. As our children grew older, Jack sat them on his lap and read to them from my diary about the history of the Cherokee, their People. I always stood in the background and looked over at my family, whispering only to myself, "Grandfather, look down, see what you have given to us."

Sincerely,

Mary Ahyoka Awiakta Clark

Acknowledgements

Although Mary Ahyoka Awiakta is fictional, her life and times are not. I have represented them as accurately as I could using many references describing the Cherokee people and farm life in early twentieth century Oklahoma.

I used her grandfather's stories, told to the young Mary, as a means to relate some of the many hardships that the indigenous people have suffered. However, I didn't want to dwell on those hardships except as they impacted Mary and Jack. After all, this is a story of self-sacrificing love.

More than 300 "Indian Schools", also known as "residential schools", were funded by the US government. They were run by various churches for the purpose of "Christianizing" those people that they thought of as heathens. In the process, they stripped those children of their own religious and cultural practices. That included cutting off their traditional hair styles, taking away their ornamentation, and clothing them in American/European dress. These schools completely ignored the traditional culture of the people who had been on this land forever. I used Mary's reaction to her lessons at school as a means to highlight the nullification of the indigenous Peoples' history. For example, she reacts to being taught about the wealth taken from "newly discovered lands", land that had already been occupied by these People for thousands of years. She is punished for her reaction.

And, as we have learned in the past few years, many of these children, entrusted to the care of the government and churches, were abused, both physically and sexually. The most recent published US data is from May of 2022 where it was reported that 500 indigenous children were buried in unmarked graves, likely killed at those schools. Investigations continue. In Canada, as many as 6,000 unmarked graves have been discovered. The treatment of the children at these schools was disgraceful, to say the least. In July of 2022, Pope Francis traveled to Canada to apologize for the "sorrow, indignation and shame" related to the Catholic Church's role in the abuse of these children.

Mary's church affiliation in this novel is Methodist. It should be understood that the choice of that church was just a matter of convenience for telling the story. There is nothing, intended or implied, by this fictional affiliation with the Methodist Church.

On one hand, the white Christians wanted to change these indigenous People in every way that they could. But, once they were "Christianized", they still treated them with disdain. In the story, I used Pastor Berkley's sermons as a means to teach the church congregation of the evils of prejudice and the value of welcoming people, different from themselves, into their church. Prejudice is what led to the unrequited love story of Mary and Jack. Unfortunately, those prejudices that kept Mary and Jack apart were common and remain so today.

Regarding the conditions that existed in the Midwest during the 1930s, I tried to paint a picture of the despair that existed, resulting from the triple threat of Depression, drought and dust. All of which, along with improved mechanization, damaged the historical farming communities through elimination of sharecropper and tenant farming, failure of smaller farms and their consolidation into larger and larger businesses. None of this could have been avoided. It was just that those conditions compressed the time frame.

I am deeply indebted to my wife Suzanne. We spent a great deal of time talking about how a woman might react to various situations. I needed her perspective, which, as you could imagine, was very different from mine. She also helped me in editing and with the artwork shown on the front cover. She is my constant source of encouragement and love. Thank you also to Harvey and Jackie, friends, who proofread the draft finding errors that I left behind.

About the Author:

PAUL MOGOLESKO grew up in Brooklyn, New York. He knew of his interest in science from his second year at Brooklyn Technical High School. He continued those studies as an undergraduate at Brooklyn College and then at MIT where he received his PhD in Chemistry. He spent his entire career in the pharmaceuticals, chemicals and plastics industries. In retirement, Paul took up two hobbies; tennis and writing.

Paul has written these other books:

CARPE DIEM: There are Few Do-Overs in Life (2015)

THE SEARCH FOR THE WHITE STORK (2019)

LET'S TALK ABOUT STEVE (a journey to hell and back) (2021)

Paul has been married to his sweetheart Suzanne for 55 years. He is the proud father of two children, their spouses and four wonderful grandchildren. Paul and Suzanne live in Boynton Beach, Florida.

BIBLIOGRAPHY

1925	https://www.thepeoplehistory.com/1925.html
1934 in Radio	https://en.wikipedia.org/wiki/1934_in_radio
American Indian Boarding Schools	https://en.wikipedia.org/wiki/American_Indian_boarding_schools#Assimilation-era_day_schools
Average Wages in 1925	https://www.google.com/search?q=average+wages+in+1925&client=safari&channel=iphone_bm&sxsrf=AOaemvL7t3pS6vExYOHCLfCWCgkMDWZdoA%3A1634734790654&source=hp&ei=xhJwYd7RJfycwbkPkN-tyAs&iflsig=ALs-wAMAAAAAYXAg1kUz7ZPv12G2NwrC3r0K1nqvQt5I&oq=average+wages+in+1925&gs_lcp=Cgdnd3Mtd2I6EAEYATIFCAAQgAQyBggAEBYQHjIFCAAQhgMyBQgAEIYDOgQJIxAnOgUIABCRAjoHCAAQsQMQQzoOCC4QgAQQsQMQxwEQowI6EQguEIAEELEDEJMBEMcBEKMCOggIABCABBCxAzoECAAQQzoOCC4QgAQQsQMQxwEQ0QM6CAguEIAEELEDEIMBOgQIAhBDOgoIABCxAxDJAxBDOgglABCxAxCRAjoKCAAQgAQQhwIQFDoHCAAQyQMQQzoICAAQFhAKEB5Q-hxYyDIgkVpoAHAAeACAAAYBiAHDCZIBAzkuNJgBAKABAQ&sclient=gws-wiz
Barn Dance	https://en.wikipedia.org/wiki/Barn_dance
Black Legion	https://en.wikipedia.org/wiki/Black_Legion_(political_movement)
Black Legion	https://en.wikipedia.org/wiki/Black_Legion_(political_movement)
Burial Traditions	https://classroom.synonym.com/burial-traditions-cherokee-indians-6872.html
Butter from Milk	https://www.wikihow.com/Make-Butter-from-Raw-Milk
Charles Coughlin	https://en.wikipedia.org/wiki/Charles_Coughlin
Cheddar Cheese	https://cheesemaking.com/products/cheddar-cheese-making-recipe
Cheese	https://www.instructables.com/Basic-Steps-of-How-to-Make-Cheese/
Cheese	https://www.instructables.com/Basic-Steps-of-How-to-Make-Cheese/#discuss
Cheese Aging	https://culturecheesemag.com/cheese-iq/ask-the-monger/temperature-affect-cheese-aging/
Cheese Making	https://www.instructables.com/Basic-Steps-of-How-to-Make-Cheese/
Cheese Making	https://culturecheesemag.com/cheese-iq/ask-the-monger/temperature-affect-cheese-aging/
Cherokee Burial Traditions	https://classroom.synonym.com/burial-traditions-cherokee-indians-6872.html
Cherokee Death Ritual	https://www.proquest.com/openview/19b92a4f1420d202c2f678d3bfbfaf93/1?pq-origsite=gscholar&cbl=18750
Cherokee Death Rituals	https://www.proquest.com/openview/19b92a4f1420d202c2f678d3bfbfaf93/1?pq-origsite=gscholar&cbl=18750
Cherokee Death Rituals	https://www.proquest.com/openview/19b92a4f1420d202c2f678d3bfbfaf93/1?pq-origsite=gscholar&cbl=18750
Cherokee Language	https://www.google.com/search?q=adsila+in+cherokee+language&rlz=1C1VDKB_enUS989US989&sxsrf=ALiCzsbJIRWafRAy-EIFkknaCt0-iZUsuQ%3A1653422118087&ei=JjiNYrXuBLTMwbkP8pyDiAQ&ved=0ahUKEwi1mYyw9fj3AhU0ZjABHXLOAEEQ4dUDCA4&oq=adsila+in+cherokee+language&gs_lcp=Cgdnd3Mtd2I6EAw6BggAEB4QBzoICAAQHhAIEAdKBAhBGABKBAhGGABQAFiGCmDXLWgAcAF4AIABVIgB2gOSAQE2mAEAoAEBwAEB&sclient=gws-wiz
Cherokee Language Tudor	http://www.nativehistoryassociation.org/tutor_tsalagi10_study.php
Cherokee Last Names	https://www.google.com/search?q=cherokee+last+names+list&sxsrf=AOaemvJGcaa9wkdaASB6TzvwiRhfPaS_pQ%3A1632164246330&source=hp&ei=ItIiYdveEcOEwbkPSuyt2Ac&iflsig=ALs-wAMAAAAAYUjnpiZN2GF4cehVZVA7eoE4beOxSrgf&oq=cher&gs_lcp=Cgdnd3Mtd2I6EAEYADIECCMQJzIECCMQJzIECCMQJzIECAAQsQMQQzIFCAAQkQJyBQgAEJECMgQIABBDMgIILhCABBCHAhCxAxAUMgQIABBDOgIILhBDOggIABCABBCxAzoKCC4QsQMQgwEQQzoICC4QsQMQgwFQIQJYqQ5g0SZoAHAAeACAAAZIBAzEuMSgBAKABAQ&sclient=gws-wiz
Cherokee Nation	https://language.cherokee.org/word-list/
Cherokee Race Relations.	https://www.hcn.org/articles/indigenous-affairs-race-and-racism-cherokee-nation-adopted-racism-from-europeans-its-time-to-reject-it
Cherokee Syllabary	https://en.wikipedia.org/wiki/Cherokee_syllabary
Cherokee; Racism	https://www.hcn.org/articles/indigenous-affairs-race-and-racism-cherokee-nation-adopted-racism-from-europeans-its-time-to-reject-it
Christmas; 1920s	https://www.hhhistory.com/2013/12/christmas-during-1920s.html
Congregation B'nai Emunah: A Brief History	https://static1.squarespace.com/static/5439f4abe4b02716f3d029d4/t/560756efe4b0c937d16be630/1443321619761/Congregation+B%27nai+Emunah+-+A+Brief+History.pdf

BIBLIOGRAPHY

Cooking in the 1800s	https://www.ncpedia.org/culture/food/cooking-in-the-1800s
Depression	https://en.wikipedia.org/wiki/Great_Depression
Dust Bowl - Wiki	https://en.wikipedia.org/wiki/Dust_Bowl
Farm Life during the Depression	https://livinghistoryfarm.org/farminginthe30s/life_01.html
Farm Relief	https://www.encyclopedia.com/education/news-and-education-magazines/farm-relief-1929-1941
Farmerettes	https://womenshistory.si.edu/herstory/community/object/farmerettes-feed-nation
Indigenous Peoples	https://www.proquest.com/openview/19b92a4f1420d202c2f678d3bfbfaf93/1?pq-origsite=gscholar&cbl=18750
Indigenous Families	https://www.hcn.org/articles/indigenous-affairs-justice-how-the-only-family-argument-is-used-against-indigenous-families
Kansas Farming	https://www.kshs.org/kansapedia/homestead-act/15142
Language	https://en.wikipedia.org/w/index.php?search=written+cherokee+language&title=Special%3ASearch&go=Go&ns0=1
Laudanum	https://en.wikipedia.org/wiki/Laudanum#History
Lincoln; Americas Strenght	https://www.nps.gov/liho/learn/historyculture/america.htm#:~:text=Our%20reliance%20is%20in%20the,in%20all%20lands%2C%20every%20where.
Lincoln; Liberty Speeches	http://www.abrahamlincolnonline.org/lincoln/speeches/liberty.htm
Lord's Prayer	https://en.wikipedia.org/wiki/Lord's_Prayer
Map of Indian Reservations	https://upload.wikimedia.org/wikipedia/commons/7/7c/Former_Indian_Reservations_in_Oklahoma.jpg
Morphine	https://en.wikipedia.org/wiki/Morphine#History
Oklahoma Land Rush	https://en.wikipedia.org/wiki/Land_Rush_of_1889
Oklahoma Land Rush; 1889	https://en.wikipedia.org/wiki/Land_Rush_of_1889#Boomers_and_Sooners
Oklahoma Land Rush; 1893	http://www.eyewitnesstohistory.com/landrush.htm
Pequot War	https://en.wikipedia.org/wiki/Pequot_War
President Jackson	https://www.battlefields.org/learn/biographies/andrew-jackson?gclid=Cj0KCQjw1dGJBhD4ARIsANb6OdlTchmv3ri_57mmlmSQ5zBUIcJpRWDrWDWpif1hC--9Gkmi2Vs4Q94aAhouEALw_wcB
Prohibition	https://www.history.com/news/10-things-you-should-know-about-prohibition
Prohibition	https://www.history.com/this-day-in-history/prohibition-ratified
Prohibition	https://www.okhistory.org/publications/enc/entry.php?entry=PR018
Prohibition Facts	https://constitutioncenter.org/blog/five-interesting-facts-about-prohibitions-end-in-1933
Radio	https://en.wikipedia.org/wiki/1934_in_radio
Roles of Farm Woman	https://www.lib.niu.edu/1999/iht719902.html
Schools	https://en.wikipedia.org/wiki/List_of_Native_American_boarding_schools
Sears, Roebuck & Company Catalog	https://www.amazon.com/Roebuck-Catalogue-Spring-Summer-Minneapolis/dp/B009JCLGF8
Struggle of the Three	https://thislandpress.com/2013/05/20/struggle-of-the-three/
Schools	https://en.wikipedia.org/wiki/List_of_Native_American_boarding_schools
Slavery	https://www.cnn.com/2022/09/06/us/cherokee-nation-museum-freedmen-exhibit-cec/index.html
Temple	https://static1.squarespace.com/static/5439f4abe4b02716f3d029d4/t/560756efe4b0c937d16be630/1443321619761/Congregation+B%27nai+Emunah+-+A+Brief+History.pdf
Thanksgiving	https://www.snopes.com/fact-check/thanksgiving-massacre-pequot-tribe/
Tillage	https://en.wikipedia.org/wiki/Tillage
Trail of Tears	https://www.nps.gov/articles/the-trail-of-tears-and-the-forced-relocation-of-the-cherokee-nation-teaching-with-historic-places.htm
Wheat Farmer	https://www.youtube.com/watch?v=7SBe7Q8hado
Wheat Prices	https://www.u-s-history.com/pages/h1532.html
Women's Wages	https://babel.hathitrust.org/cgi/pt?id=uiug.30112104140170&view=1up&seq=23&skin=2021
Yarrow	https://www.oklahoman.com/story/news/2001/02/08/yarrow-is-true-survivor/62159615007/